A REASON TO BELIEVE

MAUREEN MCKADE

BERKLEY SENSATION, NEW YORK

THE BERKLEY PUBLISHING GROUP
Published by the Penguin Group
Penguin Group (USA) Inc.
375 Hudson Street, New York, New York 10014, USA
Penguin Group (Canada), 90 Eglinton Avenue East, Suite 700, Toronto, Ontario M4P 2Y3, Canada
(a division of Pearson Penguin Canada Inc.)
Penguin Books Ltd., 80 Strand, London WC2R 0RL, England
Penguin Group Ireland, 25 St. Stephen's Green, Dublin 2, Ireland (a division of Penguin Books Ltd.)
Penguin Group (Australia), 250 Camberwell Road, Camberwell, Victoria 3124, Australia
(a division of Pearson Australia Group Pty. Ltd.)
Penguin Books India Pvt. Ltd., 11 Community Centre, Panchsheel Park, New Delhi—110 017, India
Penguin Group (NZ), 67 Apollo Drive, Rosedale, North Shore 0745, Auckland, New Zealand
(a division of Pearson New Zealand Ltd.)
Penguin Books (South Africa) (Pty.) Ltd., 24 Sturdee Avenue, Rosebank, Johannesburg 2196,
South Africa

Penguin Books Ltd., Registered Offices: 80 Strand, London WC2R 0RL, England

A REASON TO BELIEVE

A Berkley Sensation Book / published by arrangement with the author

PRINTING HISTORY
Berkley Sensation mass-market edition / August 2007

ISBN: 978-0-425-21662-0

BERKLEY® SENSATION
Berkley Sensation Books are published by The Berkley Publishing Group,
a division of Penguin Group (USA) Inc.,
375 Hudson Street, New York, New York 10014.
BERKLEY SENSATION and the "B" design are trademarks of Penguin Group (USA) Inc.

PRINTED IN THE UNITED STATES OF AMERICA

10 9 8 7 6 5 4 3 2 1

ACKNOWLEDGMENTS

To the Wyrd Sisters—especially Karen Fox, Pam Mc-Cutcheon, Angel Smits, and Deb Stover—for your fresh eyes, creative input, and encouragement.

A special thanks to my agent, Natasha Kern, and my editor, Cindy Hwang, for their unflagging faith.

And, as always, to Alan and our four-footed children.

ONE

DULCIE McDaniel squinted against the hot, harsh sun and refused to give in to the desperation tightening her chest. Instead, she studied the rustling leaves overhead and the robin perched on a branch, cocking its head at the scene below.

A hand tugged at Dulcie's skirt. "Maaa."

Madeline's crabby whine brought Dulcie back to the present. She looked down at her four-year-old daughter. "What is it, honey?"

"Wanna go home."

Dulcie wanted to do the same, but she couldn't leave her father alone while two strangers lowered his pine box into the ground. Bitterness rose like bile, and she choked it back.

Her throat constricted, and she blinked tears into submission. Her father had been a falling-down drunk who hadn't done an honest day's work since Dulcie's mother died. But he'd been her father, and she owed him something for that.

"Ma, wanna go. Hot."

"A few more minutes."

The girl fiddled with her bonnet strings.

"Leave it on, honey, or the sun will burn your face."

Madeline sighed audibly but stopped playing with the ribbons.

Dulcie squared her shoulders and brought her gaze back to the two men lowering the wooden casket into the earth.

Ashes to ashes, dust to dust.

Trying not to think about how many of her precious coins were used to give her father this simple burial, Dulcie focused on the plain cross marking the new grave beside her mother's final resting place.

Frank R. Pollard.

Rest in Peace.

Resentment filled Dulcie, and she bit the inside of her cheek. First her husband and now her father. Although both had been miserable excuses for human beings, her father had given her life and her husband had given her Madeline. But now, she had no one but Madeline, and her father and husband had the peace that was denied the living.

A dull *thwump* brought Dulcie out of her bitter musings. *Thwump.* Another shovelful of dirt hit the wood coffin. Madeline's small fingers tightened around Dulcie's hand and the girl whimpered.

Dulcie's stomach tossed and rolled, threatening to lose its meager contents.

"It's all right, honey," she said, surprised by her calm, even voice. "You can have bread with honey when we get home."

Madeline snuffled, the promise of a treat quieting her restlessness.

When they were done, the men slung their shovels over their shoulders and plodded away without a word, leaving Dulcie and Madeline alone by the fresh grave. An expectancy hung in the air, as if Dulcie's father were waiting for something.

Dulcie thought about her mother's Bible lying in the trunk at the cabin. She had considered bringing it and speaking some words over her father, but it didn't seem fitting. Not even the minister could be bothered to bury a lynched murderer.

"I hope you and Ma are together now," Dulcie said awkwardly. "And that there's no more whiskey to tempt you."

She stiffened her backbone. She'd done all she could and probably more than her father deserved. But then, even though he was a drunk, he wasn't a murderer. He hadn't deserved to die at the end of a rope with masked men surrounding him.

"Is Grandda sleeping?" Madeline asked.

Dulcie pressed her lips together and nodded. "Yes, honey, Grandda's asleep." *And he won't ever wake up.*

Dulcie turned away from the grave and, with Madeline skipping alongside her, trudged back to the mule-drawn wagon.

RYE Forrester thought he'd left hell behind. Instead, it had followed him from Kansas all the way down to Texas, bedeviling him with scorching heat during the long, dusty days. He adjusted his battered, wide-brimmed hat and tried to ignore the sweat that trickled down his cheeks and jaw. His shirt stuck to his back, clammy and wet against his skin. His inner thighs were damp from pressing against leather.

His mare tossed her head and snorted, letting him know what she thought of traveling in this ungodly heat. Rye patted Smoke's sweat-soaked neck and considered looking for some shade. However, his destination was close, and there they'd find shelter, water, and food. There'd also be saloons that served warm beer and burning rotgut.

Rye shoved temptation aside. The sooner he found the woman, the sooner he could atone and move on. He shifted uneasily. There'd probably be tears and accusations, but he'd known this wouldn't be easy. Hell, his whole life hadn't been easy. Why should this be any different?

He continued on, giving his attention to his surroundings rather than the worn-out memories scrabbling for purchase. Fields littered the area, scattered between bursts of trees, giving the land a latticed appearance. Crops were nearly ripe and it wouldn't be long before harvest began. Unless the merciless sun stripped them away and replaced the living plants with brown, withered stalks.

The town appeared as a blur on the horizon, and it took nearly half an hour to reach the outskirts of the sleepy village. His eyes shaded by his hat brim, Rye catalogued Locust as simply another town like so many others, inhabited by mostly God-fearing folks who gave their lives to parcels of land worth less than his horse.

As he studied the town, he was aware of being the center of attention. Even two years after the War between the States, every stranger in these southern towns was regarded as an enemy until proven otherwise. Rye never stuck around long enough to prove one way or the other.

He glanced around and caught movement on a hillside at the edge of town. A woman with a young girl stood in a cemetery as two men shoveled dirt into a grave. It seemed odd, just the two mourners. . . . But then, it wasn't any of his concern.

Rye steered Smoke to the livery and dismounted in the shade of the barn.

A man wearing overalls stuffed with a low-hanging belly ambled out. He pulled a soiled handkerchief from his pocket and mopped his wrinkled brow. "Four bits a day. Includes a can of oats," the man said after a jaw-cracking yawn.

Rye suspected the can was the size of a tomato tin, but he wasn't in any position to argue. And the liveryman knew it. Rye tossed him two coins, and the man caught them with his thick, stubby fingers. "For that price you'd best be giving a rubdown, too."

It wasn't a question, but the stout man gave a choppy nod. Rye tossed his saddlebags over his shoulder and untied the rifle from the saddle, hefting the scabbard comfortably with one hand. He gave the liveryman the reins. Rye's nose wrinkled at the stench of old sweat, manure, and other odors he didn't want to mull over, having smelled them too often in army barracks.

"There a place to sleep in this town?" Rye asked.

"There's rooms upstairs in the saloon."

Rye frowned. "Isn't there a hotel or rooming house?"

The liveryman shrugged and picked at a scab on his beefy forearm. "Ain't got enough folks comin' through. 'Sides, most that do are men lookin' for whiskey and a woman—saloon got both."

Six months ago Rye would've been looking for the same. He nodded to the man and ambled away, his legs stiff from sitting in the saddle for so long. Out of the shade the sun's heat struck him like a blow, and the hot air stole any moisture left in his mouth.

Going into a saloon thirsty and tired wasn't the best idea, but Rye didn't have a choice. He paused in the doorway, his forearms holding open the swinging doors. The stench of stale beer and whiskey, along with unwashed bodies and old tobacco, invoked memories of nights spent drinking himself into oblivion. He breathed through his mouth to lessen the effect, wondering if maybe he shouldn't just camp under the stars again. But the thought of sleeping on a mattress was too tempting, and that was a temptation Rye could surrender to.

He wove between chairs and tables, his footsteps muffled by the sawdust on the floor.

The tall, thin bartender placed his hands against the bar. "What can I get you, mister?"

"A room," Rye replied.

"We got four. You want the one closest to the stairs or the farthest one back?"

With morbid fascination, Rye watched the man's long mustache bounce with every word. He mentally shook himself. "I just want to get some sleep."

"Farthest one, then. That'd be two dollars for the night."

Rye glared at the man. "It got a solid gold bed?"

The bartender laughed, exposing rotting teeth. "We get that much for letting a whore rent the room for her business."

"Provided she's on her back from sundown to sunup."

"Take it or leave it, mister."

As much as Rye wanted to tell him where to shove his room, he wanted a night in a real bed more. "Clean sheets?"

"We got 'em, but it's two bits extra and you got to make up the bed."

Rye grabbed the man's shirtfront and jerked him forward, bringing them face-to-face. "You give me the clean sheets for the price of the room and I won't break your goddamned nose. Take it or leave it, mister," he said, throwing the bartender's words back at him.

"You're bluffin'." The quaver in the man's voice gave lie to his bravado.

"You and me both know you won't get two dollars from a whore on a Tuesday night in this one-horse town."

The bartender gave a jerky nod. "All right."

Rye released him, and the man stepped back, his Adam's apple bobbing up and down in his cranelike neck.

Rye tossed two silver dollars on the bar, wincing inwardly. He'd have to find another job soon to restore his scant money supply.

The bartender scooped up the coins and reached under the bar for a key. He handed it to Rye then went into the back room. He appeared a few moments later with an armload of fresh bedclothes. "Here."

Rye accepted them without comment. He turned to head up the stairs, but remembered his reason for being there. "You know a woman named Dulcie McDaniel?"

The bartender frowned. "No McDaniel around here." He paused. "Seems to me Dulcie Pollard married some soldier fellah, but I don't recall his name."

Rye suspected that was the woman he was searching for. "She live around here?"

The man crossed his long, thin arms. "Ever since she come back here 'bout four months ago. Lives on the farm three miles west of town." He shook his head. "Buried her pa today. Bastard murdered a good man. Got hanged for what he done."

It took a moment for Rye to digest the news. The woman he'd seen at the cemetery must've been McDaniel's widow, and the little girl his daughter. He didn't know whether he should be surprised or not. The fact was he'd never met her, and Jerry hadn't talked much about his family. He'd been too busy drinking and whoring.

"Damned shame," the bartender commented, shaking his head. "Frank Pollard was a good customer. Used to buy his whiskey here."

Obviously the bartender could care less about Mrs. Mc-Daniel's grief, which angered and disgusted Rye. "A woman lost her father and all you can think of is that you lost a customer?"

The man's thin lips turned downward, his mustache making his face—and frown—appear longer. "You're a stranger 'round here, mister, so you don't know how it is. If you did, you wouldn't go 'round defendin' her."

"*She* didn't kill anyone."

"Apple don't fall far from the tree."

Rye stared at him, wondering if most of the town felt the same way. As if reading Rye's thoughts, the bartender added, "The man her pa killed was well-liked. Everyone respected him. That's more than could be said for Pollard and his daughter."

Rye turned and trudged up the creaking stairs. It sounded like McDaniel's wife wasn't exactly what he thought she'd be. Maybe it'd be best if he didn't see her and simply moved on. After burying her hanged father, she probably didn't need one of her husband's old drinking friends stopping by to tell her he was responsible for Jerry's death.

Once in his room, Rye removed the smelly sheets from the bed and threw them into the hallway. As he remade the bed, he argued with his conscience. Visiting with Mrs. McDaniel was the decent thing to do, but it had been nearly six months since Jerry died. What good did it do to unearth the past and add to her grief when she had just lost her father?

Rye checked the corners of the mattress, ensuring the sheets were tucked in neat and snug. Ten years in an orphanage and fourteen more in the army made the inspection second nature. Assured the bed was regulation standard, he placed the room key in his pocket and the saddlebag over his arm. He'd seen a bathhouse on the way into town, and even though he'd use more of his dwindling money, the indulgence would be worth it.

Five minutes later he arrived at the bathhouse, not surprised to find he was the only customer. After meeting the liveryman and the bartender, Rye figured cleanliness didn't count for much in Locust. A bearded man took his money and yelled for a boy about eight years old to fill one of the tubs.

"Make it one at the back," Rye said.

The gimlet-eyed caretaker winked slyly. "Sure, mister, whatever you want."

Rye didn't bother to dissuade the man from his presumptions. It was easier than the truth.

The boy strained to carry two pails of steaming water, and some sloshed over, making the kid hiss.

"Let me take one of those," Rye said gruffly.

The dark-haired boy shot a quick fearful glance back at his boss and shook his head. "I got 'em."

Rye didn't argue but simply took one from him, casting a glare back at the man, who looked away. They emptied the pails into an oval wooden tub at the back of the room.

"I'll give you a hand with the rest of the water," Rye said to the boy.

"Don't have to, mister. I can do it."

Rye shrugged, noting the boy's ragged overalls and bare feet. His hair was long and shaggy, brushing his shoulders and falling across his eyes. "I don't mind."

Following the kid to the stove out back that held three kettles of hot water, Rye remembered another boy wearing hand-me-down overalls that were always too short or too long. That boy only wore shoes when the ground was covered with snow or ice.

"What's your name?" Rye asked him.

"Collie," the boy replied in a barely audible voice.

"My name's Rye."

Collie didn't acknowledge him, but reached for a hot kettle, using two old cloths so he wouldn't burn himself on the handles.

"Let me do that," Rye said.

Collie glanced at him. "If I don't do it, old man Knobby won't give me no money."

Although Rye suspected that was the case, his temper crackled. He kept his anger hidden from the boy, not wanting to frighten him. "I'll make sure you get paid."

Rye took the cloths from Collie and poured hot water

from the kettle into the two pails, plus a third one. He carried two back while Collie handled one. It took two more trips, the last one carrying cold water, to fill the wooden tub.

Rye dug twenty-five cents out of his pocket and handed it to the boy. "Thanks, Collie."

The kid stared at the two bit coin, his brown eyes shining. "Thanks, mister."

"You worked hard. Your folks live in town?"

Collie slipped the coin in his pocket, and his hand lingered, fingering it as if afraid it would disappear. "They're gone."

Rye frowned, wondering if they'd left him behind or were dead. "So where do you live?"

"With the Gearsons." His tone told Rye he wasn't thrilled with the arrangement. Collie picked up the empty pails. "I gotta go."

Before Rye could say anything more, the boy was gone. It didn't pay to worry about kids like Collie. They either learned how to take care of themselves or they didn't. Rye had been one of the former.

Shaking his head, he removed his gunbelt but kept it near the tub. He stripped off his grimy, dusty clothes and stepped into the tub. Sighing in pleasure, he lowered himself into the water and tipped his head back.

Although he'd been burning under the sun less than an hour ago, Rye luxuriated in the hot water. He used the harsh soap to get rid of the accumulated sweat and dirt on his skin. Using the mirror and razor in his saddlebag, he shaved.

Some time later, he rose from the tub and dried off with the rough towel that hung on a wall peg. He kept his back to the wall as he donned his clean clothes. As he put on his shirt, he brushed the mark on his shoulder, the reason he'd asked for a bath away from prying eyes.

Regrets rose and nearly strangled him. He'd ruined his army career because he was a damned coward, and he had the scar to prove it. Leaving town without seeing the widow of the man whose death he'd caused would be the coward's way out.

Rye finished dressing and strode out of the bathhouse.

The day he'd walked out of the stockade he made a promise never to let cowardice rule him again.

THE Pollard farm was easy to find. Rye reined in his horse a hundred yards from the dilapidated cabin. Out of habit, he reconnoitered the farm in the waning afternoon light. Sagging corral fences, holes in the porch, a broken cabin window repaired with uneven slats, and the barn door leaned up against the wall told Rye that Frank Pollard had spent all his money on whiskey. A swaybacked mule rubbed its rump against a corral post that threatened to topple at any moment and a milk cow stood nearby, chewing its cud. A half dozen scrawny chickens scratched at the dry soil.

From what Rye could figure, the farm hadn't been kept up for some time now. He flicked his gaze to the field behind the house and whistled low. Maybe the buildings needed major repairs, but the grain crop was thick and golden under the sun. Somebody had managed to get the field plowed and planted last spring.

He couldn't put off the meeting any longer. After wiping his damp brow with the scarf tied around his neck, he tapped Smoke's sides. The horse carried him into the yard.

The cabin door opened, and the barrel of a shotgun emerged a moment before the owner. "Hold up," came the sharp command.

Rye halted his mare, startled rather than frightened by the shotgun and the accompanying order.

"Keep your hands where I can see them."

This time Rye realized the voice was a woman's, even though the shotgun holder wore breeches. "Are you—"

"Get your hands up." The words were supplemented by the unmistaken hammer cock of the shotgun.

Rye did as she said and took a few moments to study the woman. Trousers and a baggy shirt camouflaged her figure, and a floppy hat hid her hair, except for a few loose reddish tendrils curling around her grim face. Dressed as she was, nobody could accuse the woman of being a beauty, but there was strength in her features.

"What do you want?" she asked, both barrels aimed un-erringly at Rye's head.

He opened his mouth to tell her who he was, but the dis-repair of the farm made him pause. From what he heard, Mrs. McDaniel and her daughter lived here alone. There was no way she'd be able to do the work required to bring in the crop and fix up the place. If he told her who he was and what he'd done, she'd likely order him away. However, his leaving wouldn't help her, nor would he be able to make amends.

"My name's Rye Forrester and I'm looking for a job, ma'am." The words slipped out before he could think them through.

Something akin to hope flared in her expression, but faded just as quickly. "If you're looking for a paying job, I don't have one."

Rye shrugged but kept his hands raised. "I'd be willing to work for room and board, ma'am."

Although the shotgun barrel didn't waver, Mrs. McDaniel seemed to be considering his offer. He waited patiently.

"The only place to sleep is the barn," she said.

"I've slept in worse."

"You'd be fed the same as my daughter and me, but you'll eat on the porch."

Rye understood her wariness, with a young daughter and having just lost her father. "That'd be fine, ma'am."

She studied him, as if gauging his sincerity . . . and de-gree of danger. He kept his expression friendly. He owed this woman.

Finally, she eased the hammer back and lowered the shot-gun. "I have one more thing to tell you, then you can decide if you want to work here or not." She lifted her chin, met his gaze squarely. "I buried my pa this morning. They said he murdered someone in town then they hanged him without a trial. If you take the job, you'll be working for that man's daughter."

Rye was surprised she told him, but then she probably knew he'd hear about it in town. Still, it was a brave thing to do. "You sound like you don't believe he was guilty."

"He wasn't." No hesitation. No tears. Merely a statement of fact. "Do you want the job or not, Mr. Forrester?"

Rye didn't have a choice, not if he wanted to hold on to whatever honor he still possessed.

"I'll take it, ma'am."

Two

DULCIE kept her relief hidden from her new employee and merely nodded with cool affirmation. "I'm Mrs. Dulcie McDaniel."

Forrester touched the brim of his hat and inclined his head slightly. "Pleased to meet you, ma'am."

The rough but not unpleasant timbre of his voice rolled through her, leaving behind pockets of warmth she refused to acknowledge. His gaze moved away from her, to the ramshackle cabin and across the general disrepair of the farm. Embarrassment heated her cheeks, and she felt compelled to add, "I'm a widow."

He shifted in his saddle. "I'm sorry, ma'am."

She frowned at the flush that touched his cheeks and the way his eyes shifted to some point over her shoulder.

Madeline scrambled through the doorway, and before Dulcie could stop her, she scampered over to Forrester's horse. "Nice horsey," she said, petting the mare's nose.

Dulcie set her shotgun against the doorframe and rushed over to snatch up her daughter with trembling arms. "Madeline Margaret McDaniel, you know better than to run up to a strange horse."

"No harm, ma'am." Forrester dismounted and held the

reins loosely in one hand. "Smoke here is about as gentle as they come."

Dulcie tilted back her head to meet his veiled gaze. Long sooty lashes framed startling blue eyes, and his sun-darkened cheeks and lesser-tanned jaw told her he'd recently shaved. The scent of soap and his faded but clean clothes were evidence that he'd also bathed not long ago. It was a relief to know her hired man wasn't averse to taking a bath now and again.

Her daughter stared at Forrester, her fist pressed to her mouth.

"Hello, Madeline," he said with a gentle smile.

She hid her face in the curve of her mother's neck.

"She's shy with strangers," Dulcie explained, noting the defensive edge that crept into her tone.

"But not horses."

A smile twitched her lips, but she didn't allow it to form. "No, not horses."

"Most youngsters are more scared of people than animals." He shrugged, a surprisingly self-deprecating gesture. "Always figured that makes them smarter 'n most of us."

Dulcie narrowed her eyes. "Do you have children of your own?"

He looked down as he fingered the reins. "No, ma'am. If it's all right with you, I'll start work tomorrow, bright and early." He stuck his boot toe in the stirrup and slung his leg over his horse's back.

Alarm tightened Dulcie's muscles. If he left, she had no guarantee he'd return. "Mr. Forrester."

He paused and gazed down at her, his head tilted in question.

"Why are you willing to work for me?" she asked.

"You were the first to offer me a job."

"And if you get a better offer?"

"I won't."

Puzzled but unwilling to turn away the badly needed help, Dulcie nodded. "Be here by six thirty, and I'll have breakfast ready."

"I'll do that, ma'am."

He touched the brim of his hat, and Dulcie stepped back

as he reined his mare around and trotted out of the yard. Madeline raised her head from her mother's shoulder and waved, but Forrester didn't look back.

Madeline squirmed in her mother's arm. "Down."

Dulcie set her daughter on the ground.

"Will the horsey come back?"

Dulcie crossed her arms over her waist. "I hope so, honey."

Few men would work for room and board, especially when the room was a leaky old barn. Still, the repercussions of the War between the States continued. Jobs were difficult to come by, and it was reasonable that a man might work for what he could get.

She absently watched Madeline chase a yellow and black butterfly while she considered her hastiness. The man was a stranger. For all she knew he might murder her and Madeline in their sleep and no one would even miss them.

Yet what choice did she have? If she lost the farm, she'd have no means to provide for her child. She'd have to remarry or sell herself. From her point of view, there wasn't much difference. Either a woman gave her body to her husband every night so she'd have a roof over her head and food to eat, or she gave her body to numerous men so she'd have the same.

Dulcie preferred neither. With the farm she didn't need a man, except as hired help to do the heavy labor. If Rye Forrester was sincere about working for room and board, she couldn't afford to send him away. She also couldn't afford to let him get too near her or Madeline.

Never again would she be any man's whore.

DULCIE smelled rain in the air when she awakened the following morning. She turned her head toward the single square window in the loft to find raindrops on the glass and gray clouds hovering in the drab dawn sky. She couldn't hear any patter on the roof and was surprised she'd slept through the shower.

Although she knew she should get up and prepare breakfast, she continued to lie on the straw tick beside her sleeping daughter. She listened to the excited chittering of birds and Flossie's low mooing that told Dulcie she was ready to be milked.

On the surface, little had changed since Dulcie was a girl growing up in this same cabin. But the years, like a flooding river, left nothing untouched. Currents and landscapes had altered, just as Dulcie's outlook and appearance had changed. No longer was she the seventeen-year-old girl who'd eloped five years ago.

The years had given her an appreciation for family, and although she had never held much respect for her father, he'd been a constant in her life. When she'd been a child and when she'd returned to this shack as a widow four months ago, he'd been here. And now he was gone. No snores emanated from the bedroom below and there would be no more curses when he woke with an aching head.

Dulcie didn't want to think about him and focused on what needed to be done today. As usual, there were more chores than hours to get them done, especially with today being wash day. Then she remembered the man who'd promised to return today. Would Forrester keep his word?

Swallowing back the gloominess that matched the day, she rose quietly so she wouldn't wake Madeline. She descended the rickety ladder and tugged her gown off over her head. With a wrinkled nose, she donned the patched breeches and baggy shirt, tucking the tails into her waistband. Faded braces over her shoulders held up the too-large pants that had been her father's. At one time she would've been scandalized to wear men's clothing, but now it was a necessity. In fact, she could count on one hand the times she'd worn a dress since she'd arrived home. Including yesterday at her father's grave.

As she brushed her hair in front of the cracked shaving mirror, she studied the dark circles beneath her eyes. Since her husband's death, she hadn't slept a night without waking at least a half dozen times. Sometimes it was nightmares and other times it was disturbing memories that jarred her from a sound sleep with the abruptness of a rifle shot. However, they were a small price to pay for Madeline's health and safety.

From a peg by the door, she retrieved her father's old jacket then jammed the floppy hat that hung beside it on her head, tucking her hair beneath it. After using the necessary, she gathered the eggs, deftly dodging the chickens' sharp beaks. She carried the eggs to the house, and ensuring Madeline remained asleep, Dulcie went back out to milk the cow.

She led the docile animal to a corral post and tied her. Grabbing the milk bucket and placing it under the cow's heavy udder, she sat on another old pail while she did the milking. Two months ago her father had almost sold Flossie to buy whiskey. Fortunately, Dulcie had talked him out of it. Madeline needed the milk, and Dulcie churned butter to trade for goods at the mercantile.

She leaned her forehead against Flossie's side as despair threatened to choke her. Her father, a tolerable man when sober, became mean-ugly when he drank. He'd angered a lot of people, and small towns nursed grudges like a grizzly nursed her young. Dulcie's mother had smoothed ruffled feathers and mended bridges, but once she was gone Dulcie's father had lost little time in un-smoothing those feathers and destroying those bridges.

When Lawrence Carpenter was murdered, it didn't take long for the townsfolk to lay the blame at Frank Pollard's feet. But then, they'd had a shove in his direction. . . .

"Mrs. McDaniel."

Dulcie jerked her head up from Flossie's side and spotted Rye Forrester standing on the other side of the corral fence. Her heart slid into her throat as relief nearly brought tears to her eyes. She hadn't realized until this moment how much she'd been counting on him returning.

"Mr. Forrester. You're early."

He shifted his weight from one foot to the other and shrugged. "Not by much. I can finish that up if you'd like."

She scrambled to her feet and wiped her hands on her thighs, grateful for the excuse to regain her composure. "I'd appreciate it," she said with stiff courtesy. "I'll get breakfast on."

Forrester stepped back, and she ducked through two of the corral rails. Straightening, she slipped in the mud, and

Forrester caught her arm, steadying her. She jerked out of his grip, her breath coming in ragged gasps.

"You all right, ma'am?" he asked.

She heard only concern in his voice but nodded curtly. "Fine. Thanks. I'll get breakfast started."

She forced herself to walk back to the cabin, although she could feel the hired man's curious gaze on her. Once inside, she closed the door and leaned against it, breathing deeply to counter her irrational fear.

Why had she reacted so strongly? He'd merely saved her from falling flat on her face. It wasn't like he was making improper advances. She snorted. The way she looked, most could hardly tell she was a woman, much less be attracted to her.

"Ma, gotta pee," Madeline announced, cupping her hands against herself and bouncing up and down in the middle of the room.

Dulcie shook off her lingering agitation and retrieved the chamber pot from beneath the bed in her parents' room. Usually she took Madeline out to the privy, but Forrester's presence and her disturbing reaction made her wary. "Use this, honey."

The young girl quickly took care of business, and Dulcie slid the pot back under the bed, making a mental reminder to take care of it later.

"Do you need help getting dressed?" Dulcie asked.

Madeline shook her head. "I'm big girl. Can do it myself." She scampered up the ladder.

Smiling, Dulcie set to work putting on coffee and making breakfast. As she stirred the porridge a knock sounded at the door and her heart leapt into her chest once more.

Forrester called out from the porch, "The milk bucket's by the door, Mrs. McDaniel. I'll be unsaddling my horse and setting a place in the barn for my gear. Then I'll let the mule and cow out to pasture."

As his boot heels thudded away on the porch, Dulcie peeked through the wood slats covering the kitchen window. His broad shoulders and long-legged, rolling gait drew her admiring attention, but she squelched her response. He was a man just like any other. And hadn't Dulcie learned more than she ever wanted about men?

She retrieved the milk bucket from the porch, careful not to spill any.

"Pretty horsey man?" Madeline asked.

Dulcie turned to see her daughter wearing her dress backward with the buttons misaligned. She shook her head in amusement. "Yes, that was him. He'll be working here for a little while."

Madeline's eyes sparkled. "With his horsey?"

Dulcie smiled even as her heart clenched. "His horsey will be staying with Flossie and Jack." She knelt in front of her daughter and unbuttoned the dress. "You have to promise me you won't try to pet his horsey before asking me."

The girl's lower lip pouted. "But I'm big girl."

"The horsey's bigger and she might hurt you." Dulcie removed Madeline's dress then had her slip it on with the buttons to the back. "Turn around."

Madeline did so and Dulcie rebuttoned the dress. Once she was done, she turned Madeline around to face her. "Will you promise me you won't pet the horsey or talk to the man unless you ask me first?"

Madeline stared at her, her chin jutting out stubbornly. "Why?"

Dulcie put on her stern face. "Because I said so."

After a moment Madeline nodded. However, Dulcie had no illusions about her independent daughter. Madeline would sneak away at the first opportunity to pet Forrester's horse. Dulcie would just have to watch her closely for the first few days. Fortunately, she doubted Madeline would be as bold with Forrester as she'd be with his horse.

Dulcie ladled the porridge into three bowls to cool and fried up a half dozen eggs. After getting Madeline settled at the table with porridge, eggs, and bread, she placed Forrester's breakfast on a baking tin and carried it out to the porch.

"I'll take that, ma'am," he said, striding the last few yards to the porch.

Dulcie gave him the tray and stepped back, sliding her

hands into her back trouser pockets. "Just knock on the door if you'd like more."

"This'll be fine, Mrs. McDaniel." He smiled, revealing amazingly white, even teeth. "Thanks."

Warmed by his friendly smile and simple but sincere gratitude, Dulcie fled back into the cabin.

RYE shrugged at the widow's hasty retreat and set the tray at the top of the porch steps. He lowered himself to sit beside it and took a sip of the hot coffee. Strong enough to starch a man's drawers, just the way he liked it. The food was plain but good, and the added treat of honey on the two slices of bread filled him comfortably.

With both hands wrapped around the cup, he savored the rest of the coffee and considered his new employer. He couldn't blame her for being as skittish as a wild mustang. With having her father accused of murder and lynched not long after her husband died, it was surprising she'd hired him. But then, there was no denying her place needed more work than a grown man could hope to accomplish in a month of Sundays, much less a woman alone.

Rye wasn't surprised the place was in ruins. He knew firsthand how alcohol and honest labor didn't mix. But it was a damned shame this was what Mrs. McDaniel and her daughter had come home to find. Maybe her life hadn't been easy with Jerry, but at least the army had ensured they had a steady paycheck and a place to live.

The door opened behind him. "More coffee?"

Remaining seated, he turned and lifted his cup. "Thank you, ma'am."

She poured from the blackened pot but didn't leave when she was done. Instead of getting a stiff neck from looking up at her, Rye turned away and surveyed the yard.

"I know it isn't much," she said defensively. "But it's all we got."

Rye restrained a smile. She might not have much, but she had more than her share of pride. "You've got a good crop standing in the field. When that comes in, you'll be able to do more around here."

"A lot of sweat went into it." Bitterness along with pride threaded through her tone. "With Pa dead, I can't harvest it myself." She paused. "You plannin' on sticking around long enough to bring it in?"

Although her words were blunt, matter-of-fact, Rye detected a hint of desperation. He stood and shifted so he could look her in the eye. "I'll stay through harvest."

Relief softened her features but her nod was terse. "There's enough around here to keep you busy until then."

"Yes, ma'am." He hooked his thumb in his pocket and took a drink of coffee. "What do you want me to start with?"

"The pasture fence needs mending. There's stringing wire in the barn."

"Yes, ma'am." He finished his coffee and set the empty cup on the tray. "I'll get started right away."

He found the wire half buried under some old hay in a corner of the barn. After some searching, he found a hammer and nails, as well as a shovel to fix loose posts. Without a wagon or wheelbarrow, he had to make two trips to get the supplies out to the pasture.

The clouds were beginning to dissipate and the moisture-laden air warmed as Rye followed the fence line. In numerous places, there was a single strand of wire barely held by a rusty nail. The fence needed new posts, too, but that would take too much time.

Rye stretched the wire taut and wrapped it around the new nail sticking out of the post. As he held the wire tight with one gloved hand, he used his other to hammer the nail into the wood until it was flush with the post.

He paused to wipe a rolling drop of sweat from his cheek, and from across the field, he spotted Mrs. McDaniel and her daughter coming around the cabin. Pressing his wide-brimmed hat back off his forehead, he watched the breeches-clad woman carry a basket over to a sagging line strung between two trees. The young girl drew pictures on the ground with a stick while Mrs. McDaniel hung the clean clothes on the line.

Rye imagined his wife Mary and their child in Mrs. McDaniel and her daughter's place. Agony tore at his chest, and for a moment, he couldn't breathe. The festering grief was always nearby, ready to ambush him when he weakened. He rubbed a hand across his moist eyes, scrubbing away the unfallen tears and the aching memories.

With renewed determination, he took hold of the wire and stretched it to the next post. He pushed himself ruthlessly the rest of the morning, concentrating only on his task.

By noon the sky was clear of clouds and Rye had given up on wiping away his sweat. His stomach rumbled, reminding him he'd had nothing to eat since breakfast. His sudden thirst convinced him to walk back to get some water and dig out some dried meat from his saddlebags. Surely Mrs. McDaniel wouldn't begrudge him a break.

Stacking his tools and equipment in a neat pile, he trudged across the pasture, past the cross-looking mule and sloe-eyed cow. The desultory breeze barely rippled the laundry on the line and did little to cool Rye. As he approached the well, Mrs. McDaniel stepped out onto the porch. In her hand was a cloth-wrapped package.

"Here's your lunch," she called out. "I'll leave it on the porch."

Rye nodded, and she disappeared back into her ramshackle home. He stopped by the well and drew up a bucket of water. Using the dipper, he drank his fill of the cold, fresh water. He crossed the yard to the porch and sat down to unwrap what Mrs. McDaniel had left him. In the cloth were two thick slices of bread with a mixture of beans and meat between them.

He removed his hat as he ate, letting his scalp cool in the porch's welcome shade.

"I wanna go out." Madeline's childish voice drifted out from the cabin.

"You haven't finished eating yet." Her mother's tone was more patient than Rye would've reckoned, given the woman's brusqueness.

"Not hungry. Wanna play."

"You can play after you eat that last piece of bread."

Rye could envision Mrs. McDaniel trying to bribe the girl and smiled. Jerry had rarely talked about his wife or daughter, and when he had it took the form of complaining. Rye had never understood why a man who'd had everything he wished for would prefer spending his time in stinking saloons with cheap whores.

"No!"

The high-pitched shout followed by a crash brought Rye to his feet. As he started to the door, it was flung open and a miniature dervish flew out. Rye snatched up the girl and swung her around before setting her back on her feet.

"Let her go," Mrs. McDaniel shouted.

The desperate panic in her voice shocked Rye and he released Madeline. Mrs. McDaniel scooped up her daughter and clutched her close. The girl wrapped her arms around her mother's neck, her shoulders shaking with quiet sobs. However, whether her tears were from her mother's agitation or because she was frightened of Rye, he didn't know.

"Don't you ever touch my daughter again," the woman ordered through gritted teeth. "Or I'll shoot you."

Shocked by her deadly threat, Rye raised his hands. "I meant no harm, Mrs. McDaniel. I figured you didn't want her running off."

"She's my daughter and I'll take care of her. You are only to do what I tell you. Is that understood?"

Rye's temper rose and he took a step toward her. Her gaze flicked away from him for a second but she held her ground even as she patted Madeline's back soothingly.

"All I did was catch her for you, ma'am. If you're going to think the worst of me, then maybe I'd best move on now." As soon as the words were out, Rye knew he wasn't going to leave. His debt was far from being paid. But how could he work for a woman who believed he could actually harm a little girl?

Her cheeks reddened but her spine remained ramrod stiff. "I didn't mean to insult you, Mr. Forrester, but Madeline's all I got. If something happened to her, I'd never forgive myself." Her mouth thinned to a flat line. "Or the person who hurt her."

Rye's anger leached away. She was only behaving like a mother. Although he could remember little about his own mother, he sometimes dreamed of a soft voice and gentle touch. "I understand, ma'am. But I want you to know I'd never hurt your little girl."

She remained wary, but if she'd accepted him at his word, his respect for her would've lessened. It was a good idea to maintain a healthy suspicion of strangers, but her reaction had gone beyond suspicion. It was as if something had happened in the past to make her unreasonably distrustful.

Mrs. McDaniel gave him a curt nod. "I'll hold you to that, Mr. Forrester. And I expect you to stay away from Madeline." Then, speaking in a low soothing tone to her daughter, she turned and went into the cabin, slamming the door behind them.

Rye sank back down onto the step, shivering at the woman's chilly tone. Maybe Jerry had had good reason to find solace in the welcoming embrace of a prostitute.

THREE

DULCIE straightened from her stooped position in the garden and suppressed a groan. Her gaze immediately went to Madeline, who continued to play with her raggedy doll beneath the shade of a sprawling oak tree. Content that her daughter was behaving, Dulcie placed her palms against her lower back and bent backward to stretch out the painful kinks in her spine. She straightened little by little, sighing in relief as the aches diminished.

By her reckoning, she'd been weeding and picking vegetables for nearly two hours. Neat piles of carrots, beans, onions, and corn awaited her. The only thing left was to dig up a hill of potatoes to have with the vegetables and salt pork tonight.

She grimaced. They'd had nothing but salt pork for weeks. Imagining the taste of fresh meat made her mouth water. If there wasn't so much to do around the place, she'd have asked Forrester if he'd be willing to go hunting. Wild game wouldn't be as tasty as beef, but venison or rabbit would be a welcome change.

With a mental shrug, she called out, "Madeline, let's get some water."

The girl scrambled to her feet, keeping her doll clutched to her chest, and took Dulcie's hand with her free one.

"What have you and Aggie been doing?" Dulcie asked.

Madeline held up her doll and seemed to listen for a few moments. "Aggie says it's secret."

Dulcie feigned disappointment. "You can't even tell me?"

Madeline drew the doll against her chest again and shook her head vehemently. "No. A secret."

Dulcie wondered if she should be worried about her daughter's active imagination. Since the girl didn't have anyone to play with, Madeline had created her own playmate. Had Dulcie done the same? It was too long ago to remember.

They arrived at the well, and Madeline pulled out of her grasp. "Want to do it."

Smiling, Dulcie allowed her to toss the bucket down the well. A moment later there was a dull splash. She handed the rope to Madeline, who set Aggie off to the side. The girl tugged at the rope and Dulcie surreptitiously helped her, letting Madeline believe she was pulling the full pail up by herself.

"You *are* getting to be a big girl," Dulcie praised. She handed the dipper to Madeline, who drank in noisy gulps. Some of the water ran down her chin and dripped onto her dress.

The girl giggled as she gave the dipper to her mother. "All wet."

"The sun will dry you in no time," Dulcie said with a smile.

She took a drink and felt the cold water flow all the way down her throat into her belly. The hot afternoon sun had sapped much of the moisture from her body.

Noticing movement inside the barn, she focused her attention in that direction. Forrester strode out, his arms filled with newly cut corral poles. He spotted her and Madeline, set down the poles, and strolled over to join them. She recognized the familiar rolling gait of a man who spent much of his time on a horse. Having been in the cavalry, her husband had possessed the same.

Ever since Forrester's first day, over a week ago, she'd made a point of keeping her distance. They talked only when Dulcie gave him his meals on the porch, and they discussed the tasks for the day. He remained courteous, and she had to admit he was a conscientious worker. He'd accomplished more in eight days than her father had in a year.

He removed his hat as he approached the well. Sweat flattened his wavy hair and his hat left a band across his forehead. Tugging off the handkerchief from around his neck, he mopped his brow and face. "Afternoon, Mrs. McDaniel, Miss Madeline."

"Mr. Forrester," Dulcie said, her own voice cool and detached. She remained between him and her daughter.

"Drink?" Madeline asked him.

He glanced down at Dulcie, his expression questioning. At his deference, she lost some of her tension, but her wariness didn't disappear completely. She nodded and stepped aside, but kept close enough to safeguard Madeline.

He hunkered down a few feet from the girl. "That would taste mighty good, Miss Madeline."

She giggled and filled the dipper. As she passed it to him, water sloshed onto the ground, but fortunately some remained in the ladle.

Forrester tipped back his head, and Dulcie's rapt gaze followed the up and down glide of his Adam's apple in his sun-darkened skin. A sweat droplet slid down his neck, leaving a slick trail in its wake. It rolled toward the vee of his open collar, settling in the hollow at the base of his throat, beckoning her. She ignored the reckless desire racing through her veins, even as she cursed her body's unwanted response.

"Thank you, Miss Madeline. That hit the spot," he said.

The smile he aimed at her daughter nearly buckled Dulcie's knees.

"You're welcome, Mister For'ster," Madeline said shyly.

Even her daughter wasn't immune to his charm, which made him even more dangerous. Instinctively, Dulcie shifted so she again stood between them.

Forrester straightened and raked a hand through his thick brown hair. His shirt stuck to his muscular shoulders and back, drawing her admiring gaze. "Hot one today."

"Sure is," Dulcie said, eyeing the sun's angle. "How is the corral coming?"

"As soon as I get the new poles up, I'll chop the old ones so you can use them in the stove."

"I appreciate it."

"It's my job, ma'am."

Madeline tapped her mother's hip. "Go play with Aggie?"

"Sure, honey," Dulcie replied absently. "Just stay in sight."

Madeline scampered off to the porch, talking to her doll the entire way.

Forrester's gaze followed the girl. "You must be proud of her, Mrs. McDaniel."

Dulcie slid her hands into the trousers' back pockets. "Usually."

Forrester grinned, his eyes creasing at the corners. "I'm sure she's a handful sometimes. I know I was when I was her age. I don't think I grew out of it until I was out of knee pants."

Dulcie should've walked away and gone back to work, but the temptation to talk to another adult was too enticing. "I was, too. Pa used to tan my hide. It didn't help. Guess I was too stubborn."

"There were times I skipped school 'cause I couldn't sit down."

Despite herself, Dulcie felt a rush of sympathy for him. "Sounds like your pa was even worse than mine."

He glanced away and donned his hat, hiding his features in shadows. "Wasn't my pa. It was the headmaster at the orphanage. I'd best get back to work."

He strode to the corral, leaving Dulcie to stare after him. She recalled a family of orphans in Locust when she'd been a child. They'd all been separated and had gone to different families. Dulcie recalled one in particular, a girl a year younger than her, who'd rarely smiled and often sat by herself during recess, staring into the distance. The girl had taken refuge in solitude, but Dulcie suspected Forrester had hidden his sadness behind boyish pranks, which had led to getting his hide tanned.

Her gaze shifted to Madeline, who conversed in a singsong voice with Aggie. She didn't want to imagine Madeline being forced to live with someone who didn't love her, or worse yet, would hurt her. Profound terror swept through Dulcie and she wrapped her arms around her cramping belly.

It was her responsibility—hers alone—to ensure that her daughter never lost her sweet smile.

WITH supper on the stove and Madeline taking a nap, Dulcie went out to the porch to clean the vegetables she'd taken from the garden earlier. She paused to watch Forrester washing up by the well, using the dented tin basin, soap, and threadbare towel which she'd put there for his use. With her floppy hat shading her eyes, she glanced over to see he'd finished replacing the corral poles, and had chopped the old ones into firewood. Impressed again by his labor, she managed a slight smile when he looked over at her.

Taking a seat at the top of the porch steps, she tried to ignore him, but could see his movements at the edge of her vision. Picking up a carrot, she trimmed it and tossed the greens into a tub. She'd only done a few carrots when she felt more than saw him approaching. Her fingers tightened on the knife handle.

"Mrs. McDaniel," he said by way of greeting.

Steeling herself against the effect he had on her, she met his blue eyes. "Mr. Forrester. I see you've finished for the day."

"I figured it was too late to start something new. Hope you don't mind."

How could she mind? She had never expected him to be such a hard worker, given his pay. She shook her head. "As long as the work gets done."

Dulcie kept her focus on the carrots as she continued to lop off the tops, but the strength of his perusal set heavy on her.

"Got another knife?" he suddenly asked.

She jerked her head up. "What?"

"If you have another knife, I can give you a hand."

She thought of the dull, worthless knives in the cabin and shook her head. "I don't need any help."

He shrugged. "I don't mind. I'm not used to being idle."

It struck her that someone like him shouldn't have any problem finding a paying job, rather than working for only room and board. However, she shied away from that thought, unwilling to look too closely lest she lose his badly needed help.

She nodded at him. "Suit yourself. If you're bent on doing something, you can snap the ends off the beans."

He grinned. "I haven't done that in years."

She snagged the large kettle that she'd put the beans in and handed it to him. He took it and lowered himself to a step, setting the kettle on the ground.

From her position above him, Dulcie could see his long fingers pick up a bean and snap one end off, then the other, tossing the ends into the tub with the carrot tops.

"Looks like you haven't lost your touch," she commented.

"The orphanage used to have a huge garden. All of us kids had to take care of it." He kept his head turned to his task so Dulcie couldn't see his expression, only the top of his damp hair. "If one of us didn't do our share, we couldn't eat. It didn't take many missed meals to get us to work."

Intrigued in spite of herself, Dulcie asked, "How many children were in the orphanage?"

A shrug of his broad shoulders. "Numbers changed, but usually anywhere from twenty to thirty."

"Did many get adopted?"

"Some. Mostly bigger kids who could do the work on a farm or ranch."

"What about you?"

He grinned boyishly. "I was a skinny runt. Those who came looking for a boy said I was too small, wouldn't be able to do my share."

Dulcie stopped cutting in midmotion and studied his broad shoulders, wide, strong hands, and the muscles that flexed beneath his tanned forearms. She couldn't imagine him as skinny or small. "These people who came to adopt didn't want children to love?"

Forrester chuckled, but it wasn't a pretty sound. "Maybe a few of them did, but mostly they just wanted cheap labor. At least I was spared that."

Dulcie continued her work, but her mind sifted through what Forrester said and, more importantly, hadn't said. Her memory flashed back to the sad orphan girl. "How old were you when you got put in the orphanage?"

Forrester paused, his motions stilled. "Six. I had two older brothers. Creede was sixteen so he didn't have to go there. Slater was eleven."

His voice was even, almost flat, but Dulcie had the impression his control was hard-earned. "At least you had Slater," she said.

"Not for long. Someone took him away a month after we got there." He resumed his task and snapped off the ends of a handful of beans before speaking again. "I haven't seen either of my brothers in twenty-five years."

Dulcie gasped, unable to imagine having family but not knowing where they were or even if they were still alive. In spite of her father's drunkenness, he'd been family. "I'm sorry, Mr. Forrester."

He glanced at her over his shoulder. "Call me Rye. And no need for you to be sorry, ma'am. It was a long time ago, and I've made my own way."

Ill at ease and uncertain what to say, Dulcie finished lopping off the carrot tops. "I can give you a hand with those beans."

Forrester—Rye—set the pan on a step where they could both reach. As they worked, the quiet snaps blended with birdsong and the far-off barking of a dog. Occasionally a hawk's haunting cry echoed down from the hot blue sky.

"So what about you?" Rye asked. "You live here all your life?"

"Most of it," Dulcie replied, uncomfortable talking about herself.

"When did your ma die?"

"Pa said a couple of years ago." Fresh anguish squeezed her lungs, bringing a lump to her throat, which she cleared with a cough. "I wasn't here."

"Were you with your husband?"

Dulcie's defenses, which had lowered, slammed back into place. "Yes."

"I didn't mean to pry, ma'am." Obviously he'd picked up on her renewed guardedness. "I just figured since you said you were a widow . . ."

She relaxed only slightly. Too accustomed to men wanting but one thing from a woman, she had to watch her words. "He was in the army. Died about five, six months back."

"So you came back here."

"It was the only place there was." She kept her focus on her hands as she worked, afraid if she caught his eye, he'd ask more questions. Questions like how had her husband died and what kind of man had he been and how she'd made the journey back home.

Time lengthened, and Dulcie finally breathed a sigh of relief when it appeared he wasn't going to continue his interrogation. He might be merely curious, but she didn't like talking about her past. Her failures were her own, not things to be held up in the light of day to gain pity or charity. Or to be used against her.

She reached into the pan to draw out another bean and her fingers brushed Rye's. Awareness tingled at her fingertips and flowed into her belly. Trembling at her reaction, she jumped to her feet and dusted off the seat of her breeches. "I'll check on supper. Could you get rid of the greens?"

Rye nodded. "I'll give them to the livestock then wash the carrots and beans."

"Thank you." She hurried into the house. The potatoes were boiling, as were the peas and corn. All she had left to do was fry the salt pork and slice the bread.

She got Madeline up so the girl had time to wake and wash up before eating. Twenty minutes later the meal was ready and Dulcie settled Madeline at the table. Before she joined her daughter, she carried Rye's meal out to him.

Rye had swept the porch, and only the two pans of washed carrots and beans remained.

"Thanks for taking care of them," she said stiffly.

"It wasn't any hardship, ma'am." He accepted the tray from her. "Smells good."

"Salt pork," she stated with a shrug. "It's all we have for meat."

"Did your father hunt?"

"He used to, but not since Madeline and I came back."

"What about you?"

She shook her head. "I never learned, and even if I had, I wouldn't have trusted Pa to stay sober long enough to watch Madeline."

"If you can spare me, I'll go out tomorrow morning and see what I can find," Rye said.

She'd hoped he might offer, but she was unable to bend her pride to give him her gratitude. "As long as you aren't gone all day."

"Yes, ma'am."

She couldn't tell if he was mocking her or not.

"Done eating, Ma," Madeline shouted.

Saved by her daughter's call, Dulcie fled back into the cabin.

That night, after the dishes were washed and Madeline was asleep, Dulcie settled in the old rocking chair with a tin cup in her hand. Silence filled the darkness, and with it came the familiar emptiness.

The memory of her body's reaction to her accidental touch of Rye's fingers tainted her. She lifted the cup to her lips and welcomed the whiskey's heat that burned her throat and belly, and dulled the unwanted and unwelcome desire.

PREDAWN found Rye riding away from Mrs. McDaniel's place. His mare, unaccustomed to days of inactivity, tugged at the reins and Rye let the horse gallop down the road. He closed his eyes to fully appreciate the cool morning breeze against his face. After three months of long, endless days where there had been only dank, stale air, Rye had sworn he'd never again take anything as simple as a morning ride for granted.

It was good to be away from the woman and her daughter, if only for a few hours. It was tough keeping up his pretense of not knowing Mrs. McDaniel's husband. The lie of omission grated on his conscience, but he was convinced he'd done the right thing in keeping the truth from her. The proud woman wouldn't have accepted his help otherwise.

Two hours later, he had two rabbits hanging from his saddle horn. He'd spotted deer tracks, but never had a decent shot. With his money and supplies low, Rye didn't want to waste even one rifle cartridge.

As he headed back to the cabin, his horse suddenly shied, and Rye, lulled by the morning's warmth and peacefulness, was nearly unseated. Regaining control, he patted the mare's neck and glanced around to see what had spooked her. A flash of color not twenty feet away caught his attention.

"Who's out there?" he yelled.

Leaves rustled and a group of finches rose up not far away, startled by something. Knowing something or somebody was there, Rye dismounted and looped Smoke's reins about a nearby branch. He ducked under branches and pushed through spiny brush.

"Who's here?"

Even as he called out, Rye cursed himself for ten kinds of a fool. If it was someone who had nothing to hide, he would've answered him. If the stranger didn't want to be found, Rye was probably going to be shot for his trouble, or at the very least, have his horse stolen.

Hoping he hadn't gotten smart too late, Rye retraced his steps back to his mare. He spotted a figure standing by Smoke and drew his revolver. As he neared the opening, he realized the person was very small or very young. Or both. Then he recognized the too-short and oft-mended overalls. He stuck his revolver back in his holster and strode through the brush, not bothering to mask his approach.

"What're you doing out here, Collie?" he asked.

The boy who worked at the bathhouse shrugged as he continued to stroke the mare. "I'm out here a lot. I heard the shots. Looks like you was hunting."

Rye had to take a moment to process the boy's seemingly unrelated statements. "I wanted some fresh meat."

"You mean you and the widow?"

Rye pressed his hat back off his forehead and crossed his arms. "So how do you know I'm working for her?"

"I seen ya."

Mrs. McDaniel's farm was three miles from town. "Why have you been out there?"

Another indolent shrug. "Nothin' else to do. Ain't many folks that use the bathhouse."

Rye wasn't surprised. "What about school?"

He wrinkled his nose. "Don't like it."

"What about the family you're staying with? Don't they worry about you?"

"Why?" Collie seemed genuinely curious. "It ain't like the Gearsons is my real folks. They only took me in 'cause they said it was their Christian duty."

Rye considered the boy's words. He'd known people like the Gearsons, and oftentimes their Christian duty included working the adopted children like slaves under the guise of teaching them a work ethic. He fought down a wave of anger. "Do they give you chores to do?"

"Nah."

Startled, Rye tried to see past Collie's indifference. "None?"

"The other kids do 'em. I'm just underfoot."

The way Collie said "underfoot" Rye suspected the Gearsons used the term a lot around the orphan. "So they don't miss you when you're gone?"

"Hard enough to keep track o' their own."

Rye eyed the boy's skinny frame. "They feed you?"

Collie turned his back to Rye and rubbed the horse's nose. "Yeah."

Something told him the kid wasn't being entirely truthful, but he didn't want to push him too hard. "Want a ride back to town?"

Collie spun around, his eyes wide. "Sure, mister."

"The name's Rye, remember?"

"Sure, Mr. Rye."

Smiling, Rye mounted his mare. He leaned down to grab Collie's wrist and hauled him up to sit on the horse's rump behind him. "Hold on to me."

Collie wrapped his thin arms around his waist and Rye tapped Smoke's sides.

"You ever ridden before?" Rye asked the boy.

"My pa used to let me sit in front of him."

Collie's wistful tone stirred Rye's own memories. "When did your folks die?"

" 'Bout a year ago."

"Do you have any brothers or sisters?"

"I had a little brother, but he got sick and died when he was a baby."

So Collie was alone.

"How many children do the Gearsons have?"

"Seven."

Rye was surprised a couple with that many of their own would offer to care for an orphan. "You like them?"

He felt Collie's shrug. If Collie spent so much time roaming alone, it was doubtful he did much with the Gearson children.

"Mrs. Gearson was Ma's friend. She said she was obla . . . obla—"

"Obligated?" Rye guessed.

"Yeah. Obligated to take care of me. Mr. Gearson didn't want to." Collie tightened his hold around Rye's waist. "At least he don't hit me."

And for a young boy alone that was probably the best he could do. Rye patted the boy's arm. "You mind stopping at Mrs. McDaniel's place before we go into town?"

Collie stiffened. "Don't want to."

"But you said you've been there already. This way you can meet the widow and her little girl."

"No!" Collie released Rye and wiggled backward off the horse, dropping to the ground.

Rye halted Smoke and turned to see the boy climbing to his feet from where he'd fallen, his eyes wide. "Why'd you do that?"

Collie merely shook his head, his shaggy hair falling across his eyes. He shoved the strands back and, without a word, turned and fled.

"Collie," Rye shouted. "Come back here. Collie!"

Only the sound of crashing brush answered him. Rye was worried about the boy, but he knew that if Collie didn't want to be found, Rye wouldn't stand a chance of locating him.

Why was he frightened of Mrs. McDaniel?

The answer was plain to see. Collie probably feared her for the same reason the townsfolk shunned her. She was the daughter of a supposed murderer.

$\mathcal{F}$OUR

HER shoulders aching, Dulcie placed a cloth over the eight loaves of bread she'd made that morning with the remaining flour. With the sun already hot, it wouldn't take long for the dough to rise. She dreaded the thought of firing up the stove, but they'd used the last of the bread this morning. Fortunately, the headache she'd awakened with had diminished to a tolerable throbbing or she'd be even more miserable.

"Mr. For'ster's back," Madeline called from the porch through the open door.

Since Forrester had left his gear in the barn, Dulcie had been fairly certain he'd return. Still, she couldn't help but be relieved that he, too, hadn't abandoned them.

She tucked her long ponytail beneath the floppy hat and walked out to the porch. She immediately spotted Rye riding in, and it looked like he'd had luck hunting. Taking Madeline's hand, Dulcie met him at the corral.

"Pet horsey?" Madeline asked hopefully.

"Is it all right if she pets your mare?" Dulcie asked, deferring to Rye.

He smiled, and she was struck anew by his rugged features, especially the startlingly blue eyes enhanced by his sun-darkened face. "That'd be fine, ma'am. Smoke here enjoys being the center of attention."

Dulcie continued to hold Madeline's hand while the girl stroked the horse's soft nose. Dulcie motioned with her chin at the sack tied to the saddle horn. "It looks like you had some luck."

Rye held up the bag and leaned closer. She forced herself to hold her ground.

"Two rabbits," he said in a low-pitched voice. "They're already skinned and gutted. Wasn't sure how your daughter would take to seeing them."

It was a thoughtful gesture that touched and surprised Dulcie. Jerry wouldn't have thought twice about tossing two bloody rabbits down in front of his young daughter. But wary of letting Forrester see too much, she schooled her expression to remain indifferent. "I appreciate it." She took the bag with her free hand. "I appreciate the fresh meat, too," she added stiffly.

"If you'd like, I'll try again in a couple of days. If I can bring down a deer, you'll have meat for a spell."

Her heart sped up. "I thought you said you'd stay 'til after harvest."

"I did, and I will." He appeared puzzled.

Dulcie felt light-headed with relief. She'd assumed he meant that the deer would be only for her and Madeline. She gave Rye an acknowledging nod, but his expression indicated he was waiting for more. Feeling foolish, she didn't let him in on her mistaken assumption.

"With the fresh vegetables, this will make a good stew," she said.

"I s'pect so, ma'am." After giving her one last measuring glance, Rye released his saddle's cinch.

"You figuring on working on the barn today?" Dulcie asked.

Rye shook his head. "Thought I'd patch your roof then start on the porch."

"There are more holes in the barn. Since you were staying in there, I figured you'd want to cover those first."

He shrugged. "I've got a sheltered corner. That's all I need. Your daughter should have a safe, dry place."

Dulcie stared at him, trying to decide if he was sincere or only playing on her concern for Madeline to gain her trust. She wasn't certain. However, allowing him to repair the cabin wasn't a threat, as long as he didn't break the rules.

"Come on, Madeline. Mr. Forrester has to put his horse into the corral," Dulcie said.

With only a slight thrusting of her lower lip, Madeline nodded.

"Bye, Mr. For'ster," she said to Rye, waving as Dulcie led her back to the house. "Bye, Smoke."

"Bye, Miss Madeline," he said with a smile and a wink.

Dulcie felt his gaze on her back as they crossed the yard. What kind of man was Rye Forrester? Was he as considerate and decent as he appeared? Or was that simply a mask he wore to hide his true character? After her experience with men, she figured she'd be able to recognize the mask and see what lay beneath it. But Forrester had her stumped. Or maybe he was just more patient and cunning than other men.

That was it. One day he'd slip up, and Dulcie would see Forrester for what he really was. But until then, she'd accept his help and keep him at a safe distance.

Remaining cautious was much better than being sorry.

RYE hammered the last nail into a shake then leaned back with one arm braced on the roof. He'd just used the last of the wood shingles he'd fashioned from three-foot logs and would have to cut more before he continued. However, the length of the shadows told him he wouldn't be doing any more today.

When he'd first climbed onto the cabin roof, he wasn't sure it would hold his weight. Fortunately, it had, although he remained wary of the places missing shingles. It surprised him that the widow hadn't complained about leaks since it was obvious there were a few.

"Mr. Forrester," Mrs. McDaniel called.

Rye cautiously leaned over the edge to find her standing below, not twelve feet away, and immediately noticed her floppy hat was missing. In the two weeks he'd been there, he hadn't seen her without it and was taken aback by her thick chestnut red hair shot through with golden threads. Her face, usually obscured by the ugly hat, was oval-shaped, and her fair skin displayed a hint of freckles across her nose and cheeks. However, it was her eyes that shocked him. With her hat shading them, they appeared a dull green with brown speckles. Here, in full sunlight, the green was as bright as spring grass with golden brown flecks.

"I asked if you were about done," she said, and it was obvious it wasn't the first time she'd spoken.

Rye shook off his stunned reaction. "Yes, ma'am. I just need to put up my tools and wash."

"I'll bring out your supper in ten minutes." Then she spun on her heel and disappeared from view.

Rye retreated from the edge of the roof and wiped the sweat from his brow. Strange how he hadn't considered Mrs. McDaniel an attractive woman, and figured she wore the men's clothing to hide her plain features. But now, after seeing her without the hat, he couldn't help but wonder what the baggy shirt and pants hid.

Shaking his thoughts free of the possibilities, he climbed down the ladder carefully. As a child, heights had bothered him. They still did, but he'd learned to handle the fear. More or less.

Mrs. McDaniel, wearing the hat again, brought out his food just as he finished drying his face and hands by the well. She waited for him to join her, which surprised him. Usually she simply left his tray on the porch and made herself scarce.

The delicious scents of rabbit stew and fresh-baked bread, the smell that had taunted him all day, reminded him how hungry he was. "Thanks, ma'am."

He sat down on the porch, his feet planted on a lower step, and removed the cloth covering an oversized bowl filled with stew with three thick slices of bread setting on a plate beside it. He expected the widow to hightail it back into the cabin, but she remained, her arms crossed as she gazed down at him.

"Thank you for the rabbits, Mr. Forrester," she said.

"You already thanked me." He glanced up at her. "Besides, that was the easy part, ma'am. You had the hard chore of cooking it." He grinned. "And didn't I ask you to call me Rye?"

A flush touched her cheeks and, knowing the freckles were there, he saw them clearly. It gave her face a girlish appearance, a look at odds with her solemn nature.

"Actually, it was a pleasure to cook something other than salt pork"—she paused—"Rye."

The sound of his name carried by her voice startled him. Although he'd told her to call him Rye, she hadn't done so until now. He considered calling her Dulcie, but he'd worked too hard to gain her trust and didn't want to lose it.

He glanced around, surprised he couldn't see or hear Madeline. "Where's your daughter?"

"Inside. Sleeping."

That was the reason it was so quiet. He stuck a spoonful of stew in his mouth and closed his eyes to savor the taste of the fresh vegetables with the meat. After swallowing, he opened his eyes and caught Mrs. McDaniel peering down at him. She averted her gaze, but not before Rye noticed the puzzlement in them.

"Something bothering you, ma'am?"

She shook her head. "No. Just thinking."

"About what?" Rye took a generous bite from a slice of bread covered with pale yellow butter.

Shifting her weight from one foot to the other, she shrugged. "My father."

Rye continued to eat his stew, letting Mrs. McDaniel pick her own time to speak.

"He didn't kill Mr. Carpenter. He couldn't have," she finally said.

Rye frowned and tilted his head back to look at her. "How can you be so sure?"

"He was a drunk, but he wasn't a murderer."

"Was he a mean drunk?"

She glared at him then looked away. "He wasn't violent."

He'd bet good money she'd answered with a half truth.

"Maybe this Carpenter fellah made him mad while he was drunk."

Mrs. McDaniel remained silent. Rye mentally shrugged and continued eating. He emptied the bowl before she spoke again.

"He and Pa had an argument the day before, but he didn't kill him." She paused. "He was in our barn, drunker than a skunk, when Carpenter was murdered."

"You told the law that, didn't you?"

She glowered down at him. "Of course." Her gaze skittered away. "The sheriff didn't believe me. Said I was protecting him."

Rye studied her thinned lips and stiff posture. "Were you?"

For a moment, he thought he'd pushed too hard.

"No. I wouldn't protect a murderer, even if he was my father." Stubborn determination was clear in the lift of her chin.

Rye believed her. "So who do you think killed Carpenter?"

"I don't know." The words were spat out, as if she'd been gnawing on them for some time without success.

"Who had a grudge against him?"

Her shoulders slumped, and she sat on the porch, her back against the cabin. "Nobody. To hear folks talk, you'd think Carpenter walked on water."

Rye snorted. "In my experience, someone without enemies is hiding something. How long did Carpenter live in town?"

"I heard he showed up about three years ago."

"So you didn't know him."

She shook her head. "That was a couple years after I left Locust and got hitched."

To Jerry. Rye cut off the thought. He couldn't afford to let it slip that he knew her husband.

She narrowed her eyes and clenched her jaw. "I'm going to find the real murderer and show everybody in this town that even though Pa was a drunk, he wasn't a killer and didn't deserve to die like one."

Rye licked the butter from his fingers, not surprised by her declaration. She was a proud woman and wouldn't take to folks believing the worst of her father and, consequently, her. "How do you plan on doing that?"

"I'm not sure yet." Her expression was hard, angry, but her words were hesitant. "But I'll find a way." Then, as if embarrassed by her outburst, she rose. "Would you like some more stew?"

"No thanks, Mrs. McDaniel. I'm full up." He handed her the tray with the empty bowl and plate. "If you'd like, I could do some asking around in town. I might be able to learn something about the murder."

"Thanks, but it's not your concern, Rye. He was *my* father." She turned but paused before going into the cabin. "My name's Dulcie."

She was gone before Rye could comment.

WITH only the light of a half moon, Dulcie paced the floor. The air within the cabin remained sweltering from having the stove fired most of the day, so she wore only a threadbare gown that fell to midcalf and stretched taut across her breasts. It was one she'd found in the old trunk in the loft, from before she'd finished growing and bore a child.

Her conversation with Rye played over and over in her mind. Not that it was a secret she didn't believe her father killed Carpenter, but she hadn't planned on Rye being such a good listener. Or maybe she was only desperate for the company of a man who wasn't a drunk or a scoundrel. Either way, it didn't excuse her lapse in baring her troubles to a hired man.

Dulcie stared out the window, at the varying shades of black and gray. A breeze rustled leaves and cast shifting shadows across the ground and sides of the barn. A coyote yipped, followed by another and another, and then there was nothing. Abrupt silence.

A dark figure emerged from the barn and Dulcie gasped, only to recognize Rye's lanky figure a moment later. She pressed her palm to her chest, between her breasts, and felt her heart hammering. But it wasn't all from being startled.

She shifted to the side of the window so he wouldn't see her, but remained where she could watch his movements. The moon provided enough illumination to tell he wore only pants and boots. He sauntered to the corral and folded his arms on the top pole, giving Dulcie a full, but murky, view of his back. Although he wasn't a large man, his shoulders were well-proportioned, angling down to a narrow waist, nicely rounded backside, and slim hips.

Familiar urges heated her blood and stuttered her breath. It was like the first time she'd lain with Jerry. Her entire body had come to life, sensitive and keening for hands upon her fevered skin and a more intimate need to be touched in places even she'd been afraid to touch.

Dulcie closed her eyes and leaned her forehead against the wall. She'd made her vow less than four months ago and already she was tempted to break it. Was she so needy she couldn't stand on her own two feet? So filled with sinful urges that she couldn't control her body's reaction to a handsome man?

She'd used her shameful nature to snag a husband and escape this place. Then she'd done so again to gain passage for her and Madeline's way back to the home she'd escaped. She'd come full circle in five years.

However, she wasn't a girl anymore, nor was she a woman desperate to return to the only home she'd known, the only place that offered a chance to raise her daughter by herself. Rye Forrester had accepted her conditions for work, and those conditions hadn't included Dulcie's body.

Yet if she offered, would Rye accept as quickly as Jerry or the peddler had? He was a man, so the answer was obvious.

A tear slid down her cheek, surprising her. She wiped it away with a vicious scrub of her palm. She thought she'd made her peace with what she'd done since she couldn't go back and change her foolish past. But she had it within her power to shape her future, as long as she denied those needs that invited nothing but trouble.

She turned away from the window, avoiding temptation, but the restlessness remained. Her bare feet carried her to her parents' room, and she opened the trunk at the foot of the bed. Very little remained within the trunk—a dried wildflower bouquet and a framed picture of a newlywed couple sitting stiffly for the camera. And a whiskey bottle.

Dulcie snagged the bottle's neck and carried it to the kitchen where she filled a cup halfway, then added a splash

more. After returning the whiskey to the trunk, she clutched
the cup to her chest and crossed back to the window. As she
stared at Rye, she sipped the whiskey.

Only after the liquor dulled her desire did she climb up
into the loft and fall asleep.

THE pounding on the roof joined with the throbbing in her
head and threatened to blow Dulcie's skull apart. With the
breakfast dishes washed and put away, she sat down and
folded her arms on the table to rest her head on them.

She'd overslept that morning, waking only when Madeline stirred. Despite her headache, she'd hurried through her
ablutions and dressed quickly. When she finally opened the
door to milk Flossie, she'd found a pail full of milk, as well
as another with the gathered eggs sitting on the porch.

From across the yard, Rye had nodded at her then returned to his task, forming shingles from logs. By the high
stack of shakes, he'd been at his chore for at least an hour.
And Dulcie had slept through it.

Merely thinking about it made her burn with embarrassment. It was her job to milk the cow and pick up the eggs,
and if she couldn't do those small chores, how could she
hope to hold onto the farm? Or find a murderer?

"Ma, wanna go outside," Madeline said, tugging on her
sleeve.

Dulcie raised her head and squinted against the harsh
sunlight coming through a crack in the cabin wall. It had to
be quieter outside than inside with Rye now working on the
roof. "All right, honey."

She remembered to place her hat on her head and tugged
it low over her eyes. She was grateful for the protection
against the bright day. If only she could find something to
dull the noise.

Once outside, Madeline skipped around the yard, scattering the scratching chickens and singing to herself. Dulcie
watched from the porch, but the hammering sounded even
louder there so she stepped out beyond the house. The pounding mercifully stopped, and she glanced up to see Rye sil-
houetted against the sun. She quickly lowered her eyes.

"Feeling puny this morning?" he asked.

She would've glared up at him if the sun wasn't right behind him. "It's not against the law to sleep late once in awhile, is it?"

"No. I just wasn't expecting it."

"Sorry you had to wait for breakfast." She cringed inwardly at her sarcasm.

"I wasn't worried about breakfast." His tone revealed impatience. And worry.

Dulcie refused to acknowledge his concern and the lump in her throat. She narrowed her eyes to mere slits and managed to hold her gaze on him. "As you can see, I'm fine. How's it going up there?" Diverting his attention would make him stop talking about things she didn't want to talk about.

"I'll have to cut more shakes this afternoon," he said. "Another day or two and I'll have the roof almost as good as new."

Impressed, Dulcie nodded. "That'll be a blessing."

He tipped his head to the side. "I never took you for a religious woman, Dulcie."

His use of her first name caught her off guard. But then she had given him permission to use it. "I'm not. At least, not anymore." Realizing she was being dragged into a conversation not related to work, she asked, "The porch next?"

"Unless you have something else you'd rather have me do."

She thought for a moment. "No, that's fine."

Rye looked past her. "Your daughter's over by the corral."

Dulcie spun around and regretted the hasty motion immediately. Luckily, she managed to gain control of her nausea so she didn't embarrass herself. Once her head and belly stopped rolling, she spotted her daughter ducking through the corral poles.

Dulcie ran across the yard, but didn't have to say a word. Madeline had slipped back out of the corral when she saw her mother coming toward her. The girl waited with an angelic expression that might have worked, except Dulcie had seen her disobeying the rules.

"I came back out," she said when Dulcie reached her.

"You shouldn't have gone through in the first place, young lady."

"Sorry, Ma."

She tried to remain angry, but feeling as she did, Dulcie didn't have the energy. She took her daughter's hand. "Why don't we go to the house and get Aggie so the two of you can play together?"

As Dulcie and Madeline started to the house, a loud crash sounded. Dulcie's eyes widened when she spotted Rye lying on the porch and a man-sized hole in the roof above him.

$\mathscr{F}$IVE

DULCIE'S heart stuttered, and she released her daughter's hand. "Stay here," she ordered.

Madeline, her eyes like saucers, bobbed her head.

Dulcie spared a moment to brush her daughter's soft crown in reassurance then hastened across the yard. She dropped to her knees beside Rye, and her hands hovered over him, uncertain what she should do. Although relieved there was no blood, she remained fearful of his stillness.

"Rye," she said with a husky voice.

His eyelids fluttered and opened. Confusion lay in the depths of his eyes as his gaze darted around and finally settled on her. "Miz McDaniel?"

She sat back on her heels and pressed her trembling hands against her thighs. "You're not dead," she whispered.

He squinted, and she suspected he had hit his head when he fell. "Reckon you're right. Dying wouldn't hurt this damned much."

Dulcie couldn't help herself. She laughed. Even knowing it was more from sheer relief than amusement, she couldn't stop. Tears rolled down her cheeks and she wiped at them, struggling to get her reaction under control.

Rye glared at her. "Glad to see someone thinks me falling off the roof is funny."

"No, no," she managed to say between hiccups. "It's not. Really. It's just . . ." She shrugged. "I'm sorry."

Rye's scowl faded, replaced by a grimace.

Dulcie leaned over him, the humor gone as abruptly as it had appeared. "Does anything feel broken?"

His brow furrowed and she could tell he was taking stock of his injuries. Trying to restrain her impatience, she heard light footsteps running toward them and looked up. Madeline stopped a few feet from the porch, her face pale and frightened.

Needing to reassure her daughter, Dulcie extended her hand. "Come here, honey."

Like the tentative approach of a fawn, Madeline neared her mother and grasped her hand. She lowered herself to Dulcie's lap, but her fretful gaze settled on Rye.

"Mr. For'ster goin' away like Pa?" Madeline asked with a watery voice.

The unexpected question caught Dulcie by surprise and an invisible fist squeezed her chest. She opened her mouth but couldn't find the right words.

Rye pushed to a sitting position, and he awkwardly patted the girl's small, clenched hands and somehow managed to smile. "I'm not going anywhere, Miss Madeline. I just got a bruise or two."

A lump settled in Dulcie's throat. Despite his hurting, Rye saw fit to soothe her upset daughter.

"But you got hurt and Ma was crying."

Dulcie frowned then realized what her daughter had misinterpreted. "I wasn't crying, honey." She shifted uneasily. "Do you remember when I tickled you and you laughed so hard that you cried?"

Madeline nodded somberly.

"That's what happened to me. I was so relieved that Mr. Forrester wasn't badly hurt that I did the same thing." She glanced at Rye, who was studying her far too intently. Her cheeks warm, she averted her gaze.

Madeline's face brightened and her unshed tears dried.

"Mr. Forrester will be fine," Dulcie said. "Be a big girl and get me a clean towel from inside."

The girl nodded solemnly and Dulcie pushed her up off her lap. Madeline paused in front of the door and peered at Rye as if uncertain she should leave him. He smiled and winked at her. The girl's face lit with a grin and she skipped inside.

The moment she disappeared, Rye's body sagged.

Dulcie sighed. She almost wished Rye was more aloof and callous. It would be easier to keep Madeline—and herself—from growing too fond of him.

"Thank you," she said reluctantly.

"For what?" Rye asked.

Dulcie lifted her hands then let them drop to her thighs. "For reassuring Madeline. But we both know you're not as fit as a fiddle," she said dryly. "I assume nothing is broken?"

His façade of composure dropped, replaced by a tightening of his mouth. "No, nothing broken. Bruised, though." He touched the back of his head and flinched then smiled wryly. "Good thing I've got a hard head."

She arched an eyebrow. "Why doesn't that surprise me?"

His chuckle became a groan. "Darned if I know, ma'am."

A smile twitched her lips. "Let me take a look at that hard head."

"Yes, ma'am."

Walking on her knees, she moved behind him and probed his skull gently. His sandy brown hair sifted through her fingers, silky and soft, so different than Jerry's coarser strands or the peddler's greasy pomade. She suddenly became aware of the glide of her camisole and shirt across her sensitive breasts and tried to temper her harsh breathing. She froze and closed her eyes to banish the cursed passion that rose like a swiftly flooding river.

"Dulcie?"

Rye's voice snapped her eyes open, and she jerked her hands back, folding them into fists.

She cleared her throat and schooled her voice to dispassion. "You were lucky. The skin wasn't broken."

"Yeah, lucky."

Rye started to climb to his feet. Dulcie rose faster and with more grace, and reached out to help him. He shrugged aside her assistance. However, once standing, Rye swayed, and she grabbed him, afraid he was going to topple face-down on the porch. When it appeared he was steady, she released him and slid her hands into her pockets.

Glowering, he examined the broken roof and porch.

She could guess his thoughts and tried to reassure him that she didn't blame him for the damage. "It wasn't in good shape before you went through it."

Besides the hole in the roof, he'd broken half a dozen floor planks where he'd landed. The repairs would take an extra day or two.

Madeline appeared in the doorway, her arms filled with towels. "I got 'em, Ma."

Dulcie managed to restrain her amusement. "Thank you. I only need one." She picked one from the pile. "You can put the rest away."

It looked like the girl was going to pout, but she simply turned around and went back into the cabin with her load.

"Sit down on the top step, Rye," Dulcie said.

"No. I'm fine. I need to clean this up. I don't want Madeline to hurt herself." He began to pick up pieces of the roof that lay on what remained of the porch.

Damn his stubbornness.

She set aside the cloth and joined him.

Rye wasn't surprised when Dulcie pitched in to help. Knowing how mulish she was, he'd only waste his breath if he tried to convince her to let him take care of his mess.

As he worked, his awareness of Dulcie sharpened at the memory of her gentle touch while she'd examined his head. Her chest had brushed his back, and there was no question she was all woman beneath the oversized shirt. Despite his aches and pains, his body had reacted to her soft flesh. It had been months since he'd lain with a woman, and he'd been drunk at the time. Hell, he couldn't even recall what she looked like. All he could remember was the desperation to find release . . . and oblivion.

The up and down motion of picking up the broken pieces

made him dizzy but he tried to ignore it. But when his stomach joined forces with his pounding head, he didn't have any choice. He managed to hold off long enough to escape around the corner of the cabin.

With one hand braced against the wall, he leaned over and retched. Cold, clammy sweat covered his face. Even as he vomited, he recognized the sickness as another symptom of a concussion. He'd had the same more than once in his life, and didn't look forward to the next few days when his head would ache like a son of a bitch.

"Are you all right?" Dulcie asked from directly behind him.

He spat one last time and wiped his mouth with the side of his hand. He turned to her, and despite the shading from the god-awful ugly hat, he could see the concern in her features. The last thing he wanted to do was give the widow more to worry about. Why had he been so stupid as to trust the flimsy roof?

"Sorry. It's normal to get sick from a blow to the head," he said. "I'll be fine."

"No reason to be sorry. You should take it easy the rest of the day."

"There's too much to do."

Her lips turned downward, and she looked over his shoulder then settled her resolute gaze on him. "You haven't had any time off since you started working here. If nothing else, you should take a day off for that reason alone."

Rye thought a moment, trying to figure out what day it was, and whether his loss of memory was from the fall or simply from losing track of time. "What is today?"

"Wednesday. You worked right through the Sabbath."

"No offense, ma'am, but so did you."

Her cheeks reddened. "This is my place."

"Even God took a day off."

Her mouth became a thin line, clearly showing her annoyance at his teasing. "God didn't have a farm to work."

Or a debt to pay.

Yet as rotten as he felt, Rye realized anything he attempted to do today would end up having to be redone. Gingerly touching the lump at the back of his head, he nodded.

"All right, ma'am. Let me finish cleaning up then I'll bring my things down from the roof."

"And let you take another tumble?" she asked in exasperation. "You're about as steady as a newborn calf. Sit down."

Her stern voice didn't leave any room for argument. Rye surrendered.

He walked back to the porch with Dulcie close by his side, probably expecting him to fall over any second. He eased himself down on the top step, settled his elbows on his thighs, and dropped his face into his cupped hands.

Although he couldn't see her, he heard Dulcie by the well and the quiet splash of water.

A few moments later, she said in a low voice, "Hold this against your hard head."

He lifted his head and found a damp folded cloth held out to him. He accepted it with a mumbled thanks and pressed it to the bump on the back of his skull.

Madeline's childish voice sounded behind Rye. "I help, Ma?"

"I'm almost done, honey. Why don't you sit beside Mr. Forrester? You can keep him company."

A moment later, the girl dropped down beside Rye, and in her hands was the rag doll he'd seen her with other times. Despite his pounding head, Rye asked, "What's your doll's name?"

"Aggie." Madeline clutched the doll to her chest. "My bestest friend."

"She's lucky."

Madeline scrunched up her forehead. "Why?"

"'Cause she has a friend like you."

Madeline propped the doll on her knees and smoothed its yarn hair. After a moment, she turned her face up to Rye. "Want to be my friend?"

Her simple but sincere question knotted his chest. "I'd like that, Miss Madeline."

She grinned and her eyes twinkled. "Me, too, Mr. For'ster."

"If we're going to be friends, you'll have to call me Rye."

She covered her mouth with her hand and giggled.

Puzzled, Rye glanced at Dulcie, who was watching them.

She shrugged. "She's never called a man by his first name before. She probably thinks it's funny." Dulcie returned to her task.

Rye frowned, trying to figure out if Dulcie was angry with him. Not about the roof, but that he was becoming friendly with her daughter. Yet it had been Dulcie who told Madeline to sit with him. His head throbbed, and he decided to forego trying to figure out Dulcie McDaniel.

Madeline spoke to her doll in a low voice, half her words made up. But it appeared Aggie understood, so Rye gave up on figuring them out, too.

Understanding females was a lot like trying to understand the army. Damned near impossible.

RYE spent the rest of the day sitting in the shade of the oak tree. From his vantage point, he watched Dulcie work in her garden, with Madeline helping. Although he wasn't sure if *helping* was the right word. Dulcie could've done the work in half the time, but she patiently explained the finer points of gardening to her daughter. Like how to tell a weed from a vegetable and when a tomato was ripe. It was enjoyable to watch the usually reserved Dulcie smile and praise Madeline.

It was also a damned fine sight when Dulcie leaned over to pick something or pull a weed. The loose trousers would snug up against her nicely rounded backside and hug her long legs. Even his headache couldn't stop him from imagining how those willowy legs would feel wrapped around his waist and her smooth ass cupped in his palms. He savagely reminded himself that she was untouchable, that he had no right to think of her that way.

He adjusted his hat, setting it at an odd angle because of the lump on his head, and felt restless and guilty for lazing around. But every time he stood, dizziness and nausea washed through him. And he cursed himself as ten kinds of a fool for being so careless. Hell, he wasn't supposed to be a burden to the widow.

He roused from his musings as Dulcie walked toward him, the water pail swinging in her hand. The breeze molded her shirt against her chest, and the suspenders further outlined her breasts. Despite the bagginess of her breeches, the cinched belt defined a slender waist. Her legs were long, but that shouldn't have surprised him. She was taller than his wife, who'd barely topped five feet and weighed a hundred pounds soaking wet.

"Water?" Dulcie asked as she neared him.

Realizing his mouth was dry, although not from the sun's heat, he nodded. "'Preciate it."

She handed him the ladle and he dipped it into the water.

"Thanks," he said after emptying the dipper.

She lowered herself to the ground a few feet from him, her legs folded to the side and one hand braced on the grass. He followed her gaze and spotted Madeline playing hopscotch on the bare dirt. Then he turned his perusal to Dulcie's heat-reddened face, noting the sooty smudges beneath her eyes.

"Been having trouble sleeping?" he asked.

She turned her head sharply, her eyes flat and her mouth a grim line. "Why?"

He drew back, startled by her belligerent response. "You look tired is all."

After staring at him a few moments longer, her antagonism faded and she gave her attention back to her daughter. "I'm fine."

Rye gritted his teeth. She'd obviously felt comfortable enough to join him, so why was she snarling like a wet cat? All he'd done was ask her how she was sleeping. Maybe she considered the question too personal for a hired man.

He leaned against the oak's rough trunk and tipped his head back, careful of the tender spot. Sunlight glittered between the shifting leaves, and the wind's gentle rustle whispered in the background. Despite having known Jerry, he knew little about Dulcie and curiosity impelled him to ask, "How long were you married?"

"Almost five years," she replied after a moment's hesitation.

"How'd you meet your husband?"

She shrugged. "He was assigned to the army post just north of here. We met in town."

The Jerry McDaniel he knew would more likely be found in the saloons, so how had Dulcie met him? Had she worked in one? The woman he knew didn't seem the type to ply men with drinks and coax them upstairs into her bed. Besides, he couldn't imagine Jerry marrying a whore, despite his appetite for their loose charms.

As if reading his mind, Dulcie said, "I was waiting for my father to come out of the saloon when he stopped by the wagon. We got to talking, and there happened to be a social the following Saturday. He invited me. I accepted. We got hitched two months later."

Rye nodded. Not knowing when they'd march off to a new post, many soldiers married fast. Too often it made for marriages that were less than happy. Lonely wives blamed their new husbands for taking them away from family and into the hostile frontier. Was that what had happened with Dulcie and Jerry?

"I couldn't wait to leave this place," Dulcie added. She looked around the ramshackle farm, a strange mix of fondness and bitterness in her expression. "Funny how I missed it, though."

"Not really. It was what you knew."

She fixed her gaze on him. "I suppose. What about you?"

He glanced away. "What about me?"

"You said you were an orphan. What did you do after you left the orphanage?"

Rye's heart kicked up a notch as he debated how much to tell her. "I looked for my brothers. Never found them."

"I'm sorry."

She sounded like she meant it. He shrugged. "Never figured I'd have much of a chance."

"Do you remember them?"

Age-worn pictures of two boys, both older than him, flickered through his memory. "Slater was five years older than me. He was always getting into some kind of mischief. Usually took me along." Rye shook his head, chuckling. "Never knew it then, but I figured out later it was so I got part of the blame. He was always thinking. Always coming up with ways to get out of work and responsibility."

"You said he was adopted?"

Rye's amusement faded. "By some folks looking for cheap labor. Maybe it was Slater's punishment for getting out of so much work when he was younger."

Dulcie didn't say anything.

"Then there was Creede," Rye continued. "My big brother. I always looked up to him. Wanted to be just like him." His thoughts carried him back, and with it came the anguish and fear he'd felt the day the men had come. "He was sixteen when Ma died. We'd been working in the field when two men came to the house. Creede always blamed himself for what happened that day."

"What happened?" Dulcie asked softly.

He blinked, and the horrific image of what they'd done to his mother disappeared. "They killed her," he answered, keeping his voice matter-of-fact.

Dulcie gasped.

Rye ignored her, knowing he'd be unable to continue if he looked at her. "After me and Slater were taken to the orphanage, Creede went after them."

"Did he find them?"

It was a question Rye had asked himself a thousand times. One he still didn't have an answer to. "Don't know. But I do know Creede wouldn't have given up. Not ever."

Unless he'd been killed.

Rye refused to believe the brother he'd idolized was dead. As for Slater, he was too smart to let anyone get the better of him.

"Have you given up on them?" Dulcie asked.

He had given up once, but that was before he'd been left with little else to do with his life. "No. I don't think I can."

He tilted his head back down to meet Dulcie's eyes, and was startled to see compassion in their depths.

"I don't have any brothers or sisters, but if I was separated from Madeline, I'd never give up looking for her," she said. "And I'd do anything to get her back. *Anything.*"

The vehemence in her tone and expression underlined her words. No matter what kind of wife she'd been, Rye didn't doubt she was a good mother.

Dulcie blinked and her cheeks flushed. She stood and grabbed the water pail. "I'd best get supper started."

She walked away with mannish strides, but the sway of her backside was pure woman.

$\mathcal{S}$IX

"MORNIN'."

From where she sat on the milking bucket, Dulcie jerked up her head to find Rye standing on the other side of the corral, his forearms resting on the top pole. She pressed a hand to her chest where her heart threatened to leap out. "Rye. I didn't expect you up so early."

He grinned and tilted his head, giving her the impression of a mischievous boy. "I was about to say the same thing to you."

Her face flamed. Oversleeping yesterday morning had been uncharacteristic, but she felt guilty enough to ignore his inference. "I thought after your fall from the roof . . ."

Flossie mooed, reminding Dulcie of her chore, and she resumed milking the cow.

"My head hurts some but it's better than yesterday," Rye said. "I figured I'd get an early start on fixing what I broke."

"I hope you aren't planning on going back up on the roof." She wasn't about to allow him to do something so foolish as to get dizzy and fall again.

He grinned crookedly. "No, ma'am. I won't be climbing any ladders today."

Embarrassed by her show of concern, Dulcie kept her

gaze on her hands. She searched for something to say, but her mind was blank.

"I'll gather the eggs," he said, breaking the awkward silence.

Dulcie shook her head. "No, that's all right. That's my job." She swallowed the lump of embarrassment. "I'm sorry you ended up doing that and the milking yesterday."

He shrugged. "I didn't mind, Dulcie."

Her name spoken in his honey-smooth voice sent a shiver down her spine. Annoyed by her body's reaction, she said curtly, "I'll take care of it today."

"Suit yourself, but I don't mind."

The raucous birds and the rhythmic sound of milk being squirted into the bucket surrounded them.

"Madeline and I'll be going into town this morning," Dulcie said when Rye didn't leave. "I need a few things."

"Would you like me to go with you?"

"No need."

"All right. I'll hitch Jack to the wagon after breakfast," Rye offered.

She glanced at him. "Thanks. I appreciate it. Is there anything you need?"

"I got nails enough to finish the roof and porch with some to spare, and I can't think of anything else."

Dulcie nodded in acknowledgement and Rye sauntered back to the barn without another word.

Although relieved he'd left, Dulcie felt abandoned and alone. Shrugging aside the foolish notion, she finished milking Flossie and stood. Later, after she'd gathered the eggs, she wasn't surprised to see Rye hewing new shingles for the porch roof.

After breakfast, while Madeline sat by the table playing with Aggie, Dulcie prepared for the trip into town. The extra butter and eggs she put in a bucket and covered with a towel. Hopefully there was enough to trade for flour, coffee, salt, and maybe some sugar.

With a quick glance at Madeline to make sure she was still involved with her doll, Dulcie opened the trunk in her parents' bedroom. The whiskey bottle was nearly empty even though it'd been over half full when her father was arrested. Maybe she'd drunk more than she thought, but after what she'd endured the past couple of weeks no one had a right to condemn her.

With a sinking sensation, she realized her difficulties weren't at an end. Although Rye's assistance had gone far to relieve much of her worries concerning the farm, his presence kept her on edge. And the whiskey blunted that edge. Could she afford to buy one more bottle? That was all she needed. Once the crop was in and Rye was gone, she wouldn't touch another drop.

She closed the trunk and slipped her hand into her trouser pocket. Her fingers closed on the small cloth bag. Five silver dollars and a few odd coins was the sum of her and Madeline's savings. Her father had left nothing but broken promises.

The jangle of metal and leather brought Dulcie out of her bitter musings. Rye was bringing the wagon up to the cabin. It was a thoughtful gesture, and one she appreciated, but her gratitude remained tempered with wariness. Men did nice things for women when they wanted something in return. And usually that something they wanted was the woman herself.

She quickly exchanged her trousers for a faded black skirt that she wore on her rare trips into town. Despite the fact that many folks didn't think much of her, she didn't want to add more fuel to the fire by appearing less than respectable. Pausing in front of a small mirror, she adjusted her hat, making sure her hair was piled beneath it.

"Let's go, honey," Dulcie said to her daughter.

Madeline hopped off her chair and joined her mother at the door. With the bucket of eggs and butter in one hand and Madeline's hand in the other, Dulcie walked outside. Rye was standing in front of the mule, rubbing its knotty nose. He looked up when they came outside and his gaze traveled across her, giving her a flush of awareness. If he was surprised she was wearing a skirt instead of her usual trousers, he didn't show it.

"Your carriage, ladies," he said, bowing at the waist and grinning.

Dulcie's cheeks heated, though she couldn't help but smile. "Pulled by the finest steed in the county, I'm sure."

Rye chuckled and patted the mule's neck. "Jack thinks so."

"Going with us, Mr. Rye?" Madeline asked.

Rye came around to join them by the wagon that had seen better years. He squatted down in front of the girl. "Somebody has to stay here so Flossie and Smoke don't get lonely."

Madeline's expression fell. "Maybe I stay, too."

"Then who'd keep your mother company?" He glanced at Dulcie then back at the girl. "Besides Jack."

Dulcie's lips twitched with laughter.

"I s'pose," Madeline said slowly.

"You s'pose right, Miss Madeline." Rye stood and hoisted her up, swinging her around once before depositing her on the wagon seat.

Madeline's face brightened with pleasure as she giggled. Dulcie reveled in the sweet sound. Before Jerry died, her daughter had laughed little and rarely when he'd been home. Despite everything, Dulcie couldn't help but wonder if Jerry's death wasn't as much a tragedy as a second chance for her and her daughter. But a second chance at what?

Rye took the pail from Dulcie and gave her a hand up into the wagon. Even though she didn't need it, she accepted his assistance with something akin to guilty pleasure. Once she was seated, he passed her the bucket, which she set between her feet.

"We'll be back before noon," Dulcie said.

Rye merely nodded.

Dulcie picked up the reins and immediately noticed the sheen to the leather. "When did you have time to clean the tack?"

He shrugged. "A few days ago. Woke up earlier'n usual so figured I'd use the time."

Dulcie rubbed the straps between her fingers. It wasn't a big thing, but that he'd done it without being asked was something she was unaccustomed to. "Thank you," she said with a husky voice that startled her.

"You're welcome." Rye stepped back.

Dulcie lightly slapped the mule's rump with the reins and the wagon jerked into motion. Rye raised his hand in farewell, and Madeline waved with all her might, as if she were going on a long journey. Dulcie didn't look back as they rolled out of the yard.

The town was only three miles away, a distance Dulcie had often walked as a child when she'd gone to school. Many of the larger trees along the way were familiar, like old friends. She recalled climbing more than one after school, less than eager to get home and do her chores. Although her pa drank back then, it wasn't like after her ma died.

"Pretty bird, Ma." Madeline pointed to a blue bird flitting from branch to branch as it squawked.

"That's a blue jay." A flash of golden feathers caught Dulcie's attention and she motioned to a bush filled with small yellow and black songbirds. "Look over there, honey. Goldfinches."

Madeline's eyes sparkled and she clapped in delight.

The road curved to the west, and Dulcie's heart skipped a beat. Jack seemed to sense her hesitancy and slowed to a plodding gait. As the wagon came abreast of the too-familiar tree, Jack stopped altogether. Dulcie didn't know if she'd reined him in or if the mule had halted on his own.

The oak tree was the oldest and largest in the area with its towering height and wide-spreading branches. The trunk was so big Dulcie and Madeline could hide behind it easily. Dulcie stared at the lowest branch, which was ten feet off the ground, and as thick as her waist. She pictured that morning with the dew glistening on the grass and the coral and orange sky on the eastern horizon. Although she'd been warned, the only thing that had prevented her horrified scream was her sleeping daughter.

They'd left him hanging there like a freshly killed deer, his open eyes bulging like a fish out of water. The evidence of his body's humiliating surrender to death was there for everyone to witness. The sheriff had helped Dulcie cut her pa down after they'd rolled the wagon beneath his swaying body. She thanked God her daughter had been asleep when she'd come upon his body.

"Why stop, Ma?" Madeline asked curiously.

Dulcie shook aside the gruesome memory. "I thought Jack might need to rest, but I think he's ready now."

After urging the mule into motion, Dulcie kept her gaze aimed straight ahead. Fiery rage burned through her veins. Men too cowardly to show their faces had hanged her father, and the sheriff assured her he'd make an effort to discover their identities. But he had made no progress by the day of her father's funeral. Dulcie doubted he'd put in much effort for someone deemed a murderer.

Locust came into view, and she stiffened her spine and pressed her shoulders back. As they rolled down the main street, she was overtly aware of the wary and unfriendly attention she garnered. But those didn't bother her as much as the pitying looks. Thankfully Madeline wasn't old enough to notice, much less understand them.

Dulcie drew to a stop in front of the general store. Her hands shook as she looped the reins around the brake handle. Before jumping down, she wiped her damp palms across her skirt. She had Madeline pass her the bucket with the precious butter and eggs then helped her daughter down.

Ignoring the few people around, she entered the store and walked directly to the counter. Mrs. Coulson, whose husband owned the mercantile, nodded, but her expression remained aloof.

"I have eggs and butter to trade," Dulcie stated without preamble.

Mrs. Coulson crossed her arms beneath her ample bosom. "We don't have much need for either today."

Dulcie's fingers tightened on the bucket handle and she glanced at Madeline, who was eyeing the candy jars. She turned back to the woman and leaned closer to her, not wanting to upset her daughter. "You've always traded before."

Mrs. Coulson shrugged, her eyes hard. "Like I said, no need."

Desperation hummed through Dulcie. "What if I come back tomorrow?"

Mrs. Coulson glanced away. "Doubt if we'll need any then either."

Anger stirred, replacing Dulcie's nervousness. "What about the day after that?"

Mrs. Coulson didn't bother to reply, but met Dulcie's gaze with a flat, inhospitable one.

After the harvest was brought in, Dulcie would have money, but until then she had only her eggs and butter to barter.

Mr. Coulson, a rotund man with twinkling eyes, came out from the back room. He paused, looking from his wife to Dulcie. "Morning, Mrs. McDaniel."

"Good morning, Mr. Coulson." Dulcie kept her voice as amiable as she could. "I came to trade eggs and butter for some dry goods."

Mr. Coulson smiled. "How much do you have with you?"

The man's wife glared at him. "I told her we didn't need any today."

The store owner had always seemed good-natured, so Dulcie was surprised to see his eyes glint with annoyance. "You're mistaken," he told his wife. "We're out of both, and Mrs. McDaniel's butter and eggs have always been of the highest quality."

Mrs. Coulson spun on her heel and marched into the back room. Her husband didn't even bat an eye, but turned back to Dulcie and smiled. "Now let's see what you have."

Relief made Dulcie's knees weak but she steadied herself and set the bucket on the counter. Mr. Coulson lifted the towel.

"I was hoping to get some flour, coffee, and salt," Dulcie said quietly.

Mr. Coulson nodded. "I'll help you."

In no time, the bags were piled on the counter. The storekeeper had been more than generous, even including some sugar in the trade.

"Would you like some?" Mr. Coulson asked Madeline, who was eyeing a jar of gumdrops.

Madeline nodded.

"We can't," Dulcie said, her voice tight.

"Nonsense," Mr. Coulson said. He lifted the lid and scooped out a liberal portion into a small brown bag, which he handed to Madeline. "There you go, little miss."

"What do you say, honey?" Dulcie asked her daughter.

Her eyes huge, Madeline said, "Thank you."

"Yes, thank you very much," Dulcie said to him.

Mr. Coulson chuckled. "Every child should have a treat now and again."

Confused, Dulcie frowned. "Why are you being so nice to us?"

The man didn't pretend to misunderstand, and he sobered. "You and your little girl didn't have anything to do with Lawrence's death, and there's no reason you should pay for what your father did."

Although pleased by Mr. Coulson's willingness to continue doing business with her, Dulcie couldn't help but feel a spark of indignant anger. "I know everybody believes my father killed Mr. Carpenter, but he didn't." Her cheeks heated with embarrassment. "He was passed out drunk in our barn."

Mr. Coulson's eyes filled with sympathy. "Liquor changes a person. Your pa wasn't the man he used to be."

"That might be, but it didn't make him a murderer."

"He argued with Lawrence an hour before he was found dead."

Dulcie clamped her teeth together. She knew who had supposedly seen her father argue with Carpenter. It had been her word against Virgil Lamont's. Even his name made her grit her teeth. Lamont had come to know her like a man knew a woman while she and Madeline had traveled with him from Kansas to Texas. It had been her decision, but Lamont had given her little choice. Then he'd threatened to tell the sheriff how she "paid" for her ride back home if she didn't stop insisting her father was innocent. Afraid for her reputation, she'd backed off. Only she hadn't expected the town to take justice into their own hands.

She couldn't afford to antagonize the store owner so she didn't press her father's innocence. "I thank you, Mr. Coulson."

Dulcie took the smaller bags of coffee, salt, and sugar, while Coulson carried the flour. Madeline's hands were busy with the candy bag and her doll.

"Thanks again," Dulcie said to him as he returned to the store.

"You and your little girl are welcome in my store any time," he said.

Dulcie blinked aside the moisture that stung her eyes. A small kindness, yet it was more than she expected.

The sheriff's office was down a block on the same side

of the street, and Dulcie took her daughter's hand. "Let's go pay Sheriff Martin a visit."

Madeline, one cheek puffed out with a gumdrop, nodded with excitement. Dulcie supposed just being in town was an adventure for the girl, just as it had been for her when she'd been a child. How long ago that seemed.

Madeline skipped down the boardwalk at Dulcie's side. Once at the office, Dulcie paused a moment to gather her composure then opened the door and stepped inside. The sheriff, his boots on the desktop, lowered his newspaper.

"Dulcie," he said and clambered to his feet. He ran a hand over his thinning hair. "What can I do for you?"

Dulcie remembered Lyle Martin from school even though he'd been three years older than her. What she recalled didn't exactly lend much faith in his abilities as a lawman.

"Hello, Lyle. Did you find the men who murdered my pa?" She didn't bother couching her question with tact.

His face reddened and he glanced down even as he shifted his feet like a schoolboy caught diddling in the school outhouse. "Well now, Dulcie, I wouldn't rightly call it murder."

The presence of Madeline kept Dulcie from throwing back her first heated response. "What would you rightly call it, Sheriff?" she asked coolly.

More feet shuffling. "I reckon the Bible would call it an eye for an eye."

"Except for one thing—Pa didn't kill anyone."

Impatience slipped across Martin's face. "Everyone knows you was just covering for your pa. A lot of folks woulda done the same iffen it was their kin. But the fact is he was seen having words with Mr. Carpenter not long afore he was killed. So I figure it'd be a waste of time to try'n track down the thirty, forty folks who done the lynching."

Dulcie narrowed her eyes. "Funny how you know the number involved. You told me you didn't see anything because they locked you up in one of your own cells."

The sheriff's cheeks flushed a brighter red. "I saw a little through the window in the back. Not enough to recognize no one though, 'specially since they wore coverins over their heads."

Dulcie stared at him as the cold ball of anger grew in her belly. "You don't plan on doing anything about Pa's murder, do you? You're just going to wash your hands of it." She took a step closer to the lawman. "You realize by doing nothing you're condoning murder in the name of justice and you're letting the real killer get away scot-free."

Martin clenched his jaw. "Now you look here, Dulcie. You was gone five years, and in that time your ma died and your pa hit the bottle hard. He wasn't the man he was afore you left."

It was the same argument Mr. Coulson at the store had used. She wondered if the townsfolk had had a meeting to figure out what to say to her when she came around asking questions. She wouldn't put it past the small-town politicians.

"I *know* that my father didn't kill him, and I'm going to prove it."

Dulcie led Madeline out of the stifling office. She paused on the boardwalk to gather her fury and regain her composure. Nobody believed her.

She looked across the street, and her gaze settled on the saloon. Her heart battered her ribs. Apprehension replaced her anger. If she wanted a bottle of whiskey the only way to get it was to step inside the bar and buy it. If her pa was still alive, she could've said it was for him.

She glanced around nervously, seeing a handful of people on the boardwalk. If she walked into a saloon in broad daylight her name wouldn't be worth the paper to write it on. The respectability she'd paid Lamont for with silence would be squandered.

No, she didn't need the liquor. However, the possibility of not having any in the cabin brought a measure of panic.

Still holding Madeline's hand, Dulcie guided her down the boardwalk. She kept her head down, knowing she'd wonder about every person she passed. Had this one been involved in the lynching? Had that man slipped the noose around his neck?

They reached the end of town and Dulcie took a deep breath before crossing the street. She spotted a boy peeking out from between two buildings. As they neared the alley,

Dulcie slowed. Her gaze met the kid's, who stared back at her. Not scared, but guarded. Not unlike a wild animal.

"Hello," Dulcie said.

The boy, dressed in hand-me-down overalls that were too short, continued to study her.

"My name's Dulcie McDaniel."

"I know who you are." His defensiveness surprised her.

"This is my daughter Madeline." Dulcie kept her voice calm and gentle.

The boy's gaze flicked to Madeline and back to Dulcie. "Folks call me Collie."

"It's nice to meet you, Collie." She glanced down at her daughter. "Say hello, Madeline."

"Hi," the girl said, eyeing Collie closely. "Want a gumdrop?"

Collie tried to hide his delight behind a façade of indifference, but Dulcie saw through the mask.

"Sure," the boy said.

Madeline opened the sack and poured two gumdrops into her small palm. She extended her hand to Collie, who took the pieces and popped them in his mouth. Madeline held the bag up to her face and pulled out a red one that she put in her mouth.

Dulcie eyed the boy, an idea forming, and she tried to quell it, telling herself he was a child, only a few years older than Madeline. "Where are your parents?" Dulcie asked him.

He shrugged. "Dead."

"I'm sorry." A memory niggled at her. "They were killed in a wagon accident, right?"

Collie stuck his hands in his pockets and nodded.

Dulcie had heard about it right after she got back to Locust. She'd heard the Gearsons had taken in the boy and felt sorry for the orphan. Yet this was the perfect opportunity to get whiskey without going in a saloon. "Would you like to do something for me?" she asked.

Collie's suspicion returned. "What?"

Dulcie took a deep breath. "Go into the saloon and buy me a bottle of whiskey."

Collie shuffled his bare feet. "What do I get?"

"Five cents."

"Don't seem like much."

She suspected Collie might have a bit of con man in him. "Fine. I'll find someone else."

Collie took a step toward her. "How do I pay for it?"

Dulcie swallowed her satisfied smile. "I've got a dollar." She dug into her pocket, thrusting her guilt aside even as she withdrew a silver coin and held it up between her thumb and forefinger. "You won't run off with it?"

Collie scowled. "I ain't no thief."

Dulcie handed him the dollar. "Buy the whiskey and bring it to the alley. I'll give you your nickel then."

The boy nodded then dashed off.

Dulcie watched him go, disgusted with herself for using a kid and spending money for whiskey when she wouldn't even buy a treat for her daughter.

However, worse than the guilt was the fear of not having whiskey to drown her ceaseless conscience.

$\mathcal{S}$EVEN

As Dulcie drove the wagon into the yard, she adjusted the cloth over the pail. The eggs and butter were gone and the bucket provided a means to carry the bottle of whiskey into the house unseen. Not that she cared one whit about Rye's opinion, but she didn't want him to think she was like her father. Because she wasn't. Not in the least.

Rye looked up from where he knelt on the porch, and although it was too shady for her to see his expression, she had the impression he was glad to see them. She couldn't deny her own pang of pleasure.

As Dulcie halted Jack in front of the cabin, Rye rose and wiped his hands across his thighs. He walked to the edge of the porch, carefully watching where he placed his booted feet among the broken and rotted planks. "That didn't take long."

Her heart beating a little faster, Dulcie said, "We didn't need much."

If he saw through her lie, he didn't say anything. He started to come around the wagon, but Dulcie leapt down before he could offer a hand. With only a slight falter, he changed direction and held up his arms to Madeline, who went to him without hesitation. After he set the girl on the ground, he swept his hand across her hair, smiling fondly.

He glanced in the back of the wagon and seemed surprised by the few items there. "Do they go in the house?"

Dulcie nodded.

She tried to ignore the flex of muscles in his forearms as he effortlessly lifted the sack of flour onto a shoulder. Using one arm to balance it, he wrapped his other arm around the bag of salt.

Realizing he meant to take them inside, Dulcie quickly opened the door. She preceded him and motioned to a corner. "You can put them there."

Rye set the sacks down, and his gaze moved about the two-roomed cabin. It was the first time he'd been inside, and Dulcie had no doubt he was taking in everything and judging. Seeing her home through his eyes, she was more aware of its shortcomings. The sparse furnishings—worn chairs and wobbly table—and the shafts of sunlight that streamed in through the slats covering a glassless window. Heat flooded her cheeks, but she wasn't about to apologize for what was hers.

"Thanks," she said curtly. "I can get the sugar and coffee."

"You got a pump in here," Rye commented, motioning toward the hand pump.

Dulcie shrugged, hiding her resentment at more evidence of her pathetic home. "It's been broke since I came back home. Pa was never sober long enough to fix it." One time her father had gotten so far as bringing tools in the cabin, but then he'd disappeared into the barn to get drunk. Dulcie had tried to do it herself but she'd only managed to scrape her knuckles and bruise her palms.

"If you'd like, I can take a look at it."

Carrying water from the outside well was a job she despised and she tried not to sound too eager. "If you don't mind."

"After I'm done with the porch and roof I'll see what I can do."

She nodded, keeping her anticipation tamped down. It never paid to get excited over a man's promise.

Dulcie followed him back outside, where Madeline played hopscotch in the dirt.

"Go into the house and change into your everyday dress, honey," Dulcie said.

Her daughter frowned and trudged past her and Rye, reluctance in every dragging step.

Rye chuckled softly after the girl disappeared into the house, and Dulcie couldn't contain her own tiny smile. Her gaze met his and they exchanged shared amusement at Madeline's dramatic exit.

Realizing she'd allowed too much familiarity with him, Dulcie turned and her smile melted away. Her heart pounded against her ribs and she chastised herself for allowing their relationship to become more personal. She set her mind to practical matters and retrieved the coffee and sugar from the wagon bed. Knowing the bucket with the whiskey remained in the box, she glanced covertly at Rye. He'd gone back to his work, and she breathed a sigh of relief. She climbed onto the wheel spoke and lifted the pail from the floor.

"Did you trade all your eggs and butter?" Rye asked.

Dulcie jerked, startled to see him looking at her from the other side of the wagon. "Yes, for the dry goods." She hoped he didn't notice her breathiness.

He continued to study her, and she restrained the impulse to squirm under his perusal. It was only her imagination that he could see through the cloth to know what nestled in the pail. She strolled into the cabin and once inside, allowed a sigh of relief.

Madeline came down from the loft, a frayed dress having taken the place of her town one, and she'd removed her shoes. They were the only pair that fit her and she wore them only for town trips or when the weather was too cool to go without. She skipped over to Dulcie and turned around so her mother could button the dress.

"Play inside while I make dinner," Dulcie said once she was done.

Familiar stubbornness glinted in her daughter's eyes. "Wanna play hopscotch."

"You can do that later when I'm out in the garden."

Madeline stomped a bare foot. "Wanna play now."

Dulcie resisted an impatient sigh. "I won't be able to watch you."

"Mr. Rye can. He's outside."

Although Dulcie wasn't as wary of him as she'd been when he'd arrived, experience taught her to remain cautious. "He's busy."

Madeline thrust out her lower lip. "Wanna go outside."

Dulcie considered Rye's apparent fondness for Madeline and the fact she could check on her daughter from the doorway, too. "We'll ask Mr. Rye. If he isn't too busy to watch you, then you can stay outside until lunch."

Madeline's pout vanished, replaced by a bright smile. She dashed out the door and, rolling her eyes, Dulcie followed.

"Mr. Rye. You watch me?" Madeline was already asking him.

Rye met Dulcie's eyes but spoke to her daughter. "Is it all right with your mother?"

Madeline bobbed her head up and down.

Dulcie gave a short nod.

Rye gazed solemnly at Madeline, although Dulcie noticed a sparkle in his eyes. "As long as you stay within sight of the porch."

Madeline scampered away and grabbed a stick to draw a new hopscotch game in the dirt, closer to the cabin.

Dulcie crossed her arms, watching her daughter's enthusiastic play. "Thank you."

Rye shrugged. "It's no bother, Dulcie."

She believed him, and she didn't know if that was a good thing or not.

"Lunch will be ready soon." She hurried back into the cabin.

Dulcie stashed her whiskey in the trunk beside the nearly empty bottle. Before she could close the lid on her secret, shame slammed through her. Shame for using a child to enter a saloon in her stead and shame for spending their precious money for liquor when Madeline went without new clothes and shoes.

Even as sickness roiled through her, she was tempted by the whiskey's promise of solace. She shoved the temptation aside. That was the last bottle of whiskey she'd bring into this house. She didn't really need it, after all.

* * *

RYE'S stomach growled but he tried to ignore it, just as he ignored his headache. While he was involved in his work, he was able to forget about his throbbing head. However, dividing his attention between his task and watching Madeline, he was acutely aware of both his hunger and his headache.

He set aside his saw and straightened his back. A pop and crack set his spine to rights again. They were also a sobering reminder of the hard years he'd lived. Thirty years old and some days he felt twice his age. Too many cold nights sleeping on the hard ground, as well as the hard labor—mucking stalls, digging latrines, building bridges—soldiers were tasked with when they weren't out on patrol. Throw in a few saloon brawls and there were times when he woke up moving like an old man.

"Watch me, Mr. Rye," Madeline called.

Rye raised his head to find the girl standing on one foot. She grinned and leaned down to pick up her rock, keeping her balance with only a slight wobble or two. Madeline held up the rock and finished her hop, jump, and two-foot landing.

Rye applauded her performance, and Madeline giggled.

He felt more than heard Dulcie come to the open doorway. He turned his head to see her standing there, once again wearing trousers, his lunch tray in her hands. Despite him having been in the cabin, she still didn't trust him to eat with them. He shrugged aside his disappointment.

"Come and eat, Madeline," she said.

Without her earlier reluctance, the girl dashed into the cabin, forcing Dulcie to lift the tray higher and turn aside lest she be bowled over.

"Someone's hungry," Rye said.

Dulcie's stomach growled.

"She's not the only one," Rye added with a wink.

Her face reddened. "You're probably hungrier than the two of us put together. You've been working all morning."

Rye didn't bother to deny it. Dulcie set the tray on an undamaged part of the porch. He stood, and when Dulcie turned around, she bumped into him. Rye steadied her with his hands at a slender waist that was camouflaged by the masculine clothing. She froze and met his gaze.

Unable to look away from her, Rye remained motionless. The golden brown flecks in her green eyes darkened. The heat radiating from her skin warmed his palms through her too-large shirt. Passion pulsed between them, thick and hot.

He stared down at her full, red lips. It would be so easy to swoop down and eliminate those last few inches separating them. Her breath came in soft, quick puffs between those parted lips, and he reckoned he could feel the moist warmth tickle across his neck. His body responded without conscience, reminding him of the long months of abstinence.

Madeline shouted from the cabin, "Ma."

Dulcie jerked and stepped back. Rye's hands slid away from her waist and fell to his sides, bereft of her womanly curves.

"I have to . . ." She fled into the cabin.

Abruptly alone, Rye fought for dominance of his wayward body. He took a deep breath, letting it out in a long, shaky exhalation. Dulcie was the widow of a man for whose death he felt responsible, and she deserved better from him even if she didn't know why he was here.

Resolutely, he focused on eating. After washing down dinner with cool water from the well, Rye immersed himself in his work. It was a hell of a lot easier than dwelling on Dulcie.

Later that night in the empty silence, Rye lay on top of his makeshift bed in the barn. The heat of the day carried into the evening and he had removed his shirt, boots, and socks. Dressed only in his breeches, he still felt the heat like a heavy blanket thrown across him. He amused himself by guessing where the next droplet of sweat would roll off his body. However, it wasn't enough to occupy his mind.

Thoughts of Dulcie he'd staved off earlier returned with keen vengeance. In his solitude, he relived the feel of her smooth curves beneath his palms and the gentle murmur of her breath across his neck. In his mind, Madeline didn't interrupt them, and he kissed Dulcie's sweet mouth, imagining her taste and passion. He unbuttoned her shapeless shirt and pressed it aside, revealing ivory skin. Flicking his tongue across the valley between her breasts, he tasted her clean saltiness. He turned his face, and his cheek rested against the warm, soft slope of her breast.

Rye's erection strained against his trousers, and his hand traveled down to his fly. It'd been a long time since he'd felt the overpowering urge to gain release, and he flicked open the top button. As he started on the next one, his motions stilled. Anger and embarrassment coursed through his blood.

He focused on the blunt memories of Dulcie's dead husband, on the unseeing eyes as Jerry lay on the ground, his neck bent at an impossible angle. The man who'd been married to Dulcie. The man who'd fathered little Madeline. The man who'd be alive today if not for Rye.

Shoving himself upright, he stalked outside. Some nights the barn walls closed in on him and reminded him of the stockade, and he had to get out to breathe in the fresh air and reassure himself that he was no longer a prisoner. However, nights like these it wasn't the walls that imprisoned him, but his own shame.

Restless, he walked across the yard, heedless of his bare feet. Seeing a dim light in the side window, he went to it and peeked inside.

His heart skipped a beat then thundered in his ears.

Dulcie lay on the bed, her gown hiked up to her thighs and one hand half hidden beneath it. Her other hand played with her breasts, and her nipples were visibly outlined under the thin cloth. Her head was thrown back and her long red hair fanned across the pillow. With her eyes closed and lips slightly parted, she looked like she was lost in the bliss of her own touch.

Rye had never seen a woman pleasure herself and it was a beautiful sight. It was also sexy as hell. All the blood in his body raced to his groin, making him dizzy with lust.

Dulcie's soft cry and her flushed face and neck told him she'd found her release.

He stumbled back, away from the window. His erection pressed painfully against his trousers. One touch and he knew he'd be lost.

Awkwardly, he made his way back to the barn and unbuttoned his pants. Even his shame couldn't stop him this time.

* * *

AS Dulcie worked in the garden the following morning, she wiped her perspiring brow. It had cooled little overnight and was already hot and muggy. The heavy air even made the insects seem to hover slower as they buzzed in swarms, occasionally landing on Dulcie's sweat-dampened face or arms.

She paused to take a break from pulling the stubborn weeds. Her gaze automatically went to Madeline, who was smart enough to play with Aggie under the shading branches of the apple tree. She was soothed by her daughter's faint singsong voice.

Turning, she sought Rye, who continued to work on the porch. She wondered if he was as miserable as she was in the stagnant heat. Working in the relative shade, he'd removed his hat but, she thought with a guilty sense of disappointment, his shirt remained in place.

Like a lightning bolt, yesterday's memory of the fire in his eyes and the way his gaze lingered on her lips struck her. She knew too well what that look meant. The low burn in her belly had been on the verge of becoming a conflagration. That ember, if sparked to life, would've burned her as surely as if she'd held her hand in a hot flame.

Despite the whiskey she'd drunk last night before going to bed, she hadn't been able to resist her body's traitorous desire. She'd imagined it was Rye lying with her, and it was his name she'd nearly cried out when she'd reached her climax. Even now, under the relentless sun, she felt the resonance of Rye's illusory touches.

Rye stepped off the porch and ambled to the well, and Dulcie was suddenly aware of her own parched throat. Despite every warning she gave herself, she rose and joined him.

Rye finished drinking from the ladle and dipped it into the pail, then offered it to Dulcie. She accepted it silently, her eyes meeting his over the ladle's rim as she drank from the same place his lips had touched.

Rye quickly looked away, as if embarrassed. "Hot work in the garden."

She dropped the dipper back in the pail and it hit the water with a muffled splash. "Has to be done."

"Maybe wait until this evening. Should be cooler then."

"I've got other chores to do then." She lifted her gaze to the unbroken blue sky. "Doesn't look like it'll cool off much anyhow."

He nodded in agreement.

Awkward in his silence, Dulcie rambled on. "It even smells hot. A person could almost wring water out of the thick air. The only thing that'll break it is a storm."

"Seen the same in Kansas and the Dakotas."

Curiosity stirred her, and she phrased her question as a statement. "You've done some traveling."

He averted his gaze. "Some."

She frowned, knowing he was holding something back. It bothered her, set her on edge, but what right did she have to know all his secrets? It wasn't as if she was going to confide hers. One thing she'd learned was that everyone had secrets, whether they realized it or not. And some of those were dirty little secrets, like festering wounds that had no place in the open.

"Madeline seems to be enjoying herself," Rye said.

"She likes being out. I just wish she had a playmate. It gets lonely out here."

Although her attention was on Madeline, she felt the power of his gaze on her. "For you, too."

The impact of his words coupled with his husky tone rolled through her, leaving a trill of arousal in its wake. Angered by both his inference and her body's reaction, she glared at him. "I don't have time to be lonely. And even if I was, there's nothing that says I have to give in to companionship." She spoke the last word with cool disdain.

He grinned with wry amusement. "Never said anything about companionship. Only that without another woman to talk to, you probably get lonely. I know most women like to visit with other womenfolk."

Dulcie's cheeks burned with chagrin. She'd been reading her own frustration into his innocent words. "Sometimes I do miss that," she murmured.

Keeping her mortified gaze averted, she headed back to her garden. Toiling in the dirt beneath a hot sun was infinitely preferable to dueling with her body's response to Rye.

Dividing her attention between him and watching Madeline, Dulcie continued removing the ripe vegetables from the garden. Although she didn't think her daughter would get into trouble around the yard, she didn't trust her to stay within the confines. There'd already been times when Madeline had disappeared and Dulcie had searched frantically for her. Each time she'd found her daughter, or Madeline had found her. However, Dulcie couldn't rely on luck indefinitely. That was one reason she wished she had womenfolk living nearer—mothers tended to look out for each other's children.

After eating, Dulcie had Madeline lie down for a nap. The girl whined and argued, but within a couple of minutes she was fast asleep on the bed, which was cooler than her regular bed in the loft.

Dulcie carried two pails outside to get some water from the well. The approaching ashy gray clouds caught her attention. Although she'd expected rain to break the heat, uneasiness trembled through her.

"Your root cellar have room for you and Madeline?" Rye asked behind her.

She spun around, startled.

"Sorry," Rye said. "Didn't mean to scare you. Need water?"

She nodded, and he took the buckets from her and lowered one into the well.

Dulcie mentally shook herself. "Yes. There's room in there for you, too."

Rye flashed a smile as he drew the pail up. "We might need it."

"What about the animals?"

"Is there room for them, too?"

Her first reaction was irritation then she realized he was only teasing her. It'd been a long time since she'd been teased good-naturedly.

Rye lowered the second pail into the well. "Better if they stay in the pasture," he replied. "If the barn came down with them in it, they wouldn't have a chance."

A sweltering breeze sighed across her face, yet Dulcie felt a chill creep down her spine. Almost against her will her attention was again drawn to the northwest.

Rye lifted the second filled pail off the hook and carried both to the porch. Dulcie shook herself free of the lethargy the weather conjured and followed him, refusing to let her gaze fall below his waist.

"Don't stray far from the house this afternoon," he said.

"I won't." She took the pails from him and went back into the house.

Inside, she filled a large kettle with water and placed it on the stove to cook some of the vegetables for supper. Despite the coming storm, Dulcie had to take care of the produce she'd picked that morning and the day before. If she put the chore off any longer, she'd lose some of her precious foodstuffs.

Dulcie checked on her daughter, who continued to sleep restlessly in the oppressive heat. Then, although reluctant to begin the time-consuming task, she rolled up her shirtsleeves.

The front and back doors were open as she sorted the vegetables, but the outside air that moved through the small cabin did nothing to cool it. Dulcie's hair curled and stuck to her sweaty face. Sometime later she carried the root vegetables to the root cellar, which smelled of rotting potatoes even though she'd cleaned them out the previous month. She left the sacks in the relative coolness.

As she returned to the cabin, she noticed the ladder leaning against the side of the house. She tipped her head back to see Rye repairing the roof, his back to her. How he could bear the heat up there she didn't know. Although since the clouds now hid the sun, he didn't have the direct rays bearing down on him.

He moved with an economy of motion, his shoulders rippling beneath his sweat-stained shirt. He muttered a colorful oath and she stifled a smile. Then he turned and spotted her. His face, already flushed from the heat, reddened even more.

"Beggin' your pardon, Dulcie, I didn't know you were there," he said.

She waved an appeasing hand. "Believe me, I've heard worse. Are you sure you should be up there already?"

He smiled crookedly. "Didn't feel dizzy yesterday so figured I was safe."

She hoped he wasn't merely trying to placate her. She didn't want him taking another dive off the roof because he had too much pride. But she also knew whatever she said might be misconstrued or flat-out ignored. That was the way of men.

Forked lightning slashed through the clouds, and she mentally counted the seconds until the thunder vibrated around them. It wasn't loud enough to wake Madeline yet. "It's about twelve, fifteen miles away," she said.

"But it looks like it's coming in fast." He quickly gathered his tools. "Look out, Dulcie. I'm tossing some things down."

She stepped under the porch eave. Once the tools were lying on the ground, Rye's feet and legs came into view on the ladder. Dulcie knew it wasn't proper, but she couldn't draw her gaze away from the long, muscular legs as he climbed down the rungs. When his thighs came into view, she lingered on his groin, noting with an increased pulse the slight bulge behind his button fly. Her mouth grew dry as passion whirled through her, like a sudden gust of wind catching a leaf in its current.

She caught herself a moment before he descended completely. Her face burned, but with shame or carnal desire, she wasn't certain, which made it even more difficult to bear. The wind picked up, feeling like hot fingers tracing her face.

"Can you help me get this stuff to the barn?" Rye asked.

Unable to trust her voice, she nodded and gathered what she could in her arms. Rye hefted the ladder. They deposited the things in the barn and went back out into the yard. Although no rain fell yet, the smell of a coming shower permeated the air.

More lightning streaked across the dark sky and there were fewer seconds before the thunder rumbled. Rye was right—the storm was traveling quickly.

"I'd better get inside. Madeline is scared of thunder," Dulcie said.

Rye gave her shoulder a gentle push. "Go on. I can get the rest."

She nodded and ran into the cabin, crossing to the bedroom

to check on Madeline. The room was empty. Dulcie's heart slid into her throat and she dropped to her knees to check under the bed, but only dust balls greeted her. She climbed the loft ladder, her palms damp and her breath rough. Madeline wasn't up there either.

Dulcie would've seen her leave through the front door, which meant she'd gone out the back. She dashed out the back door and hollered, "Madeline. Madeline, honey, where are you?"

No answer.

"Madeline!"

$\mathcal{E}$IGHT

THE clouds grew more ominous, more black than gray, with an odd tinge of greenish yellow as Rye carried the last load of tools to the barn. A worried frown tugged at his lips. Usually clouds like this heralded more than rain, thunder, and lightning.

As he started out to the pasture to check on the animals, he heard Dulcie's frantic shout for Madeline. His blood turned icy and he ducked through the corral poles. He raced around to the back of the cabin, skidding to a stop at Dulcie's fear-filled face.

"What's wrong? Where's Madeline?" he demanded.

She stared at him as if he were a stranger. He grabbed her arms and forced her to focus on him. "Did something happen to Madeline?"

"I-I d-don't know," she stuttered, her eyes wide. "When I-I went to check on her, she was g-gone."

Rye forced his own fear aside and kept his expression steady. "When did you last see her?"

Dulcie seemed to take strength from him, and she straightened, pulling her shoulders back. "Right before I took the vegetables to the root cellar. She was sleeping. When I came back in, she was gone."

"You searched the cabin?"

She nodded, her lips thinning as characteristic impatience returned. "Of course. She's not there."

Rye's mind raced. "You were only gone about five minutes. She couldn't have gone far. Does she have any favorite places to hide?"

He could see Dulcie's thoughts clicking, returning to the problem rather than giving in to her fear. "There's a few." Thunder clapped, and Dulcie's salvaged composure faltered. She latched onto Rye's forearms, her fingernails digging into his skin. "We have to find her."

"We'll find her," he reassured her with more confidence than he possessed. "We can split up and check her hiding places. Where are they?"

She shook her head. "It'll be faster if we go together. Come on."

Dulcie took the lead just as the first raindrop struck him. Rye was hard-pressed to keep up with her. Maybe it was the breeches she wore or maybe the terror of her lost child, but he'd never seen a woman move so quickly.

They stopped near a stream some hundred yards from the cabin. Rye scanned the area, looking for any sign the girl might have been there. He met Dulcie's expectant gaze and shook his head. She pressed her lips together and continued to the next place, a small clearing with rocks that became chairs in a child's imagination.

"This is her favorite place," Dulcie said between pants.

Raindrops rattled the leaves above them and plopped dully on the ground.

Rye moved in a small circle, looking around. "She's not here. Where else?" he asked, keeping his voice calm and firm.

Rye couldn't tell if the moisture on her cheeks was from tears or the rain. "There's only one other place I can think of."

"Let's go."

By the time they arrived beside a small pond, he and Dulcie were drenched. There was no sign of the little girl.

A flash of motion caught Rye's attention. "Madeline!"

He plunged into the brush after her with Dulcie close behind him. Although the ground was slick with mud, Rye caught up to the slight figure. As soon as he was close enough to see clearly he knew it wasn't Dulcie's daughter. He caught the back of the boy's overalls.

"Collie," Rye said, trying to evade the kid's thrashing limbs. "Take it easy. No one's going to hurt you."

The boy quieted, but Rye continued to hold him. Collie glared at him, defiance in his tilted chin. "I ain't done nothin' wrong."

"What're you doing out here?"

"Didn't know a storm was comin'."

"We're looking for Mrs. McDaniel's little girl. Have you seen her?"

Collie's gaze darted to Dulcie, who stood behind Rye. "I ain't seen her, but I can help look for her."

"You should get home," Dulcie spoke to the boy.

"Nah. They ain't gonna miss me. I know some hiding places she mighta got to."

Rye turned to Dulcie, silently asking if they should allow him to help. But she looked away without giving any indication of her thoughts. Puzzled, Rye gave his attention to Collie again. "All right. You lead."

The boy tore away and Rye and Dulcie followed. For the next five minutes they checked two more places, but there was no sign of Madeline. The rain fell heavily now, and the rapidly cooling air made Rye shiver when he'd been sweating less than half an hour ago. He wondered how Collie was doing with his bare feet, then remembered Madeline would be barefooted, too, and wearing only a threadbare dress.

Collie came to a halt, and Rye stopped. Dulcie brushed against Rye's arm as she stood beside him.

"Where could she be?" Dulcie asked, desperation edging her voice. She'd forgotten her hat, and her hair had come loose from its band and straggly tendrils stuck to her face.

Collie scowled and his brow furrowed. "There's another place—"

Before Rye could ask, Collie trotted off, and Rye had no choice but to follow. They'd only gone a hundred feet when Collie veered off the path. Rye squinted through the rain and grayness to see an overhang on the rocky slope that seemed to be the boy's destination. His boot soles slipped on the slick gravel as he scrambled after Collie.

A few moments later he drew up short at the sight that greeted him. Madeline, soaked and miserable, was hunched over and Collie was standing beside her, awkwardly patting her shaking shoulders.

"Madeline," Dulcie cried and pushed past Rye.

Collie, appearing relieved to have Dulcie take over the comforting, shifted to stand beside Rye. Dulcie gathered her daughter in her arms. Rye felt the urge to join them, to wrap his arms around them at his own relief. Instead, he put an arm around Collie's thin shoulders. The boy shivered, and Rye pulled him close against his side, hoping to share some of his warmth.

Thunder's percussion vibrated through Rye. Balls of ice began to mix with the rain, striking Rye's hat and shoulders like pebbles flung at him.

Swearing silently, Rye pressed Collie under the scant overhang with Dulcie and Madeline. "Duck down and cover your heads," he shouted above the storm's rising din.

Dulcie gathered Madeline close and bent over her, sheltering her daughter from the increasingly large hailstones. Rye joined them, putting one arm around Collie and the other around Dulcie and Madeline, and pressed them close to the rocky wall beneath the narrow ledge. He covered them with his upper body, shielding them as Dulcie protected her daughter.

The wind shrieked and pitched hail against them. It was like being hit by a shotgun blast of rock salt. Rye tightened his protective embrace around the woman and two children, hoping to spare them the worst of the stinging hits. The natural shelter helped shield his head, but his back and shoulders weren't so fortunate. He had no doubt he'd be bruised and sore.

The storm's intensity raged for what seemed like hours. Madeline hiccup-sobbed while Collie tried to hide his fear, but Rye felt the boy's anxiety in his shuddering and hitched breaths. Dulcie remained steadfast, but she couldn't restrain the occasional gasp.

With his body pressed tightly against hers, Rye couldn't

help but feel the soft curves hidden beneath her masculine clothing. Despite the cold air and rain, heat exploded wherever their bodies touched. His memory supplied him with the vision of her lying in her bed, her gown rucked up as she pleasured herself. He'd never seen anything as beautiful as Dulcie when she found her release. Stifling a groan, he eased up to put some space between them, and he hoped like hell she hadn't noticed his hard flesh against her backside.

Pebbles skittered down the incline around them. A flash of lightning immediately followed by a sharp crack of thunder wrought a shrill scream from Madeline, which nearly deafened Rye. A few moments later he smelled burnt wood mixed with an acrid odor. A faint sizzle told him a nearby tree had been hit by lightning, but Rye doubted there was a threat of fire with the curtains of rain coming down.

Finally, the hail tapered off and the rain eased to a sprinkle. The thunder grew fainter as the storm moved on to its next target.

Clenching his teeth, Rye forced his cramped muscles to obey him. He straightened and sat back on his heels. There wasn't a square inch on his back and shoulders that didn't smart.

"Jumpin' junipers, that was a storm," Collie exclaimed, his eyes shining with excitement.

"Yeah, jumpin' junipers," Rye repeated wryly. He turned to Dulcie and Madeline. "You all right?"

Dulcie bent over her daughter, sweeping Madeline's wet stringy hair back from her teary face. "Honey, are you hurt?"

Her eyes wide with lingering terror, Madeline hiccupped. Dulcie framed the girl's face between her palms, forcing Madeline to meet her gaze.

"Do you hurt anywhere, Madeline?" Dulcie asked.

Awareness eased back into the girl's expression. "Feet," she said in a small voice.

Rye examined her feet and found a few cuts on her soles. He was shocked by their icy coldness and carefully rubbed them to bring warmth back.

Madeline whimpered, and Dulcie gathered her close, rocking her in her arms. Dulcie gazed at Rye over the girl's head, her gaze both questioning and apprehensive.

"Nothing serious," Rye said. "But she needs to get someplace warm."

Dulcie nodded and pressed her lips to Madeline's crown.

"Let's go back to the cabin and change into dry clothing." He extended his hands toward Madeline. "I can carry her."

Dulcie shook her head. "I will." She kept her arms around her daughter.

Rye clasped Dulcie's arm and helped her stand. Madeline's thin legs wound around Dulcie's waist while her arms encircled her mother's neck. Without a word, Dulcie strode away. Rye scowled at her back. Sometimes the woman was too stubborn by half.

"I'd best get back to town," Collie said.

The boy's disconsolate voice drew Rye's attention from Dulcie's infuriatingly stiff back and exasperating pride. "The farm's closer."

Collie's hair stuck to his face and neck. He slid his hands into his pockets. "Nah. I'll be all right." A sneeze and a shudder belied his words.

Rye hooked an arm around the boy's shoulders and steered him in the wake of Dulcie and Madeline. Collie attempted to duck away, but Rye merely swung the kid up into his arms. The boy didn't fight him and Rye had the impression he wasn't anxious to return to his foster family.

They caught up to Dulcie, and Rye slowed his pace to follow her, trying to ignore the subtle swing of her hips. He listened to their dull footfalls on the damp earth, the far-off rumble of thunder, and Dulcie's murmurs as she reassured her daughter. Melting hailstones littered the ground, giving the terrain a strange, winterlike appearance. In places steam rose, caused by the mating of ice and heated soil.

Dulcie stopped. A large branch lay across their path, the black wood still smoking from where lightning had severed it from a mulberry tree.

Rye took the lead and picked a path around the fallen branch. Collie remained silent, but his taut body told Rye he wasn't nearly as unaffected by the storm and its aftermath as he'd made out. Sometimes bravado was the only thing an orphan had to call his own.

Finally they arrived back at Dulcie's farm. No hailstones

remained in the yard, but water stood in puddles. Leaves, torn from their branches, lay on the ground and were plastered against the barn and cabin walls. Two corral sections sagged but hadn't fallen.

"Thank heavens, the cabin's still standing," Dulcie said.

Collie wriggled, and Rye set him on his feet but kept a firm hand on his shoulder so he couldn't escape.

"Looks like I won't even have to repair the roof again," Rye said, keeping his tone light.

She glanced at him and seemed to notice Collie for the first time. "He didn't go home?"

Annoyance stung Rye. "I wouldn't let him since your place was closer. He's soaked clean through."

"I don't have any clothes that will fit him."

"All he needs is a blanket to wrap up in while his things dry."

"It'll be late by that time."

Rye's temper flared and he gnashed his teeth, barely restraining his annoyance. She hadn't even thanked the boy for his help. "You'd best get Madeline inside."

He spun around and headed to the barn with Collie in tow.

"Rye," Dulcie called.

He didn't turn around but continued on and led Collie to the stall where his bedroll lay upon a pile of fresh straw. Rye hunkered down in front of the boy. "Take off your wet things and wrap the blanket around you. I'll hang your clothes outside on the corral. The sun will dry them in no time."

"Wanna go back to town."

Rye pointed at him. "As soon as your overalls are dry, I'll take you back. I'll talk to the Gearsons and tell them what happened."

He stood and turned, but Collie grabbed his arm. The boy's expression was anxious but he tried to hide it. "You don't need to go with me. I can take care of myself," Collie said.

"I didn't say you couldn't, but I figured they might be fretting over you."

"Nah. They don't care."

The boy's bluster didn't fool him. Rye shrugged. "Didn't

say they did. Just thought they'd like to know how you saved Madeline's life."

The boy blinked in surprise, then drew back his shoulders. "Maybe it won't be so bad, long as you don't run off at the mouth."

Rye squelched a smile. "I'll try not to. Now get out of those wet clothes before you catch something."

Collie scowled, but he set to work removing his overalls. While the boy did that, Rye exchanged his own drenched shirt and pants for a dry set. As Rye fastened the last button on his shirt, a soggy bundle struck the back of his head. He spun around and made a teasing lunge for the boy, but even wrapped in the blanket, Collie was fast on his feet. Giggling, the boy ducked into another stall.

Rye, his sore body protesting a game of tag, surrendered without a fight. He picked up Collie's soaked clothing and his own and carried them outside. After he'd strung them over the corral poles, he looked toward the cabin. Dulcie's inhospitality to Collie continued to puzzle and anger him. The boy had helped find Madeline, yet Dulcie couldn't seem to wait to have Collie gone. No thank you, no warm food, and no dry clothing before sending him on the three-mile barefoot hike back to town. Had Rye misjudged Dulcie that badly?

He'd be damned if he waved Collie away like some bothersome mosquito. Rye knew only too well what it felt like to be treated as an inconvenience instead of a living, breathing person.

INSIDE the cabin, Dulcie dressed Madeline in a dry dress and added two pair of stockings to warm her chilly feet. The girl weaved and her eyes fluttered shut. Dulcie barely got her settled into the bed before Madeline dropped off to sleep.

Dulcie leaned against the doorjamb and studied her daughter's pale face. Terror and fear clawed at her, reminding her how close she'd come to losing the one person in the world she loved. She told herself over and over that Madeline was alive and well. The storm hadn't stolen her.

Thanks to the boy Collie.

Dulcie's cheeks burned with renewed shame. What if Collie told Rye he'd bought her whiskey? Might he think she was just like her father?

But I'm not. If I was, I'd need a drink right now. But I don't. So I'm not like him.

Feeling calmer, Dulcie went to the bedside and kissed Madeline's brow. The sleeping girl didn't move.

Dulcie gathered their wet clothes and carried them outside. She spotted Rye by the corral and her gaze met his. No welcoming smile touched his lips, and she knew the reason. Without Collie, they wouldn't have found Madeline before the worst of the storm hit, and Dulcie hadn't even thanked the boy. Her guilty conscience had made her defensive.

He turned back to the barn.

"Rye," she shouted. "Wait."

Some of her anguish must have leaked into her voice because he stopped and turned around. She left the wet clothing on the porch rail and hurried across the yard. She stumbled to a stop in front of him. His arms were crossed over his chest and only coolness showed in his face.

"How's Collie?" she asked.

"Fine."

His terse answer was like a slap across the face. Humiliated, she slid her gaze past him, to the corral where their drenched clothing hung. "It can't be very warm in the barn."

"It's not."

He obviously wasn't going to make it easy for her, yet could she blame him? She'd behaved like a callous witch. "I'm sorry."

"For what?"

"For not thanking Collie. For not inviting him into the cabin."

Rye's eyes narrowed, but he remained silent.

Annoyance crept into Dulcie. "I was worried about Madeline, and I wasn't very nice to Collie."

"It's not me you should be apologizing to."

She lowered her gaze, chastised by his matter-of-fact words. "He's in the barn?"

Rye nodded.

Dulcie took a deep breath. She entered the barn, blinking in the relative dimness.

"Rye?" Collie called.

Dulcie cleared her throat and glanced back to ensure Rye remained standing in the yard. "No, it's Mrs. McDaniel."

She heard a rustle in one of the stalls and went to it. Her eyes adjusted to the sparse light and she spotted Collie standing in a corner. Around him were Rye's belongings— saddle, saddlebags, razor, tin cup, and a newspaper. Little to show for a man's life.

She drew her attention away from Rye's things and focused on the boy who knew of her secret. Maybe if she acted as if it hadn't happened, he would, too. "I want to thank you for finding Madeline."

With a blanket wrapped around him, it was hard to see his shrug. "Weren't nothin'."

"It was something to me. I don't know what would've happened to her if you hadn't found her. How did you know where to look?"

Collie shrugged.

"Were you spying on us?"

Although his face was draped in shadow, she caught a glimpse of guilt. "I don't like school so I go 'round to different places."

Dulcie studied him, seeing him as a young boy rather than a symbol of her cowardice. He was about six inches taller than Madeline and too thin for his height. In fact, she recalled how his overalls ended above his ankles. If he'd been her son, she'd ensure he had clothes that fit, even if they were secondhand.

She heard the creak of the door, and Rye stepped into the barn. She ignored him and spoke to Collie. "It's cool in here. Why don't you come into the house to wait for your clothes to dry?" At his wary expression, she added, "Would you be interested in some bread and honey?"

His eyes widened, but he shook his head. "I'll jest wait here."

"Go on with Mrs. McDaniel," Rye said. "It'd be better than waiting in this drafty barn."

Collie's gaze bounced from Dulcie to Rye and back. "All right," he said with obvious reluctance. "You gonna come inside too, Rye?"

"I've got things to do," Rye said. "But you go on now. I'll take you home later."

Dulcie swung open the stall door and waited. Collie took a deep breath and shuffled out, clinging to his blanket.

As she passed Rye, she caught the warm approval in his eyes. She told herself it didn't matter, but her heart refused to listen.

𝓝INE

DULCIE guided Collie into the cabin, her hand pressed gently but firmly against his shoulder. She felt resistance in his rigid muscles and dragging feet, but she couldn't blame him. Her guilty conscience reminded her that it was her earlier behavior that made him reluctant.

She drew a chair close to the stove. "Sit here, Collie." She smiled in what she hoped was a friendly manner.

Cautiously, like a gopher sticking its head out of a hole, Collie perched on the edge of the chair.

Dulcie kept her gaze averted, suspecting he'd only be more uncomfortable if she gave him her full attention. She added wood to the still-hot embers, and it wasn't long before heat emanated from the stove. Although the storm and hunt for Madeline had lasted little more than an hour, it felt like yesterday that she'd begun preserving the vegetables. Despite her aching exhaustion, she had to finish the chore.

"You aimin' on picklin' them carrots?" Collie asked, startling her.

"Do you like pickled carrots?"

He glanced away. "Ma used to make 'em."

"You miss her, don't you?" As soon as the question left her lips, she wished she could take it back. Of course the boy missed his mother, and asking him about it would only reawaken the pain.

He shrugged. "Some, I guess. But it don't make no difference. She's gone and ain't no cryin' or carryin' on will bring her back."

Dulcie swallowed the lump in her throat. She had an idea those words weren't Collie's, but something he'd heard from the Gearsons. As much as she'd hated her father's drunkenness, he'd been her father and she missed him. Anger swelled through her at the Gearsons' cruelty. A boy should be able to mourn the death of his parents.

"Where's Madeline?" he asked.

"She's sleeping. If you'd like to lie down, too, you can go up into the loft."

"Nah." He stood. "My clothes should be about dry by now."

Dulcie pressed him back into the chair. "I doubt that. Besides, I haven't properly thanked you for finding Madeline." Her breath stammered in her throat. "She's all the family I have and if I'd lost her . . ." Her voice quavered and she cleared her throat. "Thank you, Collie."

His cheeks reddened and his gaze dropped to his lap. " 'Tweren't nothing, ma'am." Then he lifted his head and studied her with eyes too old for his seven years. "I heard about your pa. Used to see him in town."

"He's gone." She had the impression he wanted to say more, but she didn't want to talk about him. "You'll eat supper here. It's the least I can do for what you done for us."

"Don't go to any bother on my account." Collie's expression didn't match his words.

"When was the last time you ate?"

The boy's gaze sidled away. "This mornin', I reckon."

It was no wonder he was all skin and growing bones. Despite herself, Dulcie liked the boy and felt a deeper pang of discomfiture at how she'd used him to buy her whiskey. He was merely a lonely child with no one who truly cared for him. Except maybe Rye, who probably saw much of himself in the orphan.

After reassuring herself that Collie didn't look like he would bolt, Dulcie cut two thick slices of bread and spread honey on them. She lifted a trapdoor on the floor and pulled the milk crock from the cool space beneath. Thanks to Flossie, milk was one of the few things she had plenty of. She poured milk into a glass and placed it and the snack on the table. "Pull your chair up, Collie. This should hold you until supper."

After only a moment's hesitation, the boy tugged his chair closer to the table and took a long drink. He picked up a slice of bread and took a monstrous bite. The ecstatic look on his face over something as simple as honey on bread gave Dulcie a pang of sympathy. Although she and Madeline didn't have much, at least they had enough to eat.

Collie downed the rest of the milk after the last bit of bread disappeared. Swiping his forearm across his mouth, he looked at Dulcie. "Thank you, ma'am."

"You're welcome." She suspected his manners came from his mother who had instilled them in him at an early age.

Dulcie went outside and retrieved more water from the well. As she brought up a pail, she surreptitiously looked around for Rye, but didn't see him. Refusing to acknowledge her odd disappointment, she carried the water into the cabin. Collie remained sitting by the table, but he'd laid his head down and his eyes were closed. The busy day followed by some food had finally tuckered him out.

Dulcie moved quietly as she prepared three crocks for the vegetables. She blanched the vegetables in boiling water then drained them and placed them in their respective crocks. Using squares of cloth, she covered the gallon-sized crocks. She added the vinegar to the carrots, and the sharp tang rising around her caused an arrow of melancholy to pierce her. Her mother used to pickle many of their vegetables. At the time, Dulcie had turned her nose up at the sour food, but now it brought back pleasant memories. Funny how she could be homesick for a time instead of a place.

Done with the daunting task, Dulcie was surprised to see Collie continued to sleep. She peered across the room into the bedroom to see Madeline hadn't moved. Dog tired, Dulcie wished she could sit down and fall asleep. But the kitchen had to be put back to rights, then she had to cook supper.

A quiet knock at the door gave her a reprieve, and she

hurried over before Collie or Madeline woke. She opened the door cautiously and found Rye on the other side, two skinned rabbits in his hand. She put a finger to her lips.

"Thought some fresh meat might taste good," he said in a low voice.

She took the rabbits from his outstretched hand. "Thank you."

"Is Collie in here?"

She nodded toward the table, and Rye leaned in the door to see the boy sleeping. He smiled but though there was fondness in it, there was also anger in his eyes.

"Those folks who look after him ought not to let him run around the countryside," he said.

He was right, but Dulcie recognized the futility of the situation. "So what're you going to do, adopt him yourself?"

He blinked, as if considering it, then shook his head. "What would I do with a kid?"

"Love him." The words slipped out before she could stop them. Uncomfortable, she looked down at her boots. "You're right. It's a foolish idea. Whoever heard of a man with no home or wife raising a child?"

Awkward silence surrounded them. Dulcie wished she could take back her words.

"You need anything from the garden?" Rye's cool expression placed distance between them as surely as if he'd walked away.

She took stock of what she had in the house, which wasn't much now that she'd preserved the vegetables. "How about potatoes and peas? Enough for four." At his raised eyebrow, she added, "Collie's eating supper with us."

Immediately, his eyes warmed and a gentle smile curved his lips. "Do you want me to leave them on the porch?"

She started to nod, but stopped. Recalling how he'd sheltered her, Madeline, and Collie without a second thought during the storm, she shed more of her vigilance. "You can bring them in."

"Yes, ma'am." Rye's boot heels rapped sharply on the porch as he left.

Dulcie cut up the meat and placed it in a heavy frying pan. Just as she was about to go out to see what was taking

Rye so long, he came up the porch steps and tentatively entered the cabin.

"Here they are," he said, holding up a pail and a basin.

He'd peeled the potatoes and shelled the peas. All that was left for Dulcie was to cook them on the stove.

"Thanks," she said.

"You're welcome."

Collie joined them, the blanket wrapped around him like a cocoon. He rubbed his eyes and yawned. "I'd best get back."

"I already told you you're eating supper with us first," Dulcie said, leaving no room for argument.

Collie looked at Rye.

"You heard Mrs. McDaniel," Rye said, inclining his head toward her. "I think your clothes are dry."

Collie brushed past Dulcie.

"Supper will be ready in about forty-five minutes," Dulcie called after them.

Rye handed Dulcie the potatoes and peas. "Just give us a holler."

Smiling, Dulcie watched Rye lead the blanket-wrapped boy to the barn. Madeline's call from the bedroom interrupted her bemusement, but the picture of Rye's hand resting on Collie's shoulder remained with her.

"HOLD it there," Rye said.

Collie held the corral pole against the post. Rye pulled a nail from his shirt pocket and pounded it into the wood. When he was done, the boy released the pole and Rye gave it a tug, but it was solid.

After Collie had donned his now-dry clothing, Rye enlisted his aid in fixing the storm-damaged corral. Rye could've done it himself in less time, but he wanted to give the boy something to do so he wouldn't run off.

Collie squished mud between his toes and grinned down at them. "That sure was a humdinger of a storm."

Rye made a face. "You're going to wash your feet before going into Mrs. McDaniel's house." The boy opened his mouth to argue, but Rye held up his forefinger. "No sass."

Rye, with Collie trudging beside him, walked back to the

barn. Soon after Rye came to work for Dulcie, he'd straightened and cleaned the room within the barn where the tools were kept. He spent evenings scrubbing them with a steel brush to get rid of the rust. A few were ruined, and he piled those in a corner. Maybe Dulcie's father wasn't a murderer, but he sure as hell was a lazy son of a bitch.

As Rye put the tools away, Collie walked around touching and picking up everything.

"Put things back where you got them," Rye said without turning.

"I ain't never seen a woman in trousers before," Collie said.

Startled by the unexpected comment, Rye looked over his shoulder at the boy, who was rubbing the handle of a scythe. "Mrs. McDaniel does a lot of work most women don't do."

"Why?"

"'Cause she doesn't have a man to help her."

Collie's brow furrowed. "She's got you."

Rye shifted uncomfortably. "I'm just passin' through. Before I came, she didn't have anyone but her father."

"Everyone says he killed Mr. Carpenter."

"That's what everyone says."

"You believe that?"

"I can't say one way or another since I wasn't around. Didn't know Dul—Mrs. McDaniel's father or this Carpenter fellah."

Collie nodded, his mind obviously racing like a dog after a rabbit. "I didn't like him much, but Mr. Carpenter used to give me a nickel. Once he even gave me fifty cents."

Rye pulled the extra nails out of his shirt pocket and put them in a tin can. "When I was your age, if I got a nickel, I'd spend it on candy. Is that what you do?"

Guilt crossed Collie's face. "No."

Puzzled, Rye gazed at the boy. "So what did you do with it?"

"Nothin'." Collie's chin lifted in challenge.

So the kid has a secret or two. But then, Rye'd had his secrets at that age, too. Still did, only grown-up secrets were more hurtful.

"Let's go get those feet cleaned up," Rye said.

Collie wrinkled his nose. "Already had me a bath today."

"Getting soaked by rain isn't the same as taking a bath."

An infectious grin lit Collie's face. "Yeah. But it's funner getting wet in the rain."

Rye laughed, unable to dispute that comment. At the well, he brought up a bucket of water and had Collie sit on the porch steps. He poured the cool water over the boy's muddy feet, eliciting a yelp from him.

"Tryin' to make me sick?" Collie asked, glaring at him.

Rye restrained a chuckle. "Tryin' to make you clean." He tossed him a lump of soap. "Scrub with this, and I'll get another bucket of water."

When Rye returned, Madeline stood behind Collie, watching in rapt fascination as the boy washed his feet.

"Hello, Miss Madeline," Rye said.

The girl grinned and ducked her head, all signs of her earlier adventure gone. "Collie's dirty."

The boy glared at her, but Madeline was impervious to his scowl.

"That's why he's washing up." Rye scrutinized the boy's feet and found them vastly improved by the soap. "I'm going to rinse them now."

Collie clenched his teeth, prepared for a fate worse than death. The water washed away the soap and dirt, leaving clean, pink feet.

Dulcie came out to join them and passed Rye a towel. "Thought you might need this."

Rye, enraptured by the flush in her cheeks and the amusement dancing in her eyes, didn't take the towel immediately.

Collie grabbed the towel from Dulcie. "I can wipe my own goldarned feet."

Rye dropped his stare, embarrassed by his reaction to her. "Don't swear in front of womenfolk, Collie."

"That ain't swearin'," Collie said.

"Close enough."

"Supper's on," Dulcie said. "I know it's a little early, but that way Collie can get home before dark."

"I'll be taking him home," Rye said.

Dulcie nodded as if she'd assumed that. She took her daughter's hand and went into the cabin.

Above Collie's protests, Rye checked his feet. Assured they were clean and dry, he allowed the boy to follow Dulcie and Madeline inside. Rye went in last. Despite Dulcie's invitation to supper, he wasn't altogether certain she meant for him to eat inside with the rest of them. However, she had four places set at the table and directed where he and Collie were to sit.

He hung his hat beside Dulcie's and gingerly sat down. Collie appeared as uncomfortable as Rye felt. It had been a long time since Rye had sat down with anyone to eat a meal, not counting the army mess hall.

Rye forced himself to relax. He waited for Dulcie to say grace, but she went right to spooning food on Madeline's plate and passing the serving bowls to Collie. Rye helped the boy, then himself to mashed potatoes with gravy, creamed peas, buttered bread, and fried rabbit.

There was little talk except to ask for more food. The more Collie ate, the more the boy's anxiety eased. When he finally pushed his plate away, he rested his hands on his belly and burped.

Madeline giggled.

Rye caught Dulcie's amused gaze, and although he wanted to laugh himself, he didn't. "What do you say, Collie?"

"Everything was real good, Mrs. McDaniel. Thanks," the boy said.

"That wasn't—"

"Close enough. My ma used to say more room outside than there is in," Dulcie said, smiling. "I'm glad you liked it, Collie."

Rye surrendered. "It was good, Dulcie. Thank you."

Her face pinkened, and Rye wanted to reach across the table to cup those smooth, flushed cheeks, trace her lower lip with his thumb. He looked away. No matter that it was impossible and unwise, Rye couldn't ignore his attraction to her.

"I'm sorry I don't have any pie or cake," Dulcie said.

"I don't know where I'd put it if you did," Rye said. He turned to Collie. "I'll give you a ride back to the Gearsons'."

Although Collie didn't appear thrilled to return to his foster home, he pushed back his chair and stood.

Dulcie rose to hug Collie, who kept his arms at his sides and fastened his wide eyes on Rye, as if begging him to rescue him. Rye ducked his head to hide his amusement.

"Thank you for your help, Collie. I won't ever forget what you did," Dulcie said.

"Yes, ma'am." His voice was muffled by Dulcie's shoulder.

She released him, and Collie scrambled back.

"You're welcome to visit any time you want," she said.

Collie rounded the table and started backing away. "Yes, ma'am." He scurried out the door.

Rye chuckled and got to his feet. "I suppose I'd better get out there before he runs all the way back to town."

"I didn't mean to scare him."

"You didn't. He just isn't used to being hugged."

She crossed her arms, her expression troubled. "That's a shame. A child should know affection."

Memories from Rye's own childhood spilled into his mind. His wife Mary had taught him to hug and that it was all right to want to touch another person. Or maybe she'd merely unlocked the dark place in his heart where loving memories of his mother and father were guarded against the sterile orphanage. And now Mary and her tender smile and gentle nature were gone, too.

He shook the painful thoughts aside. "I'll be back soon."

Dulcie nodded and gathered the dirty dishes. Rye retrieved his hat on the way out and settled it on his head. He was relieved to see Collie hadn't run, but instead, was standing by the corral.

Rye whistled shrilly and his mare came running despite the green, inviting grass in the pasture. Once Smoke was saddled, Rye mounted and drew her up alongside the corral where Collie waited on the top pole. The boy climbed onto the mare's rump, behind Rye.

"Hold on," Rye said.

Collie's arms went around his waist and Rye heeled Smoke into motion. He let her run some then slowed to a walk for the last half mile. As they drew closer to the Gearsons', Collie grew quiet and his thin arms tightened around Rye. He hadn't seen any sign that they beat the boy, but there were other ways for folks to hurt children. Rye knew most of them.

Dusk was turning to night when they arrived at the Gearsons'. Rye hung onto Collie's forearm, easing the boy down to the ground. He stood close to Smoke as Rye dismounted.

Two chubby blond boys rushed out the door as Rye guided Collie toward it. The twin boys, slightly older than Collie, stopped and stared.

"You're in trouble, dog-boy," one of them taunted.

"Yeah. Ma ain't happy," the other said.

Collie stiffened beneath Rye's palm, but he remained silent and lowered his gaze. Rye bit the inside of his cheek, knowing he'd only make it more difficult for the boy if he defended him.

Before Rye could knock on the door, it was opened by a heavyset woman with a red, sweat-coated face. "It's about time you got back, Collier. What would your mother think if she knew you was out past dark? Go on inside."

Collie glanced up at Rye with an apologetic look then disappeared into the house.

Mrs. Gearson mopped her brow with a dirty, limp handkerchief. "What did Collier get into this time?"

Rye removed his hat and held it between his hands, which trembled with resentment of the woman's callous tone. "Collie helped find a young girl that ran away right before the storm hit."

The woman blinked her narrow eyes. "Who're you?"

"Rye Forrester, ma'am." Rye remained courteous for Collie's sake. "I work for Mrs. McDaniel. It was her daughter that Collie saved."

"McDaniel. I don't know no McDaniel 'round here."

"She's old man Pollard's daughter." The man who spoke came up behind Mrs. Gearson from inside the house. He was as rail thin as his wife was round, and was even more dour-faced. "You know you're workin' on a murderer's farm?"

"Mrs. McDaniel didn't kill anyone." Rye said, his mild tone a direct contrast to his churning fury.

"Well, no, but she ain't no saint herself."

His wife tut-tutted. "Hush, Hubert. That was five years ago."

"You heard what they said about her and—"

She elbowed him in the ribs. "I said hush."

Hubert rubbed his chest and glared at his wife, but didn't say anything else.

Small towns were often rife with gossip, and with Dulcie being the daughter of a supposed murderer, Rye was certain she had more than her share of rumors circulating about her. He didn't care to hear any of them. "Like I was saying, Collie found Mrs. McDaniel's four-year-old girl before the storm. I figured he saved her life."

"That good-for-nothin'—" Hubert began.

Again her elbow stopped him. "It was a sad day when Collier's ma and pa died. It's good to know their boy might not be as dimwitted as we feared."

"He's not slow-witted," Rye said sharply. "He's a little boy who misses his folks."

Gearson grumbled. "Boy ought to be over 'em by now."

Rye didn't dare speak for a long moment, afraid of what he might say. Instead, he donned his hat. "I just wanted you to know where he was and what he did. And Mrs. McDaniel fed him supper."

"That's good 'cause we already ate. If he shows up late for a meal here, he goes without."

Rye counted to five, but his temper remained at the boiling point. "Seems to me none of your own go without, and don't tell me they always show up on time for meals."

Gearson took a threatening step forward. "How we raise our own ain't any of your concern."

"Maybe not, but seems to me you shouldn't be keeping Collie if you ain't going to raise *him* like one of your own." He marched down the steps.

The Gearsons remained on the porch, glaring at him as

he mounted Smoke. As he rode away, he glanced back and spotted Collie's pale face peering out a window.

Rye spurred Smoke into a gallop, but he couldn't outrun the look of abandonment in the boy's eyes.

$\mathscr{T}_{EN}$

DESPITE her long nap before supper, Madeline was asleep on the large bed again by the time Dulcie put away the last of the dishes. Dulcie didn't want to disturb her rest by having her climb up to the loft, so she removed the sleepy girl's dress and slipped on her nightgown. Madeline fell back into a sound sleep in a matter of seconds.

Dulcie swept back her daughter's fine hair and kissed her unblemished brow. "Good-night, honey," she whispered. She rose and placed Madeline's dress over the footboard so it would be there for her in the morning.

Although it was only eight o'clock, Dulcie yawned and rubbed her gritty eyes. She, too, was tired. The lingering fear from Madeline's disappearance and of the storm itself had worn her out. She gazed longingly at the bed, but the sudden recollection of Rye protecting them from the hail and the awareness of his lean muscles pressing against her produced another kind of longing. Her body hummed with familiar restlessness. Her camisole brushed her breasts like a lover's caress and the almost-ache between her legs pulsed in time with her heart.

Dulcie turned away from the bedroom and dropped into a rocking chair. She thought she'd left her wicked nature in the past, with that foolish girl who'd demanded a dashing army private take her virginity. He'd eliminated her maidenhead in one night, but losing her innocence had taken longer—two years to realize that dashing private was nothing but a randy young man who took his pleasure with any willing woman. She'd wanted to yell at him and deny him his husbandly rights, but she couldn't stop her body from wanting what he gave her. She couldn't fight the waves of pleasure, the cresting of passion, when he took her. Yet afterward, shame would wash through her. Was she no better than the whores who found their pleasure with any man?

It was only after Jerry had hit Madeline that she'd denied him. He'd never struck their daughter again, and rarely did he come to his wife's bed.

She tipped her head back and closed her eyes. The peddler was more evidence of her immoral character. He'd threatened to abandon them in the middle of nowhere to get Dulcie into his bed. She'd hated lying there beneath him and hated the way her body betrayed her under his knowing touches. But she hated herself the most for riding the passion and crying out when the ecstasy crashed through her.

The moment Virgil Lamont dropped them off at the farm, Dulcie swore to deny that depravity within her. She had everything she needed with the farm and Madeline. And if there were some nights when her body burned, she'd learned how to quench the fire herself.

Dulcie's mouth was parched, and she rose to get some water from the pitcher. As she drank, she gazed out into the darkening night. Rye should be back soon. As if her thoughts conjured him, he and his gray mare materialized out of the darkness. He drew his horse up by the barn and dismounted.

Dulcie set the empty cup down and was halfway across the yard before she realized what she was doing. She paused, noticing the cool evening air on her warm cheeks and the low clucking of the chickens. Her restless gaze settled on Rye, and she continued over to him.

"Did you have any trouble with the Gearsons?" she asked.

He didn't seem surprised to see her. "Not exactly."

His answer didn't allay her concern. "Did they hurt him?"

"No." Rye undid the saddle cinch. "I don't think they've ever hit him." He lifted the saddle and blanket off Smoke's back and carried them into the barn.

Dulcie followed him inside, where a kerosene lamp offered a circle of light. She shoved her hands into her trouser pockets, uncertain why she was out here after dark, without the buffer of Madeline between them.

"I can't figure out why they took him in if they didn't want him," Rye said.

"Obligation."

The lantern's light lent menacing shadows across his face as he gazed down at her. "That's not enough."

"Sometimes that's all there is." She tipped her head to the side, studying the frustration coloring his expression. "He reminds you of yourself, doesn't he?"

Rye stilled, then his long, sure fingers untangled the saddle strings. "I suppose."

For a moment, she wanted to comfort him like she comforted Madeline when she was sad. Instead, she pressed her hands deeper into her pockets.

Rye straightened, grabbed a currycomb, and strode out of the barn. Frowning, Dulcie hurried to catch up to him. She leaned against the corral and watched him brush his mare.

"Maybe if you got hitched, you could take Collie yourself," she remarked.

Rye paused in his task to gaze at her, his eyes burning with something akin to passion. Dulcie's body responded to his hot look and she swayed toward him.

Suddenly he grinned. "You askin' me for my hand, Dulcie?"

Embarrassment scalded her face. "Of course not. I was only thinking out loud."

"That's good, 'cause I don't aim to get married again."

Surprised, she asked, "You were married?"

"She died," he answered, his flat tone clearly indicating he didn't want to talk about his wife.

Although curious, she respected his privacy.

He curried his mare with long, slow strokes, his free hand

following the path of the brush to smooth his horse's smoky coat. Dulcie studied his hands, the easy motions and light, sure touches. Would he be as gentle with a woman?

What would it have been like to be married to a man like Rye instead of someone like Jerry? She imagined him lying with his wife. She suspected he'd been tender, then more insistent, but never demanding, never hurting. He wouldn't take, even from his duty-bound wife, but ask with a husky, passionate voice.

"Is Madeline asleep?" Rye asked.

She cleared her throat. "Yes. The storm really frightened her."

"Scared me, too. Especially with us out in the open like that."

"I never thanked you for what you did." She shifted uncomfortably, not used to being grateful to someone. "You protected us when the hail started. If those stones had been any larger, you could've been badly injured."

"They would've hurt you and the children a lot more than they hurt me."

Dulcie's heart slid into her throat, and she looked away. Without asking for anything in return, Rye had risked his life for theirs.

He moved toward her, stopped only inches in front of her. Worry furrowed in his brow. "Are you all right?"

She wanted to look away so he wouldn't see her need, but her eyes refused to obey. "Fine," she whispered.

Recognition of her desire dawned in his eyes and in the sudden flare of his nostrils. But there was also denial, a rejection of the mirroring passion she knew he felt. She touched his chest, feeling the heat of his skin and the beat of his heart through his shirt.

Humiliation burned within her, and she drew her hand away. "I should get back inside," she said with a hoarse voice.

Before she could see the disgust in his eyes, she strode across the yard, her vision blurring. She closed the door behind her and leaned against it. Struggling alone to raise a daughter and make a living on a farm, she had no cause to dwell on such selfish yearnings.

Her gaze strayed to the bedroom, to the trunk at the foot of the bed. As if of their own volition, her feet carried her to it and she lifted the lid. The whiskey beckoned her, promised her respite from the chaotic swirl of shame and desire and guilt. Without hesitation, she plucked the brown glass bottle from the trunk.

As Dulcie tugged the stopper out, her conscience gave her pause. But then the biting scent of the alcohol hit her.

I'll only have a couple of sips, just enough to help me sleep.

RYE gathered his tools the next morning, determined to finish his work on the porch and roof. Fortunately, he'd had enough completed that no water had leaked through the roof into the cabin during the storm. As he walked out of the barn with his arms full, he was surprised to see Flossie where he'd tied her to the corral, her udder heavy. A glance at the quiet cabin told him Dulcie wasn't up yet.

Frowning, he carried his things to the porch and set them down quietly. He had planned to start work early since Dulcie was usually up by now, but maybe after yesterday's scare, both she and Madeline needed the extra rest.

He sat down on the step to wait, and unease flitted through him. His exchange with Dulcie last night had left him restless and tense, in more ways than one. He was no stranger to that look she'd had in her eyes, and if she'd been anyone but Jerry's widow, he would've taken her up on her offer. Hell, a man only had so much self-control and, intentional or not, Dulcie was driving him to the brink of that control.

He hadn't meant to hurt her, but better she be miffed now than embarrassed and angry later. She was a lady who'd had some tough times, and he wasn't about to take advantage of her. A year ago he might have thought different, but he'd had a lot of time to think while he'd been in the stockade. And he'd thought long and hard.

The door creaked open behind him and he turned, expecting to see Dulcie. Instead, Madeline poked her head out.

Rye greeted her with a smile. "Morning, sunshine."

The girl grinned and tiptoed out to sit by Rye. Still wearing her nightgown, she leaned against his side.

"Your ma still asleep?" Rye asked.

Madeline nodded vehemently.

"Sleeping in the rocking chair." She giggled. "With her clothes on."

Rye kept his growing unease masked from the girl. "Maybe she woke up earlier and put on her clothes."

"No."

Although Rye wondered how she could be sure, he didn't ask her. Kids often sensed and knew more than adults gave them credit for.

Flossie bawled mournfully from the corral.

"Why don't you get dressed and you can help me milk Flossie?" Rye suggested to the girl.

"Okay." Madeline jumped to her feet and scrambled back into the cabin.

When she rejoined him, she stood with her back to him. "Button," she said.

Smiling at the bossiness so like her mother's, Rye did as she commanded. His big fingers fumbled with the tiny buttons, but he finally managed to get them.

"All done," he said.

Madeline spun around to face him, and her tangled hair framed her innocent features. "Gotta go."

Rye frowned. "Go where?"

She rolled her eyes as if he were as dumb as dirt. "Privy."

His face heated. "Oh. I'll wait here."

On bare feet, she dashed to the outhouse and disappeared inside. Rye stood, wondering if she might need help. For all he knew about four-year-old girls, she might fall in or something.

The cabin door flew open and Dulcie rushed out, her hair even wilder than her daughter's. "Is Madeline out here?"

Rye caught Dulcie's arms as she stumbled down the steps and the smell of stale whiskey on her breath nearly bowled him over. He turned away, disgusted by the evidence of her drinking. "She's in the privy."

Dulcie sagged, then as if remembering herself, jerked out of his hold and backed away. "I-I must've overslept." Her voice was tentative, guarded.

Whiskey will do that to a person.

"You were tired," Rye said. He kept the irritation out of his voice. "I'll take Madeline with me to milk Flossie. That'll give you some time to clean up."

Bloodshot eyes met his and she glanced away. "Thanks."

She shuffled back inside, leaving Rye more angry than sympathetic. If it was only herself she was hurting, he'd simply be disappointed that she'd followed her father's path. But Madeline could wander off, get hurt, or a dozen other things while Dulcie was drunk. Didn't she think of that?

Shaking aside his misgivings, Rye started walking toward the privy. Madeline hopped out before he reached it, her nose wrinkled. She quickly dipped her hands in the basin of water set out on an upright chunk of wood and shook the droplets off.

"Milk Flossie now?" she asked, her eyes shining with excitement.

"Flossie would appreciate it," Rye said.

As he walked, Madeline placed her small damp hand in his larger one. A lump climbed into his throat, and he gently closed his fingers around hers. She skipped along beside him, thankfully oblivious to his mixed-up feelings.

"You stay on this side of the corral and pet Flossie while I milk her," Rye said.

Madeline immediately stroked the cow's nose, smiling and whispering to the animal as if Flossie understood her.

Rye went to work relieving Flossie of the pressure in her udder. The cow remained placid, probably enjoying both the petting and the relief of getting milked.

"Your ma sleep late very often?" Rye asked, keeping his tone light.

"Sometimes." She resumed her one-sided conversation with the cow.

"A lot of times?"

Madeline shrugged. "No. Only when she's sad. I can tell."

Considering she'd lost her husband and her father in the past six months, she had a right to be sad now and again. "Does she miss your father?"

Madeline pressed her lips together and shrugged. "He yelled at me," she said.

It took a moment for Rye to figure out who she was referring to. His insides clenched. "Did he ever hurt you?"

One small shoulder lifted in a half shrug.

Rye leaned his forehead against Flossie's side. The milk pail was over a quarter full and he fought the urge to kick it over.

It hadn't even entered his mind that his drinking and whoring friend might hurt his daughter. At the time, he'd been blind to everything but his own grief.

Rye finished milking Flossie and stood, picking up the milk pail. He set it on the other side of the corral and untied Flossie so she could wander back into the pasture to graze.

Madeline tried to pick up the pail, but Rye intercepted her. "I'll carry that, Madeline."

She surrendered it without an argument and fell into step beside him.

Dulcie came out as they walked across the yard. She'd brushed her hair and changed into a different shirt, but the familiar signs of the previous night's drinking remained in her pale face. The lines in her brow and at the corners of her eyes bespoke a pounding headache. Despite himself, Rye felt a twinge of sympathy. He recalled those mornings too well.

Madeline raced ahead and greeted her mother with a hug, which Dulcie returned. Bittersweet warmth kindled in Rye to see mother and daughter embracing. It reminded him too much of what he'd lost.

"Thanks for taking care of Flossie, Rye," Dulcie said.

"She was getting impatient," he said.

Dulcie's face reddened, and she reached for the pail. "I'll take it in."

"I've got it. You might want to feed the chickens and collect the eggs."

She didn't meet his gaze, but only nodded. "C'mon, Madeline. You can help."

The girl seemed overjoyed to be given such an important job. Rye smiled at her and carried the milk to the cabin, setting it on the porch by the door.

A cry spun him around, his heart nearly pounding out of his chest. Madeline pressed against Dulcie's leg, as the chickens pecked close to her feet. Rye hurried over to them.

"You have to throw the feed out farther," Dulcie said to her daughter. "That way they won't go after your toes."

Wide-eyed and her lips turned downward, Madeline stared in fear at the hungry chickens. The rooster strutted over to the girl, so close his feathers brushed her legs. Madeline whimpered and clung to Dulcie's waist.

Rye marched through the chickens, scattering them in all directions. He picked up the girl, and she wrapped her arms around his neck, burrowing her face in his shoulder.

"Why'd you do that?" Dulcie demanded.

"She was scared." Anger vibrated through his voice.

"They weren't going to hurt her. She has to get used to them."

"She's barefoot, Dulcie. They could've drawn blood."

Dulcie's gaze went to her daughter's feet and her eyes widened. The only color in her face was two red splotches on her cheeks. "I-I didn't—"

"No, you didn't." Rye bit the inside of his cheek, torn between fury and pity for the woman. "I'll watch Madeline until you're done gathering eggs."

Temper flashed in Dulcie's expression, but she turned away and went into the ramshackle coop to collect the eggs.

"Help Ma get eggs?" Madeline asked, watching her mother with wounded eyes.

Rye shook his head, his throat tight with empathy. "How about you and I go check on Jack and Smoke?"

"I pet them?"

"They'd be sad if you didn't."

Excitement replaced Madeline's gloominess. Rye leaned over to set her on the ground and she clung to his neck.

"I'll keep the hens away from you," Rye said. "I promise."

After a moment, she released him, but held tightly to his hand. Rye gazed down at Madeline, humbled by her trust. It had been a long time since anyone had depended on him.

And it felt damned good.

* * *

"DAMNATION," Dulcie swore, staring down at the three broken eggs. She resisted the urge to dash the basket on the ground.

Gritting her teeth, she cleaned out the slimy mess from the basket then continued going through the piles of straw. She found three more eggs to add to the four unbroken ones and hurried out of the coop's stuffy confines.

Breathing in the fresh air eased the pounding in her temples only slightly and did even less for her sour mood. She searched the yard for Madeline and Rye, then the pasture, and spotted them by the livestock. Madeline was safely held in Rye's arms.

Dulcie swallowed back the impulse to retch. She knew how vicious the chickens and their sharp beaks could be. How many small scars did her own hands bear from them? Yet she hadn't even thought of Madeline's bare feet. It was Rye who'd saved her daughter from harm.

Her throat closed and tears burned her eyes. Although she recognized her weak nature with men, she'd believed she was a good mother. Yet, in addition to the incident with the hens, Dulcie had slept through Madeline rising and leaving the cabin that morning. What if Rye hadn't been here? Where would the girl have gone? Would she have disappeared like she'd done before the storm?

Dulcie had drunk more whiskey than she'd intended last night. If she'd only had a few sips to ease her nerves as she'd planned, none of this would've happened. It was Rye's presence that made her turn to alcohol to find sleep. If he wasn't around, she wouldn't have touched the whiskey, wouldn't have overslept, and Madeline wouldn't have been out by the chickens.

It was all *his* fault.

But if he hadn't been here, Madeline might still be lost and maybe hurt or worse. The cabin would be falling down around them and the corral wouldn't be standing. And her corn and wheat would rot in the fields.

My crops. A chill swept through her. She'd put all her

hopes in them—hope for new shoes, clothing, and food, as well as hope for independence. What had the storm done to them? Had the hail destroyed them? No, the stones hadn't been that large. At least, she didn't think so.

Her heart beating a harsh staccato in her chest, she set the basket of eggs on the porch and started down the path that led to the fields.

"Dulcie." Rye, carrying Madeline on his broad shoulders, strode through the pasture toward her. She waited impatiently for him to draw near.

"Where are you going?" he asked.

"I want to make sure the hail didn't harm the crops," she replied.

"It didn't."

His certain reply brought her gaze back to him. "How do you know?"

"When I came back from town last night, I swung past them. A few cornstalks were down from the wind, but that was all the damage I saw."

Dulcie's temper flared. "Why didn't you tell me?"

He shrugged, a gesture almost amusing with Madeline on his shoulders. Except Dulcie wasn't laughing.

"I forgot." He perused her silently, his features a bland mask. "I'm surprised you didn't think of it yesterday."

She jerked, as if he'd slapped her. Damn him for being right. And damn him for being so smug about it. Except maybe he wasn't being smug. Maybe it was her own guilt making her feel so defensive.

"I was worried about Madeline." It was more or less the truth.

"You should've worried more about her this morning," he said in a low voice.

Dulcie's cheeks grew hot with humiliation. "I was tired."

He merely stared at her, challenging her to confess her lie. But she didn't. She couldn't. Good women didn't drink whiskey. Nor did they harbor wicked thoughts about their hired men. "I'll take Madeline into the house."

After a moment, Rye leaned down and lifted Madeline off his shoulders, setting her on the ground. She turned around and held up her arms. "Want another ride."

Rye smiled down at the girl, his eyes crinkling at the corners. "Later. Right now your ma needs your help."

Madeline thrust out her lower lip, but Dulcie curtailed her argument by taking her hand. "You can stir the porridge."

The girl brightened and followed Dulcie without balking. Dulcie was aware of Rye's disappointment with her earlier behavior, but she told herself she didn't care.

What was another lie to add to her growing list?

ELEVEN

LATER in the day, as Dulcie worked on her hands and knees in the garden, Rye joined her.

"Do you want me to recover that window?" he asked.

She squinted against the sun over his shoulder. "No, I plan to get glass for it." She lowered her gaze. "Soon as the corn and wheat are in."

He shrugged. "Suit yourself." He walked away.

Dulcie scrambled to her feet. "Rye?"

He stopped and turned.

She approached him and took a moment to make sure Madeline still played with her doll. Shoving her hands in her back pockets, she took a deep breath. "This morning, with the chickens and Madeline . . ."

She hoped he would say something, to spare her from having to speak the words, but he crossed his arms and simply gazed at her. Although his expression wasn't judgmental, she knew he was measuring her, and she suspected she was coming up woefully short in his estimation. Steeling herself against his silent criticism, she plunged ahead. "I'm sorry. You were right. I shouldn't have had her help me feed them. She's too young."

"You should be apologizing to your daughter."

Surprised, Dulcie tried to tell if he was serious or merely unforgiving. Or different than any other man she'd known. "You're the one who was angry."

"I'm not the one who was scared and crying."

She gauged his sincerity. "You mean that."

Impatience flashed across his features, but it was replaced with sudden understanding. "I'm not your father, Dulcie. You might make me mad, but I'd never harm you."

Her mouth opened to snap back a retort, but she abruptly closed it. How had he known she'd always been careful not to upset her father? Frank Pollard had a temper, especially when he was drinking, and she'd learned that if she angered him, an apology would usually calm him. "You're nothing like him," she said quietly. "Or my husband." She glanced away, angered by the tears stinging her eyes. "Sometimes I'm glad Jerry's gone."

Awkward silence surrounded them.

"Did you love him?" Rye asked so softly she almost missed the question.

The answer was easy. The reasons weren't. "I thought I did. A long time ago." She glanced at him. "Did you love your wife?"

He nodded without hesitation. "I still do."

Dulcie's heart squeezed painfully. "She was a lucky woman."

"If lucky is dying during childbirth when you're twenty-three-years-old, then I suppose she was." Bitterness bled from his words. He cleared his throat. "I'd best get back to work."

He spun around and nearly ran back to the cabin porch.

Dulcie wrapped her arms around her waist, feeling a chill despite the heat of the September sun. If Jerry had loved her like Rye had loved his wife, her answer to Rye's question would've been different. And Jerry would probably still be alive.

She returned to her garden and let the scent of the rich soil and growing plants soothe her. Dirt coated her hands and got under her fingernails, but it was clean dirt. Not like the dirt that stained a person's soul or dirt that marred a conscience. Those couldn't be washed with soap and water, and rarely ever got clean again.

The afternoon passed, and Dulcie's headache leached away. With an end to the dull throbbing came another assault from her conscience. She gazed at her daughter, who helped her carry the harvested vegetables to the porch. Dulcie had made a horrible mistake last night by drinking too much whiskey. "Would you like to walk down to the creek?" she asked.

Madeline's eyes lit up and her face broke into a blinding smile.

Dulcie's own heart lightened, and she held out her hand. Madeline clasped it, and mother and daughter headed to the creek.

RYE, his arms filled with boards, came out of the barn and paused. Dulcie and Madeline were walking down the path. For a moment, he thought his eyes were playing tricks on him, but Dulcie was actually skipping with her daughter. He smiled, pleased to see this carefree side of Dulcie.

Curious as to where they were going, Rye set his things down and followed. Their giggles reached him before he spotted them beside the narrow creek. He drew closer, but kept hidden in the brush some twenty-five feet from the water. Feeling slightly guilty for intruding, Rye told himself he was only watching out for Madeline. After what had happened that morning, he didn't fully trust Dulcie.

He knelt down and settled back on his heels as he observed their fun. Madeline stood in the shallow stream, the water at her knees. She splashed about, getting herself and her mother wet. Dulcie laughed and sat back on the bank to remove her boots and stockings. She rolled up her trousers and Rye couldn't help but admire her slender ankles and gently curved calves. Then she removed her hat and tossed it down beside her shoes. Her hair, bound in a ponytail, spilled past her shoulders and halfway down her back. She joined her daughter in the water, laughing like a young girl.

Blood surged through Rye's veins. The sun kissed Dulcie's face, and he could almost see the sprinkling of freckles across her nose and cheeks. His gaze moved downward, to the two buttons she'd opened at her collar to the tempting shadows of the slope of her breasts and the valley between them. And lower still, to her slender waist and gentle flare of her hips, down her willowy legs, exposed below her knees.

Dulcie and Madeline scampered about in the clear water. Tendrils of hair clung to their faces but neither woman nor girl cared. For a moment out of time, their world consisted of sunshine, cool water, and each other.

Anguish punched Rye and stole his breath. If Mary and their child had lived, this would be Rye's world, too. Instead, he lurked on the fringes, sitting in the place of a man who'd died because of him. If what Dulcie said was true, he doubted Jerry would've recognized the value of this moment—a moment Rye would sell his soul to possess.

The ache expanded, and he rubbed his fist against his chest to try to ease the pain. But he knew nothing would ever take away the horrible emptiness. Just as nothing would ever remove the brand on his shoulder. Both would be with him the rest of his life.

Rye crept away and returned to the farmyard, where he used work to forget. He focused on pulling off the crooked and rotting boards that covered the broken window. Although Dulcie had told him not to redo the repair job, he couldn't leave it like it was. Just as he finished putting the last board in place, a man rode into the yard. Rye didn't recognize him, but he did recognize the glint of silver on his vest. He set his hammer down and ambled out to meet the lawman.

"Afternoon," Rye said.

The sheriff stared down at him. "I'm lookin' for Mrs. McDaniel."

"She and her daughter went for a walk. They should be back soon."

"Who're you?"

Irritated by his officious tone, Rye replied, "Forrester, Rye Forrester. I work for Mrs. McDaniel."

"She didn't mention anythin' to me about a hired man."

Rye shrugged, but his voice was steely. "She probably figured it wasn't any of your business."

The lawman frowned and his face reddened. "You've got a smart mouth on you, mister."

"Forrester. Mister Forrester." Rye didn't bother to hide his annoyance. "What is it you want to talk to Mrs. McDaniel about?"

"That's between her and me."

Rye studied his doughy face and narrow-set eyes. He doubted the sheriff had arrested anybody for anything worse than being a nuisance. "Did you find the men who hanged her father?"

The sheriff jerked his attention back to Rye. "You from around here?"

Rye tipped back his hat. "No, but a person can't help but hear things."

"What've you heard?"

"Only that Mrs. McDaniel's father was lynched, and she says he was innocent."

The sheriff barked a laugh that held no humor. "Yeah, she tells everyone the same thing, but someone seen him arguin' with Carpenter not long afore he was murdered. He was guilty."

"Because if he wasn't, you let an innocent man be hanged?" Rye kept his tone mild.

The man's face turned crimson. "There was nothing I could do. There were too many of them."

"I find it damned hard to believe that in a town this small, you didn't recognize any of them."

The lawman glared at him and opened his mouth, but nothing came out.

Rye spotted Dulcie and Madeline walking back from the creek. Dulcie had put her shoes and stockings back on, as well as rolled down her trousers. However, she carried her hat, and her cheeks were flushed with laughter. When she noticed the sheriff, her amusement abruptly disappeared and furrows returned to her smooth brow. Dulcie spoke to Madeline and the girl trotted off into the cabin.

The sheriff dismounted as Dulcie approached.

"What brings you all the way out here, Sheriff Martin?" Dulcie asked, her tone thick with sarcasm.

Martin removed his hat, but a scowl curled his lips. "I jest wanted to let you know that I ain't been able to find anyone who was involved with the lynchin'." He shrugged. "I figure it'd be a waste of time to keep on lookin'. Asides, everybody but you figures he was guilty."

Rye, knowing Dulcie's temper, saw it flare in the flattening of her lips and the stiffening of her shoulders.

"You took one man's word that Pa done it. What if that man was lying?" Dulcie demanded.

"Why would Virgil Lamont lie?"

Dulcie's angry expression faltered a moment, but her challenging tone remained. "Maybe he killed Mr. Carpenter."

"And why would he do that?" Martin shook his head and placed his hat back on his head. "The whiskey changed your pa, Dulcie. Maybe you didn't want to see it, but when your ma died, he didn't do nothin' but drink. The only way he could buy whiskey was to do odd jobs around town. Carpenter tried to get him to quit drinkin'. Your pa didn't like his meddlin'." Martin shrugged. "Frank was probably drunk when he killed him."

"He was drunk all right, but he was in our barn out cold, not in town killing anybody." Dulcie's voice trembled.

"There's only your word."

Rye sensed Dulcie's anger and humiliation. "You're saying Mrs. McDaniel's word is no good?"

"I'm sayin' that Frank was her father and she'd say anything to protect him." Martin glanced at Dulcie almost apologetically. "And herself."

Dulcie spun away.

Rye watched her leave then turned back to the sheriff. "Instead of looking for those who lynched her father, maybe you should be looking for the real murderer."

"That'd be a waste of time, Forrester." Martin shifted his weight from one foot to the other. When he looked at Rye, his face held regret and something more. "Me and Dulcie went to school together. She was the prettiest girl in school, but she had some of her pa's wild streak in her. She had this restlessness in her. When she run away to marry the soldier fellah, everybody knew why." His face reddened slightly.

It took Rye a few moments to figure out what the sheriff was telling him. Knowing Jerry, it shouldn't have surprised Rye that he didn't wait for a wedding to bed Dulcie. However, he suspected Dulcie wasn't unwilling. She'd wanted to leave Locust, and she'd found the easiest way to do that.

He shook aside the thought. That was part of the past. "Do you mind if I nose around a bit?"

Martin studied him. "You'd be wastin' your time."

"It's mine to waste."

"Suit yourself." He mounted his horse and gazed down at Rye. "But don't be surprised if folks ain't willing to talk to you." The lawman rode away.

"He's a jackass," Dulcie said.

He turned to find her standing behind him. "He said you two went to school together."

She shrugged. "You grow up in this town and everybody knows everybody."

He considered getting her reaction to what else the sheriff had said, but rejected it. He'd made his own share of mistakes with his life. How could he blame Dulcie for the same? There was no evidence now to suggest she was a loose woman, and Jerry had never accused her of being unfaithful, although he had often been.

"He's giving up, isn't he?" Dulcie asked.

"Sounds like it."

"He always did take the easy way. He used to cheat on tests in school."

Rye couldn't help but chuckle. "I have to admit I might have done that once or twice myself."

Dulcie allowed a wry smile. "I guess we all have. It's just that . . ."

"You want your father's name cleared," Rye finished softly.

"Yes."

"I told the sheriff I was going to ask around, find out if anyone else might have had a grudge against this Carpenter."

"You believe me?"

The hope in her eyes was almost too painful for Rye to bear. "I believe that you believe he was innocent."

She searched his face, and he forced himself not to squirm under her scrutiny. She sighed and looked away. "I can't blame you. You've only heard that he was a no-account drunk."

"I admit I don't think much of a man who would let a place like this go to ruin." He looked around the farm deliberately. "But there's a lot of difference between being lazy and being a murderer."

"Calling Pa lazy was about the best I could do, too, but he'd never kill anyone." Determination gleamed in her eyes. "That I'm certain of."

Loyalty was an admirable trait, but blind loyalty could be dangerous. He hoped Dulcie knew the difference.

DULCIE didn't sleep well, but she managed a night without the assistance of whiskey. She awakened early and instead of lying in bed to toss and turn for another hour, she rose and put on coffee. Once it was ready, she poured herself a cup and carried it outside to drink in the hazy sunrise.

She sat sideways on the step so she could examine the repaired porch. Even though her feelings were mixed up concerning her hired man, she had to admit Rye knew how to wield a hammer. Every task he'd undertaken, he'd completed, and his work was better than her father could've done when he was sober. She was damned lucky the day Rye Forrester had shown up looking for work, even though she wondered why he'd chosen her place. If he was thinking of taking advantage of her, he'd done nothing to further that goal.

Except gain my trust.

She tried to ignore the voice of suspicion, but she knew enough about people to know nothing was ever free. There was always a price, and she doubted Rye's price was a room in a leaky barn and three meals eaten on the porch. Yet if there was more, she had yet to see any sign of it.

The barn door swung open and Rye stepped out. Although he was dressed, his shirt was unbuttoned and untucked, the tail fluttering about his lean hips. The broad expanse of his chest narrowed to his flat belly. Heat flared in Dulcie and she shifted, bringing her legs together.

Rye lifted his head and looked right at her, as if sensing her presence. He froze, like a buck scenting a doe. Dulcie could do nothing but hold his gaze as her stomach clenched and her breathing grew more rapid.

Suddenly, he returned to the barn. Dulcie gasped, as if she'd been holding her breath, which she might have done. His masculinity frightened her, but not nearly as much as her own passion. Was it only physical attraction? Dealing with her yearnings was difficult enough, but what if there was more to it than lust? If she cared for him, it would be more difficult to resist, and twice as dangerous to give in.

Rye reemerged from the barn, but this time his shirt was buttoned and tucked into his trousers. As he sluiced water across his face by the well, Dulcie rose and went back into the cabin. She should milk Flossie, but it was still early enough that she could enjoy another cup of coffee. With Rye.

Ignoring the warning voice inside her, Dulcie refilled her cup and poured coffee for Rye. She carried them onto the porch and sat back down on the step, deliberately setting Rye's cup in plain view.

After a moment of startled hesitation, Rye dried his face and ambled over to join her.

"Morning, Rye," she said, forcing herself to look up and meet his eyes. He didn't wear his hat and water droplets in his hair glinted in the morning sunlight.

"You're up early."

Her cheeks heated and she peered down at her hands, which were wrapped around her cup. "It's a beautiful morning." She held up his cup of coffee and lifted a brow in question.

He smiled, revealing white teeth free of tobacco stains, unlike so many other men. "Thanks."

He took the cup from her and eased down on the far side

of their shared step. The cacophony of birdsong surrounded them, with the occasional moo from Flossie, as they sipped their steaming coffee.

"I don't usually have time to drink coffee before tending Flossie and gathering the eggs," she said. "I figured since I was awake early, I'd take advantage of it and enjoy the peace and quiet." She realized she was rambling and bit the inside of her cheek.

Rye didn't seem to mind. "Reminds me of mornings when I was just a mite, probably a year or two older than Madeline." His gaze took on a faraway look. "My folks were early risers, so us kids were, too." He chuckled. "Slater never took to getting up early so it was up to me and Creede to pull him out of bed. Creede had to take the brunt of his orneriness."

"Sounds like your family was close."

"We were. Guess that's why it hurts so much to think about them." He gazed into the distance. "And why it's so hard to forget."

"Have you looked for them?"

"Long time ago. Never found either one."

"Maybe you should try again."

"It's been nearly twenty-five years, Dulcie. For all I know, they both could be dead now." He glanced away, but she didn't miss the flash of pain across his face.

"Or they could both be alive, and thinking the same as you."

"Then why haven't they come looking for me?"

"Maybe they did, but you've come a long way from the orphanage, with no word of where you went."

Rye stared down at his empty coffee cup. "I reckon that's possible. If I had any word of them, I'd go searching, but there's been nothing in all these years." He lifted his head. "Would you if you were in my position?"

She frowned, unsure how to answer. "I don't know. I don't have any brothers or sisters."

"Maybe not, but you have a daughter. Would you ever give up on her?"

Her heart tripped in her chest, reminding her how close

she'd come to losing Madeline before the storm. "No. Never. She's my daughter. My flesh and blood."

Rye nodded knowingly. "Even though I haven't seen them since I was a kid, my brothers are still my only family. My own flesh and blood." His gaze took on a distant look. "I haven't given up. I don't think I can."

Dulcie laid her hand on Rye's. "There's no sin in holding on to hope."

The warmth of his skin pulsed through her. The peace of the morning and the knowledge that no one was near added to the awareness. It would be so easy to simply lean forward and kiss his inviting lips and press her tongue to the tiny indent in his chin.

Despite the voice yelling at her to stop, she yielded to the swirling passion. At first his mouth was hard. But, using her knowledge of men, she flicked her tongue along his upper lip and his mouth submitted to hers. His hand curved around her cheek and she moaned, giving in to the pleasure of a man's touch—of *Rye's* touch. Straining forward, she brushed her breasts against his chest, and his sharp inhalation revealed her power over him. A part of her reveled in the triumph of her charms, while a larger part was disappointed he fell so easily.

Suddenly, he pulled away. "Stop it, Dulcie. This isn't right."

Her desire thwarted, Dulcie glared at him. "I'm not good enough for you?"

His mouth dropped open with shock. "No, that's not it." He licked his lips. "I won't be staying, and it's not right to take advantage of you."

She wanted to laugh. How could a woman be taken advantage of when she wanted it? Yet something in Rye's tone and expression stopped her. Reminded her she had a responsibility to her daughter and to this farm. And to herself.

Humiliated by her actions, she shot to her feet and strode across the yard to milk Flossie. Grateful he didn't follow her, Dulcie mechanically milked the cow. Leaning her forehead against Flossie's side, Dulcie allowed the monotony of the chore to numb her thoughts.

When Rye came to stand outside the corral, she sensed

him before seeing him. She steeled herself and met his gaze. "Breakfast will be ready in about half an hour."

"That isn't why I came over here."

She shrugged, hiding her tension.

"It's not that . . ." Rye cleared his throat and tugged at his hat. It seemed she wasn't the only one who was nervous. "It's not that I don't think you're a pretty woman and all, but it's just that, well, there're things you don't know about me."

Her interested piqued, Dulcie studied his tense figure. "What kind of things?"

He laughed, although there was more anxiety than amusement in the sound. "Things I don't like to talk about." He sobered. "If you want me to leave, I will."

Alarmed, she finished milking and stood. Her knees shook slightly, and she locked them in place. She hadn't expected the offer and wasn't certain she wanted to accept it. Her mind told her that if he had secrets, he should leave. Yet her heart told her whatever secrets he possessed, they weren't harmful to her or Madeline. His concern for her daughter seemed sincere. She didn't think a person could act so convincingly, but she'd been wrong in the past.

"Truth be told, I'm still not sure if I can trust you," she said. "You seem trustworthy, but you might be looking for something else."

"All I want is a roof over my head and three meals a day. I have that."

She picked up the pail and walked over to stand directly across from him. "Most men want more."

"Maybe I'm not most men."

"Or maybe you have another reason." She peered at him, trying to read behind his bland mask.

"Maybe, but even if I do, you can be certain I won't hurt you or Madeline."

Dulcie studied him a moment longer then passed him the milk pail. He stepped back as she slipped between the corral poles.

"Maybe I'm being a fool, but I don't want you to leave," she admitted.

He smiled, his expression giving way to relief. "I'm glad.

I promised to help you through the harvest, and I hate to break my promise."

Her apprehension eased. Maybe he was a man who took promises seriously. If he was, he was a rare man indeed.

$\mathcal{T}$WELVE

THE afternoon was hot and stagnant as Rye put the pump in the cabin back together. Months of disuse had made it difficult to take apart, but he'd finally managed to do so that morning, skinning and bruising his knuckles in the process. He'd found the broken piece and fashioned a new one from some metal lying around in the barn.

Dulcie and Madeline stayed outside, and Rye suspected it was because he'd unwittingly given Dulcie reason to distrust him. She'd forced him into a corner, and since he didn't dare tell her the truth, he'd given her cause to question him. Not that she hadn't before, but she'd begun to trust him. And now that bridge would have to be rebuilt. Of course, he didn't need her trust to pay his debt, but he'd begun to care for both her and her daughter.

The kiss told him he cared too much. He'd nearly lost the battle against his conscience, but he'd managed to draw back before being carried away by their combined desire. There was no doubt Dulcie was a passionate woman, but she was probably lonely, too. He wasn't a man to take advantage of a lonely woman, especially when he was the cause of her loneliness.

Sighing, Rye dismissed his regrets and concentrated on

tightening the last piece of the pump. He oiled the parts, primed the pump, and worked the handle. Sweat dripped from his chin onto his chest. Finally, he heard the gurgle and rise of water through the spout. A surge of mud came through, splashing his face, and he wiped his eyes. Grumbling, he continued to work the handle.

Eventually, the water ran cold and clear down the pipe that drained the water outside. Rye cheered loud enough to bring Dulcie and Madeline running into the cabin. They stopped just inside the door and stared at him.

"It's working." He knew he was grinning like a fool but didn't care.

They continued to stare at him.

"What?" he asked, annoyed.

Dulcie didn't speak but motioned to her own face.

"Coon," Madeline said, her eyes wide.

Dulcie's snort was followed by laughter. She covered her mouth, but her eyes twinkled. "Your face is covered with mud except for your eyes." She paused. "You look like a raccoon."

Rye frowned and felt the pull of drying mud on his face. He touched his cheek and grimaced, but when he looked at Madeline, he grinned. "I'd best wash up before the other coons come to take me away."

"You got it working?" Dulcie asked, shifting her attention to the pump.

Rye stepped back. "Try it."

Dulcie took Rye's place by the pump. Water free of dirt came through. She whooped and smiled widely. For a moment, he thought she was going to hug him, but she drew back. Her eyes glittered with gratitude and pleasure. "Thank you. I won't have to carry water inside anymore."

"I should've fixed this sooner. It would've saved you a lot of extra work."

"I'm just glad you fixed it." She turned to her daughter. "Would you like to try it?"

Rye stepped back as Madeline, with Dulcie's sneaky assistance, worked the handle until more water came through the spout. The girl laughed in undisguised delight and put her hands under the stream. Dulcie grabbed a towel before Madeline made a mess.

As she dried the girl's hands, Dulcie looked at Rye. "It might seem like a little thing to you, but I can't tell you how much it means to me."

Rye's throat thickened. "I understand, Dulcie." He paused. "I really do."

She studied him a moment longer and nodded. "It's still a few hours before supper, so I think I'll give the pump a good workout. I've got more vegetables to put up." She glanced away, appearing nervous. "Why don't you take the rest of the day off? You can get rid of your raccoon face and do what you'd like for a change."

Rye's first impulse was to turn down her offer, but the temptation of bathing in the creek was too strong. And if he went into town, he might be able to learn more about Carpenter's death and Dulcie's father's lynching. "If you don't mind, I'll take you up on that."

"Why would I mind? I was the one who suggested it."

Rye nodded. "Thanks." He glanced around, suddenly uncertain of his decision. There were a lot of things left to do to get the place back into shape.

"Go on. You deserve some time off," Dulcie urged, guessing his thoughts.

Ducking his head, Rye grinned. "I'll just get my tools put away and head to the creek."

Three quarters of an hour later, his hair still wet, Rye saddled Smoke. He'd bathed, as well as washed the clothes he'd been wearing, in the running stream. After donning the clean but wrinkled clothes from his saddlebag, he brought the wet ones back to dry on the clothesline.

Rye ensured the cinch was snug and led Smoke out of the corral. He glanced at the cabin. The food from the garden was gone from the porch and he assumed Dulcie had taken it inside to start putting it up.

He mounted Smoke and rode down the narrow, rutted road that led to Locust. A leisurely half hour later, he tied Smoke's reins to a hitching post in front of the saloon. Since he hadn't touched booze in over six months, he knew it would be difficult to enter the bar. However, it was the best place to pick up information.

He steeled himself against the lure of alcohol and pressed through the batwing doors. It was dim inside, especially after the afternoon's brightness. There were two men drinking beer at the bar, and he went to stand a few feet from one of them. He ordered coffee from the bartender, relieved to see it wasn't the same one he'd dickered with for the room.

"Have to make a fresh pot," the man said.

"I'll wait."

The bartender gave him a dirty look, but Rye merely looked at him. When he went into the back room, Rye pretended to study the bottles behind the bar.

"You're new around here," one of the two beer drinkers said.

Rye turned to face the redheaded man and rested his arm on the bar. "That's right. I'm working for Mrs. McDaniel." At their puzzled looks, he added, "Pollard's daughter."

The man sneered. "The murderer's daughter."

At his slur, Rye's hands fisted but he made them relax. "I heard tell he was lynched."

"It was justice, pure and simple," the other man, who sported a shaggy beard and mustache, said.

"Not so pure and simple. He didn't get a trial."

"Didn't need one. He was guilty, no matter what his girl said."

"So you don't think the wrong man was lynched?"

The first man snorted. "Don't seem likely."

"Why do you say that?"

He shrugged. "A peddler seen him with Carpenter right before the murder."

"Peddler still around town?"

"Left right after the hangin'."

"Maybe it was the peddler who'd done it and covered his ass by blaming it on that other fellah."

"Why would he?"

"Why would Pollard?"

"There was bad blood between him and Carpenter. Don't know of no one else who had a beef with him."

"So he just killed him out of meanness?"

"Prob'ly. Like Ernie said, there was bad blood 'tween 'em."

"I hear Pollard's daughter claims her father was innocent. Claims he was in their own barn, passed out drunk."

The redheaded man guffawed. "'Course she'd say that. Pollard was a drunk, but he was still her pa."

The bartender came out of the back. "Coffee'll be ready in fifteen minutes."

Rye grinned. "I've changed my mind. I don't feel like coffee anymore."

He touched the brim of his hat, and the bartender's muttered curses followed him outside. He breathed deeply of the hot but fresh air, untainted by stale alcohol, dirty sawdust, and sweat.

It seemed Sheriff Martin's attitude was probably a common one. Rye figured he'd get pretty much the same from most of the townsfolk.

A sign that read Carpenter's Hardware caught his attention. He headed to the store and entered, surprised by the array of goods displayed. Most hardware stores weren't nearly as well stocked, nor as clean and neat.

A young man, around eighteen or nineteen, came out of the back, an apron protecting his starched white shirt and black trousers. "What can I help you find?"

"Are you the owner?" Rye asked.

Grief flashed across his face. "I guess. It was my father's, but he was murdered. I'm Peter Carpenter."

Rye shook his hand. "Rye Forrester. I work for Mrs. McDaniel." He paused. "Frank Pollard's daughter."

Peter flushed red. "The man who killed my father."

"So I've heard." Rye flinched inwardly, realizing some of his sarcasm had slipped through. "She says he didn't do it."

Peter made a chopping motion. "Nobody believes her."

"What if she's right?"

"She's not. Mr. Lamont said he saw my father and Pollard together not long before the murder."

"Pretty convenient."

"Get out of here, mister," Peter ordered.

A woman joined Peter. She looked to be a few years older than him, and the top of her head didn't even come to his shoulder. "What's going on out here?" she asked.

Peter moved to her side protectively. "Nothing you need to concern yourself with, Martha."

"And you are?" Rye asked.

"Lawrence was my husband," Martha said, her voice as stiff as her starched collar.

Rye's gaze arced between her and Peter, comparing her lustrous black hair and flashing green eyes to Peter's dark hair and hazel eyes. He'd assumed they were brother and sister, but obviously he was wrong.

"How long were you married?" Rye asked.

"We married three years ago, right before we moved here." Martha crossed her arms and exchanged a glance with her stepson. "Peter was seventeen at the time."

Studying her, Rye doubted she was more than twenty or twenty-one when she married the elder Lawrence. "I'm sorry about your husband's death, Mrs. Carpenter, but I'm sorry for Mrs. McDaniel, too. It was her father who was lynched."

"Whoever lynched him did so without conferring with Peter or me. I don't condone lynchings, but in this case, Frank Pollard deserved it." For such a petite woman, she carried a whole lot of hatred.

Rye wanted to argue, but suspected neither the widow nor son would listen. They were both convinced of Pollard's guilt.

"I'm sorry to have bothered you." He turned to leave.

"Mister?"

Rye paused and looked over his shoulder at the woman. "Yes, ma'am?"

"Tell Mrs. McDaniel I'm sorry for her loss, but I'm not sorry he's dead." Steel edged her tone. "He was a murderer and he deserved to hang."

Rye's temper flared, but he restrained it. "Next time you see her, *you* tell her."

With that, Rye stalked out of the store. He'd heard Carpenter was well-liked in town and wondered if that sentiment extended to his young widow and son. In Rye's opinion, they weren't folks to be admired. In fact, they were downright mean. Of course, grief could turn a person, too. Still, to give Dulcie such a message was cruel and uncharitable.

He looked around and spotted a boy walking with his mother across the street. Maybe he'd head over to the Gearsons' and check on Collie, find out if his foster parents were keeping a closer watch on him. Instead of riding his horse, he walked the short distance and found a passel of kids playing in front of their house. He searched for Collie among them, but the boy was absent.

Frowning, Rye continued over to the group and recognized the chubby twins from his previous visit. "Hey," he called, and when they looked up, he asked, "Do you know where Collie is?"

They glanced around then shrugged. "Dunno," one of them said.

Impatient, Rye swept his gaze across the other children. "Have any of you seen Collie?"

A girl about eight years old stepped forward. "I seen him by the livery," she said shyly.

Rye smiled at the girl. "Thanks."

He strode back the way he'd come. In the livery, he found the same man who'd been working the day he arrived in Locust.

"You seen a kid about so tall, light hair, wearing overalls?" Rye asked him.

The big-bellied man angled a glare at him. "Why you lookin' for Collie?"

"I want to make sure he's okay."

He shrugged meaty shoulders. "Fine last time I seen him. That was 'bout an hour ago."

"Do you know where he went?"

"Try the bathhouse."

"Thanks. I'll do that." He started to turn away but stopped. "You around here the day Carpenter was murdered?"

The man moved tobacco from one cheek to the other and spat brown juice to the ground. "Yep."

Rye heard heavy suspicion in the single word. "You see anything?"

"Nope."

Rye studied him. "Would you tell me if you had?"

One milky eye narrowed. "Heard you was askin' questions."

Word traveled fast in a small town. "I'm only trying to learn the truth."

"The truth is Pollard killed him and then he got what he deserved." The burly man shook his head. "Carpenter was good for this town. He was the one who put up most of the money for the new school. And when the church needed fixin', he was right there. He's gonna be missed, which is a lot more 'n I can say for Pollard."

Rye hadn't realized Carpenter was near to being a saint in Locust. So why would anyone, including Pollard, have killed him? Maybe Pollard had wanted money and Carpenter refused to give him any. "I didn't know the hardware business was so profitable."

"Folks say he come from back East where his family was well-to-do."

Rye nodded to the man and strolled to the bathhouse, his mind churning. If Carpenter came from a wealthy family, that explained how he could throw money around. He would've thought the townsfolk would want the right man to be brought to justice for his murder, but he also understood how angry people could become an unthinking mob.

Rye arrived at his destination and pushed open the door. Knobby was slouched in a chair tipped back against the wall. His snores nearly lifted the roof.

Rye kicked his feet, and the man flailed his arms as the front chair legs hit the floor with a loud thump.

"You wantin' a bath?" the bleary-eyed man asked.

"I'm looking for Collie."

Knobby scowled at him. "Probably out back where he usually is when we ain't busy."

Which was probably most of the time. Rye nodded and walked around to the back. Collie was adding more wood to the stove where pots of steaming water sat. As the boy turned toward him, Rye expected to see a bruise or two.

However, Collie's face was untouched, and Rye let out the breath he'd been holding.

Collie's eyes widened, then he affected aloofness. "You needin' a bath?"

Rye studied him, recognizing the hurt in his eyes. Although he'd had no choice but to return the boy to the Gearsons, Rye felt guilty. "No, I came to see you."

Collie stuck his hands in his pockets and lifted his chin. "Now you seen me."

"Were you punished that night for being at Mrs. McDaniel's place?"

The boy shuffled his bare feet. "Mrs. Gearson just talked, like she always does."

"What about Mr. Gearson?"

He shrugged his thin shoulders. "He yelled a lot."

Rye crossed his arms and leaned a shoulder against the wall. "He didn't hurt you, did he?"

"Nah." Collie turned away and leaned over to check the stove. As he did, Rye caught sight of a bruise on his upper arm.

"Where'd you get that?" he asked, keeping his voice steady and pointing at the mark.

Collie twisted his neck to see it. His face reddened. "Nowhere."

Rye squatted down in front of the boy and carefully took hold of his shoulders. "Who hurt you?"

He jerked out of Rye's grasp. "I ran into a tree."

Rye's anger sizzled. "Show me the tree."

Panic clouded Collie's expression. "It ain't nothin'." He darted into the alley.

Rye followed, his longer legs a match for Collie's desperate pace. When the alley ended, Collie headed toward the woods at the edge of town. But Rye closed the gap and grabbed Collie, enfolding him in his arms. Collie fought like a tomcat, but Rye endured his flailing feet and fists.

"Easy, Collie. I don't want to hurt you," Rye soothed.

The boy continued to thrash.

"That's enough," Rye ordered.

His tone of voice penetrated Collie's frenzy, and the boy calmed and sagged in Rye's grip. Rye turned his restraining hold into a loose embrace. The boy pressed his head against Rye's waist, but kept his hands hanging loosely at his sides.

Rye patted his back. "Who hit you, Collie?" he asked softly.

For a long moment, there was no reaction from Collie, then he murmured, "Timmy and Tommy."

"The twins?"

Collie straightened and stepped back. When he looked up at Rye, his face was dry but flushed. "Yeah."

Although kids didn't always tell the truth, Rye knew Collie wasn't lying. "Did you tell Mrs. Gearson?"

"I did the first time. They lied. Said I started it. She believed them." He spoke matter-of-factly, as if being called a liar didn't bother him.

Rye suspected otherwise.

Timmy and Tommy were the Gearsons' flesh and blood, so the parents would naturally take their sons' side rather than Collie's. Rye rubbed his aching brow. "Can you stay away from them?"

"I usually do during the day."

But at night, Collie had nowhere to go. Helplessness gnawed at Rye's insides. He had no idea how to get Collie away from the Gearsons, and even if he did, who would be willing to take him in?

"Don't worry 'bout me. I can take care of myself," Collie said with false bravado.

The boy's pride had made him run before admitting the twins had hurt him, and pride continued to shield him. But Rye saw his lurking fear. "Two against one isn't a fair fight, especially when they're bigger than you," he said gently.

The boy's gaze sidled away. "Ain't nothin' you can do, Rye. Ain't nothin' nobody but me can do."

Collie was too young to be taking on the world, yet having lost his parents he had no one to help shoulder that burden. No one except Rye.

"Do you think the Gearsons would let you stay out at Mrs. McDaniel's place for a few days?" he asked.

Collie blinked in surprise. "Why?"

Rye had to tread carefully since Collie wouldn't take to

being coddled. "I could use your help around her place." He smiled and lowered his voice. "You saw how much needs to be done. Too much work for one person."

The boy regarded him warily. "I ain't that strong."

"Maybe not as strong as me, but you helped me just fine with the corral."

Collie's brow furrowed. "Mrs. McDaniel won't mind?"

Good question. "As long as you got nothing against sleeping in the barn."

His face brightened, then darkened once more. "Mrs. Gearson won't let me go."

Rye grinned, putting more confidence than he felt in the expression. "Leave her to me." He put his hand on Collie's shoulder and steered him in the direction of his foster parents' home.

Collie dragged his feet as they neared the house, which was quiet now with all the playing children gone.

Mrs. Gearson opened the door as they came up to the porch. "Now what did he do?" she demanded.

Rye's temper climbed, but he kept his expression calm. "*He* didn't do anything, ma'am. I was just wondering if you could spare Collie for a few days. Mrs. McDaniel's got some work he can do, and instead of going back and forth every day, Collie could stay out there."

"What about his chores around here?"

Rye forced a smile. "I'm sure one of your own could do them for a few days."

She didn't look convinced.

He leaned closer. "One less mouth to feed, and you wouldn't have to worry about what mischief he's into."

"Well, maybe it wouldn't be so bad for a few days." She was obviously swayed by the temptation of saving food and her own peace of mind rather than any concern over Collie.

Rye's muscles hurt from smiling. "I appreciate that, ma'am." He turned to Collie. "Go on inside and get what you'll need."

Collie looked at Mrs. Gearson as if expecting her to launch into a tirade, but when she only nodded, he slipped past her into the house.

The rotund woman stepped out onto the porch. "I'd best warn that you he's a handful. He sasses back and lies about fighting with the other kids. That boy is headed for no good."

Rye bit the inside of his cheek. The woman had a blind spot a mile wide. Although taking the boy to Dulcie's place for a few days wouldn't solve the problem, it would give Collie some time away from his tormentors.

Collie returned with a cloth bag slung over his shoulder.

"Ready?" Rye asked.

Collie nodded.

"You mind your manners, Collier, and don't be giving those folks any grief," Mrs. Gearson said.

"Yes, ma'am." His voice was barely audible.

"Good-bye, ma'am," Rye said.

Rye steered Collie through town to where he'd left his horse. "Have you had supper?"

The boy shook his head.

"What do you say we eat in town first?"

"Really?" Excitement shined in his eyes.

"Have you ever eaten in a restaurant?"

Collie shook his head.

Rye slapped his back and smiled. "Then you're in for a treat. But first thing you need is a bath."

AFTER Collie cleaned up in the bathhouse, which Knobby grudgingly allowed him to do for free, he dressed in a clean pair of trousers and a shirt from his bag. Rye combed the boy's dark hair back from his face and grinned at the transformation.

"You look respectable," Rye said.

Collie made a face. "I don't know why I needed a bath. The rain soaked me good yesterday."

Rye laughed. "You didn't use soap then."

Collie stuck his tongue out at him. Laughing, Rye led him into the hotel and to the dining area. He was glad there was no one around to notice Collie's bare feet. After they sat down, Collie continued to look around in fascination. He ran his fingers along the tablecloth and touched the salt and pepper shakers.

A woman scurried over to their table. "What can I get you?"

"What've you got?" Rye asked, giving her his friendliest smile.

"Today's supper is beef stew with biscuits."

"We'll each have a plate. And milk for Collie and coffee for me."

The woman peered at him and smiled. "Why, that is you, Collie. I hardly recognized you all gussied up. My, you are a handsome one."

The tips of Collie's ears reddened and he ducked his head. "Rye made me take a bath."

Rye chuckled at the boy's disgusted tone.

Over Collie's lowered head, the waitress winked at Rye. "I'll have it out soon."

Rye leaned toward Collie and teased, "I didn't know you had a sweetheart."

Collie glared at him and muttered, "Miss Janey ain't no such thing."

Rye knew better than to laugh.

As they waited for their food, Rye listened to Collie tell stories about Knobby and Burt, the liveryman, and others Rye hadn't met. Since Collie didn't go to school, it seemed he used his time to spy on the townsfolk.

Halfway through another of Collie's tales, Rye glanced out the window to see Mrs. Carpenter and her stepson leaving the hardware store. She had her hand through the crook of his arm and their heads were bent close as they talked.

"Yuck," Collie said, drawing Rye's attention.

"What?"

Collie pointed toward the Carpenters. "They're always doin' that, whisperin' and talkin' like that."

Rye's question was stalled by the arrival of Miss Janey and their food. As soon as she set Collie's plate in front of him, the boy dug in like he hadn't eaten in weeks.

"You need anything else, just let me know," the waitress said.

Rye grinned at Collie's enthusiasm. "This looks real good. Thanks."

"You're welcome." Miss Janey gazed boldly at Rye a moment longer than necessary.

Rye watched the exaggerated sway of her hips but found himself imagining breeches-clad hips and fiery chestnut hair. Even away from Dulcie, he couldn't stop thinking about her. Something told him he was on the trail to trouble.

$\mathcal{T}$HIRTEEN

ALTHOUGH Dulcie suspected Rye wouldn't be back for supper, she made enough for him, too. As she and Madeline ate in the cabin, she again marveled at the luxury of not having to go outside for water. Merely fixing the pump would've been enough to justify Rye's room and board for a month.

Madeline smushed the green beans into the mashed potatoes with her fork.

"Quit playing with your food, honey," Dulcie scolded absently.

The girl dropped her fork on the plate. "Where's Mr. Rye?"

Dulcie restrained a sigh. Madeline had only asked that question a dozen times already. "He rode into town."

"Why?"

"Because he deserved some time to himself."

"Don't he like us?"

"*Doesn't* he like us," Dulcie corrected automatically. She thought a moment, wondering how to answer the innocent question. "I'm sure he does, but a man likes to get away for a little while."

"Like Pa done?"

Dulcie was surprised Madeline, as young as she was, would remember how often her father had been gone in the evenings. "I suppose."

Madeline bowed her head so Dulcie couldn't see her expression. She reached over and placed her hand on her daughter's crown. "What's wrong, honey?" She shook her head, but Dulcie knew there was something bothering her. "Do you miss Mr. Rye?"

Madeline shrugged, but remained mute.

Concerned, Dulcie hooked her finger under Madeline's chin and raised her head. A tear coursed down the girl's pink cheek. "Why are you crying?"

"I'm not."

The feisty reply brought a smile to Dulcie. "Then where did that tear come from?"

Madeline dashed it away. "Mr. Rye said he was my friend."

Uncertain what she meant, Dulcie nodded slowly. "That's right."

"Then why'd he leave?"

Dulcie's heart twisted, and she knelt beside her daughter's chair. She'd suspected Madeline was infatuated with Rye, but had hoped it wasn't serious. However, it appeared she'd grown too fond of him too quickly.

"He'll be back, honey." Dulcie hoped it wasn't an empty reassurance. She managed a smile. "If you're done eating, you can help me with the dishes."

"Can I pump the water?" the girl asked, her expression brightening.

Dulcie playfully poked her side. "We'll take turns."

Madeline jumped up, causing Dulcie to scramble to her feet. As they worked, Dulcie was grateful for a child's resiliency. They washed and dried the dishes together, with Dulcie allowing Madeline to do more than usual. It gave the girl something to keep her mind and hands occupied.

As the last dish was put away, Dulcie heard a wagon roll into the yard. She peeked out the window and recognized the man and woman in the buggy. Her heart lurched and her hands trembled.

She understood how her daughter felt about Rye since

Dulcie, too, liked the stranger who'd come into their empty lives and brought hope with him. If she was honest with herself, she liked him more than she had a right to. His easy smile and eagerness to help wasn't deterred by her wariness. In fact, he seemed to go out of his way to be helpful and to ease her burden. No other man had ever done that for her— neither her father nor her husband.

"Stay inside, Madeline. I'll be back in a few minutes," Dulcie said, keeping the dread out of her tone.

Her daughter didn't look happy, but went to play with her doll.

Her heart thundering, Dulcie walked outside. "Good evening, Mrs. Carpenter, Peter."

The Carpenters nodded curtly.

"Would you like to come inside for coffee?" Dulcie asked, hoping they'd refuse.

"No," Martha Carpenter replied. "Your hired man stopped in the store this afternoon."

Startled, Dulcie asked, "Why?"

"To ask us about Lawrence's death. He said you're still insisting your father was innocent."

Dulcie stiffened her spine. "He didn't kill your husband."

"Why do you keep saying that?" Peter asked.

She turned to the younger man. "Because it's the truth."

"My husband is gone," Mrs. Carpenter said. "Your father killed him and he's paid for his crime. I don't appreciate you or someone on your behalf dredging it up again."

Dulcie took a step closer to the wagon and glared up at the diminutive woman. "And I don't appreciate everyone in that lynch mob getting away with the murder of an innocent man. I'll do whatever has to be done to find the real murderer and clear my father's name."

"I told you she wouldn't listen to reason, Martha," Peter said, his voice low and worried.

Martha kept her steely gaze on Dulcie. "She'll listen to me whether she wants to or not. As I told your hired man, I'm sorry for your loss, but I'm not sorry your father is dead. He deserved to hang."

Hot anger boiled in Dulcie. "When I find the real killer, I'm also going to learn who took part in the hanging. If I find out you were involved, I'll do my best to make sure you're punished."

Martha's lips pressed together, forming a grim slash across her face. "Let it go, Mrs. McDaniel, or you'll be sorry."

Dulcie kept her gaze locked on the woman. "Is that a threat, Mrs. Carpenter?"

A syrupy sweet, insincere smile crossed Martha's face. "A promise, Mrs. McDaniel."

Peter slapped the reins against the horse's rump, and Dulcie had to scramble back or be knocked down by the buggy. With her hand on her hips and fury churning in her chest, Dulcie watched them leave.

If their intent was to stop her from seeking the truth, they'd done the opposite. When someone told her she couldn't do something, she did everything in her power to accomplish it. Like coming back home to a rundown farm that nobody, including her father, believed could be salvaged. But with Rye's assistance, the farm was getting fixed up.

And it looked like Rye was helping to repair her father's name, too.

WITH a coffee cup in her hands, Dulcie sat on the porch step. Half her concentration was on Madeline playing hopscotch and the other was pondering the Carpenters' startling visit. Lurking behind those thoughts was Rye. She was anxious to hear what he'd learned when he'd visited the Carpenters.

Would he spend the night in town or come back to sleep in the barn? Imagining him in a saloon with a short-skirted whore perched on his lap twisted her lips into a scowl. Rye wasn't her husband and it was no business of hers what he did with whom. So why did the thought of him making time with a saloon gal bring sharp jealousy?

"Ma, Mr. Rye's back," Madeline shouted, bringing Dulcie out of her dark musings.

Her heart leapt, and she stood, rubbing her suddenly damp palms against her trouser-clad thighs.

As Rye neared, she noticed someone riding behind him. Someone small. *Collie.*

Although uncomfortable around Collie because he'd bought her whiskey, she sincerely liked the boy. Finding Madeline before the storm was another point in his favor. But why was he with Rye?

She and Madeline joined them at the corral. They stood back as Rye lowered Collie to the ground then dismounted.

"Hello, Collie," Dulcie said warmly.

"Miz McDaniel," he said, his eyes lowered.

Madeline tugged on his shirtsleeve. "Hi, Collie."

A smile touched the boy's lips. "Whatcha doing?"

"Playing hopscotch. Wanna play?"

Collie shrugged, but his expression lost its apprehension. "Sure."

Madeline grabbed his hand and pulled him away.

Dulcie watched them go and smiled when the boy tossed his rock onto the first square. She turned to Rye and her eyes collided with his.

"I hope you don't mind that I brought him here," Rye said.

Frowning, Dulcie replied, "Why should I?"

Rye fiddled with his horse's reins, then met her gaze squarely. "He'll be here for a few days."

She hadn't expected that. "Why?"

His gaze sidled away. "He needs to be away from the Gearsons for a while."

She tried to read his expression but he hid his thoughts too well. "Did something happen to him?"

Rye turned his attention to Collie and Madeline, and it seemed he was seeing something Dulcie didn't. "He's a good worker and I can use his help."

It wasn't an answer but she stifled her annoyance. "Where will he sleep?"

"He can bunk in the barn with me. Do you have a spare blanket?"

"Yes. I'll get a couple for him. The nights can get cool."

"Thanks."

"He's a good boy." Dulcie jammed her hands deep in her pockets. "I had two visitors here about an hour ago."

Rye paused in loosening the saddle cinch. "Who?"

"Lawrence Carpenter's widow and son."

Rye's lips flattened into a scowl. "Did they tell you I talked to them this afternoon?"

She nodded. "They weren't very happy about it."

"I didn't mean—"

She raised her chin. "I'm glad you did. They're so certain my father was a murderer they won't listen to anyone who says otherwise." She paused. "Mrs. Carpenter said if we didn't stop asking questions and dredging up the murder, I'd be sorry."

"She threatened you?"

"Sounded that way to me."

Rye chewed on the inside of his cheek, his expression both thoughtful and furious. "Sounds to me like she might be trying to hide something."

Dulcie swept a loose tendril behind her ear. "That's what I thought, too. But why would she kill her husband?"

"How was he killed?"

"Stabbed."

"How big was he?"

"Almost as tall as you but heavier."

Rye shook his head. "I doubt a woman the size of Mrs. Carpenter could have done it. Maybe it was the son and she's protecting him."

"Then the peddler is protecting him, too. He's the one who swore my father was with Carpenter not long before the murder."

"The peddler is the one I need to talk to. What's his name?"

Panic flooded Dulcie. As much as she wanted to prove her father's innocence, she was more afraid of Rye finding out she'd lain with the peddler. She cared what Rye thought of her—more than she ought to. "Virgil Lamont." Speaking his name aloud left a bitter taste in her mouth.

Rye nodded. "That's right. Someone mentioned his name in town."

"He's gone. He left the day after the murder."

"If this Lamont was coming back to testify during the trial, he probably told the sheriff how to get hold of him.

Peddlers don't travel fast. I might be able to find him and be back in a day."

"And what good would that do? He'd lie to you, too, and the sheriff wouldn't believe you anymore than he believed me."

"You sound like you don't want to prove your father's innocence," Rye said, his eyes narrowed.

Dulcie looked away, afraid he'd see her guilt in her eyes. "I just don't know how talking to him will help." Indecision clouded Rye's expression and she pressed her advantage. "You said yourself there's a lot to be done here, including the crops that are ready to be harvested." She swallowed past the tightness in her throat. "Without the corn and wheat, I'll lose this place, and I don't know how I'll provide for Madeline."

Rye's gentle hands on her arms were almost too much to bear, and she fought the sting of tears.

"I understand," he said softly. "Besides, I have a feeling the peddler will come back through again soon enough. They usually have their circuits they follow."

Relieved she'd been given a reprieve, Dulcie nodded. He released her and turned to take care of his horse.

Bereft of his touch, Dulcie shivered despite the warmth of the evening air. The meeting with Lamont was only delayed. If she truly wanted to clear her father's name, Virgil Lamont was the key. But her humiliation mocked her, made her heart pound with the fear that he would expose her secret.

She gathered her composure and asked, "Did you and Collie have supper?"

Rye removed the saddle from Smoke's back. "We ate at the hotel in town. Collie'd never eaten in a restaurant before."

Although the fondness in his voice didn't surprise her, for a moment she envied Collie. To have Rye's affection was something she dared not think about. It would be too easy to allow him to take over her life, do with her what he wished. She'd made that mistake twice already.

Rye carried his saddle into the barn, leaving Dulcie alone and uncertain what to do. Restless, she walked back to the porch and sat down to watch the children play. Although Collie was a few years older than Madeline, he seemed to enjoy their game.

Dulcie had made a promise to herself, to be independent and free of a man's control. However, that promise didn't come without a cost. Madeline would have no brothers or sisters to play with, giving her the same lonely childhood Dulcie had experienced.

Rye came out of the barn and led Smoke into the corral. Her chest ached, but Dulcie couldn't figure out if her grief was for Madeline or for herself.

RYE awakened early by habit and lay on his bedroll listening to the quiet snores coming from the next stall, where Collie slept. The excitement of staying in a barn had kept him awake long after he should have been asleep. Rye himself was somewhat bleary after answering the boy's endless questions late into the night.

He eased up off his bedroll and tugged on his pants and boots. He considered leaving his shirt off, but after Dulcie had surprised him one morning, he decided not to risk it. The brand on his shoulder blade would invite too many questions he didn't want to answer.

Leaving his shirt unbuttoned, he grabbed his razor and left the barn. The humid air struck him like a wall. Clouds with gray underbellies filled the sky, casting a sickly pallor across the land. But behind them was a wide strip of blue sky, an indication the clouds would pass and bring another hot day.

He crossed to the well and filled the bucket. Shaving by rote, Rye gazed at the fields beyond the pasture. Dulcie was right about it being time to start harvesting. The wheat waved in the light breeze, creating an undulating river of gold. The nearby cornstalks were tall and green and appeared heavy with ears of corn. It was time to begin the laborious task of cutting the wheat and picking the corn.

As he wiped his face after shaving, Dulcie came out onto the porch. Even from where he stood, he could tell she wasn't feeling well again. She squinted against the dull gray sky, and her mouth formed a thin-lipped line. He suspected her whiskey bottle was emptier than it had been yesterday. Disappointed, he wheeled around and returned to the barn.

If she wanted to destroy her life with liquor, who was he to stop her? Yet what about Madeline? What would happen to her? Didn't Dulcie know how much she was risking? He knew firsthand that drinking never solved a thing, and, more likely than not, it brought on new troubles—*worse* troubles. Maybe if he talked to her, pretended his life was someone else's and told her about how the whiskey had nearly destroyed him.

Collie sat up on his bedroll, relegating Rye's concerns to the back of his mind.

"Morning, Collie," Rye said.

The boy blinked in his direction and looked around as if trying to figure out why he was sleeping in a barn. It was only a few moments, however, before recognition stole across him. "Mornin', Rye. Is the sun up?"

"Hours ago," Rye teased. "Rise and shine, Collie, you're wasting daylight."

The boy took his words to heart and scrambled up. He drew on his oft-mended shirt and too-short overalls.

"You can wash up at the well before breakfast," Rye said.

Dulcie was already in the corral, milking Flossie with mechanical motions. She gave them a half-hearted smile and then turned her attention back to the cow.

Collie washed up with cool water from the well, getting as much water on his clothing as on his face and hands. Rye didn't scold him, knowing the boy probably had too much of that at the Gearsons'. Besides, the air was warm and his clothes would dry quickly.

"What do we do now?" Collie asked.

Rye dipped his hand in the water bucket and smoothed down the boy's hair, which stuck out in twenty different directions. "Now we get to fill up the water tank in the corral."

Rye found another pail and he and Collie began the long process of hauling water from the well to the corral. He enjoyed the boy's company and the chore took less time than usual with Collie's help. While they did that, Dulcie finished milking Flossie and took care of the chickens and gathering eggs.

She didn't speak to them other than a mumbled good morning. Rye didn't trust himself to say anything more than the same.

Once the animals were watered, Rye and Collie inspected the farming tools in the barn. Rye found a long-handled scythe that appeared to be at least twenty years old, but there was little rust and the blade had probably been sharpened last year during harvest time. Rye used a whetstone to sharpen it.

"It's gonna take a long time to cut the grain," Collie said, eyeing the scythe and shaking his head. "Mr. Gearson got a machine to cut it."

"Do you think he'd let us borrow it?"

Collie scrunched up his face and shook his head. "He don't like Miz McDaniel."

Rye expected as much and surrendered to having sore muscles and blistered hands for the next couple of weeks. He just hoped they'd save enough of the crop to give Dulcie the income she needed to get through the year.

Just as he finished sharpening the scythe, Dulcie called them to breakfast. When he and Collie got to the porch, there weren't any plates sitting there and the front door was open.

She obviously trusted him enough to allow him in the house now. Rye ushered the boy in ahead of him. Madeline was already sitting at the table, a piece of bread in one hand and her fork in the other.

"Hi Mr. Rye. Hi Collie," she said, an impish grin on her face.

"Morning, Miss Madeline," Rye said, winking at her.

She giggled and crammed the piece of bread in her mouth.

"Sit down," Dulcie said as she brought over a pan and shoveled cooked eggs onto their plates, which already held fried potatoes and salt pork.

There was also hot cereal, bread, butter, honey, and fried apples.

Collie stared at the pile of food around him as if unsure he was allowed to eat it.

"Go ahead," Rye urged the boy.

Collie didn't need to be told twice and attacked the fried apples first.

The food disappeared rapidly, and Rye rose and went to the stove. "Would you like some more?" he asked Dulcie, holding up the coffeepot.

She nodded, and Rye filled her cup then his own and placed the black pot back on the stovetop. He sat down and sipped, watching Collie, who was working on another piece of bread and honey.

"I appreciate you letting us eat inside," he said in a low voice to Dulcie.

She fiddled with her fork, setting it on the plate and picking it up again. "I guess you've earned my trust."

He cleared his throat to keep from chuckling at her grudging tone. "I think that was a compliment."

She glared at him. "Think what you want."

This time he did laugh. "Someone woke up on the wrong side of the bed." Her glare lost some of its venom but didn't disappear completely, and Rye figured he'd best change the subject. Especially since he had a strong hunch it wasn't the side of the bed, but too much whiskey that made her irritable. "I'm going to check the corn and wheat to see if they're ready. Would you and Madeline like to walk to the fields with us?"

"Yes. Give me a few minutes to clean up the breakfast dishes and we'll be ready to go."

"I can give you a hand," he said.

Dulcie seemed startled by the offer. "All right."

While Madeline and Collie kept one another company, Rye and Dulcie cleared the table. Dulcie washed the dishes in a large pan of soapy water and slid them in the rinse pan. Rye plucked them out of the steaming water and wiped them dry.

She was a puzzling woman, intriguing Rye with her different layers. Fierce, protective, and prickly as a mad porcupine, but beneath that and her masculine clothing lurked a woman's passionate nature. He'd witnessed the power of her passion that night when he'd seen her through the window, pleasuring herself. It was a sight he wouldn't forget.

So why did she deny her femininity in the light of day? Why hide who she was?

"You seem to know your way around dirty dishes," Dulcie commented.

Rye opened his mouth to tell her he'd done his share of kitchen duty while in the army. Abruptly, he clamped his lips together. "My wife wouldn't let me get away with not helping out," he said awkwardly.

Dulcie's hands stilled. "I tried to get Jerry to help with the house chores after Madeline was born. He laughed at me. Said that was my job and since I didn't do his job, he wasn't going to do mine."

Rye gripped the plate in his hands tightly. The more he learned about Jerry, the more Rye realized how wrong he'd been in befriending him. Rye should've realized a man with a wife and child ought to be home with them instead of frequenting saloons. But at the time Rye had only seen someone as desperate as himself to fill his off-hours with whiskey.

Maybe he was a coward for not revealing the real reason he'd shown up at her farm, but at least his cowardice would enable him to help her without having to endure her loathing. And despite what she said about Jerry, the man had been her husband, and Rye's actions had killed him.

After the last pot was dried and put away, Dulcie donned her floppy hat. Rye ushered the children outside and Dulcie joined them. The gray clouds had meandered to the west, leaving a crisp blue sky in their wake and the sun's heat pouring down on them, just as Rye had reckoned.

Madeline sneezed once, then again.

"Ewwww," Collie said, backing away from her.

Rye glanced at Dulcie questioningly.

"She gets sneezy this time of year," Dulcie said with a shrug. "Come along, Madeline. We're going for a walk."

The girl took her hand and tried to grasp Collie's hand with her other, but the boy backed away. Rye grinned inwardly. Collie played with frogs and snakes, but he wouldn't touch the hand of someone who'd just sneezed.

They walked four abreast down the road, and when Dulcie veered off to the fields, Rye and Collie walked behind her and her daughter. Although he knew Dulcie wasn't feeling her best this morning, she didn't let it slow her pace. He tried not to notice the swing of her breeches-clad hips or the pendulum motion of her long ponytail across her back. The sun shimmered across her red hair, creating a waterfall of fire and gold.

What was it about her that drew him so powerfully? She was brash and headstrong. She dressed and walked like a man. She tested his patience every day.

He mentally shook his head. He knew what simple lust felt like, and there was more to it than that. Perhaps it was the glimpses of vulnerability in her eyes that softened his feelings toward her. Or maybe it was her obvious love and patience with her daughter. Or it could be her damnable pride that both irritated him and made him respect her grit.

Why didn't matter. The temptation remained. He couldn't ignore it, but he couldn't act upon it either. He glanced at Collie and was glad the boy was here to distract him.

They stopped at a corner where the corn met the wheat. The cornstalks were as tall as Rye, and his speculation earlier that they were thick with ears of corn was proven correct.

Rye reached for an ear and tugged down the husk, pushing aside the silky tassels. The kernels were pale yellow and full on the cob. Dulcie leaned over his arm to take a look, her breath warming his skin.

"The corn's almost ready," she said.

Rye nodded and released the cob, stepping away from her. "Another week and it'll be time to pick it."

He leaned down and fingered the plump heads of wheat, finding them dry and ready for harvest.

"I'm doing my share, too," Dulcie said firmly. "I used to pick corn and bundle the wheat stalks when I was a child."

"It's going to take a lot of sweat."

"I have sweat. It's money I need."

Rye chuckled. "And you should get it if we can get this all harvested." He sobered. "We'll have to start cutting and bundling the wheat, then while the shocks are drying, we'll pick the corn."

Dulcie's expression was grim but determined. "We'll get it done."

"Right now, let's go back and get what we need to start working," Rye said. "It's going to be the first in a string of long days."

FOURTEEN

DULCIE straightened and stifled a groan when her backbone popped in three separate places. She glanced at Rye, impressed anew by his strength and endurance. During the long day, he'd swung the scythe in wide sweeping arcs, dropping the grain into the cradle and laying it in a windrow, which she swept into piles. Behind her, Collie twisted the stalks into bundles. The boy looked as miserable under the hot sun as she felt.

Madeline was the only one who wasn't toiling. She sat under the closest tree with her doll, but her play seemed lackluster. It was more than likely she was a bit under the weather. Dulcie wouldn't have brought her, but the girl was too young to be left alone.

Rye stopped and leaned on the handle of the scythe. The back of his shirt was drenched with sweat and he removed his hat to wipe the moisture at his brow and the base of his neck.

"It's near sunset," Dulcie said, raising her voice to be heard. "We've done enough for one day."

Collie scrambled to his feet, his face red despite the floppy brimmed hat she'd found for him to wear. The anticipation in his expression told Dulcie he was ready to call it a day.

"You go ahead. I want to finish this row before I quit."
Rye continued swishing the scythe back and forth, the grain
falling more evenly than when he'd started that morning.

Dulcie indulged in admiring the play of muscles across
his back and arms as he worked. He wasn't a large man,
though he was taller than her husband had been. However,
where Jerry had been thin, Rye was lean and muscled. She
easily recalled the sight of his flat belly from when he'd
gone to the well with his shirt undone. At the time she'd
been hard-pressed to look away, to deny her longing.

Collie sighed and dropped back to his knees to continue
twisting the straw into bundles. Behind him at ten-foot inter-
vals were shocks of five or six bundles, the wheat heads facing upward to dry. They'd all worked hard, but fifty acres
was a large amount for one man to cut by hand.

Yet, without Rye's help, she wouldn't have even this acre
cut. His arrival had been a blessing when Dulcie had been
ready to give up on blessings. Though he only received room
and board as his pay, Rye never ended a workday early. Even
now, when she knew he had to be exhausted, hot, and
aching, he continued to work.

She promised herself that once the wheat and corn were
sold, she'd give Rye a portion of the money. He'd more than
earned it.

Sighing, Dulcie headed toward Madeline with her rake in
hand. As she passed Collie, she touched his shoulder. "Come
on to the house and you can help me with supper."

Collie's gaze shifted to Rye and his shoulders straightened, losing their slump. "I'll stay with Rye."

Dulcie smiled gently, expecting his answer. "Make sure
you both don't work too much longer. The wheat will still be
here come morning."

"Yes, ma'am."

Dulcie gathered Madeline and they trudged back to the
cabin. Dulcie ached in places she didn't know could ache
and knew it would be worse tomorrow. She was grateful her
headache had finally disappeared around midday, leaving
her with only the stress of the labor and the heat of the sun.

Why had she given in to the whiskey last night? Because

she hadn't been able to turn off the memories had seemed a good reason then, but not now.

Arriving at the cabin, Madeline immediately went to the bedroom and lay down. Concerned, Dulcie perched on the edge of the bed and rested a palm on her daughter's brow. She felt warm, but being outside all day would account for that.

"Are you sick, honey?" she asked Madeline.

Madeline pushed her mother's hand away from her forehead and mumbled, "Tired." She rolled onto her side and closed her eyes, hugging her doll close to her chest.

Dulcie stared down at her, trying to determine if her daughter was sick or, as she said, simply tired. Madeline had stayed up past her bedtime last night, playing with Collie. That could account for her weariness today.

If sleep was all Madeline needed, she would be better tomorrow. If she wasn't, then Dulcie would decide what to do. She hoped she wouldn't have to make that decision.

BY sheer force of will, Rye managed to swing the scythe one more time. The last of the wheat in the row fell. His arms dropped, unable to hold the tool up a second longer.

He hung his head, unsure if he'd be able to raise it again. He couldn't remember a time he'd felt as utterly worn out as he did at this moment. His arms and shoulders ached, as did his legs and sides. The thought of walking back to the cabin brought a jab of apprehension—he didn't think he could move even an inch.

"Rye, you all right?"

Collie's question produced a surge of strength, and Rye managed to lift his head and shift his stance to meet the kid's worried face. "I'm all right, Collie," he answered. "Just tired."

Collie nodded and removed the hat. His sweat-dampened hair lay flat against his scalp. "Me, too." He turned and pointed at the many shocks of bundled wheat behind them. "But I got lots done, didn't I, Rye?"

Despite his exhaustion, Rye smiled. "You done real good, Collie. Real good."

The boy seemed to puff up with pride. Collie had a right to be proud of what he'd done. Rye had told him more than once he didn't have to work all day, but the youngster insisted that if Rye was working, he'd work, too.

Collie's stomach growled. "I could eat a horse."

Rye feigned a scowl. "I don't think Smoke would like that too well."

Collie giggled, the childish sound clutching at something inside Rye. This was the first time he'd heard the boy laugh with genuine amusement.

His throat oddly tight, Rye put his free arm around the boy's shoulders. "What do you say we take a dunk in the pond before heading back to the house?"

Collie grinned his answer.

Despite his overwhelming fatigue, Rye managed to walk to the pond and strip to his drawers before jumping into the pond. The cool water refreshed him, and he and Collie splashed each other, laughing and washing at the same time. Rye was glad he'd suggested the pond, even if he'd merely intended to please Collie. His soreness remained but didn't seem as overwhelming, and he was no longer as exhausted.

Dusk was fading to twilight when they climbed out of the pond and headed back to the farm, carrying their clothes and wearing only their hats and drawers. By the time they got to the barn, they'd dried in the warm air.

Leaving their smelly clothes on the corral pole, they donned clean clothing.

As they neared the porch, Dulcie opened the door wide. "I was wondering when you two would wander in."

"We went swimmin'," Collie said. "Me and Rye stunk something awful so we figured we'd best wash up."

Dulcie glanced at Rye, and he nodded in confirmation. "A skunk smelled downright sweet compared to us. Hope we didn't keep you waiting," he said.

She shook her head, an amused smile tugging at the corners of her lips. "No. I was just, uh, wondering when you were going to come in from the field."

"I finished that row, and Collie, he finished bundling all the grain you'd raked." He gazed down at the boy proudly. "You got yourself a good hired hand with him, Dulcie."

"I think I have the two best hired men in Texas," she said. "Come in. I know you have to be hungry."

Startled by her praise, Rye followed her and Collie inside. He didn't see Dulcie's daughter seated at the table. "Where's Madeline?"

"Sleeping." A tinge of trepidation touched her expression. "When we got back, she lay down and fell right to sleep. Hasn't stirred since."

"Is she under the weather?"

"I'm not sure. If she's still so tired tomorrow, I'll keep her in the house all day." She gnawed at her lower lip. "I won't be able to help in the fields then."

"Don't worry about that. Madeline's more important."

She blinked a few times, as if blinking back tears, and her smile was shaky. "Yes, she is."

Recognizing her embarrassed gratitude, he made a show of sniffing. "Something smells tasty."

"Fried chicken," Collie guessed.

"You butchered one of your hens?" Rye asked, surprised.

"It was an older one that wasn't laying anymore. Figured it'd make a good meal after all the work done today," Dulcie explained.

Besides fried chicken, there was gravy, potatoes, boiled peas, carrots and beans with butter melted over them, fried okra, baked apples with honey, and bread topped with butter. Dulcie brought three glasses to the table and set one by each of their places. "I figured you all might prefer some buttermilk for a change."

Touched by her thoughtfulness even though he knew she was tired, too, Rye dug into the banquet. They'd all worked up an appetite toiling in the field and nobody spoke as they ate.

Rye used the last piece of his bread to sop up the gravy and melted butter from his plate. He popped it in his mouth and pushed his empty plate aside. "Thanks, Dulcie. It tasted mighty good." He elbowed Collie lightly.

"Uh, thanks, Miz McDaniel. I ain't ate this much good food ever," the boy said, his face flushed.

Dulcie smiled. "It's nice to cook for men who appreciate it." Her expression faltered and she shrugged. "My husband never did."

"He was a fool, Dulcie," Rye said, and he meant it.

She stared down at the tabletop. "I was a fool for marrying him. I just wanted to get away from Locust so bad I was willing to accept the first man's offer."

Rye wasn't certain how to respond.

"Not that I regret it. I'd marry him again even knowing what I know now just so I'd have Madeline."

"She's a lucky girl."

"Yeah. She's got her ma," Collie said softly.

Dulcie reached out and laid her hand on the boy's. "I want you to know you're always welcome here, Collie. Even after Rye moves on, you just come by any time you want."

Collie's eyes widened and his alarmed gaze sought Rye. "You're leavin'?"

"Not for a while," Rye assured. "I promised Mrs. McDaniel I'd help get her crops in."

Although Collie seemed to accept that, his troubled expression told Rye he was still upset.

"We have another long day ahead of us tomorrow," Rye said. "We'd best get some sleep." He pushed back his chair and stood.

Collie reluctantly did the same.

"Goodnight," Rye said to Dulcie.

Collie mumbled something that sounded the same and led the way out of the cabin. As Rye started out the door, Dulcie grabbed his arm. He stopped, and she released him.

"I'm not very good at telling folks thanks, and I know I don't say things very well. Most of the time I probably sound mad and maybe selfish, but I want you to know that I really appreciate all you've done, Rye. You work harder than anyone I've ever known, and you're not even getting paid for it." Her words were rifled out, as if she were afraid she wouldn't be able to get them out fast enough.

Rye held up a hand. If she knew the real reason he was here, she wouldn't be so free with her praise. "I agreed to work for room and board, and you've held to your end of the bargain. The least I can do is hold to mine." He cupped her chin and brushed his thumb across her soft cheek. "Never apologize to me or anyone else for who you are, Dulcie McDaniel."

Her eyes glimmered with moisture as she nodded jerkily.

Unable to curb his feelings for her, Rye leaned forward and brushed his lips across her silky cheek. "Goodnight, Dulcie."

He spun away and hurried out before he lost the battle to take her in his arms and kiss her like she deserved to be kissed. The way he wanted to kiss her.

DESPITE the liniment he'd rubbed on his arms and shoulders before dropping off to sleep, Rye could barely move the next morning. He raised his arms, the limbs feeling ten times heavier than usual. And when he finally managed to stand, he tottered like an old man.

It took him twice as long—and some quietly uttered curses—to dress. By the time he tugged on his boots, his muscles were loosening up. At the well, he washed up and shaved. He was surprised Dulcie wasn't up yet and hoped it wasn't because she'd drunk herself to sleep.

When he returned to the barn, he decided to let Collie sleep until breakfast was ready. The poor kid had fallen asleep the minute he hit his bedroll.

Rye carried pails of water to the livestock, and his muscles lost most of the tightness that remained. With still no sign of Dulcie, he milked the cow and carried the pail to the porch. He pressed an ear against the door and heard the sound of coughing and Dulcie's low voice, although he couldn't understand what she was saying. A frisson of foreboding slid down his backbone.

He knocked on the door. "Dulcie, you awake?"

He waited impatiently and raised his hand to pound louder this time, but the sound of footsteps stilled him. The door swung open and Dulcie stood in the opening, dressed in her usual over-large shirt and breeches. However, her fiery hair was unbound and spilled around her shoulders and over her breasts like a cascading waterfall. But the panicked look in her eyes stole his attention.

"Is it Madeline?" Rye asked. The girl's well-being was the only thing that would unnerve Dulcie so completely.

Strands of hair fell across her face as she nodded and

swept them back. "Yes. She's burning up, and she started coughing a little after midnight." She twisted her hands together. "I don't know what to do."

"Is there a doctor in town?"

"Dr. Wickberg."

"I'll run into town and get him. Will you be all right until we get back?"

Her green eyes appeared huge and haunted and her freckles stood out starkly on her pale face. "Yes. Please hurry."

Rye clutched her arms, forced her to meet his gaze. "Everything will be fine. Just stay calm and keep Madeline comfortable."

Madeline coughed from the bedroom and Dulcie half turned toward the sound. Rye shook her, bringing her attention back to him. "Did you hear what I said, Dulcie?"

She nodded jerkily. "Yes."

"Remember, stay calm, or Madeline's going to pick up on your fear and you don't want that, do you?"

Dulcie visibly drew herself together and her expression became resolute. "No. I'll make sure she stays quiet."

"Good girl. I'll send Collie up."

"No, don't." She grasped his hands, and her fingers were ice cold. "If Madeline has some catching sickness, I don't want him to get it."

The fact that Dulcie would be in danger, too, didn't even occur to her, and it wouldn't make any difference if it did.

"I'll tell him to stay away from the house." Rye pulled away from her. "I'll be back as soon as I can."

He ran across the yard to the barn and leaned over the sleeping boy. "Wake up, Collie."

The boy blinked blearily. "What?"

"Madeline is sick and I have to go into town for the doctor."

Collie rubbed sleep from his eyes. "Sick?"

"Yes. Don't go near the house, but maybe you can gather the eggs and feed the chickens."

"Okay."

"I'll be back as soon as I can."

Rye saddled Smoke and heeled her into a gallop. It took less than ten minutes to get to Locust, and it was another few minutes for Rye to track down the doctor's place. He reined in Smoke in front of the house and jumped out of the saddle before she came to a stop. He took the three steps in one leap, nearly bumping his head on the hanging sign that read "Dr. Nathan Wickberg," and pounded on the door, panting like he'd run the entire distance into town.

Nobody answered and he used his palm to slap the door.

"Hold on, hold on," came a grumble from inside the house.

Rye clenched and unclenched his hands at his sides. Finally, a middle-aged man with muttonchop whiskers swept open the door.

"Mrs. McDaniel's daughter's sick," Rye said. "She's got a high fever and a bad cough."

Dr. Wickberg hitched his suspenders onto his shoulders. "Frank's granddaughter."

"Yes." Rye narrowed his eyes. "Is that a problem?"

"No, not at all. I liked Frank . . . when he was sober. Give me a minute to grab my bag and tell my wife where I'm going. My buggy's in the back if you could hitch it up for me."

Rye nodded and ran around to do as the doctor asked. Dr. Wickberg joined him just as Rye finished hitching the man's horse to the buggy.

"Thanks, son." Dr. Wickberg climbed up onto the seat and slapped the reins against the horse's rump.

Left in the dust, Rye hurried back to Smoke and caught up to the doctor. They traveled the short distance in silence. Rye prayed Madeline's illness wasn't serious, but the memory of Dulcie's fearful pallor caused his gut to clench. If Dulcie lost her little girl, Rye suspected she'd lose interest in everything, including her own life.

Collie met them in front of the cabin, his pinched expression revealing his unease.

"Hello, Collie," Dr. Wickberg greeted the boy.

"You gonna help Madeline, Dr. Wickberg?" The hope in Collie's face told Rye how scared he was for the girl.

"I'm going to do everything I can," the doctor assured. He patted Collie's shoulder and bustled into the house, his medical bag in hand.

Rye's knees trembled, and he sank down onto the porch

step. He hadn't had time to be afraid until now. Although he'd only known Madeline a short time, he cared for the girl a great deal. He recalled her giggles and pictured the mischievous twinkle in her eyes when she was about to do something she shouldn't.

Collie sat down beside Rye. "Is she gonna be okay?"

Rye wanted to tell him Madeline would be as good as new in a day or two, but he couldn't. "I don't know. I didn't see her, but Mrs. McDaniel said she was pretty sick."

Collie edged closer to Rye and the older man put his arm around the boy's skinny shoulders. "I don't want her to die like my ma and pa done."

Rye's heart slipped into his throat and he swallowed before speaking. "We'll do everything we can to help her."

They sat in silence, hearing murmurs from the cabin but unable to discern the words.

"Do you got a ma and pa?" Collie asked in a low voice.

"No. They died a long time ago. When I was about your age."

"Did you have any brothers or sisters?"

The hollow ache in Rye's chest returned. "Yes. Two brothers."

Collie leaned his head against Rye. "I wish you were my brother."

Rye hugged the boy closer to his side and wished he was worthy of being Collie's brother. He took a deep breath and released the boy. "I'm going to take Smoke down to the corral. Why don't you give the doctor's horse some water?"

Collie nodded.

After the horses were taken care of, Rye and Collie went back to their vigil. Rye paced on the porch while Collie threw rocks down the dirt road.

It was midmorning when Dr. Wickberg finally came out with Dulcie behind him.

"With that laudanum, she'll sleep for a few hours. Keep bathing her with cool water. That'll help the fever," the doctor said. "Use the laudanum only in the evening to help her sleep."

Dulcie, her face pale but determined, nodded.

"If she gets worse, send for me," Dr. Wickberg said.

"I will, Doctor. Thank you," Dulcie said.

Dr. Wickberg smiled paternally and laid a hand on her shoulder. "You get some rest, too, or you won't be any help for that sweet little daughter."

She managed a weak smile. "I'll try."

Dr. Wickberg nodded, and Rye walked him to his buggy.

"Make sure Dulcie gets some sleep," the doctor said in a low voice to Rye. "She's going to make herself sick if she doesn't."

"I'll make sure she does. What's wrong with Madeline?"

"Could be a bad cold. Might be the flu. As long as her fever breaks within the next couple of days and she coughs up that stuff in her lungs, she's got a good chance of recovering."

"And if those things don't happen?"

"Don't go building bridges you might not have to cross," Dr. Wickberg said sternly. "Madeline is a strong little girl. Give her a chance."

Ashamed of his pessimism, Rye nodded. "Thanks for coming out, Dr. Wickberg."

"That's my job, son." He leaned down and spoke in a low voice only Rye could hear. "What's Collie doing out here? I thought he was staying with the Gearsons."

"He needed some time away from that brood," Rye said, growing angry despite himself. "Those twins are a mean pair."

"Ahhh, Timmy and Tommy," Dr. Wickberg said with a knowing grimace. "They didn't hurt Collie, did they?"

"Just some bruises this time. He told Mrs. Gearson, but she believed her boys, who said they didn't do anything to him."

"Blind spot, pure and simple." The doctor shook his graying head. "I never thought Collie should go with the Gearsons, but nobody else spoke up for him."

I know what that feels like. Rye shook the memories aside. "Thanks for coming, Doctor."

"You just keep an eye on them and make sure you come and get me if Madeline takes a turn for the worse."

"I will."

Rye stepped back as the doctor drove his rig out of the

yard. He turned back to see Collie on the porch and no sign of Dulcie.

Although they weren't his family, Rye couldn't help but feel responsible for them. It had been a long time since anyone had needed him.

FIFTEEN

DULCIE wasn't surprised to hear a tentative knock not long after Dr. Wickberg left.

"Come in," she called softly from Madeline's bedside.

Rye entered the room, removing his hat as he did. His gaze flew to Madeline. "How is she?"

Dulcie shrugged, fighting another spate of tears. "She's sleeping, and the doctor said rest will help her get better."

He remained by the doorway, looking ill at ease, but Dulcie didn't have the strength to reassure him.

Rye fingered his hat's brim. "You ought to get some rest, too. You won't do Madeline any good otherwise."

"Dr. Wickberg talked to you." It wasn't a question, but she knew she was right when Rye's face reddened.

"He mentioned that you might have to be persuaded to get some sleep yourself."

She chuckled. "Knowing Dr. Wickberg, he ordered you to make sure I didn't wear myself out."

Rye grinned lopsidedly. "Maybe he suggested it awfully strong." He relaxed his stance. "You've known him long?"

"He brought me into the world," she replied. "Ma didn't have an easy time of it. Fact is, she would've died if Dr. Wickberg hadn't been with her." Her expression sobered.

"But Ma wasn't able to have any more children. I know Pa wasn't happy about that, especially since he wanted a son."

"Is that when he started drinking?"

She shrugged. "Maybe. I don't remember a time when he didn't have whiskey around the house, but it didn't get bad until I was twelve or thirteen years old." A sudden craving for the liquor in the trunk swamped her and she fought the urge. She couldn't touch the whiskey when Madeline needed her. Still, the temptation lingered.

"Whiskey never solved anything," Rye said.

Startled, she glanced at him. Had he read her mind? Had he learned of her occasional nip? How could he? She only drank when she was alone in the cabin at night.

Rye's gaze darted over her and settled on a faded needle-point hanging above the bed. "I knew this fellah who hardly ever touched whiskey." His chuckle sounded forced. "He didn't even like the taste of it. But one day something happened, and the only thing that made him forget was whiskey. He took to drinking it whenever he wasn't working. Spent all his money on it. He got so bad that one day instead of doing his job, he went to a saloon and drank until he was falling-down drunk."

Rye paused and a faraway glint came to his eyes. "While he was drunk, he did something stupid, and a man died." He cleared his throat, and his gaze returned to the present. "He hasn't touched liquor since that night."

Dulcie studied him, the grief in his expression and the stiff way he held himself. Either that man had been a good friend or he was Rye himself. She suspected the latter. "What happened to him?"

"Last I heard he was trying to make a new life for himself."

"At least he quit drinking. My pa never did."

Some emotion flashed through Rye's features. "It's a good lesson for anyone who thinks whiskey can take away a person's problems. The only thing whiskey does is bury the pain a little deeper, but the pain never goes away. A person just has to learn how to live with it."

The intensity of his gaze forced Dulcie to look away. He knew about her drinking, just as surely as she knew it was no friend, but he who caused a man's death. But she wasn't like her father; she'd never be like him.

Rye gazed at Madeline, his expression gentling. "I'll stick close to the house today, so if you need anything or if you'd just like me to watch Madeline, I'll be here."

She clasped her hands together as her throat grew tight. Even after all the times she'd been curt with him and made him eat his meals alone on the porch, Rye was genuinely concerned about Madeline . . . and her.

"I appreciate that, truly I do, but Madeline will probably sleep for most of the morning." Dulcie met his compassionate gaze. "What I'd like is if you'd go back to cutting the wheat." She cleared her throat. "When Madeline gets to feeling better, she's going to need new clothes and we'll need food for the winter. And we won't have that unless the wheat and corn can be sold."

Dulcie thought he might misunderstand, think she was more worried about the harvest than Madeline, but Madeline was the reason for everything, including the harvest.

"All right," Rye agreed after only a few moments. "That makes sense, but Collie or I will come check on you every couple of hours."

Gratitude warmed her and she nodded without hesitation.

He turned to leave, but Dulcie caught his wrist. "Could you watch Madeline while I make breakfast?"

"You don't have—"

"You and Collie can't work with empty bellies." Dulcie rose.

Rye inclined his head and moved to sit on a chair pulled close to the bed.

She took a last look at her daughter's pale face and bit back a sob. Madeline looked so helpless. Dulcie spun away to carry out her task.

Rye heard her call Collie in and ask him to set the table and butter the bread. She explained what was happening with Madeline and also reassured him that she would be fine. Her voice was calm, steady, and reassuring but Rye knew she was hiding her fear from Collie.

His original impression of Dulcie was that she cared little about others, and oftentimes her bluntness irritated him.

However, listening to her gentle words to Collie he couldn't help but wonder what made her so rude and inconsiderate at times. Perhaps it was the same reason that made her turn to whiskey.

"Breakfast is ready."

Startled by Collie's voice, he turned to see the boy standing hesitantly in the doorway. Collie glanced at Madeline then looked away, as if fearful that he might hurt her by simply gazing at her.

"She's sleeping," Rye said softly.

Collie nodded and bolted away from the room.

Rye cupped Madeline's warm cheek. "We'll be close by," he whispered to the sleeping girl.

He rose and joined Collie at the table.

"She's still sleeping," Rye told Dulcie.

She brought their filled plates to the table then started to the bedroom.

"You need to eat, too, Dulcie," Rye reminded.

"I'm not hungry." Her tone left no room for argument, and she disappeared into the small bedroom to sit with her daughter.

Rye forced himself to eat and glanced at Collie, who was merely moving his food around with his fork.

"You'd best eat, Collie," Rye said. "We'll be working in the field the rest of the day." He suddenly realized he was treating Collie like a slave rather than a guest. "You don't have to go out to the field with me. I don't want you to think I brought you out here just to work."

"I like working with you."

Collie's simple declaration touched Rye, and he smiled warmly at the boy. "I like working with you, too."

Collie grinned widely and shoveled food into his mouth.

After he finished eating Rye stepped into the bedroom to find Dulcie staring down at her daughter as if she might disappear at any moment. The vulnerability he saw in the woman shook him. Dulcie was always so certain of herself, but beneath that shield lay the tender heart of a woman.

"She'll be okay, Dulcie," he said.

Her lips trembled and she curled her hands into fists. "I keep telling myself that, but it's so hard to see her this way."

Rye sat down beside her on the bed and put his arm around her shoulders. "I know, but there's nothing else you can do."

She leaned against him, resting her head against his shoulder. "This can't be easy for you, not after losing your wife and baby. I'm sorry."

He didn't know if she was sorry about him losing his family or sorry he had to see Madeline this way. Either way, he wasn't sorry he was here for them. "The only thing that matters right now is Madeline. You just concentrate on doing what Dr. Wickberg said."

She nodded against him. "I'll try."

Despite the circumstances, Rye savored the feel of her body against his. She was warm, and her soft curves fit against his lean hardness. It'd been a long time since he'd held a woman to offer comfort and not as a prelude to buying her time.

"I'm ready, Rye," Collie said, standing in the doorway.

Dulcie pulled away from him.

"Why don't you go out and fill up a bucket of water to take with us?" Rye suggested to Collie.

The boy left to carry out the task.

"We'll check on you every couple of hours," Rye said.

"We'll be fine."

He smiled at the typical Dulcie response. "I know."

Rye carried the scythe and pail of water, leaving Collie to bring the rake. Once in the field, they fell into a routine. Rye swung the scythe back and forth while Collie raked the windrows into piles behind him. Then once a row was cut, both Rye and Collie bundled the stalks and set them up to dry.

Near dinner time, Rye sent Collie back to the cabin to see how they were doing. The boy returned half an hour later with buttered bread, dried apples, pickles, and hard-boiled eggs. They ate the simple fare and went back to work. When midafternoon arrived, Rye had Collie sit in the shade under a tree while he took his turn running back to the cabin.

"Dulcie?" Rye called out quietly from the open doorway.

"Come in."

Rye entered the bedroom to find Madeline awake but obviously not feeling well. Her eyes were puffy and red, as if she'd been crying, and her face was flushed with fever.

"Hey, Madeline," Rye said, smiling at the girl.

Madeline's smile wasn't her usual, but it was enough to relieve Rye. "Hi Mr. Rye. Where's Collie?"

"Working in the field. He said to say hello."

Madeline coughed and sweat covered her face. Dulcie dampened a cloth in a pan of water and gently wiped away the moisture. The girl closed her eyes.

"How is it going in the field?" Dulcie asked, but Rye didn't know if it was because she was interested or she simply didn't want to talk about Madeline's condition in front of the girl.

"We're getting it done one row at a time. I'd best be getting back out there," he said.

Madeline opened her eyes. "Wanna go with."

Rye leaned over the girl. "Not today, but maybe tomorrow."

"Hate being sick."

"Me, too." Rye laid his hand on her head. "Your job is to get better."

"'Kay."

Rye resisted the impulse to kiss the girl's hot brow. She wasn't his daughter, and he had no right pretending to be her father. Especially since he was the reason her father was dead. That thought made him retreat two steps.

"We'll be back later," Rye said.

Dulcie merely nodded, and Madeline looked like she was about to cry. Rye hurried out, hoping his visit hadn't upset Madeline too much.

The rest of the day passed in the monotonous routine of the harvest. Even though Rye worked fewer hours today, he was more tired than he'd been last night. He and Collie stopped at the pond again to bathe, but this time they didn't take the time to splash water at one another. They simply washed the sweat from their skin and trudged back to the cabin.

Dulcie hadn't made supper, but Rye would've been surprised if she had. He and Collie entered the silent cabin on their tiptoes. Collie stayed behind Rye as they tiptoed to the bedroom door. Both mother and daughter were asleep.

Dulcie's arm was curled around Madeline's body, holding her close.

Rye's heart missed a beat then hammered against his ribs. Terrified of the strangling emotion, he backed out of the room, nearly stumbling over Collie.

"Is she . . ." Collie couldn't finish his question.

Rye cleared his throat. "They're sleeping. Both of them must be tuckered out."

Collie sighed in relief.

"What do you say we cook supper tonight?" Rye asked the boy, hoping to keep his mind off Madeline.

He canted his head. "Men don't cook."

"Who told you that?"

"Nobody. I just never seen a man cook before."

"Then you're in for a special treat." Rye pasted a smile on his face and kept his tone light.

Dulcie and Madeline continued to sleep as Rye prepared supper. He ensured Collie was always busy, whether it be stirring something or pumping water or setting the table.

Dulcie walked out of the bedroom as Rye and Collie sat down to eat. Rye immediately rose and filled a plate for her.

She blinked at the food and her face flushed. "I'm sorry. You shouldn't have had to cook your own supper."

"It wasn't any problem. Collie helped."

"But—"

"Eat." Rye guided her to a chair.

She sat down and picked up her fork but didn't attempt to do anything with it.

"It don't taste bad," Collie said, misunderstanding her hesitation.

She smiled at the boy. "I'm sure it's good. I don't have much of an appetite."

"It doesn't matter if you do or don't. You have to eat," Rye said firmly. "Madeline is depending on you."

His words seemed to penetrate her preoccupation, and Dulcie tried some of the creamed peas and potatoes. Her eyes widened. "This is good."

Rye grinned inwardly as he feigned a glare. "You didn't think a man could fix something that tasted good?"

Her cheeks flushed. "To be honest, I never knew a man who cooked."

"I thought it was woman's work," Collie piped up and shoveled another spoonful into his mouth.

Rye winked at Collie. "If that were the case, a man who isn't married would likely starve."

"That why you can cook, 'cause you ain't married?"

Pain arrowed through Rye, but it wasn't as sharp as it would've been a month ago. "That's partly right. But the fact is, I even cooked for my wife a time or two."

"What happened to her?"

"She died." Rye forced a smile. "But not from my food. Now eat before it gets cold."

Collie stared at him a moment longer, then dug into his food. Rye's gaze caught Dulcie's sympathetic eyes and he quickly looked away. It'd been nearly two years since he lost Mary. Sometimes it seemed forever, and other times it felt like it was only yesterday.

He cleaned off his plate, but tasted little of the fresh vegetables and salty meat. Glancing at Dulcie's plate, he was pleased to see she'd finished her meal, too. However, her face was too wan and her eyes red and puffy.

She pushed back her chair and stood. "I'll wash the dishes."

Rye rose and grasped the plate in her hand. "Collie and I will take care of them. Sit down and rest."

Familiar impatience flashed in her features. "All I've done today is sit around. You and Collie are the ones who've been working all day."

She tried to pull the plate from his hold, but he wouldn't release it.

"Worrying is harder on a person than honest labor," he said gently. He studied the stiff set of her shoulders and stubbornness in her face. "You don't have to do everything yourself, Dulcie."

For a moment, it didn't seem as if she'd heard him, then she crumpled in front of him. "I-I'm not used to depending on other folks."

Not even your husband? But even as he thought it, he knew the answer. Jerry McDaniel was a poor excuse for a husband and father. And it said a lot about Rye that he'd considered the son of a bitch his friend.

Shaking the regrets aside, Rye tugged the plate from Dulcie's hand. "Go on, Dulcie."

She nodded and returned to the bedroom to continue her vigil over her daughter.

"I can help," Collie said, standing beside Rye's elbow.

Rye reined in his thoughts about Dulcie and her husband. He smiled at the boy. "I was hoping you'd say that."

Rye washed the dishes and Collie dried them. Fifteen minutes later, they had everything cleaned up.

Collie stood by the door awkwardly, his hands in his pockets. "We gonna stay in here tonight?"

Dulcie appeared in the bedroom doorway. "You can both sleep in the loft. That's where Madeline and I usually sleep."

Startled she'd allow him to stay in the cabin overnight, Rye asked, "Are you sure?"

Although her face was pale, her nod was firm. "Yes." She took a deep breath. "I trust you."

Instead of satisfaction, Rye felt only guilt. If she knew the truth, she would never give him her trust.

DULCIE jerked out of her slumber. Her neck twinged sharply and she pressed a hand to it. Disoriented, she took a few moments to determine where she was and why she'd been sleeping in a chair. A single candle burned, filling the bedroom with various shades of light and dark.

A small snuffle startled her and she rose, moving to Madeline's side. She gently rested her palm against the girl's brow. Hot. Too hot. Madeline coughed, a weak but jagged sound.

Renewed fear constricted Dulcie's throat and a hiccupped sob slipped out. She pressed her fist to her mouth, felt her teeth digging into her lower lip but welcomed the pain. It was easier to bear than the thought of her daughter dying.

Hating herself for her momentary lapse into despair, Dulcie gathered her composure. She picked up the pan of now lukewarm water and carried it to the door. Tossing it out beyond the porch, she paused a moment, gazing at the star-filled sky. Although it was a warm night, a chill chased across her skin and goose bumps rose on her arms.

If she lost Madeline . . .

A tear rolled down her cheek.

"Dulcie?"

She spun around. Rye stood just inside the door, wearing only trousers and a partially buttoned shirt. Her heart pounded with startled fright even as she remembered she'd allowed him and Collie to sleep in the loft.

"Are you all right?" Rye asked, stepping onto the porch.

She nodded and cleared her throat. "You scared me."

"I'm sorry." He frowned and stretched out his hand, his fingers brushing her cheek. "You're crying."

She retreated from his touch and dashed her hand across her damp face. "I got some dirt in my eye."

"How's Madeline?" Rye obviously saw through her lie.

"Her fever's worse." She slipped past him into the cabin and hurried over to the pump to fill the basin with fresh, cold water.

Rye, his bare feet silent on the wood floor and his body a murky shadow in the dim cabin, joined her.

Caught in her anguish, Dulcie worked the pump handle until water overflowed the basin, shocking her back to the present. She stopped pumping and leaned over the handle, hanging her head. "She's burning up, and she's coughing more, too."

Silence greeted her words but she sensed Rye moving closer. Then a gentle hand settled on her bowed back. "Did he tell you what to do for the coughing?"

Dulcie forced herself to think, not feel. "To put hot cloths on her chest."

He grasped her shoulders and drew her to an upright position with a firm hold. "Go sit with Madeline. I'll heat some water."

Dulcie nodded, too worried and tired to care that Rye was giving her orders. In the bedroom, she dampened a cloth and laid the wet rag on Madeline's forehead. Perching on the mattress, Dulcie swept back her daughter's fine hair from her face and tried not to think.

Madeline coughed raggedly.

"Shhh, it's okay, honey," Dulcie reassured, even as she battled the panic that crawled up her throat.

The fit continued and Madeline's face reddened as tears escaped her closed eyes. Dulcie pulled Madeline into her arms and patted her back, her own heart threatening to shatter. Finally, Madeline quieted, but Dulcie continued to hold her, rocking her.

"She's all right, Dulcie," Rye said from her side. "You can lay her back down now."

She couldn't unlock her arms. Fear like she'd never known filled every part of her. As frightened as she was after Jerry died, leaving her alone to raise their daughter, it didn't come close to the abject terror she now felt. Madeline was the only person in the world she loved and who loved her in return.

"We need to put warm cloths on her chest, Dulcie," Rye said. "Please, let her go."

Rye's voice sounded strained, as if he, too, were fighting his emotions. Dulcie concentrated and finally loosened her muscles to ease Madeline down to the propped-up pillows. It took every ounce of willpower she possessed to release her.

And it was a shock to see Madeline's fever-bright eyes open and staring at her.

"How're you feeling, honey?" Dulcie asked, hoping her daughter didn't hear the tremor in her voice.

Madeline whimpered. "Hot. Hurts."

Dulcie bent close. "I know, sweetheart, but we're going to make you all better."

The girl shoved off her blankets and grumbled. "Too hot."

Dulcie tugged the muslin sheet back over her. "Just this one cover, okay?"

"No." Her plaintive moan was followed by a kick to remove the sheet.

Dulcie's fear made her impatient. "Please, honey, you have to stay covered."

"Don't wanna."

Tears threatened Dulcie's precarious control.

"Let me try," Rye said.

She glanced at him, gauged his intentions, then reluctantly rose to allow him to take her place.

"Hey, Miss Madeline," Rye cajoled. "You seem to be a bit under the weather."

The girl pouted. "Don't like being sick."

"I'll tell you a secret." Rye leaned close. "I hate being sick, too," he said in a loud whisper.

"You're never sick."

"Maybe not since I came here, but before I used to get sick a lot."

Intrigued, Dulcie stepped closer.

"You're lying," Madeline said, crabby.

Rye drew an *X* on his chest. "I promise you I'm not lying."

Madeline stared at him. "Were you sick like me?"

"One time I was. But I used to get stomachaches a lot."

"Ma gives me licorice when I have a tummyache."

Rye smiled, his eyes crinkling at the corners. "Next time I get a tummyache, I'll ask her for some." His smile faded. "Do you want to feel better?"

She nodded, her lips pressed into a line of stubbornness.

"Then you have to keep covered up even though I know you're hot," Rye said.

She opened her mouth as if to argue, but a cough erupted. Dulcie reached for her, but Rye pulled the girl up against his chest. He rubbed her back, his voice calm and steady. "Easy, Maddy. I've got you."

Moisture stung Dulcie's eyes. Her experience with men had taught her that they weren't capable of tenderness or compassion. Yet here was Rye, again forcing her to reevaluate her opinion.

He crooned softly to Madeline until she stopped coughing and was able to draw a deep breath. He laid her back down, and Dulcie set the cool, wet cloth back on Madeline's brow.

"How're you doing, sweetheart?" Dulcie asked, her voice hoarse with unshed tears.

Madeline managed a little nod and her eyelids slid closed. Her breathing grew steady.

Rye stood and heaved a shaky sigh. "We should put those hot towels on her while she's sleeping."

Working together, Dulcie and Rye unbuttoned Madeline's gown and placed the hot compress on her chest, then re-covered her. Madeline continued to sleep restlessly.

Even with Madeline so ill, Dulcie couldn't help but notice how small the bedroom seemed with Rye sharing it. He'd buttoned his shirt, tucked the tails into his trousers, and pulled on his boots at some point, yet she couldn't deny her body's reaction to his nearness. She cursed her weak nature and tried to ignore the restlessness that settled deep in her belly.

Maybe Madeline's deathly illness was Dulcie's punishment for her sins. First for lying with Jerry before they were married, then for whoring herself with Virgil Lamont.

Please, God, don't punish my daughter for what I've done.

SIXTEEN

DULCIE studied Rye's shadow-shrouded features, seeing pain that went beyond Madeline's illness. She averted her gaze. "I'm glad you're here."

Rye cleared his throat. "I am, too."

He took the chair Dulcie had awakened in, in what seemed hours ago. Although she was overly aware of him, she couldn't deny his presence was appreciated. She didn't feel so alone, solely responsible for her child's life. It didn't make sense since Rye wasn't kin, but then a lot of things didn't make sense when it came to the mysterious man.

Caught in the fever's clutches, Madeline murmured non-sensical phrases and occasionally cried out. Dulcie's stomach twisted with dread. She rewet the cloth and laid it on Madeline's too-hot brow. As she stroked her daughter's hair, she hummed a nearly forgotten lullaby.

From the day Madeline was born, Dulcie had rarely been separated from her daughter. Madeline gave her hope. Madeline gave her love. Madeline gave her a reason to believe life would be good once more. However, there'd been countless times that Dulcie had reason to doubt the future, and this was the most crushing. If her daughter died, Dulcie would be left with no hope, no reason to believe, and no love.

A hundred memories, from Madeline's birth to the day she and Madeline capered in the water, ambushed her thoughts, and she stopped her soft lulling. They were too swift and too numerous to pick out individual images—she tried to focus on a specific memory, the day Madeline was born.

The need to share her thoughts overcame her, and, keeping her gaze on her daughter, she spoke. "Jerry was on patrol the day Madeline was born. We'd just moved to the fort, so I only knew our neighbors, a sergeant and his wife who were at least ten years older than me."

Dulcie knew Rye was listening and silently thanked him for not interrupting. "When my water broke, I was terrified. No one had bothered to tell me that would happen. I thought I was losing my baby." She paused, her heart pounded, reliving the moment. After regaining her composure, Dulcie continued. "I ran over to the neighbors' and pounded on the door. The sergeant's wife took one look at me and knew what happened. I don't think I was the first young wife to come to her for help. Everything from then on is a blur, up until she put Madeline in my arms."

Dulcie smiled, recalling the joy she'd felt, and a tear slid down her cheek and dripped onto the blanket covering her daughter. She brushed the moisture away. "Do you know what I remember most when I looked at Madeline for the first time?"

"No. What?" Rye asked, his voice barely above a whisper.

"I thought she was the ugliest thing I'd ever seen in my life. She had all this wrinkled skin and a funny-shaped head. But the sergeant's wife told me all babies started out looking that way. I didn't believe her until Madeline was a few weeks old."

She chanced a look at Rye and saw his understanding smile, but also the poignant sadness in his eyes. He never had a chance to see his child. "I'm sorry. I shouldn't have—"

"No, it's all right, Dulcie. It was their time, and I've finally made peace with their passing." His gaze strayed to Madeline and determination filled his eyes. "But it's not Madeline's. Not yet."

Rye's conviction gave Dulcie strength and she nodded stubbornly. "Damned right, it's not."

He smiled. "You just hang onto that, Dulcie."
And she did.

RYE stood and stretched his stiff muscles. For the last two hours, Dulcie had been making certain the rag on Madeline's forehead stayed cool and the cloth on her chest warm.

"I'll get some more hot water," he said, leaning over Dulcie.

She blinked in surprise, as if she'd forgotten he was in the room. After a moment, she handed him the basin. Her fingers brushed his, and he felt a slight ripple of arousal then cursed himself for his unseemly reaction.

He slipped out of the bedroom with the basin. After tossing the old water out, he refilled the basin from a steaming kettle on the stovetop.

"Thanks," Dulcie mumbled.

Rye placed his hand on her stiff shoulder. "I can do that for a while so you can sleep."

She stared at him, as if trying to figure out his words. As exhausted as she was, he doubted she was thinking straight. She blinked and nodded. "All right." She stretched out on the bed alongside Madeline. "I'm just going to rest my eyes, but I won't sleep."

Rye brushed the ponytail that flowed down her back. "That's fine."

Dulcie closed her eyes . . . and was asleep in less than a minute.

Rye drew the chair nearer to the bed and gazed down at mother and daughter. In the candle's flickering light he could see the resemblance in the cheekbones, nose, mouth, and chin. He hoped she would grow up to be as strong-willed as her mother instead of possessing her father's weaknesses.

Despite knowing Dulcie and Madeline for less than a month, Rye's emotions were entangled with them. Just the thought of the little girl losing her battle brought the sting of tears. He angrily swiped at his eyes with the back of his hand. He knew firsthand what it was like to lose loved ones, and he didn't want Dulcie to have to go through the hell he had.

The night swept by, but time held little meaning for Rye. His world narrowed to Madeline and her feverish ramblings and restless movements. He did his best to keep her quiet so she didn't wake Dulcie, who needed the sleep.

As the rising sun peeked in the window, Rye stretched cramped muscles. Muted footsteps approached the bedroom, alerting Rye to Collie's arrival. He met the boy outside the bedroom.

"You weren't in your bedroll," Collie said accusingly.

"I was helping Mrs. McDaniel with Madeline."

Collie peeked around Rye. "Is she better?"

"She's got a fever."

Fearful eyes met his. "Folks die from fever."

Rye hunkered down in front of the boy and rested his hands on his slender shoulders. "That may be so, but we're not going to let Madeline die, you hear me?"

Collie's expression twisted into anger. "If someone's gonna die of fever, ain't nothing you or me or no one can do about it."

"We can fight the fever," Dulcie said.

Rye and Collie turned to see her standing in the doorway.

"Madeline will not die," she said, her tone no less fierce than her expression.

Collie seemed to shrink before her. "I-I didn't mean nothin', Miz McDaniel."

Before Rye could reassure the boy, Dulcie dropped to a knee in front of Collie, who stared at the floor. Her intense expression was replaced by sympathy and concern. "I know you didn't, Collie. I understand how hard it must be after you lost your mother and father. But I'm not going to let Madeline go without a fight." She paused and used a crooked finger to raise his chin. "I hope I can count on you to help me."

Collie drew back his shoulders. "I'll do anything you ask."

Dulcie cupped his chin in her palm and smiled. "Thank you." She rose. "If you two could milk Flossie and take care of the chickens, I'll get breakfast on."

The sleep had done Dulcie a world of good. She seemed more composed, more like herself.

Rye guided Collie out the door and to the well to wash up.

Collie splashed water on his face, wetting his shaggy hair. "Miz McDaniel isn't like folks say."

Rye paused, his hands in the dented water pan. "What do folks say?"

Collie shrugged. "That she's mean and don't like people. Some say she's like her pa."

"Do you believe that?"

"Not really. She's never hit me or yelled at me, but—" He clamped his mouth shut.

"But what, Collie?"

He scrubbed his face with his palms and reached for the towel. "I promised I wouldn't say nothin'."

"Who did you promise?"

"Miz McDaniel."

Rye frowned. "Did she do something bad?"

The lad squirmed. "I dunno."

Although Rye hated to make the boy break a promise, he had to know Dulcie's secret. "If I promise not to tell anyone, will you tell me?"

Collie's internal battle was clear in his distressed features.

"I'm sorry, Collie," Rye said guiltily. "I shouldn't ask you to break a promise."

The boy lifted his gaze. "Even if it's something bad?"

Rye's heartbeat skittered, but he hoped he kept the apprehension from his face. "That depends, Collie. There are some bad things that are really bad, and some that aren't as bad as a person might think."

Collie's face squinched up. "It might not be so bad." His brow furrowed. "Or maybe it is."

Frustration knotted Rye's gut. He wanted to know, but didn't feel right pushing the kid. "You don't have to tell me."

"I think it'll be okay." He took a deep breath. "Miz McDaniel had me buy her a bottle of whiskey. She gave me a whole nickel for getting it for her."

Disappointment rang through Rye, not for the boy's confession, but for Dulcie and the problem she refused to acknowledge. Had that been the only bottle? Or had there been others?

"Did I do wrong telling you?"

Rye glanced down to see worry fringing the boy's eyes. He forced a smile. "No, pard, you did good. And I promise I won't tell Mrs. McDaniel you told me."

Collie's apprehension faded. "I'll feed the chickens and gather the eggs."

"Thanks, Collie."

The boy headed to the old lean-to where the eggs would be found.

Rye rubbed his grizzled jaw and stared at the cabin. "Once Madeline is better, you and I are going to have a talk, Dulcie McDaniel."

WITH the brutal sun high in the sky, Rye stopped swinging the scythe and dropped his arms. Sweat rolled down the side of his face in a maddening tickle but he didn't have the strength to wipe it away. Finally, his breathing slowed, and he turned to Collie, who raked the cut grain in neat straight rows behind him. The boy had worked diligently since their late start that morning, and guilt assailed Rye.

"Sit down for a few minutes," Rye said to the boy.

Collie stopped raking to angle him a look. "You going to rest a spell?"

"I'm not tired," Rye lied.

"Me neither." The lad continued raking.

Rye set his scythe on the ground and grabbed hold of the rake handle.

"What did you do that for?" the boy demanded.

"You're going to fall down if you don't rest."

"I ain't neither." He jerked on the rake, but Rye held it in a tight grasp. Collie tried again and lost his balance. Rye shot out a hand and caught him before he fell.

"Just sit down for a few minutes, Collie," he said in exasperation.

The boy narrowed his eyes. "Only if you do."

Rye sighed and dropped the rake on a pile of wheat. He guided Collie out of the field to a cluster of trees, where the boy grabbed the dipper out of the pail and guzzled the lukewarm water. Collie filled it again, but handed it to Rye, who accepted it with a nod of thanks. As Rye drank the blessed water, Collie sat down and leaned against the rough trunk of an oak tree. His thirst sated, Rye pulled on his shirt that he'd hung from a low-hanging branch earlier, then joined Collie.

"It's hard work," Rye commented, removing his hat and placing it on his drawn-up knee.

"It ain't so bad."

Rye resisted a smile at the boy's youthful pride. "Maybe not for you, but I'm about tuckered out."

"That's 'cause you're old."

Rye opened his mouth to argue, but abruptly closed it. Hell, he was thirty years old. And what did he have to show for living over half a lifetime?

A horse, a saddle, and the clothes on his back. Nothing that meant anything.

"Did you get that mark from an Indian?" Collie asked.

Startled, Rye glanced down into the boy's sparkling eyes. It took a moment to realize Collie had seen the scar on his shoulder. "No," he simply replied, hoping the kid would let the subject drop.

"A bad man?"

Rye recalled the man who'd held the red-hot iron against his shoulder. He'd known the sergeant for years, from before he had married and lost his family, from when Rye had been a damned good soldier. The sergeant had kept his face expressionless, but Rye saw the compassion and apology in his eyes as he'd lifted the glowing iron from the fire.

He shook himself free of the bitter memory and answered honestly, "No, he wasn't a bad man."

Disappointment clouded Collie's face. He'd obviously hoped Rye had an exciting adventure to tell him.

They sat in companionable silence listening to the buzzing insects and the slight breeze rustling the leaves. Rye's thoughts veered to Madeline. While he worked, he'd been able to keep his mind off her and Dulcie. But now he couldn't help but wonder how the young girl was faring.

Collie's stomach growled loudly, drawing Rye's attention. They'd eaten a late breakfast, but that had been over six hours ago. Disgusted by his thoughtlessness, Rye forced a smile. "What do you say we head to the cabin and get something to eat?"

Collie scrambled to his feet, and the eager look in his face made Rye feel even more lowdown. Collie extended a small hand to Rye. "What're you waiting for?"

Chuckling, Rye let the boy help him up. Collie hissed slightly, and Rye, concerned, held onto the kid's hand, turning it over in his larger one. Broken blisters between his thumb and forefinger oozed blood.

"Why didn't you say something?" Rye asked.

Collie shrugged. "It's okay."

"No, it's not." Another notch on his conscience. "We'll take care of it at the house."

Rye, angry at himself, brooded all the way back to the cabin. He was no different than those people who adopted children simply for another hired hand to work their farms. What he ought to do was take Collie back to the Gearsons. At least there he wasn't worked from dawn to dusk.

Rye made Collie stop at the well, and he cleaned the boy's open sores with cold water. Although Collie flinched when the water touched the broken blisters, he remained stoic. Rye retrieved some salve from his saddlebag in the barn and slathered it on the boy's hand then wrapped one of his old cavalry scarves around it.

"There, that should protect it," Rye said.

Collie flexed and unflexed his hand. "Feels better."

Rye smiled and ruffled his thick hair. "Good. What do you think of going back to the Gearsons' today? You've already been here three days."

Something akin to betrayal cut through Collie's expression. He stared at Rye, who forced himself to smile encouragingly.

"Don't wanna," Collie mumbled.

"It's not so bad there. Three meals a day, plus a real bed and a roof over your head."

Collie scuffed his toe in the dirt and shrugged. "I s'pose."

Rye had to do what was best for the boy, even though he hated taking him back to a family who merely tolerated him. He steered Collie toward the cabin. "Let's see how Madeline is getting on then rustle up something to eat."

Without his earlier enthusiasm, Collie shuffled into the house. Their long shadows moved ahead of them as they crossed the yard. Inside the house, the acrid scent of sweat and sickness struck Rye and he quickly moved to the bedroom. The smell was stronger there.

Dulcie's frightened gaze met his. "I think her fever's up."

Rye moved to the bedside and placed a palm on the girl's brow. It was definitely hotter. "I'll get the doctor."

Dulcie nodded tersely.

Rye turned and nearly bowled over Collie. Impatient and scared for Madeline's life, Rye grabbed the boy's shoulders and lifted him out of the way, setting him in a corner. "Stay there, and don't get in Mrs. McDaniel's way," he commanded.

His eyes wide, Collie nodded and seemed to shrink in the corner. Satisfied the boy wouldn't be a nuisance, Rye hurried out to saddle Smoke.

Apprehension driving him, Rye rode hard for Dr. Wickberg's office. The doctor's wife answered the door.

"He's not home. He had to go out to the Cook place early this morning. Karl got stomped by a horse," the woman said, not without sympathy.

"Where do they live?" Rye demanded.

"About twenty miles west of here."

Rye managed to stifle the cuss that rose to his lips. Torn between going after the doctor and returning to help Dulcie, he considered where he could do the most good. "When the doctor gets back, tell him Madeline McDaniel is burning up with fever."

The doctor's wife laid a hand on his arm. "I've helped my husband with some fevers. If wiping her down with a cool cloth doesn't help, bathe her in cold water."

"Thank you." Rye remembered to tip his hat before he spun around and remounted Smoke.

A short time later, Rye hurried into Dulcie's cabin, sweat coating his face and dampening his shirt. Collie was still in the corner where Rye had left him. The boy looked small and scared, and his vulnerability pierced Rye's concern for Madeline.

"Where's the doctor?" Dulcie asked, grabbing his attention.

"Twenty miles away." He tried to remember the family's name. "At the Cooks'."

Dulcie's face, already wan, paled even further. "When will he—"

"Mrs. Wickberg didn't know. I can ride out to get him, but it'll take time."

"Time we don't have." Dulcie gazed down at Madeline's fever-flushed face.

"The doc's wife said that if a cool cloth doesn't bring the fever down, bathe her in cold water."

Dulcie nodded, resoluteness replacing her apprehension. "All right. Let's do it now. Get the tub from out back and fill it with water from the well."

As Rye turned to carry out the task, he noticed Collie once more. "C'mon, Collie. You can help as long as you're careful with that hand."

The boy nodded shortly and followed Rye. After Rye carried the tub inside, Collie worked the pump handle and filled kettles with the chilly well water. Rye carried the kettles to the tub and dumped the water in it.

Finally the tub was full, and Rye hurried back to the bedroom. "It's ready," he said.

Dulcie nodded and picked up Madeline, cradling her in her arms. Madeline's head lolled against her chest and the girl murmured feverishly. Dulcie didn't waste any time placing her daughter, still wearing her nightgown, in the tub.

Madeline jerked awake and wrapped her arms around her small torso. "Too c-cold."

"I know, honey, but we have to do this to bring down your fever."

"C-cold. Out." Madeline struggled to climb out, splashing water onto the floor and Dulcie.

Rye knelt down to help hold Madeline in the tub. Goose bumps arose on the young girl's arms and legs, but fever heat continued to radiate from her. Madeline coughed and ceased fighting them, but her lethargy was almost worse.

Dulcie used a washcloth to sluice water over Madeline's thin shoulders and arms while Rye held the girl so she didn't slip under the water's surface. Only when Madeline's lips took on a faint bluish hue did they stop.

Rye lifted Madeline out of the tub and Dulcie wrapped a blanket around her, then took her daughter from Rye and hugged her close. Dulcie's red-rimmed eyes met Rye's. "She doesn't feel as hot."

Rye laid his palm on the girl's brow. "Feels like it's come down."

Dulcie didn't look reassured. "But will it stay down?"

Rye wished to God he could tell her what she wanted to hear. "I don't know."

Dulcie carried Madeline back into the bedroom.

Rye glanced at Collie, who'd hovered on the fringes while they'd taken care of Madeline. The boy's face was pale and he had the look of a caged wild animal. "You ought to have something to eat."

"I'm not hungry." Collie's gaze settled on the bedroom door where Dulcie had taken her daughter. He looked like he wanted to ask a question and Rye waited, but the boy remained silent.

Rye steered Collie to the table and set him down on a chair. He glanced at the bedroom door across the room but knew he could do nothing more for Madeline or Dulcie.

"You gonna take me back to the Gearsons now?" Collie asked, his voice dull.

Although it'd been his idea to take the boy back, Rye wasn't so certain about his decision. "Do you want to go back?"

Collie looked away. "No, but I'm just in the way 'round here."

Rye tried to see past the boy's apathy. Was Collie jealous of the attention Madeline was getting? "Who told you that?"

"You." His indifference was replaced by accusation.

Startled, Rye tried to remember what he might have done or said that gave Collie that impression. "I don't want you working in the field until those blisters heal, but I don't remember saying anything about you being in the way."

"Then why'd you put me in a corner before you rode off to get the doctor?" Collie asked resentfully.

So you wouldn't be in the way.

Guilt-ridden, Rye ran a hand through his hair. "I was worried about Madeline. I'm sorry."

Collie merely grunted.

Unable to think of anything else to say, Rye put a skillet on the stove. Five minutes later, he placed a couple of fried eggs between two slices of bread and gave it to Collie. Although he ignored the sandwich for nearly a minute, Collie finally gave in to his hunger and ate it, washing it down with a glass of milk. Rye managed to eat a slice of bread and two eggs, as well as drink a cup of bitter black coffee.

"Would you like to stay here for another day or two?" Rye asked after they had eaten.

Hope flared in the boy's face, but it was extinguished almost immediately. "You don't want me here."

Rye squatted down in front of the seated boy and grasped his arms. "You're wrong, Collie. I like having you here. So do Mrs. McDaniel and Madeline."

"Then why do I have to go back?"

Because the Gearsons were responsible for him, Collie would have to return at some point. So was it better to let him stay longer, or leave now before the lad became too attached to them? Or maybe *Rye* was afraid of becoming too attached to the boy.

"Let me stay, Rye. I promise I won't get in the way."

"I wouldn't be taking you back to the Gearsons' because I want to. I'd be taking you back because I don't want you to work so hard."

"But I like working with you."

The boy's plaintive plea caused Rye to look away for a moment to regain his composure. "I'm glad, but I didn't bring you out here to make you work all day. You'll be able to rest at the Gearsons' and let that hand heal."

Collie picked at the bandanna wrapped around his hand. "It don't hurt much." He turned earnest eyes to Rye. "And if I promise not to work for a little while, will you let me stay? Please?"

Rye dropped his head in resignation. He couldn't deny those pleading eyes. He lifted his head and met the boy's gaze. "All right. You can stay, but no field work."

Collie's face lit up. "I promise I won't do no work until you tell me it's all right."

Rye couldn't help but grin. "I thought boys were always trying to get out of work."

"It ain't that I like it, but I don't mind if it's with you and Miz McDaniel and Madeline."

Rye tousled the boy's hair. "Right now, you can help me take care of the tub and clean the kitchen."

Collie held up his wrapped hand, his eyes glittering with mischief. "Can't. Gotta let my hand heal."

Rye burst into laughter but didn't argue.

Once the chores were done, Rye went into the bedroom. Dulcie's face was turned away from him, and he feared the worst. "How is she?" he asked softly.

She turned slowly to meet his gaze. "She finally stopped shivering, and the fever hasn't come back. She might even be breathing a little easier."

Rye sagged in relief. "Thank God."

"I doubt He had much say in it." Dulcie's tone was bone-dry.

The woman's uncertainty and fear had vanished, replaced with her familiar cynicism, which boded well for Madeline's recovery.

"Is there anything I can do?" he asked.

Her expression gentled. "Get some rest. You didn't sleep much last night."

Rye shrugged. "I've survived on less. I'd go back out to the field but it'll be dark in an hour." He paused. "It's a good time to do some hunting. Maybe I can get some fresh meat."

Dulcie nodded. "I'd appreciate it, Rye." Her face reddened. "I'm down to a few pounds of salt pork."

Rye nodded without comment then went to round up Collie.

$\mathscr{S}$EVENTEEN

AFTER a late supper of fresh venison steaks and a variety of vegetables from the garden, Dulcie rose to clear the table. "You're welcome to stay in the loft again," she said to Rye and Collie.

"I think someone's ready to go up there already," Rye said, looking deliberately at Collie, whose eyelids were at half-mast.

"I ain't tired." Collie's yawn contradicted his words.

Dulcie fought a smile. "Maybe you'd like to wash the dishes then."

Collie's panicked gaze leapt to Rye. "Maybe I'd best go on up." He held up a hand wrapped in a scarf. "Gotta heal so I can help in the field tomorrow."

"We'll see how it looks in the morning," Rye said, canting an eyebrow at the boy. "Go on up and hit the sack."

Collie didn't appear too pleased by Rye's words, but he didn't argue. He climbed the ladder into the loft.

"What happened to his hand?" Dulcie asked in a low voice so she wouldn't be overheard.

"Broken blisters from raking. Kid didn't even say anything, just kept on working."

Dulcie slid plates into the dishwater, her conscience baiting her. "I hope he knows he doesn't have to earn his keep."

Rye paused. "Thanks, Dulcie."

His sincere tone warmed her face, and she sought another subject. "Where will you go after the harvest is in?"

Rye moved close to Dulcie, and she could smell soap and leather and an enticing scent all his own. "Haven't figured that out yet."

"You could stay here." The words were out before Dulcie could stop them. "I mean, there are always things to be done, and as long as you're willing to work for room and board . . ."

Rye faced her, his gaze steady but oddly sad. "As much as I like you and Madeline, I have to find a paying job."

Dulcie choked back her disappointment and plunged her hands into the soapy water. She washed a dish and slid it into the pan of clear, hot water. Without asking, Rye picked up a towel and wiped the plate.

They worked in silence that wasn't quite comfortable, but wasn't taut either. Instead, it felt expectant, like the calm before a thunderstorm. Finally, Rye wiped the last dish, and Dulcie put it away. Each carrying a pan, they tossed the dishwater and rinse water out into the yard.

Back in the cabin, without the children or chores to distract them, Dulcie grew increasingly restless. She was aware of a thrumming in her body, a reaction to Rye's presence.

"I'd best get some sleep, too," Rye said.

The lamp's light cast sinister shadows across Rye's handsome features, but the shadows lied. Dulcie had trusted Rye with her most precious possession, and he'd proven he was a man like no other man she'd known.

"I can't sleep yet and I wouldn't mind some company," she said softly, her heart kicking against her ribs.

Rye studied her, the blue of his eyes nearly eclipsed by the black circles. "All right." He walked with stealthy grace to one of the rocking chairs and sat down.

Dulcie's heart thundered in her ears and her palms grew moist. She was courting peril, tempting herself with the nearness of a man. But Rye wasn't just any man. She trusted him as she'd trusted no other. Yet that wasn't the danger. It was herself she didn't trust.

If she truly wanted to preserve her pride and independence, she wouldn't have asked him to sit with her. Although angry with herself, undeniable excitement thrummed through her.

To try to gain back her composure, she tiptoed into the bedroom. She gazed down at Madeline, sleeping peacefully for the first time in three days. Tears filled her eyes, and one trailed down her cheek to drip onto the sheet covering her daughter. Dulcie swept the tear away and bent down to kiss Madeline's cool brow.

As she straightened, she glanced at the trunk at the end of the bed. The whiskey called to her, tempted her with its numbing promise. For one night she wanted to forget her horrific fear for Madeline's life; she wanted to lay aside her responsibility of providing for her daughter; and she wanted to smother her sinful yearnings for Rye.

Her gaze flicked to the man in the other room and collided with his. His expression was hidden in the dull lamplight, but his eyes burned with a need she recognized too well. She'd seen it often enough in the mirror.

A wildfire passed through her, leaving banked embers in its wake, and she knew that tonight even whiskey couldn't contain her body's wantonness. Lifting her chin, she left the bedroom and sat down on the other rocking chair across from Rye.

"How is she?" he asked in a low voice.

"Sound asleep. Doesn't feel like the fever has come back."

Rye nodded. "Good." He grew serious. "It's going to take at least two weeks to cut your wheat by hand. If we had a reaper, it'd only be a couple of days."

Dulcie blinked at the unexpected remark. Had she misread the look in his eyes? Or had she merely seen what she wanted to see? She swallowed her self-loathing. "Pa had one. He told me he sold it after Ma died."

"So he could buy whiskey?"

She nodded, humiliated that Rye knew her father's weakness so well.

"Why did he drink?" Rye asked.

Bitterness welled up in her. "Because he liked it."

"Why?"

Dulcie scowled. "What difference does it make? He was a drunk."

His expression became pensive and his sight turned inward. "People drink for different reasons, Dulcie. Some drink because they're scared, others drink to forget, and some drink because they hate themselves." His pointed gaze pinned her. "Why do you drink, Dulcie?"

Her blood ran cold, and the room zoomed in and out of focus. "Why would I drink?" she asked, hoping he couldn't hear the thudding of her heart.

Rye studied her, and she had the impression he saw things in her that nobody else did. "You tell me, Dulcie."

She dropped her gaze to her clenched hands in her lap. A half truth was better than lying. "Sometimes I get lonely."

"Everybody gets lonely one time or another."

She lifted her head, and pain and solitude reflected in his eyes, a mirror of her own. Perhaps she hadn't been mistaken. Maybe his need was based on loneliness, too.

Without conscious thought, she stood and walked to him, then knelt between his legs. She leaned forward, wrapped her arms around his waist, and rested her head against his flat belly. She felt him lengthen and harden against her cheek. Passion flowed through her veins, hot and needy and reckless.

"Do you get lonely, Rye?" she asked.

"Yes." The single word seemed to have been wrenched from someplace deep within him.

Dulcie remained where she was, her need pulsing through her. She recalled her first time with Jerry, how it had been uncomfortable in the beginning, then there'd been only ecstasy. It was a pleasure she came to crave, but even when she'd learned of her husband's infidelity, she never sought out another man. And while she'd hated Lamont for exacting her favors in return for passage home, Dulcie hated her body's betrayal even more.

However, Rye never demanded anything from her. She wanted to give him her body—herself—because he was kind, gentle, and compassionate. And because she desired his touch, desired him more than she'd desired any other man.

Rye laid his hand on her head, his fingers caressing her

scalp and combing through her hair. She trembled at the act that felt even more intimate than sex.

"I want you, Rye." The words came unbidden, yet they held the truth.

His muscles tensed and his erection throbbed. "It's not right. The children—"

"Are asleep," she finished. Not looking at his face, she could speak more freely. "It's been a long time since I've felt like a woman."

For a moment, she thought he was going to push her away.

"You don't know me, Dulcie." It sounded as if the words were torn from him.

She took a deep breath and raised her head to meet his hooded gaze. "I know you're kind and gentle and would never hurt Madeline or me. And I know you want me as much as I want you."

Rye tangled his fingers in Dulcie's hair and clenched the strands within his fists. He stared into her wide, luminous eyes, saw the need and desperation that drove her. He remembered too clearly how she'd looked through the window that night, lying on the bed, her legs spread and her hand beneath her gown. He'd barely been able to resist then. . . .

God in heaven, he knew it was wrong, but his own needs overrode his conscience. He pulled her toward him, his hands buried in her soft hair. If he wanted, he could count every freckle that dotted her nose and cheeks, but anything as complicated as counting was lost to him. Canting his head slightly, he pressed his lips to hers. She moaned her approval, and her warm mouth slid across his.

Dulcie returned his tender kiss then grew bolder as she traced his lower lip. He opened to her exploration and their tongues met, tentative at first, but timidity disappeared as passion flared, growing hotter.

Dulcie rose gracefully and he clasped her hips, pulling her toward him. She wrapped her arms around his neck and sat on his lap as they continued to kiss. With her backside pressed against his groin, Rye squeezed his eyes shut, fighting for control. He drew his mouth from hers, afraid her kisses would take him over the edge.

Rye gasped. "Have to . . . slow down."

With flushed cheeks, Dulcie leaned back slightly. A wicked smile touched her kiss-swollen lips, and she shifted to kneel in front of him again. Before Rye could react, she attacked his trouser buttons and reached in to touch him.

Rye arched upward, his hips coming off the chair. He grabbed her wrists. "What're you doing?" he asked and was embarrassed by his trembling voice.

She smiled, a light teasing grin. "If you have to ask, then it's been too long."

Dulcie pulled out of his grasp and slowly unbuttoned his shirt. Her fingertips brushed his skin below and little arcs of pleasure rippled through him. When his shirt was completely undone, Dulcie stretched out to slip it off his shoulders.

Rye stiffened, knowing what his shirt hid. If she saw the brand . . . He clasped her arms and stood, pulling her to her feet with him. Her body pressed against his from knee to chest.

"You're wearing too many clothes," Rye whispered. He'd simply meant to distract her, but as he took his turn in removing her shirt, his excitement built. He unbuttoned the first few buttons then pulled the tails out of her waistband and lifted the shirt off over her head and tossed it aside. A dingy white camisole did little to hide her hard nipples.

With shaking fingers, he untied the bow between her breasts, and kissed the freckles scattered between them. Her sharp inhalation made him smile against her milky skin. He reached up to draw the camisole straps down and inched them down her arms. More of her breasts were revealed until the cloth fell below her nipples. He growled low in his throat and captured a peak between his lips, gently worrying it with his tongue and mouth.

She placed her hands on his head, but Rye couldn't figure out if she wanted him to stop or keep going. As much as he wanted to continue, he released her nipple and looked up, questioning her with his expression.

"Don't stop." The words exploded from her, along with a gasp.

Relieved, Rye returned to lave her nipples, but even through the haze of passion, he remembered to keep his shirt covering his back. Some part of him reminded him he had no right making love to the widow of the man he'd killed, but his body was past listening to his conscience.

Dulcie splayed her fingers through Rye's hair and held him close. She arched her back, eagerly pressing her breasts against him. He could smell her feminine scent, and his blood roared through his veins.

But before he could make another move, Dulcie pushed him away. "Don't move."

Startled and confused, Rye stood motionless as Dulcie hurried into the bedroom and returned with a blanket, which she spread out on the floor. He released a pent-up sigh of relief. She hadn't changed her mind.

The lamp's glow seemed to bring fire to Dulcie's hair, with flames of red and gold flickering through her tendrils and forming a halo around her head. The lamp dusted her face and bare breasts with golden light. His arousal, which had faded slightly, sharpened once more.

Dulcie grabbed his waistband, tugging him down onto the blanket until they knelt facing one another. He kissed her lips then kissed a trail down to her breasts, and finally to her belly. However, before he could release the buttons on her trousers, she pressed him to lie on his back. She tugged down his pants, leaving his drawers, which outlined his erection. Before he could reach for her, she wrapped her hand around him with only the thin cloth between them.

Rye had sown his wild oats before he married, but he'd met few women as assertive in making love. However, he found himself elated by Dulcie's brazenness, liked that she took pleasure in touching him.

Suddenly she freed him from his underwear and her warm, wet mouth closed around him. Intense pleasure streaked through him, and he twined his fingers in her thick hair. He tried to hold back, tried to prolong his rise, but Dulcie's mouth was too inviting. His release exploded, shattering him into a hundred pieces.

For minutes Rye lay there, aware of Dulcie's soft breasts against him and her head pillowed on his chest. He unclenched his hands and let loose her hair. Laying one hand on her silky cheek, he stroked her sleek back with the other.

Her soft moans sent an arrow of renewed lust through him. He slid his hand across her cheek and down her smooth neck to her breast. Pinching her nipple gently, he listened to her breathing grow more ragged. Her scent drifted to him, enticed him.

Rye gently rolled her onto her back and wasted little time removing what remained of his clothes, except for his shirt. He moved between her legs and gently brushed across her damp flesh. Her thighs stiffened, and her moan rolled through him. Shifting to lie down, he flicked his tongue across her, tasting her femininity.

"What're you doing?" Dulcie asked in a ragged voice.

Rye raised his head and looked past her breasts to her wide eyes. "Giving you what you gave me," he said softly.

He returned to his delectable task, his hands splayed across her hips to hold her still. Dulcie shuddered continuously, her low moans bringing Rye to hardness once more.

Dulcie had known pleasure with a man buried within her, but neither Jerry nor the peddler had ever kissed her this way. She shuddered as Rye's tongue stroked across her in broad sweeps, slowing to give extra attention to the sensitive nubbin. On nights when she couldn't fight the loneliness, she would touch herself in the same place, but never had it taken her voice and left her only with inarticulate moans.

He reached up, pinched a nipple, and her belly and thighs quivered, tensing even more. Suddenly he sucked on the hard bud as his hands kneaded her breasts. Dulcie threw her hips upward as the tension exploded. She bit down on her fist, managing to hold back her cry so she wouldn't wake the sleeping children.

She fell back onto the blanket, her muscles limp and her heartbeat pounding in her ears. Before she could regain her breath, Rye moved up over her body, his weight balanced on his arms and knees as he straddled her. Although it was odd he kept his shirt on, Dulcie liked how it hung from his torso and brushed her sensitive skin.

He kissed her and she tasted herself on his lips. But she also tasted Rye beneath it, and excitement pulsed through her once more.

"Ready?" His whispered question was followed by a delicious swipe of his tongue across her earlobe.

Shuddering with desire, Dulcie nodded. Rye kissed her and slid into her in one smooth motion. She moaned around their kiss. Wrapping her legs around him, she locked her ankles at the back of his waist. He withdrew and began to thrust in slow, easy motions. Aftershocks rippled through her even as the coil in her belly tightened once more.

Dulcie pressed her head against the floor and closed her eyes, feeling him in her and around her. The tension grew, down her spine and into her buttocks, clenching and tightening, like a spring being wound tighter and tighter.

"Look at me," Rye said in a passion-husky voice.

She opened her eyes. His hair stuck to his forehead and his face was flushed. He was panting, but a devilish smile curved his lips.

"Let it go, Dulcie. I promise I'll catch you." Then he reached down between their bodies and rubbed her sensitive spot.

Dulcie went over the edge and opened her mouth in a soundless scream. Her limbs stiffened and blackness dotted her vision. She was vaguely aware of Rye spilling into her.

Dulcie lay limp and exhausted as Rye rolled off her, panting. She stared at the ceiling, trying to recall if she'd ever been so satisfied, so content. Rolling onto her side, she propped her head on her hand and gazed down at Rye. She smiled, amused that he still wore his shirt but nothing else.

Rye opened his eyes, which were smoky with sated passion.

"Nobody's ever . . ." She broke off, embarrassed.

Rye snagged her waist with his arm and pulled her over to lie snug against his side. "I'm glad."

He kissed her crown and closed his eyes. Dulcie tipped her head back and studied his face, which was still slightly flushed. A sweat-dampened curl fell across his brow and his long lashes brushed his cheeks. The faint shadow of whiskers covered his straight jaw and outlined his nicely shaped lips. Remembering the feel of those lips on her, she shivered as aftershocks from their lovemaking echoed through her.

Curling close to Rye's side, she realized she didn't need whiskey to fall asleep tonight. Tomorrow would be soon enough for the guilt to return.

RYE woke and lay still in the faint lamplight as he tried to determine where he was. Throughout his years in the army, he'd awakened in various places, but he didn't think this was one of them. He turned his head to see red hair fanned across his arm and chest.

Dulcie.

He nearly groaned aloud. He'd done what he swore he wouldn't—taken advantage of a woman he'd made a widow. Yet even as he berated himself for his weakness, he recalled Dulcie's assertiveness and what she'd done. He grew aroused at the memory of her mouth on him. In his experience, only whores knew about pleasuring a man that way. His wife had been innocent of anything to do with sexual relations, and he'd taught her how to make love. He hadn't even considered teaching her that method. Had Jerry taught Dulcie? Or, knowing Jerry as he did, had he met her in a saloon?

What did it matter? Dulcie was a woman he could easily fall in love with, and her experience was only a small part of who she was. Besides, being honest with himself, he liked what she'd done.

He looked outside and gauged the time to be around four in the morning. Although he would've preferred sleeping with Dulcie for another hour or two, Rye didn't want the children seeing them together. They were damned lucky neither Madeline nor Collie had awakened during the night. Reluctantly, he reached for his discarded clothing and began to dress.

Dulcie opened her eyes and blinked up at him. "Rye?"

The sleepy bewilderment in her expression made him want to kiss away her slumber and he looked away before he surrendered to temptation. He'd given in to temptation too many times already.

"We have to go to our own beds, before Collie and Madeline wake up," he said.

Dulcie's eyes widened as if suddenly realizing where they were . . . and that she was naked. She quickly retrieved her shirt.

As much as Rye wanted to watch her, he turned away to button his own shirt.

"What time is it?" she asked.

"Around four."

Rye stood and extended a hand to Dulcie, but she ignored it, scrambling to her feet. The over-large shirt hid everything from her neck to her knees. He tried not to remember how her slender legs had wrapped around his waist, or how her breasts had felt within his palms.

"This"—Dulcie motioned to the blanket—"this can't happen again."

Although Rye agreed, for reasons she would never know, he wished it could be different. If Jerry had died doing his duty, and not because of a drunken dare, Rye could court her like she deserved. But he was still a deserter, and he could never escape the brand on his shoulder.

He stepped over to her, wrapped his arms around her waist, and kissed her gently. "You're right. It can't."

She stared up at him, her brows furrowed in question, one she didn't ask.

Rye forced himself to release her and step back. "I'd best get up in the loft before Collie wakes up."

She nodded and gathered up her clothing and the blanket they'd made love on. Without looking at him, she hurried into the bedroom where Madeline slept.

Regret lodged in Rye's chest. What would he do when the harvest was in and Dulcie didn't need him anymore? What could he do but move on?

$\mathcal{E}$IGHTEEN

THE approach of a wagon brought Dulcie out of her garden and she shook out the folds of her skirt. Although the skirt felt odd around her legs, she had to admit it was cooler than trousers. It also made her feel more like a woman than she had in months. Heat touched her cheeks as she remembered how Rye had made her feel like a woman last night. As much as she tried to forget their lovemaking, she couldn't help but recall his kisses and how he'd touched her *there* with his mouth.

She forced the memories aside as she walked around to the front of the cabin. Dr. Wickberg drew back the reins and gazed down at her. "Hello, Dulcie. You look nice today."

She blushed and wondered how a skirt could make her feel so different. "Thank you, Doctor. Are you here to see Madeline?"

He nodded, and worry blunted his features. "My wife told me about Madeline's fever."

Dulcie smiled. "We followed your wife's advice and put Madeline in a cold bath. It broke her fever, and she's doing much better." She glanced down at her dirty hands and said ruefully, "Since she was sleeping, I thought I'd catch up on the garden work."

The doctor smiled, his relief clear. "Good. If you don't mind, I'd like to check on her."

"I'd be grateful."

Dr. Wickberg climbed down from the buggy and grabbed his bag from under the seat. "What about her cough?"

"We put hot compresses on her chest the night before last and that helped."

"Did the bath make it worse?"

"No. In fact, her cough hasn't been nearly as bad since her fever broke." Removing her wide-brimmed straw hat, Dulcie led the way into the cabin that smelled of apples and cinnamon, and motioned him to the bedroom. The bed was bare except for an old quilt that Madeline slept on. "She's slept quite a bit since the fever broke."

"That's a good sign," Dr. Wickberg said quietly. He opened his medical bag and pulled out a stethoscope. After listening to her chest, Dr. Wickberg broke into a genuine smile. "Her chest sounds less congested." He laid his hand on the girl's brow for a few moments. "Her temperature feels normal, too."

Although Dulcie knew she was better, she was relieved to have the doctor confirm it. Dr. Wickberg closed his bag and followed Dulcie out of the bedroom.

"Do you think the fever and cough will come back?" she asked hesitantly.

"It's possible, but I doubt it. You did a good job, Dulcie."

Although his praise warmed her, she knew she wouldn't have been able to take care of Madeline on her own. "Without Rye's help, I wouldn't have been able to do it."

"Is that your hired man?"

She nodded. "Rye Forrester." Her cheeks heated, and she glanced away. "Would you like some apple pie? It's fresh out of the oven."

"You got some coffee to go along with it?"

She smiled. "Of course."

"Then I'll take you up on that offer."

Dr. Wickberg sat down by the table while Dulcie washed her hands then cut the pie and placed a generous piece on a plate. She set it in front of him, along with a cup of coffee. She poured herself some but didn't have any pie.

"Been awhile since I had warm apple pie," the doctor commented, his expression showing his enjoyment.

"It's been awhile since I made it." Dulcie rose and returned to the bedroom to open the trunk at the end of the bed. She lifted out her bag of precious coins and found a silver dollar. Rejoining the doctor, she placed the coin on the table by his plate and folded her hands in her lap. "I appreciate you coming out. And I promise I'll pay the rest of whatever I owe you when I sell the crop."

The doctor smiled kindly. "Whenever you can, Dulcie. The missus wouldn't mind some of your eggs and milk as payment. She used to get them at Coulson's store."

"Mrs. Coulson doesn't like me much." She shrugged, surprised by the pain of her admission. "She's one of those who thinks the apple doesn't fall far from the tree."

Dr. Wickberg glanced down. "I've heard the gossip, Dulcie, and I'm not surprised there are some folks who'd like to see you gone from the area. That's simply human nature. But not everyone feels that way."

Although intrigued that there might be those in town who didn't wish her ill, she had another matter that required her attention more. She wrapped her hands around her coffee cup and stared down into it. "Do you believe my father killed Mr. Carpenter?"

Dr. Wickberg finished his pie. "I wouldn't have thought Frank was capable of killing anyone, but he'd been drinking more since your ma died, and liquor changes folks. I've seen more'n my share of wives beat up by their liquored-up husbands. Once the men sober up, most of them don't even remember what they did."

Dulcie lifted her gaze and leaned forward. "He didn't kill him. He was passed out drunk in our barn."

Dr. Wickberg's eyes widened. "Did you tell anyone?"

"The sheriff. He said I was just protecting Pa, but I wasn't. He was innocent."

"What of the man who swore he saw your father and Lawrence arguing? I believe it was that peddler."

"Virgil Lamont." Even saying his name made Dulcie's insides churn with disgust.

"Why would he lie?"

"I don't know." Dulcie glanced at the doctor, but she couldn't hold his gaze. If she did, he'd see her shame in her eyes. "Pa didn't kill Mr. Carpenter."

"Then what of those folks who hanged him?"

This time Dulcie didn't have to hide her feelings. "They're guilty of murder," she said grimly. The doctor flinched slightly, and her heart skipped a beat. With a trembling voice, she asked, "Were you one of those who lynched him?"

He met her eyes. "No, Dulcie. I wasn't party to your father's death."

Although relieved, she suspected he was hiding something. "But you know who was."

"Your father's gone, Dulcie. Dredging up his unfortunate death isn't going to help anyone."

Disillusioned, she stared at the doctor. "That's what Mrs. Carpenter and her stepson told me. In fact, they insinuated that if I continue to try to prove my father's innocence, something might happen to me." Indignant anger burned in her belly. "But then, what's another innocent life? Those involved in the lynching are murderers, pure and simple."

Dr. Wickberg's expression hardened. "Those people believed they were dispatching justice. It didn't help that Lawrence was well-liked and your father had a reputation as a lazy drunk."

"It doesn't matter what kind of man he was, my father didn't deserve to be hanged."

The doctor laid a calming hand on her shoulder and she shook it off. "You can't change what happened," he said.

"No, I can't. But I can see that those people who lynched Pa are punished."

Dr. Wickberg smiled sadly. "You'll never learn who they were, Dulcie." He finished his coffee and stood. "I'd best get back to town."

She accompanied him outside and watched as he climbed into his buggy and drove off.

Dulcie's vision blurred as she watched him go. She was grateful to Dr. Wickberg for helping Madeline, but he was just like the other townsfolk. So determined to avenge Lawrence Carpenter's death, they wouldn't even consider they'd hanged the wrong person.

When would they realize the real murderer was still out there?

AS tired as Rye was when he and Collie entered the yard, he still noticed the sheets flapping on the line in the noonday breeze. If Dulcie had been able to wash the bedsheets, it was a sign that Madeline was well enough to be out of bed.

At the well, Rye cleaned the grime and sweat from his face and arms. "You need to clean up, too," he told Collie.

"But I didn't do nothin' but lay around and watch you work."

"You caught grasshoppers and played with a snake. Wash up, young man."

With a long-suffering sigh, Collie did as Rye said. Rye had examined the broken blisters on Collie's hand after breakfast and had ordered him to take it easy that day so they'd heal. The boy had argued, but Rye reminded him of his other option—returning to the Gearsons'. Collie had followed his order to rest without any more opposition.

Rye wiped his face and hands dry, then inspected the boy's hands, noting the bandanna didn't appear too dirty. It would last the rest of the day.

The cabin door was open as they approached, and the tantalizing smell of apple pie made Rye's stomach growl. Collie slipped past him to enter first.

"Hi, Collie. Hi, Mr. Rye." Madeline, wearing a clean dress with her hair freshly washed and brushed, sat by the table. Her voice was somewhat hoarse but her face had a healthy color and her eyes were bright, but not with fever.

"Look at you, Miss Madeline," Rye said, grinning. "All better?"

The girl nodded. "Ma said Dr. Wickberg said I was lots better."

Rye turned his attention to Dulcie and blinked in shock. Instead of her usual trousers and baggy shirt, she wore an apron over a gingham blouse tucked into a dark blue skirt. Her chestnut red hair was tied back loosely, leaving wavy tendrils to frame her face, softening her features. Her cheeks were flushed, making her freckles stand out, and her green eyes sparkled.

"You look real purty, Miz McDaniel," Collie said, beating Rye to the compliment.

"Thank you, Collie. After nearly three days in the same clothes, I couldn't stand another minute," she said with a nervous laugh.

The way she kept smoothing her skirt and brushing back her hair, Rye knew she wasn't as comfortable as she'd been in her former trousers. But Rye found her hesitancy endearing, adding another facet to her already complicated nature. He also couldn't help admiring her womanly curves, remembering too well how those curves looked without the clothing hiding them.

"Sit down and dig in," Dulcie said, her voice breathy.

Despite his vow that last night wouldn't be repeated, Rye couldn't keep his eyes off her as he sat down in what was becoming *his* place at the table. Collie sat to his right and Madeline to his left.

"When did Dr. Wickberg come by?" Rye asked, wanting something to take his mind off Dulcie's transformation.

"About an hour ago. He said Madeline will be just fine."

Rye heard a distinct lack of enthusiasm in her voice. Was there something she wasn't saying—something to do with Madeline's health? Or something else? He glanced up to question her, but she gave him a slight shake of her head and looked deliberately at the children.

Dulcie sat down and helped Madeline spoon food on her plate. Rye did the same with Collie, and a memory of himself and his two brothers eating with their parents stole across him. His oldest brother Creede had sat next to him and helped Rye with his food. The picture was so vivid that he could recall every detail of Creede's face. A memory from twenty-five years ago. How did Creede and Slater look now? Would he even recognize them if he passed them on a street?

"Could you pass the peas, Rye?" Dulcie asked, and he knew it wasn't the first time she'd spoken.

"Sorry," he murmured and handed her the bowl of peas.

As they ate the meal Dulcie had fixed, she asked Rye, "How did the cutting go?"

"We have about four acres done. It's all bundled, too."

Her expression lost some of its animation. "There's still forty-five acres to go."

"I'm working as fast as I can," he said, unable to curb his irritation. "If we had a reaper . . ."

"I know you're working hard, and I'm grateful for what you've done. But I don't know if it'll be enough." Her voice was a mixture of gratitude and frustration.

"There's got to be somebody with a reaper who'd be willing to help you out," Rye said.

She shook her head. "Before I started planting, I tried to get some help, but we couldn't pay anyone. And those who knew Pa were of the mind that he should be doing his own planting instead of drinking."

"I don't know much about farming, but couldn't you offer a percentage of the crop as payment for the use of a reaper?"

"I could, but I might not be left with enough to get through the winter and buy more seed for next year's planting." The exasperation and stubbornness in her expression were familiar.

Rye pushed back his empty plate, comfortably full. "You might have to take that chance, Dulcie, or you won't get enough to even make it through the winter."

She pushed her food around. "I really thought I had a chance to make it on my own out here. That I could take care of Madeline and myself without anyone's help." She laughed, but it was with a touch of self-reproach. "I'm such a fool."

"No, you're not, Dulcie. Just because you hire someone to help you doesn't mean they own your farm."

She shuddered and murmured, "No, just me."

Rye looked at her quizzically, certain he hadn't heard her correctly. "What?"

Dulcie shook her head and didn't meet his gaze. "Nothing. You're right." She rose and carried her plate to the pan of hot water. "I'll get the apple pie."

She served the children, then Rye and herself. As Rye savored the pie, he pondered her odd reaction. What had she meant? Was her strange comment related to last night's love-making? He suspected she regretted what they'd done just as he did. However, it didn't stop him from wishing for another night with her.

"Your pie's as good as Ma's was," Collie said, his mouth full.

Dulcie smiled warmly at the boy. "Thank you, Collie. I'm glad to hear that."

Collie licked his upper lip. "Maybe even better. She burned it once. Said she got busy." He frowned thoughtfully. "Pa said it was his fault, but don't know how it was."

Rye suspected Collie's parents were busy together, and when he looked at Dulcie's red cheeks, he knew she was thinking the same thing. Rye cleared his throat. "You know how busy us grown-ups can get."

Dulcie abruptly asked, "Would anyone like more pie?"

"I would, Miz McDaniel," Collie said, then added, "Please."

Dulcie placed another piece on his plate and asked without looking at him, "What about you, Rye?"

"No thanks, Dulcie. I won't be able to move if I have another bite and I'd like to get another acre cut this afternoon."

Since Madeline hadn't finished her first piece, Dulcie carried the pie tin back to the pantry.

Rye helped clear the table and put away the leftover food. Collie and Madeline remained by the table, talking and giggling.

"How're you feeling, honey?" Dulcie asked her daughter.

"Not tired," the girl piped up, obviously knowing what her mother was really asking.

"Are you hot?"

Madeline shook her head, her long hair flying around her head like a carousel. "No." The girl coughed, but it ended quickly. "Wanna play outside."

Dulcie looked at Rye imploringly.

"How about if you and Collie play on the porch?" Rye suggested, then spoke to Dulcie. "It's just as warm out there as it is in here, so she won't catch a chill."

"Would you mind playing with her, Collie?" Dulcie asked.

The boy nodded. Rye reckoned he'd have more fun here with Madeline than sitting and watching him work.

Dulcie wiped her daughter's hands with a damp cloth, then Madeline jumped down from the chair and grabbed Collie's hand. She tugged him to his feet. "C'mon. Let's go outside."

Allowing himself to be led away, Collie didn't appear too dismayed to go with her.

Rye shook his head, chuckling. "I'd best get back to work." He started toward the door, then stopped. "What else did Dr. Wickberg say?"

Dulcie placed her hands in the warm soapy water and began to wash the dishes. "I asked him if he knew who was involved in my father's lynching."

Rye moved closer so the children wouldn't overhear them. "What was his answer?"

She stilled and turned her head to meet his gaze. "He swore he wasn't involved. He never came flat out and said he knew who murdered my father, but I could tell he knows some of them."

"So why wouldn't he tell you?"

"He believes my father killed Mr. Carpenter, so he tried to convince me the townsfolk were only 'dispatching justice.' If I can't get Dr. Wickberg to tell me anything, how can I get anyone else to talk to me?" Bitter frustration welled in her voice. She cleared her throat. "When I was a child, I used to wish for a different father, one who didn't drink or yell or slap Ma or me. Sometimes I used to imagine hitting him back, but I never did. I know Pa wasn't worth much, but he was the only father I had, and I owe him something for that."

Rye ached for Dulcie, for the girl she'd been and the woman she'd become in spite of a son of a bitch for a father. He clenched his hands at his sides, suddenly fearful of the intensity of his emotions. "I understand." He headed to the door, to escape this woman who affected him more deeply than even his wife had.

"Rye," Dulcie called.

He stopped and turned toward her.

"About last night . . ." Her stricken expression made his gut clench. "That wasn't part of our working agreement."

Rye frowned. "I never thought it was."

Her relief bewildered him, but he didn't dare stay in her presence any longer. He might forget all the reasons why it was wrong to kiss her again.

DULCIE finished washing the dishes then checked on the children, who were playing a game with sticks and rocks on the porch. She didn't interrupt them but listened unashamedly from the door.

"No, you can't do that. You have to have both a stick and a rock," Madeline explained in a surprisingly adult tone.

"Oh, okay," Collie said in an easygoing manner.

Dulcie put a hand up to hide her smile. She wondered if she was as bossy as Madeline at that age.

"Will you be staying here for always?" Madeline asked Collie.

"Nah."

Dulcie doubted that Madeline heard the yearning behind the bravado in the boy's voice. For a moment, she wished she could give Collie a home here, but she couldn't even guarantee a home for Madeline. How would she provide for two children?

If Rye stayed, we could do it together.

No, she couldn't even allow herself to think such thoughts. Not after swearing never to depend on a man again.

"Rye wanted to take me back to the Gearsons' yesterday," Collie said. "I think he was mad at himself for what I done to my hand when I was working."

Dulcie's breath caught in her throat. Rye truly cared about Collie . . . and Madeline. His concern for two children not his own puzzled Dulcie, but made her respect him more. If she had known there were men like Rye out there, she wouldn't have been so quick to raise her skirts for the first one who showed an interest in her.

Refusing to ruin the bright day by dwelling on her mistakes, Dulcie went out to the line to retrieve the sheets and make up the bed.

As soon as she finished, Madeline and Collie trooped into the house.

"We're hungry, Ma," Madeline said.

Dulcie spread honey on two thick slices of bread and gave one to each of them. While they ate their snack at the table, Dulcie drank coffee and watched Madeline's eyelids droop.

"Time for a nap," Dulcie said to her daughter.

After only a token resistance, Madeline laid down on the newly made bed and closed her eyes. It wasn't long before the girl was asleep.

Dulcie tiptoed out of the room and joined Collie, who still sat by the table, looking forlorn. "Would you mind helping me pick the cucumbers?"

He jumped to his feet. "No, ma'am. I used to help Ma in the garden."

Glad she'd asked him, Dulcie placed her wide-brimmed hat on her head and grabbed two pails from the porch. Collie took one from her, and, swinging the pails at their sides, she and the boy headed to the garden.

They knelt among the vines, picking cucumbers, Collie's wrapped hand not slowing him down. As they worked, Dulcie's eyes kept returning to the rolled-up scarf around Collie's hand. It looked oddly familiar.

Later, after they carried the two pails of cucumbers into the house, she said, "Maybe we should unwrap your hand and make sure those sores underneath didn't get dirty."

Collie shrugged and held out his hand. Dulcie untied the scarf's knot with shaking fingers. As she unwound it, the sense that she'd seen the bandanna before grew stronger. She shook it out, and her breath stuttered in her throat. It was a regulation scarf from a cavalry unit—the same unit Jerry had belonged to. Rye had never said anything about being in the army, much less knowing her husband.

Maybe he found it or bought it from a soldier.

Dulcie held up the scarf. "Did he tell you where he got this?" she asked Collie, keeping her voice even.

"No."

"Was he a soldier?"

Collie shrugged. "Don't know. He never said nothin' 'bout it."

Dulcie let out a breath she didn't realize she was holding.

He must've bought it from a soldier, or maybe he'd found it. "Let's see how those blisters are faring."

Once she was satisfied the sores weren't dirty and that they were healing fine, she rewrapped the scarf around his hand. Her doubts intensified. Although Rye had told her about his brothers and his wife and child, he was surprisingly closemouthed about what he'd done for the past few years. What if he had been in the army? Maybe he'd known Jerry. But if he had, wouldn't he have told her?

She checked on Madeline and found her sleeping soundly. "Collie, would you mind watching Madeline? I have to run out and ask Rye something. I won't be gone long."

"Okay."

Dulcie went outside and walked swiftly down the path leading to the wheat field. Her toe caught in her hem, nearly tripping her. She'd forgotten what a bother skirts were when a person was in a hurry. Muttering some unladylike phrases, she hiked up her skirt hem to her knees and continued on.

Flossie and Smoke grazed contentedly in the pasture and Dulcie paused to scrutinize Smoke's coat, to see if the mare had a cavalry brand on her. There was a brand, but it wasn't the U.S. Cavalry.

Feeling foolish, Dulcie almost turned back to the cabin. However, as she recalled what Rye had told her about his life, she thought again about the large gap he hadn't explained. Maybe he'd simply drifted, working as a hired hand at various places. Yet that didn't seem right either. Her gut and heart told her there was more to Rye Forrester than met the eye.

Taking a deep breath, Dulcie continued onward to the field but slowed to a more ladylike pace. Arriving at the edge of the field, she spotted Rye's shirt hanging from a tree branch. Her gaze found him kneeling on the ground with his bare back toward her. She stopped and took guilty pleasure in admiring his broad shoulders and smooth back that tapered to a trim waist. She hadn't been able to touch that back because he'd kept his shirt on the entire time they'd made love. Unease flittered through her once more—why hadn't he removed his shirt?

She squinted to scrutinize his back and found a mark on

his shoulder. Feeling like she should know what it was, she drew closer to see it more clearly. She didn't call out as she walked toward him, intent on examining the scar.

Recognition struck her like a blow, and she reeled from the knowledge.

No, I don't believe it.

Suddenly Rye came to his feet, turning to face her. "Dulcie, what're you doing here?"

"I-I came to see you," she replied, wishing with all her heart she hadn't recognized the mark. "That brand. You're a d-deserter."

Rye's face paled beneath his dark tan and he opened his mouth but nothing came out.

"I saw the scarf on Collie's hand. Is it yours?" Dulcie demanded.

Rye took a deep breath and nodded.

"Why didn't you tell me?" Dulcie's voice rose with outrage despite her attempt to remain calm. "I told you about my husband and how he was in the army. Why did you lie to me?"

He lifted his head, and his eyes were filled with a world of hurt. "I didn't lie. I just didn't tell you the whole truth."

"Tell me now! And it better be the *whole* truth this time."

"I am a deserter, and I did know your husband." He paused. Dulcie thought she saw a gleam of moisture in his eyes, but it must have been a trick of the light. "We used to drink together."

Rage and indignation filled Dulcie. She slapped Rye's cheek. "You son of a bitch. You knew how my husband cheated on me with all those saloon whores. You must've had quite a laugh over Dulcie McDaniel, who couldn't even keep her own husband satisfied in their bed."

He lifted his hands, palms out. "No, I swear it wasn't like that."

She wanted to believe him, wanted to with all her heart. She wanted Rye to be different than the others. But he wasn't. He'd gotten what he wanted, which was in her drawers. It was just that he'd been more underhanded than Jerry and Virgil Lamont.

"I want you off my land," she ordered, her voice as frozen as her insides.

"What about the crops?"

"I'd rather have them rot than have a liar and a deserter staying under my roof."

Rye flinched, and his face lost all expression. He spun around and strode to the tree that held his shirt. He didn't stop to put it on, but kept marching without looking back.

Dulcie gritted her teeth to hold back the sob that climbed up her throat. She'd been so stupid, believing that someone would work for merely room and board. Had he simply been amusing himself by seducing his former drinking buddy's wife? Had he found her as wanting in bed as her husband had?

Damn him to hell.

NINETEEN

RYE'S heart thundered in his chest, the beat keeping time with his thudding footsteps. She hadn't even given him a chance to explain.

Explain what? That her husband and I were supposed to be on guard duty that night instead of drinking? That I dared Jerry to walk the edge of a saloon roof? That he and I were so drunk that we didn't even notice the rotting wood?

It was a stupid, senseless death that never would have happened if Rye hadn't been drinking. Rye had lost everything but his life that night—his excellent army record, his rank, and his self-respect. His branding followed three months in the stockade before he was allowed to walk out of the fort with only the clothes on his back and an old Navy Colt revolver in his belt.

While serving his time he'd made a vow never to drink again, and despite the constant temptation, he remained true to that vow. But at this moment, if there was a bottle of whiskey in front of him, he wouldn't think twice about breaking that promise.

As he passed Smoke in the pasture, he whistled. The mare trotted up to the corral, beating Rye to the barn. As Rye crammed his things into his saddlebag, he remembered his bedroll was in the cabin's loft.

Anger still pounded through him as he strode to the house, but he halted at the sight of Collie sleeping in one of the rocking chairs. Rye's fury disappeared and his shoulders sagged. He leaned against the doorframe and removed his hat, scrubbing a hand through his damp hair.

He'd have to explain to the boy why he had to return to the Gearsons' and why he'd never see Rye again. The kid didn't deserve to be tossed aside like an old boot. Why had Rye ever befriended Collie? He knew he couldn't stay in Locust, yet he'd toyed with the boy's affections and allowed himself to get close to the kid.

He turned his head and spotted Madeline sleeping on the bed. His heart dropped into his gut. He'd spent hours by the girl's side, soothing and comforting her during her illness. Maybe for a few minutes he'd even allowed himself to think of her as his own daughter.

And now, because he'd been a coward—afraid to tell Dulcie the truth in the beginning—he'd lost any chance of starting fresh. The possibility of remaining here with Dulcie, Madeline, and Collie was gone, and he hadn't even known how much he'd wanted this family. Not until this very moment.

He felt Dulcie's presence and turned to see her running across the yard, her skirt held in tight-fisted hands. She fairly flew up the steps and halted just outside the door. No sign of the Dulcie he'd known last night remained.

"I assume you're just picking up your things," she said coldly.

He nodded, not knowing how to deal with her anger and sense of betrayal while his own guilt ate at his insides.

Her gaze skipped past him to Collie, and her expression thawed, becoming regretful. "I'm sorry he got involved in all this."

"I am, too."

She clenched her teeth and her features became icy once more. "Get out of here, Rye. I don't want to see you ever again."

His conscience didn't allow him to argue. Instead, he woke Collie. "We're leaving."

The boy blinked the sleep away. "What?"

"Go up to the loft and get your things. We're going back to town now," Rye said.

"You said—"

"I don't care what I said," he cut in, forcing sharpness into his tone. "We have to leave now."

Collie's gaze flicked to Dulcie then back to Rye. He obviously sensed the angry undercurrents that ran between them. He pressed his lips together and nodded.

Rye followed the boy up to the loft. He grabbed his bedroll then waited for Collie to pack his few belongings in the worn bag he'd brought with him from the Gearsons'. They climbed down the ladder and Dulcie was no longer where she'd been. As Rye guided Collie out of the cabin with a hand on his shoulder, he saw Dulcie sitting ramrod straight on the edge of the bed by her sleeping daughter. She didn't even look up as they left.

"Did I do something bad?" Collie asked, his voice trembling.

Rye's conscience stabbed him and he stopped in the middle of the yard to face the boy. He placed his hands on Collie's shoulders. "No, Collie. Mrs. McDaniel is mad at me, not you."

"Did you do something bad?" The boy's expression was a mixture of apprehension and surprise.

Rye owed Collie the truth. "I lied about something important. Mrs. McDaniel just found out, and she's very angry with me."

Collie glanced down at his wrapped hand. "Did it have something to do with your scarf?"

Startled by his perceptiveness, Rye hunkered down in front of the boy. "It's from the cavalry unit I was in. Mrs. McDaniel's husband was in the same unit. I didn't tell her I'd known him." *And I still haven't told her that I caused his death.*

"If I hadn't hurt my hand, she wouldn't have known." Collie's tone vibrated with self-reproach.

"No. It's not your fault. It had nothing to do with you,

Collie." Rye licked his dry lips. "If it were up to me, I'd stay here and get the Gearsons to let you stay here, too. But I have to move on now."

Collie looked like he was going to cry but valiantly held the tears in check. He nodded. "I understand."

Rye believed he actually did. He gave the boy's arm a quick squeeze then straightened and headed to the corral. Less than five minutes later, he mounted Smoke and pulled Collie up behind him.

Rye took a precious minute to study the silent cabin. At least he'd been able to fix it up for Dulcie and her daughter—they'd be snug and dry this winter. He stared at the window into the bedroom, hoping to see a sign of Dulcie behind the glass, but she remained out of sight.

Feeling as if the stockade door was slamming behind him again, Rye touched his heels to Smoke's flanks and headed to Locust.

DULCIE eased the curtain back in place as Rye and Collie disappeared down the road. She fought the tears that threatened to spill over and won the battle. However, her throat felt raw and scratchy from restraining her bitter disappointment.

How had she been so wrong about Rye? She'd been so careful in the beginning, watching and waiting for him to make a mistake, but he'd been so hardworking and unceasingly polite. She thought he'd even come to respect her. Instead, he'd simply been biding his time to get what all men wanted from a woman, and she'd been foolish enough to give it to him.

Her gaze went to the trunk. It had been days since she'd pulled out the whiskey bottle and, more shocking, she hadn't even missed it. Especially after making love with Rye.

Self-disgust curdled in her belly.

Madeline made a soft noise in her sleep, and Dulcie studied her daughter's innocent face. She'd been so close to losing her. . . . If she had, Dulcie knew nothing, especially not whiskey, would be able to fill the emptiness.

Steeling herself against the liquor's temptation, she concentrated on how she could provide for her daughter. With the garden, they'd have plenty of preserved vegetables and fruit until next year. Yet, without money, she wouldn't have meat or the dry goods they'd need.

Most of the ripe wheat still stood in the field. Rye's suggestion to get someone with a reaper to cut it made sense. However, the thought of going into town and trying to find someone made her palms sweat.

Her gaze again settled on Madeline, and Dulcie's resolve strengthened. She could do it. She had to do it. For Madeline's sake.

LEAVING Collie at the Gearsons' proved more difficult than Rye anticipated. If the boy had carried on, it might have been easier. Instead, Collie remained mute and rigid, letting nothing of how he felt show in his face.

Mrs. Gearson had the two youngest children at home while the older ones were in school.

"Go on up and put your things away," she ordered Collie without any sign that he'd even been gone.

"Yes, ma'am." The lad didn't look back when he trudged into the house.

"What happened to his hand?" Mrs. Gearson asked, more out of curiosity than concern.

"A couple of blisters broke. Didn't want them getting infected," Rye replied, fidgeting in the saddle. "He's a good kid. Hard worker."

Mrs. Gearson nodded. "When it's something he wants to do, he can work." She narrowed her gaze. "You movin' on then?"

"In a day or two."

"Surprised you didn't stay to help Pollard's daughter with the crop."

He looked past her, into the dim interior of the house where Collie had vanished. "Time to be leaving." He focused on her again. "Take care of him."

"No need to fret about him. We'll give him a place to sleep, clothes on his back, and food for his belly. It's our Christian duty."

He noticed she didn't mention anything about love or affection. Again, he was struck by the wrongness of leaving Collie with this family.

"If someone else would be willing to take him, would you let him go?" he asked.

She narrowed her eyes. "Depends on who it was. If it's a drifter like yourself, I wouldn't. I owe his folks a decent place for him to be raised."

Rye suspected Collie's parents would also want their son to be loved. But Mrs. Gearson was right. Collie deserved to know where he'd be sleeping every night. He took a deep breath to ease the burning in his chest. "I'd best find a place to stay tonight."

She returned to the house as Rye rode away. He blanked his mind, tried not to think of Collie or Dulcie or Madeline. He stopped at the livery and arranged for a place for Smoke as well as permission to sleep there himself. With very little money left, Rye couldn't afford both a hotel room and a meal.

As Rye cleaned up in the livery using a pail of water, the brawny liveryman, Burt, kept him company.

"I seen you in town before," Burt commented in between puffs from his rolled smoke.

"I've been working at the Pollard place," Rye said.

"For Dulcie?"

Rye paused to glance at the man. "You know her?"

Burt shrugged. "Sure. She grew up here. Lots of folks know her. She was kind of a wild filly."

"What do you mean?"

The man held up his beefy hands with fingers stained with tobacco and dirt. "Nothin'. Only that you could tell she was lookin' for a way outta Locust. Found one, too, with some soldier boy passin' through."

Burt's voice insinuated he knew something more.

"A lot of girls want to get hitched and get their own home," Rye commented.

"But not all of them get knocked up before they stand in front of the preacher."

Knowing Jerry, Rye shouldn't have been surprised. However, the Dulcie he knew was nothing like that girl Burt was telling him about. At least, she hadn't been when he first met her. Another possibility occurred to him—maybe she had been intending to trap him all along.

It would explain her forwardness. If she caught him, she'd have a man to take care of the farm. Yet, if that was her intention in the beginning, why did she wear men's clothing that covered her figure? No, he didn't believe it. Dulcie wasn't a woman to use herself to gain favor.

"When she come back this spring with that peddler fellah, I could see they knew each other pretty well, too, if you get my meanin'." Burt winked at him.

Rye's hand curled into a fist, but he managed to curb his impulse. "No, I don't," he said coldly.

Burt's lewd expression faltered and he covered it with a shrug. "Well, Lamont is back, so it'll be interestin' to see what happens."

It was Lamont who'd told the sheriff he'd seen Pollard arguing with Carpenter when Dulcie said her father was passed out drunk in their barn.

If Burt was right about Dulcie and Lamont, it would explain why she'd been so reluctant to tell Rye about him. Still, if she wanted to clear her father's name, she'd have to face Lamont at some point.

"You must've known her father then," Rye said, keeping his voice casual.

Burt nodded. "I knew him. Always a drinker but got worse the last year or so, after the missus died. Seen it happen more than once. A man loses his woman and crawls into a bottle, like he's goin' to find her there."

Rye flinched inwardly at the man's too-accurate words. "From what I heard, he was a murderer, too," he said, keeping his tone bland.

Burt shifted, and his gaze turned downward. "That's what everyone said."

Rye faced him. "You didn't believe he was?"

"He used to do some muckin' out in here so he could buy his whiskey. He had a temper, but I never seen him hit no one."

"Why didn't you speak up?"

Burt dropped the end of his smoke and ground it under his heel. "Wouldn't have made no difference. Everyone figgered he killed Carpenter."

"Were you one of those who put a noose around his neck?"

Burt swallowed and shook his head. "No, but I didn't do nothin' to stop them that did neither."

"Do you know those who were involved in the lynching?"

"Don't matter anymore. Frank's gone."

"It matters to Dulcie," Rye said quietly.

The big man sighed. "Yeah, I reckon it does." He scratched his whiskers. "Y'hear that the Carpenters is leavin' town?"

Startled, Rye shook his head.

"Heard tell they're movin' to Denver. Too many bad memories here, I s'pose." Burt wandered off.

Rye absently tucked the tails of his shirt in his pants. He couldn't really blame Carpenter's widow and stepson for leaving. If he was in their place, he might do the same.

Adjusting his hat, he considered what to do next. If he wanted to find the instigators behind Pollard's lynching, he'd have to go where men's talk tended to be careless.

Rye strode across the street and entered the saloon. He walked directly to the bar and ordered coffee and a meal. After the bartender handed him the cup of coffee, Rye went to an empty table at the back to wait for his food. As he sipped the hot bitter sludge, he looked around. About a dozen men sat around in groups of twos and threes, talking in low voices punctuated by occasional bellows of laughter or a loud belch. The stink of stale liquor, dirty sawdust, and unwashed bodies nearly undid Rye's conviction to learn the truth. But then he remembered the betrayal in Dulcie's face and his resolve strengthened. After he'd hurt her so badly, he wanted—*needed*—to do this for her.

Fifteen minutes after he sat down, a plump woman wearing a stained apron brought out a plate of overcooked steak, watery potatoes and gravy, and some beans that looked like they'd been boiled to mush. He ate the bland food, trying not to remember the meal he'd eaten earlier that day with Dulcie and the children.

When Rye was done eating, he carried his plate to the bar and got a refill for his coffee. He remained standing by the bar, trying not to notice how the lamplight turned the whiskey bottles on the shelf a rich amber color, or how the smell got into him, searching for that familiar place that couldn't deny the whiskey.

Rye's hands trembled as he fought the restless urge to grab one of those brown bottles and lift it to his mouth. He licked his lips and could almost taste the sharp burn, the promise of oblivion.

No!

It wouldn't win. Rye had paid a steep price for his weakness. He had no intention of paying again.

He finished his coffee, not even noticing the caustic taste. "More," he said to the bartender.

The man shook his head, obviously not liking to serve coffee when he had watered-down whiskey and piss-weak beer to serve his customers. But he returned from the back room with the pot and sloshed more coffee into Rye's cup. Rye gave him a nod.

"You got somethin' against liquor?" the bartender asked.

Rye shrugged. "Nope. As long as I'm not drinking it."

The man grunted and returned the coffeepot to the back.

"Quiet tonight," Rye commented.

The bartender shrugged. "Usual. Come Saturday night things liven up."

"Bet it was pretty lively the night of the hangin'," Rye commented.

"You around then?"

"Heard about it. Frontier justice at its best."

"Hell, the circuit judge don't come by but every two, three months. No reason to waste good food on a murderer since he was gonna hang anyhow."

The bartender's callous disregard for a man's life made Rye's stomach churn and the coffee burned from the inside out.

Rye forced himself to lean forward and smile conspiratorially. "You help take care of the killer?"

The bartender glanced around warily. "It weren't just one person."

Rye guffawed. "Well, I figured that." He turned and leaned against the bar, making a show of looking at every man in the saloon. "I'll bet most of these fellahs helped out justice."

"Maybe. And maybe most of the town was involved, too."

Rye's mouth grew dry, and he kept his back to the bartender. "That so? That'd make it mighty difficult to arrest anyone."

The bartender chuckled. "Who says the sheriff wasn't a part of it, too?"

Rye turned around slowly. Although the bartender was grinning, Rye suspected he wasn't joking. No wonder Dulcie had never learned anything. Everybody protected everybody else with a conspiracy of silence. He felt sick and empty, like right after Slater had been taken away by his new parents.

A suited man about Rye's age entered the saloon. He removed his narrow-brimmed derby hat and brushed some dust from its crown as he made his way to the bar.

"I heard you were back, Lamont," the bartender said.

"Word gets around fast," the man said. He smiled, revealing a gold tooth.

So this was the peddler Dulcie might have— If Rye finished the thought, he'd wind up punching the bastard. Instead, he had to find out why the man had lied about Dulcie's father. He pasted on a smile and turned to the peddler, hating his too-handsome face and perfectly coiffed hair.

"So you're the peddler I've heard about," Rye began.

Lamont turned to him with a salesman's smile. "My reputation precedes me."

Rye shrugged. "I heard you were the one who got a man hanged."

Lamont's expression faltered. "That man was a murderer."

"I heard he was nowhere near Carpenter when the man was murdered."

The peddler straightened his lapels and glared at Rye. "I only told the sheriff what I saw."

Rye calmed himself, not wanting to scare the man off. "Then I guess he got what he had coming."

Lamont visibly relaxed. "I don't think we've met. Virgil Lamont, peddler of the ordinary and extraordinary."

Rye restrained a humorless laugh. "Rye Forrester, drifter."

Lamont narrowed his eyes. "Forrester, you say?"

Rye nodded warily.

"Any relation to the family down Robles way?"

Rye's breath stuttered. "I don't know. I have two brothers, but I haven't seen them in a long time. Slater and Creede."

"Creede. That was his name, and his lovely wife Laurel."

The breath left Rye's lungs. Was this Creede Forrester his long-lost brother? He drew in a shaky breath and forced nonchalance. "Near Robles, you said?"

The peddler nodded. "Cotton farmer. I heard his wife was from some city out east. Can't imagine why she chose to live in the middle of nowhere with a farmer."

"Maybe because she loves her husband," Rye said, his thoughts still caught up in maybe finding his brother after all these years.

Lamont tilted his head and studied Rye like he was some odd insect. "Don't you know love is just like those goods in my wagon? It can be bought and sold for the right price."

Rye smiled grimly. "That's not love, Lamont. That's rutting."

Lamont laughed as if Rye just told a joke. "Call it what you will, Forrester, and I'll do the same."

Suddenly feeling overwhelmed by the day's events as well as the possibility that his brother could be only a few days' ride away, Rye pushed away from the bar.

"Leaving so soon?" Lamont asked.

"Long day. Gonna be around for a while?"

Lamont nodded. "I'll be peddling my wares here for a few days."

Rye smiled a predator's smile. "I'm sure we'll run into each other again."

Rye felt Lamont's narrow-eyed gaze on his back as he left the saloon. Once outside, he took a deep cleansing breath to ease his trembling. Part of him wanted to get on Smoke and ride to Robles. If he rode hard, he could be there tomorrow night. To find one of his brothers was a dream he'd long ago let die. Only it had been smoldering, not dead, and the peddler had fanned that dream back to life.

But he owed Dulcie. He'd taken away Dulcie's husband and Madeline's father, as well as their provider. Now all she had was a farm and no way to do the work needed to make a living on it.

He refused to dwell on the most important reason to stay in Locust—his heart.

$\mathcal{T}$WENTY

ALTHOUGH she was fairly certain Madeline was well on her way to recovery, Dulcie still didn't like taking her into town. Fortunately it was only a few miles, and the sun shone bright, warming the air.

As the mule plodded along, Dulcie tried to keep her daughter talking. It was better to answer a slew of questions than think about what lay ahead or to dwell on Rye. She hoped he'd left town, yet if that were so, she mourned ever seeing him again.

"Where do clouds come from, Ma?" Madeline asked, her head tipped back to look at the sky.

Dulcie glanced up at the fluffy white cloud lazily floating across the wide blue sky. "My ma used to tell me God made clouds. When He's happy He makes ones like that. When He's angry, He makes them dark and scary."

The girl pointed at some wispy clouds. "What about those? When does He make them?"

Dulcie studied the horsetail-shaped clouds. "He makes those when He's smiling," she replied quietly.

"So God's smiling and happy today."

"I suppose so, honey."

Madeline wriggled closer to Dulcie. "I'll be happy, too, if we see Collie and Mr. Rye."

Dulcie had been trying hard not to think of them, yet she knew how much her daughter adored both. "We might see Collie since he lives in town, but Mr. Rye was leaving."

"He didn't even say bye."

Dulcie hadn't given Rye much choice when she'd ordered him off her land, but it would've hurt Madeline more if he had said good-bye.

"Remember when your pa had to leave, and he didn't have time to say good-bye?"

"But Mr. Rye's lots nicer than Pa. Pa didn't really care 'bout me."

Dulcie nearly choked on the lump in her throat. Even his young daughter had known what a poor excuse for a father Jerry had been. And that was the man Dulcie had given herself to—a man even a four-year-old knew was no good. Yet she couldn't regret that foolish part of her past. If she hadn't met Jerry, Madeline wouldn't have been born.

"If Mr. Rye stayed in town, you might get to see him again." Dulcie knew she shouldn't get her daughter's hopes up, but she hated seeing Madeline so unhappy.

Locust came into sight, reminding Dulcie why they'd made the trip. As much as she dreaded the process of finding someone to cut her wheat, Dulcie had to try. She drew the plodding mule to a stop in front of Coulson's mercantile and hoped Wendell was working rather than his shrewish wife. After climbing down from the wagon, she lifted Madeline down beside her. The girl took Dulcie's hand without prompting.

Taking a deep breath and ignoring the looks sent her way, Dulcie led Madeline into the store. At the sight of Mr. Coulson behind the counter, she drew a sigh of relief. He was talking to a suited man with his back toward her. A sense of familiarity swept through her as she tried to determine who he was.

Coulson caught sight of her and smiled. "Mrs. McDaniel, you have any eggs or butter for me today?"

"No, I'm afra—"

The man turned around, shocking her into silence.

"You know Virgil Lamont, the peddler, don't you?"

She barely heard Coulson's question over the roaring in her ears.

"Madeline, how are you?" Lamont greeted her daughter as if they were long-lost relatives.

Madeline hid her face in Dulcie's skirts.

"Shy, isn't she?" Lamont had the guts to comment. He stepped closer to Dulcie, who barely managed to remain in place. "Mrs. McDaniel, it's a pleasure to see you again."

Neither his oily undertone nor his lewd scrutiny was lost on Dulcie. She shivered, but regained her composure. "Mr. Lamont. I'd say it was a pleasure, but the last time you were here, you got my father killed."

"From what you told me about him, it was no loss."

Dulcie reacted without thought, but Lamont caught her wrist before her hand landed on his cheek. "I see your temper hasn't improved overly much."

She trembled with rage. "Let go."

He held her for a second longer then abruptly released her. Until this moment, she hadn't realized how much she hated him. Yet she hated herself, too, for letting him do what he'd done to her.

"Why did you lie to the sheriff about seeing my father with Mr. Carpenter?" she asked, hoping he didn't notice the tremor in her voice.

"Why would I lie? I didn't know your father, except for what you told me about him."

Dulcie's face heated with guilt. She'd been lonely, and it had been too easy to talk after Lamont had taken her, with night hiding her sin. "He might not have been a good father, but he wasn't a murderer either."

He shrugged. "You have to admit your life is better without him."

Her stomach pitched and she swallowed back the bile that rose in her gorge. Biting back her rage, she spoke to Madeline. "Why don't you go look at the candy? Mr. Coulson will show you what he has."

The girl's gaze jumped from Dulcie to Lamont and back, then she walked to the front counter. Once Madeline and

Coulson were talking, Dulcie turned back to the peddler and spoke in a low voice. "You never cared for me, which means you lied for someone else."

His expression faltered for a moment, confirming Dulcie's theory. However, she didn't know who he would've lied for, or why. Or maybe it was as simple as Lamont killing Carpenter himself and using her father as the scapegoat, since he knew the man from Dulcie's description. Which meant she was in part responsible for her father's death.

All thoughts of finding someone with a reaper fled. The only thing that mattered was getting away from Lamont. She joined her daughter, who was chomping on a piece of licorice. "What do I owe you, Mr. Coulson?"

"Don't worry about it, Mrs. McDaniel."

"Thank you," she said with heartfelt gratitude.

She turned to leave with Madeline's hand in hers. Lamont hurried ahead of her to open the door. Dulcie paused, not wanting to accept anything from him, even the small courtesy. But she didn't want to make a scene, so she stepped through without acknowledging him.

Before she could lift Madeline back into the wagon, Lamont snapped the girl up and onto the seat. Fortunately, it was so fast Madeline didn't have time to be startled. Dulcie refused to thank him and moved around to the other side of the wagon. Lamont beat her there and stood leaning against the wagon's side.

"You used to be a lot friendlier," he said.

Her face hot, Dulcie glanced around to see if anyone was within earshot. Nobody was near, except Madeline. She kept her voice down. "I didn't have a choice then."

Leering, he leaned nearer. "Sure you did. I still remember you begging for more."

Dulcie burned with shame, yet shook with suppressed rage. She crossed her arms to keep from hitting him. "You used me."

"You didn't complain too much."

"I only did it because if I hadn't you would've left Madeline and me behind," she said in a hoarse voice.

He shrugged. "You wanted something from me, and you had to pay my price. It was a business transaction."

She hated herself because he was right and she'd willingly gone to his bed all those nights. Being a wife or working in a saloon were the only jobs she was fit for after Jerry died. Sleeping with Lamont to get back to Texas hadn't seemed too bad a bargain at the time.

"Excuse me. I have to go now," she said through stiff lips.

"What do you say to one more night, for old times' sake?" Lamont asked, his voice low and obscenely intimate.

"You don't have anything I want this time." She tried to push him aside, but he remained immovable.

"My silence."

She froze and met his smug expression.

"I'll come by your place tonight," he said.

Rage vibrated through her. "I have a shotgun."

"If you use it, you'll never learn who really killed Carpenter."

Her father was dead. Nothing would bring him back, but the way he'd died wasn't right. The real murderer remained out there, and for all she knew, it could be Lamont. However, if she let Lamont into her bed tonight, she'd lose every ounce of self-respect she managed to regain. "What if I refuse to let you in?"

He shrugged his shoulders. "Then I'll let it be known what you did to get back here."

"I'll call you a liar."

Lamont chuckled. "Even if you do, who's to say folks won't believe me instead of you? Besides, my reputation won't be harmed, but yours . . ." He shook his head, his meaning clear.

"If I agree, will you tell me who killed Carpenter?" she asked.

"Maybe."

His smile, which she used to think was roguish, disgusted her now. As did his too-handsome features. Rye's rugged features were infinitely more appealing.

"You need some help, Mrs. McDaniel?"

A voice startled Dulcie, and she turned to Rye standing on the boardwalk behind them, as if he'd materialized from her thoughts. Her heart sped up and her knees trembled. "Uh, no. I'm fine."

"Really? It looked like this man was bothering you."

Although Rye's voice was casual, the cold look in his eyes told her he was angry. However, she didn't know if the emotion was aimed at her or Lamont.

"This isn't any of your concern, Forrester," Lamont said.

Dulcie's heart dropped into her belly. They knew one another.

"I think that's up to the lady," Rye said.

Dulcie looked back at Lamont, whose expression reminded her of his threat. If Rye didn't know about them yet, he soon would, as would the rest of the town, if she didn't agree to Lamont's demand. "Virgil Lamont and I are old friends," she managed to say without throwing up.

The disappointment in Rye's face was too hurtful to see and she dropped her gaze.

"If you say so," Rye said coolly. He turned his attention to Madeline, who was staring at Rye like he was one of those knights come to save the damsel. "Good morning, Miss Madeline."

The girl's lower lip thrust out. "You didn't say bye."

Rye walked to her side of the wagon. "You were sleeping and I didn't want to wake you up."

Madeline stomped her foot on the wagon floor. "I thought you were my friend."

"I am." He swept his hat off and held it against his heart. His wavy hair lay flat, which Dulcie found more attractive than Lamont's stiffly pomaded hair. "I'm sorry for leaving without saying good-bye, Miss Madeline," he said to the girl.

She stood up in the box and leaned toward him. He caught her as Madeline wrapped her arms around his neck. She whispered something to Rye that Dulcie couldn't hear, but she did hear what he said in reply.

"I'll miss you, too, sweetheart." Then he kissed her cheek and settled her back onto the wagon seat.

Dulcie cleared her full throat. How had she believed Rye was anything like Virgil Lamont? Rye hadn't pretended his affection for Madeline. Did that mean he hadn't faked his feelings for her, too? Not that he spoke of love, but all he'd done bespoke of fondness and consideration.

So why hadn't he told her he'd known Jerry?

Unable to remain in either man's presence for a moment longer, she pressed Lamont aside and climbed into the wagon. She took the reins in her hand and clicked her tongue to get Jack moving.

As they rolled away slowly, Dulcie heard Lamont call after her, "I'll be by around six for supper."

Afraid to see Rye's reaction, Dulcie didn't look back.

THE knowledge that the peddler was going over to Dulcie's that evening ate at Rye. If what Burt said was true, Dulcie, Madeline, and Lamont had traveled together to Locust, spending long days and nights in each other's company. Rye tried to tell himself he didn't care what had happened between them and what might happen again tonight. It didn't work.

What about Madeline? She'd looked frightened of Lamont. Had he hurt her? If he ever laid a hand on her, Rye would tear the man apart. But then, he wouldn't be around to protect her. The realization left a bitter taste in his mouth.

Why had Dulcie invited the man whose lie had led to her father's lynching to supper? Was she hoping to learn the truth? In his mind's eye, he saw Dulcie and the suave peddler lying in bed and Dulcie asking him questions in between kissing and touching him. The picture brought red-hot fury and seething jealousy.

After Rye calmed down, he went in search of Lamont and found him on the edge of town with his wagon, surrounded by a dozen people checking out his wares and making their purchases. Rye sidled in beside another man to look at the knives, but his attention was on Lamont's voice as he extolled the virtues of a new kettle.

There was no question the man was a slick talker. Had Dulcie been swayed by his fancy words?

The crowd tapered off until only Rye remained.

"See anything you'd like?" Lamont asked.

"A lot of things, but the pockets are empty," Rye said, forcing a friendly smile.

Lamont, knowing he wouldn't get any money from Rye, began to repack the items he'd displayed to the small crowd.

"So you know Mrs. McDaniel and her daughter?" Rye asked.

"Gave them a ride back to Texas after she lost her husband. Poor woman. All alone with a child to support."

So Burt wasn't making up a story. "Her father was here."

Lamont finished wrapping up a glass lamp. "I know. She told me about him. Said he was a drunk."

"But not a killer." Rye paused. "You didn't see her father arguing with Carpenter, did you?"

"I told the sheriff I did."

Rye smiled coldly. "You lied."

Lamont dusted his hands off and smiled just as frigidly. "Prove it."

The man as good as admitted he didn't see Pollard with Carpenter the day of the murder, but Lamont was a slippery bastard. "You see everything as something to buy or sell."

"I'm a peddler by trade, Forrester. Buy and sell is what I do."

"What about your word? You ever sell that?"

"I don't know what you mean."

Rye grinned without warmth. "Sure you do. Lies can be bought and sold, and I bet you'd be a good one to sell them."

"You're grasping at straws, Forrester."

"Do you know Carpenter's widow and son?"

"As well as I know any of the folks around here," Lamont replied without hesitation. "Surely you don't think upstanding folks like them would pay me to lie?" His eyes glittered with humor.

Rye had hoped Lamont might show his hand, but the man had ice water in his veins. He managed a nonchalant shrug. "Mrs. McDaniel seemed pretty convincing when she told me her father was innocent."

"Mrs. McDaniel has a way of making men do things."

Rye gnashed his teeth at the man's underhanded meaning. He hated to believe Dulcie had lain with him, but his gut was telling him otherwise. Still, knowing Dulcie, she must've had a damned good reason.

"I wouldn't know," Rye said coolly. "Good day, Lamont."

Rye turned and strode back to the heart of town. His mind raced as he tried to unravel the tangled web. What if her father *had* committed the murder, and Dulcie was trying to clear his name for her own peace of mind?

No. He was allowing Lamont to make him doubt Dulcie. Her obvious love for her daughter and her desperation to provide for Madeline without asking for help told him far more than Lamont's smooth words.

Rye found a chair on the boardwalk where he could see most of the town. He'd keep an eye on Lamont and see what he was up to. Putting a booted foot against a post, he crossed his other ankle over it and rocked back on his chair.

Ten minutes later, Lamont walked into town from the edge where his wagon was parked. At the door of the saloon, Lamont stopped and turned to look directly at Rye. He smiled and tipped his hat. Rye touched the brim of his own hat, and his smile was as artificial as Lamont's.

The sun moved to its zenith and started its downward slide. A boy peeked out of the alley not far from Rye. He recognized the shaggy dark hair immediately. "C'mon out, Collie."

His hands stuck in his overall pockets, Collie trudged over to Rye. "You said you was leavin'." There was accusation in the boy's tone and belligerent expression.

"I am, but I have something to do first," Rye said. He surveyed the boy, glad to see he didn't sport any new bruises. "How was your first night back at the Gearsons'?"

Collie shrugged and sank to a cross-legged position beside Rye's chair. "It was okay. The food ain't as good as Mrs. McDaniel's though."

Rye smiled. "Yeah, I know what you mean. How's your hand?"

Collie held out his still-wrapped hand. "You wanna look at it?"

Rye leaned forward and unwrapped the bandanna. He held the scarf up for a moment, remembering Dulcie's anger and wishing he'd told her the truth when he'd first met her. But he'd been scared, scared that she wouldn't allow him to work off his debt . . . and guilt.

He examined the sores on the boy's hand and was pleased to see they were well on their way to healing. "You don't have to wear this anymore."

"Can I have it?" Collie asked, pointing to the bandanna.

"Why?"

Collie lifted one shoulder. "I kinda like it."

It was also something for the boy to remember him by. Rye understood too well how a stranger's kindness to an orphan would be recalled years later. He folded the scarf and handed it to Collie. "Have Mrs. Gearson wash it."

"I'll wash it."

In other words, Collie was afraid the woman would give it to one of her own rather than back to him. Rye cleared his throat. "That'd be fine, too."

For a long time, they sat in silence, with Collie on the boardwalk by Rye's chair. Rye had never known the boy to remain still for so long, and it bothered him. Yet he liked his company, even if they didn't talk.

"I seen Mrs. McDaniel and Maddie," Collie said some minutes later. "Seen that peddler with them, too."

"You don't like him?"

"He's not very nice."

"Did he do something to you?"

"Called me a thief and told me to stay away from his wagon."

"When was this?"

"Last time he was here. I didn't go by his stupid wagon anymore, but I watched him. He never knew I was there," he said proudly.

"So you saw what he did and where he went?" Rye asked, trying to tamp down his excitement.

Collie nodded. "Mostly."

"You know he told people he saw Mrs. McDaniel's father fighting with Mr. Carpenter. Did you see that, too?"

Collie fiddled with the cavalry scarf. "No. And I never figgered how he did."

"What do you mean?"

Collie lifted his head, and his brows were furrowed. "That day Mr. Carpenter was killed, I followed the peddler. He spent lots of time around his wagon, selling stuff to folks and straightenin' things up. He didn't go nowhere until after Mr. Carpenter was dead."

Rye set his feet flat on the boardwalk and rested his elbows on his knees as he leaned close to the kid. "So he couldn't have seen Mr. Pollard arguing with Mr. Carpenter."

"Don't rightly see how with him never near Mr. Carpenter."

Dulcie was right. Her father wasn't a murderer.

"Did you tell the sheriff?" Rye asked.

"Told the Gearsons, but they said I was makin' things up."

Anger flooded Rye. Children lied sometimes, but the Gearsons should have taken Collie to the sheriff and let the sheriff figure it out. Between Collie and Dulcie, Pollard should never have been arrested. But that would've meant they'd have no one to blame for Carpenter's death, and having the wrong man was better than having nobody.

Rye composed himself, not wanting Collie to see how much his words had affected him. "Did you ever see the peddler visit folks?"

"Not much. Everyone went to him, 'cept Mrs. Carpenter. She had him bring his wagon to her house. Guess she thought she was better'n other folks."

"Was Mr. Carpenter with her when the peddler was there?"

Collie thought for a moment then shook his head. "No, she was alone." The boy squirmed. "I seen him and Mrs. Carpenter kiss once."

Stunned, Rye stared at the boy. "Are you sure?"

Collie made a face. "I know what I seen."

Mrs. Carpenter and Virgil Lamont? A scandalous picture fell into place. Mrs. Carpenter, much younger than her husband, found she preferred someone closer to her age. And in order to have Lamont *and* her husband's money, she'd have to find a way to get rid of Lawrence Carpenter. All she needed was for someone to kill him and somebody else to be accused of the crime. Frank Pollard was the perfect choice for the scapegoat, and Virgil Lamont was given the task of placing the blame on him. However, since Collie knew Lamont hadn't been near Carpenter all day that meant somebody else had killed Carpenter.

Who?

TWENTY-ONE

RYE abruptly stood. "Let's go talk to the sheriff."

Startled, Collie stared up at him. "Why?"

"So you can tell him what you told me about the peddler."

Collie wrapped his thin arms around his drawn-up knees. "The Gearsons is right. He ain't never gonna believe me."

Angered by both the Gearsons' disregard for their foster child and the miscarriage of justice, Rye had to take a moment to calm himself. He hunkered down in front of the boy. "Mrs. McDaniel told the sheriff that her father was at home when Mr. Carpenter was killed, but he didn't believe her. But if you tell him that the peddler couldn't have seen her father and Mr. Carpenter fighting, he'll have to believe both of you."

Collie scrutinized him. "I'm not lying, Rye."

Rye smiled. "I know you're not, and that's why we're going to see the sheriff." He levered himself up and extended a hand to the sitting boy. "Come on."

Collie grasped his hand and Rye pulled him to his feet. With a hand on his back, Rye guided the boy to the sheriff's office. Entering, they found Sheriff Martin sleeping with his hat pulled over his eyes and his feet propped up on the battered desk.

Rye slapped Martin's boot and the lawman jerked, his eyes snapping open. "What?"

"Collie here has something to tell you," Rye said. He turned to the boy and said gently, "Go ahead."

Martin listened to the boy's story, his expression clearly revealing his skepticism. Once Collie was done, the sheriff spoke. "Did this fellah tell you to tell me this?" he asked, motioning to Rye.

Collie shook his head. "No, sir. When I heard Mr. Pollard was 'rested, I told the Gearsons that the peddler couldn't have seen him and Mr. Carpenter fightin', but they said I was lyin' and that you wouldn't believe me."

"They were right. I don't."

"Look, Sheriff, between what Mrs. McDaniel and Collie have told you, even you can see Frank Pollard couldn't have killed Carpenter." Rye tried to keep the irritation from his voice but knew he wasn't succeeding.

"Virgil Lamont said—" the sheriff began.

"A peddler's job is to stretch the truth. Why would you take his word over theirs?"

Martin slammed his fist down on the desk and jumped to his feet. "Why would Lamont lie? He'd only been here a time or two before and got along with everyone. And Dulcie, she was gone for over five years, and when she come back, she don't hardly talk to anyone until her pa is in trouble."

"So you're saying just because Dulcie kept to herself, you took Lamont's word over hers?"

Martin glanced away, but not before Rye saw the confirmation in his eyes. "It wasn't like that."

"No? Then tell me how it was." Rye didn't bother covering his angry frustration. "Tell me why you allowed an innocent man to be taken out of your jail and hanged. Tell me why you didn't arrest those who did the hanging. And tell me why you still won't even consider that Dulcie and Collie are telling the truth."

Martin glared at him. "This is a small town, mister. Carpenter was well-liked 'round here. Somebody had to pay for killin' him."

Rye gnashed his teeth. "And that somebody was Frank Pollard, because he was a good-for-nothing drunk and nobody would stand up for him. Nobody but his daughter, who you wouldn't even consider was telling the truth.

"And what about the real murderer? He's running around scot-free, and you don't care that an innocent man was lynched in his place."

Martin's face reddened, but he didn't say anything.

Furious, Rye slapped the desktop and spun around. "Let's go, Collie. I can't stand the stink in here."

The boy hurried to the door, clearly wanting to get away from the sheriff as much as Rye. Once the door was slammed behind them, Rye stood motionless on the boardwalk. Rage clouded his vision as he struggled to keep from striking something.

"Why won't he believe us?" Collie asked.

The boy's tentative question dissipated Rye's remaining anger. "Because he knows he let an innocent man die and he won't own up to it."

Collie frowned. "I never liked Mr. Pollard, but I didn't like seein' him hang neither." He shuddered.

Rye stared down at the boy, suddenly realizing Collie must have witnessed the hanging. Remembering his own childhood when he'd sneaked out of the orphanage late at night, he wanted to kick himself for not considering the possibility. "Did you recognize anyone who hanged him?" he asked.

Collie stared into the distance, his young face drawn. "There were lots of people. They all wore something over their faces, so mostly I couldn't tell who they were."

Rye sensed Collie knew more and waited for the boy to continue.

"Mr. Gearson was there. I saw him when he went back to the house. So was Knobby from the bathhouse and"—he swallowed—"Mrs. Carpenter was there, too. There was lots more, too."

"What about the sheriff?"

Collie turned to glance through the lawman's window and shivered despite the warmth of the sun. "I think so."

If the sheriff was involved in the lynching, there was no way to bring justice to the vigilantes. It would be Collie's word against the word of everyone, including the sheriff.

The simple fact was Dulcie's father was dead and no one would be charged with his murder.

However, there was still the mystery of who actually killed Carpenter. If Rye figured that out, then he'd have something to give Dulcie before leaving Locust.

AFTER she returned home, Dulcie moved mechanically, keeping her mind empty except for whatever task she worked. Madeline was oddly quiet, playing with her doll and making up stories she told Aggie in a low, singsong voice. Although they ate dinner, Dulcie couldn't recall what it was she'd made for her and her daughter.

While Madeline napped in the afternoon, Dulcie picked apples. As she did, she worried about the wheat still standing in the field, as well as the corn on the stalks. If only she hadn't been so quick to judge Rye. The deserter brand was reason enough for him to keep quiet about having been in the army. He was obviously ashamed of the scar since he'd kept his shirt on even when they'd made love.

She paused, her hand on an apple, as she recalled that evening and what he'd done to her. Her cheeks heated and she squeezed her thighs together. If he'd only been looking to get her into bed, he wouldn't have taken the time to pleasure her. And he had pleasured her, more than she imagined a man could.

She pulled the apple off the branch and crammed it into the bag slung over her arm and head. Her thoughts turned to Lamont's blackmail—his silence in exchange for a night in her bed. What about the next time he was in Locust? And the next? Would his silence cost a night each time he was passing through town?

Her stomach heaved, and she pressed her arms against her belly. Was her reputation worth her self-respect? She'd whored herself with Lamont before, but that had been for Madeline, and she'd do it again to protect her daughter. But for herself? Didn't she deserve more? Didn't she deserve a man like Rye Forrester?

Her vision blurred and she swept her wrist across her eyes. Resolve stiffened her spine. This evening she'd accept

Lamont into her home and feed him supper. She'd learn why he lied about seeing her father argue with Carpenter, and she'd do it without letting him use her again.

Maybe Jerry had thought she was a worthless wife, and maybe Lamont thought she was little more than a whore. But Rye had made love with her, treated her like she was special. And after experiencing Rye's loving, she'd accept nothing less ever again.

AFTER feeding Collie at the restaurant and sending him on his way, Rye entered Carpenter's hardware store. Although startled to see Lamont inside, he wasn't surprised that the peddler and Mrs. Carpenter had their heads bent close as they talked. It only strengthened his theory that they were in cahoots.

Mrs. Carpenter, facing the door, quickly moved away from Lamont. "Can I help you?" Her tone was as chilly as a Dakota winter.

"Mr. Lamont. I'm surprised to see you here," Rye said, ignoring the woman.

Virgil Lamont turned languidly, and his artificial smile made Rye grit his teeth. "I'm merely trying to persuade Mrs. Carpenter to purchase some of my goods."

"It seems to me a woman who's planning on leaving doesn't have much use for your load of "—he paused deliberately—"goods."

Lamont's face flushed, but he also appeared startled by the news of her moving. "I hadn't realized she was leaving Locust."

Mrs. Carpenter's haughty expression slipped. "I was about to inform you when we were so rudely interrupted," she assured Lamont. "In fact, I was going to ask you if you would like to buy some of our goods at lowered prices."

Rye leaned against a barrel filled with chains and crossed his arms. "Consider it another form of payment for services rendered."

"I don't understand," Lamont said, brushing some dust from his sleeve.

Rye shrugged nonchalantly. "I figured it out. Mrs. Carpenter wanted her husband dead, but she needed someone to take the blame since he was so well-liked around these parts. So she struck a deal with you to lie about Pollard."

Mrs. Carpenter narrowed her eyes. "Are you insinuating I killed my own husband?"

Rye's chuckle was as icy as her glare. "No, ma'am. You aren't big enough or strong enough to have killed him."

Peter Carpenter came out of the back room and froze, his gaze roving from Rye to his stepmother to Lamont and back to Rye. "What's going on?"

"Nothing," Mrs. Carpenter quickly replied.

Rye drew his brows together as his gaze went from the woman to her stepson. What if Mrs. Carpenter had wielded her charms on Peter? Being young and impressionable, he might do anything for her. Including kill his own father.

Rye's stomach rolled in revulsion and he swallowed the caustic rise in his throat. He pushed away from the barrel and approached the counter, his gaze locked on Peter's face. "Is she worth it? Is she worth having your father's murder on your conscience?"

Peter's face paled, confirming Rye's horrible suspicion. Rye would've given anything to still have his own father, and this foolish young man had killed his.

Rye took a deep breath and surveyed the three people staring at him—Lamont with coolness, Mrs. Carpenter with loathing, and Peter with trepidation. He shook his head in disgust and strode out.

Even though he was now fairly certain of who was involved in the murder, he found himself in the same helpless position he'd found himself with the sheriff. He had no way of proving their guilt. However, there was a weak link in their triad of murder.

And Rye had to break that link to learn the truth, for Dulcie's sake.

DULCIE heard the approaching jangle of a wagon and her heart leapt in her breast. Her gaze flicked to the table, which was set for three, and her daughter, who'd made her displeasure for the peddler known with whines and pouts. If there was anyone she could have left Madeline with this evening, Dulcie would have done so.

Dulcie smoothed a hand over her daughter's hair then kissed her crown. "It'll be all right, honey. After we eat, I want you to go up to the loft and play. If you get tired, you can lie down up there and go to sleep."

Madeline scowled. "I know, Ma."

"I'm sorry, honey." Dulcie had given her the same instructions at least a half dozen times.

"I don't like him."

Dulcie clamped down on the hysterical urge to laugh. "I'm not fond of him myself, but we have to be polite."

Madeline looked like she wanted to argue, but footsteps on the porch made Dulcie raise her finger. "Be good," she told her daughter.

As Dulcie walked to the door, she glanced into the bedroom to reassure herself that the loaded shotgun stood in the corner. Her gaze landed on the trunk, where the whiskey bottle was hidden, untouched for days. She would've liked a swallow for courage, but it was too late now. A knock sounded, and Dulcie fisted her hands at her sides and took a deep breath. Slowly, she uncurled her fingers and opened the door.

Virgil Lamont, wearing a dark suit, swept her dress-clad figure with a lecherous gaze. "Hello, Dulcie."

"Mr. Lamont," she greeted him formally, her heart racing and her palms damp with apprehension. She motioned for him to enter.

He stepped into the small cabin and wrinkled his nose. "This is what you wanted to return to?"

She lifted her chin. "It's our home. Mine and Madeline's."

Lamont merely grunted. He spotted Madeline sitting in a rocking chair and approached her.

Dulcie quickly insinuated herself between him and her daughter. "Supper is ready."

The man narrowed his eyes but nodded.

She motioned for him to sit then ushered Madeline into the seat across from him. Aware of his gaze on her, Dulcie tried not to shudder with revulsion. How had she ever lain with him?

Because he threatened to strand Madeline and me in the middle of nowhere . . . and because my body liked what he did.

Self-hatred made her grimace, but she pressed the disgust aside. She had to pretend to go along with his blackmail if she hoped to get any information from him.

Once the plates were filled, Dulcie sat down to eat. Although it was one of the better meals she'd prepared, it tasted like sawdust and settled like a rock in her belly. As she forced herself to eat, she rehearsed in her mind how she'd get him to admit he'd lied about seeing her father and Carpenter arguing.

"I saw your friend Forrester in the hardware store right before I came out here," Lamont remarked.

Dulcie faltered for a second and hoped the peddler didn't notice. "Forrester was my hired man."

"Funny. I got the impression there was more between you two."

Dulcie's heart skipped a beat and she kept her gaze lowered, fearful Lamont would see the truth in her eyes. "You're wrong."

There was a moment of dense silence, then Lamont said, "He accused Mrs. Carpenter and her son of killing Lawrence Carpenter."

Dulcie's heart jumped and she caught the peddler's narrowed eyes and held them. "He must've had good reason."

"Do you know what I think, Dulcie? I think Forrester is sweet on you and trying to get in your good graces by proving your father didn't kill Carpenter."

Maybe the other night *had* meant more to Rye than simply lying with a willing—more than willing—woman. But she wasn't about to tell Lamont. "You're imagining things."

"I'm done, Ma. May I go?" Madeline asked.

Dulcie glanced at the girl's plate, which was still half full. But she didn't want her daughter to hear any more of their conversation. "Go ahead."

Madeline scrambled down from her chair, and no residual effects from her illness were evident as she scampered up the ladder.

"She's going to be a beauty, just like you," Lamont said.

Dulcie swallowed the bile rising in her throat. "She's a good girl."

Lamont finished eating and pushed his plate away. "You aren't a bad cook"—his eyes glittered like obsidian—"but you're better in bed."

She flushed hotly. "You threatened to leave Madeline and me behind if I didn't—"

Lamont laughed. "Come now, Dulcie. You weren't a blushing virgin. You knew what you were getting into, and from what I recall, you didn't mind sharing my bed."

Dulcie closed her eyes as humiliation threatened to choke her. She reminded herself she'd done what she had to and pushed back her shame. She concentrated on her task. "I wonder what Mr. Forrester's reason was for accusing the Carpenters of murder."

Lamont leaned back and negligently slung an arm over another chair. "I believe he thinks the widow cuckolded the old man." His eyes flashed with dark humor. "And bedded her stepson."

Shocked, Dulcie's eyes widened. Mrs. Carpenter was much younger than her husband had been, but to sleep with Peter and be party to killing her husband . . . Dulcie had done some things she wasn't proud of, but she could never be that brazen.

"You look surprised, Dulcie. Surely you know how powerful passion can be," Lamont said, his tone mocking.

She refused to be baited. "Did she pay you to lie?"

Lamont's composure slipped and an insincere smile tried to cover it. "You're getting ahead of yourself, Dulcie. Our deal is one night together, then I'll tell you what you want to know."

As surely as Dulcie knew the sun would rise in the east, she knew Lamont wouldn't reveal the truth. Not now and not in the morning after he received his "payment." With that realization, she felt a lifting of the weight from her shoulders. "You're lying. You're planning to have your fun tonight and leave tomorrow morning without telling me a thing. And the next time you're in the area, you'll be calling on me again, wanting another 'payment' for your silence, and promising me something else you never intend on giving."

Lamont studied her, and a reluctant smile touched his lips. "Maybe. But it doesn't change a thing. If I leave here now, everyone in town will know of your loose morals."

The fear Dulcie expected didn't materialize. Instead, she thought of Rye and how well he'd treated her and Madeline. If she gave in to Lamont's demand, she would lose Rye's respect, and that would hurt more than the entire town of Locust thinking less of her. Besides, the townsfolk already looked down upon her for being the daughter of Frank Pollard. But they didn't know her or her reasons for what she'd done or why she'd returned to Locust, to a father who was a drunk and a farm that was falling down.

They didn't know that she loved her daughter more than her reputation.

Dulcie stood and walked to the door. She opened it wide and made a sweeping gesture toward it. "Get out of here, Lamont."

He eyed Dulcie like he'd never seen her before. "Are you sure, Dulcie?"

She smiled and nodded, feeling as if she was awakening from a nightmare. "I've never been more certain. Go ahead and spread your rumors. I don't care what you or anyone else thinks of me. *I* know who and what I am."

Lamont rose slowly and crossed to the door. He stood gazing down at Dulcie. "I'm almost sorry we met like we did." He turned to leave but paused on the porch. "You're a hell of a woman, Dulcie McDaniel."

She stared after him, startled by the reluctant admiration in his voice. Before she realized what she was doing, she ran out to his wagon and grabbed the nearest trace to hold the horses. Lamont tipped his head in question as he looked down at her.

"Did you kill Mr. Carpenter?" She held her breath.

He was still for a long moment then slowly shook his head. "I had no reason to. He was a good customer."

"You didn't see my father arguing with Carpenter, did you?" Dulcie knew she was pressing her luck, but some strange compulsion wouldn't let her stop.

Lamont stared at her, as if trying to determine what to tell her. "That part's true, only it was the day before Carpenter was killed."

"How much did Mrs. Carpenter pay you to lie to the sheriff?"

Lamont chuckled without humor. "I was expecting my money this time, but she's still paying interest."

Dulcie's face heated, realizing *how* she paid the interest. Was Mrs. Carpenter so ruthless as to bed both Lamont and Peter so she could be rid of her husband? Thinking of the beautiful but cold features of the woman, Dulcie knew she *could* be that heartless. "Rye's right, isn't he? Mrs. Carpenter and Peter killed him, and you were paid to cast the blame on my father."

Lamont merely gazed at her, his silence as good as a confirmation.

Although she'd insisted all along that her father was innocent of murder, there was a part of her that wasn't certain. It was the part that remained a little girl, afraid of his drunken wrath. And now, though she was relieved to know she was right, she didn't know whether to be relieved or sickened by the ugliness of the crime. "Your lie got my father killed."

"Your father was hanged by all those righteous townsfolk." His voice was rife with sarcasm.

"He wouldn't have been in jail if you hadn't lied to the sheriff."

Lamont shook his head. "They wanted somebody to blame. Your father was an easy target." He leaned down toward her. "Get out of Locust, Dulcie, before you become their next sacrificial lamb."

TWENTY-TWO

RYE watched Virgil Lamont leave town. He knew where the man was headed and hated the jealousy that cut through him. Dulcie had made her feelings clear concerning him, and what she did with another man wasn't any of his concern. Except he couldn't even think about her with Lamont without wanting to thrash the peddler.

He shifted his weight from one foot to the other as he leaned against a building, his figure hidden by the alley's shadows. He expected one or both of the Carpenters to leave the store and walk home soon. However, the only one he cared about was Peter, the weak link.

Voices drifted out of the saloon across the street, along with the scent of whiskey and beer. The hunger, never far away, beckoned him. One shot of whiskey wouldn't do any harm, and it would help him get past the jealousy gnawing at his insides. Except he knew one shot wouldn't do anything but make him want another and another.

He clamped down on the craving, ignoring it like he learned to ignore many things while locked in the stockade. More minutes crawled by, and Rye's calf cramped. He walked in tight circles to relieve it, keeping to the shadows.

Finally, after full dark had fallen and only the moon and

stars lit the night, Mrs. Carpenter came out of the store. She marched away in the direction of her home. Through the hardware store's window, he could see a light shining dimly from the back room.

Rye settled his hat brim lower on his brow and crossed the street. He ducked into the alley and went around to the back door of the hardware store. Hoping it was unlocked, he turned the knob and pressed the door inward. It creaked softly and Rye froze. After a few moments of silence, Rye breathed again and pushed the door open far enough that he could slip inside.

He spotted Peter immediately, the younger man's back to him as he packed items into a crate. Approaching Peter with stealthy steps, Rye managed to get within five feet of him before the young man turned around.

Peter's eyes widened and he stumbled back. "What're you doing in here?"

Rye pulled his Navy Colt out of its holster and aimed it at Carpenter. "You and I are going to call on a friend." He motioned for Peter to move toward the back door. "Let's go."

The young man shook his head. "I'm not going anywhere with you."

Rye eased the revolver's hammer back. "I think you will, because if you don't I'm going to put a bullet through your hand. It'd be awfully hard to keep Mrs. Carpenter happy if you only have the use of one hand. She'd probably have to find someone even younger than you." Peter's complexion became scarlet, but Rye had to give him credit—he didn't rise to the bait. "Are you coming the easy way or the hard way?"

Peter untied his apron, his hands shaking. "Where are we going?"

"It's a surprise."

Rye prodded the younger man out the back door ahead of him. He'd tied Smoke and another horse in the trees on the edge of town so no one would see them leave. Once the two men were mounted, Rye took the reins of Peter's horse.

"We're going to the Pollard place," Peter guessed after a few minutes.

"Yep."

Rye didn't feel inclined to talk. He wasn't looking forward to seeing the peddler's wagon parked in front of Dulcie's cabin, and he was even less excited about seeing him and Dulcie together.

Carpenter remained silent the rest of the way, but Rye sensed his growing unease. The cabin came into view, as well as the wagon parked in the front. However, he saw Lamont in the wagon and Dulcie standing beside him. Bewildered, he and Peter rode into the yard.

Dulcie stepped away from Lamont and looked from Rye to Peter and back. "What's going on?" Her voice was wary.

Rye dismounted and motioned for Peter to do the same. For a moment, it looked as if Peter might bolt, but he did as Rye said. The young man's gaze skittered to Lamont, his apprehension obvious.

"Peter here has something to tell you," Rye answered.

"No, I don't," Peter denied.

"I should get back to town," Lamont said.

"I don't think so," Rye said. "You'll join us." When Lamont lifted the reins, Rye pulled out his Navy Colt. "That wasn't a suggestion."

Lamont scowled, but climbed down from the wagon.

"Is Madeline inside?" Rye asked Dulcie.

"She's asleep in the loft."

"We'll talk in the barn." Rye prodded both Carpenter and Lamont ahead of him.

Dulcie fell into step beside Rye and asked in a low voice, "Peter and Mrs. Carpenter killed him, didn't they?"

Surprised, Rye glanced sharply at her. "How—"

"Lamont told me, more or less. He said Mrs. Carpenter paid him to lie to the sheriff, too."

"I guess you didn't need my help after all."

Dulcie smiled ruefully. "I could use your help convincing the sheriff."

"That's why I brought Peter here. I'm hoping we can convince him to confess."

"I'd like to try," Dulcie said, determination and a hint of fear in her expression.

Rye didn't think she could get Peter to talk, but it was her father and she deserved the chance. "All right."

Once inside the barn, Rye kept his revolver trained on the two men. "Mrs. McDaniel would like to say something, and you're both going to listen like gentlemen."

Dulcie crossed her arms to cover her trembling and looked at Peter. "How's your stepmother?"

"Fine," Peter mumbled.

Lamont snorted a laugh.

Dulcie knew she risked Rye learning of her shame with Lamont, but she couldn't let cowardice sway her. "You would know about Mrs. Carpenter, wouldn't you, Lamont? Seeing as how she's been paying you with her favors."

Just as I paid him with my favors.

"You're lying." Peter's accusation sounded more desperate than confident.

"Have you and Mrs. Carpenter"—Dulcie's face heated—"been together, Lamont?"

The peddler remained silent for a long moment. He glanced at Peter then shrugged and nodded. "Yes."

"No!" Peter launched himself at Lamont, and they both fell to the ground. The two men were close to the same size but Peter's rage gave him the advantage as they fought.

As much as Dulcie wouldn't have minded letting them continue fighting, she needed them in one piece to talk to the sheriff. "Rye?"

He nodded, understanding what she wanted, and waded into the fisticuffs. Grabbing the back of Carpenter's shirt, he pulled him off Lamont. The peddler's nose was bleeding and it appeared Peter had broken it.

Peter fought against Rye's hold, and Rye pressed his gun barrel against the younger man's side. "Hold it, Carpenter."

The enraged man stopped fighting and Rye released him. Peter hunched his shoulders as he panted and glared at Lamont. The peddler struggled to stand, a hand to his bleeding nose.

Clenching her hands at her sides, Dulcie almost felt sorry for Peter. However, she took selfish delight in seeing Lamont's handsome face marred by a broken nose.

Lamont glowered at Peter. "Martha Carpenter played you for the fool. All she wants is your father's money, and she used you to get it."

"We're going to get married after we leave Locust," Peter argued.

Dulcie wisely remained silent.

Lamont laughed. "More likely she'll seduce another man to kill *you* next time."

Peter suddenly looked very young and confused. "She said she loved me."

"You said you loved me." Dulcie heard the echo of a memory in his voice, only it was to Jerry she'd said the words.

"Did she convince you to kill your own father?" Dulcie asked the young man softly.

Peter stared at the ground and nodded. "She said we could take his money and get married and live in a city. It would be just the two of us."

Lamont opened his mouth, but Dulcie shook her head in warning. Although what the younger man had done was appalling, Dulcie understood the sway of passion and false words of love.

"My father and your father are dead because Martha used you, Peter," Dulcie said. "You have to tell the sheriff what happened. You have to stop Martha from doing this to someone else."

Dulcie glanced at Rye and caught him studying her, but she couldn't tell what he was thinking. Maybe it was better she didn't know. She'd said terrible things to him, words she regretted, but she'd felt betrayed.

Peter sniffed and drew his wrist across his eyes. "I-I've been having nightmares since I k-killed him. Maybe they'll go away if I confess."

His plaintive tone made Dulcie's eyes sting with tears. "Maybe they will, Peter," she said gently.

Rye ushered both Lamont and Peter back out to the yard. As they readied to return to town, Dulcie moved over to Smoke and laid a hand on Rye's calf. She looked up at him. "Come back after you're done at the sheriff's office."

Rye blinked. "Are you sure?"

"Yes. There are some things I have to tell you."

Rye lifted his head and looked out into the dusky evening. "There's something I have to tell you, too."

"I'll be waiting."

As Rye rode away with the two men, Dulcie wrapped her arms around her waist in the cool evening air. Her father's name would be cleared, but what of those who lynched him? How would they be punished for their crime?

However, the most important question remained. Could Rye forgive her?

IT was long after dark when Rye finally left the sheriff's office and rode back to Dulcie's. Nervousness battered him as he headed back, but he forced himself to ignore it.

As he dismounted in front of her cabin, the door opened and a rectangle of light spilled out. His breath caught in his throat at the feminine vision that stepped onto the porch. Dulcie's long hair cascaded over her shoulders and a halo of reddish gold surrounded her face. A dark green dress hugged her breasts and followed the smooth curves to her slender waist and rounded hips. Desire kicked him below his belt.

"I was afraid you changed your mind," Dulcie said with a tremulous smile.

He managed a grin. "I was thinking the same of you."

"Come on in."

Rye climbed the steps and removed his hat. Self-conscious despite the many times he'd been in the cabin, Rye stood awkwardly by the door.

"Have you eaten supper?" she asked.

Startled, Rye shook his head.

She gave him a look that reminded him of when she scolded her daughter. "Sit down and I'll get a plate for you."

"You don't have—"

"I know I don't have to."

Still ill at ease, Rye hung his hat on a hook and crossed to the table where he sat down.

Dulcie set a plate loaded with fresh vegetables, a thick slice of bread, and venison in front of him. She returned a few moments later with two cups of coffee, one of which she set by his food. The other she clasped between her hands as she sat across from him. "How did it go at the sheriff's office?"

"Peter Carpenter told him what happened. Lamont swore he made a mistake with the day he saw your father and Carpenter arguing. He's lying, but the sheriff really didn't have anything to hold him on. He brought Martha Carpenter in and she denied everything, but between Peter and Lamont's testimonies, she'll spend some time in jail, too." Rye shoveled some food into his mouth. Her cooking tasted sinfully good after the two meals he'd eaten in town.

"What will happen to Peter?"

"Since he confessed and turned himself in, he might just end up in prison the rest of his life instead of being hanged."

Dulcie scowled. "Martha is guiltier than him."

"I know, but that's the way it is." Rye finished eating.

Dulcie appeared troubled, but didn't comment. "Would you like some more?" she asked.

"No thanks. It was good, Dulcie. Real good."

She glanced down, but not before Rye caught the rose blush in her cheeks. "I'm glad you liked it." She licked her lips, her tongue drawing Rye's attention to her mouth. "Now that my father is cleared of the murder, do you think the sheriff will arrest anyone for the lynching?"

Rye wished he had better news. "No. He told me again tonight there were too many involved and he didn't recognize any of them." He paused. "I'm sorry, Dulcie, but I think your father's death will go unpunished."

"I was afraid of that."

"Is Madeline still asleep?" Rye asked, hoping to draw Dulcie out of her melancholy.

"In the loft." She refilled their coffee cups. After a few minutes, she spoke. "I'm sorry."

Startled, Rye asked, "For what?"

"For being so quick to judge you." Her small laugh was mocking. "As if I have a right to judge anybody."

"You have nothing to be sorry for, Dulcie. I should have told you the truth when I first got here."

She studied him, her teeth nibbling on her lower lip. "You know the place in the Bible where it talks about casting stones?"

Rye nodded, puzzled.

"I've made some terrible mistakes, Rye," Dulcie said, her

voice rough with hidden emotion. "I tricked Jerry into marrying me. I don't think he was looking for more than a good time, but I was determined to get out of Locust." Her face flushed. "I got with child, and he did the decent thing." She laughed without humor. "Probably the first and only decent thing he ever did."

Uncomfortable, Rye glanced down. Her sin was slight compared to his.

"Did you know Jerry very well?" she asked.

A heavy weight settled on his chest. She deserved the entire truth this time. "Not really." He scrubbed his damp palms on his thighs and listened to his heart drum in his ears. Facing the hot brand was nothing compared to facing Dulcie. "I was with him the night he died."

Her eyes widened, her expression wary.

Rye could barely talk past the dryness in his mouth and throat. "I dared him to walk on the roof."

"Were you drunk, too?"

Rye closed his eyes, wishing he'd never come here, never faced Jerry's widow. But then, he never would've met Dulcie either. "Yes. After Mary and our baby died, I started drinking."

The air around them seemed to disappear in the brittle silence. Then he felt a soft hand on his and he opened his eyes to find Dulcie leaning across the table and gazing at him intently.

"If it wasn't you, it would've been someone else. Or he might've done something foolish some other time simply to impress a woman." Dulcie's voice was strong and her expression without the angry hatred he expected.

For so long he'd pictured what her reaction would be when she learned the truth of his guilt. Yet none of those imagined came close to her calm acceptance. "He was your husband," he said, feeling foolish.

"He was a drunk and a whoremonger. You were a better father to Madeline these past weeks than Jerry ever was," Dulcie said without hesitation.

Dizzy with relief, he squeezed her hand that rested on his.

"There's something else I have to tell you," Dulcie said. "Something else I'm ashamed of." Her voice broke.

Rye thought of Burt and what he'd said about Dulcie and

Lamont. "Does it have to do with Virgil Lamont and how you got back to Locust after Jerry died?"

Dulcie's complexion paled, leaving her freckles standing in stark relief on her face. "Lamont told you?"

"No, he never said a word. I heard some things in town."

Suddenly she laughed, but it was tinged with hysteria. "Lamont wanted me to sleep with him tonight in exchange for his silence. But it seems everybody already knows."

"It was only gossip, Dulcie."

She sobered. "No, it's the truth. Virgil Lamont was selling his goods around the fort right after Jerry died. I asked him where he was headed next, and he said south, to Texas." Dulcie held onto his hand tightly. "He said he'd give us a ride. I didn't even question him. The next day, he said he expected some payment for us traveling with him. I didn't have any money.

"Lamont threatened to leave Madeline and me in the middle of nowhere if I didn't agree to sleep with him." Her voice broke, and she cleared her throat. "I had to do it. If it was only myself I would've taken my chances, but Madeline's life was more important than anything."

Rye barely managed to restrain his fury. "I'll kill the bastard."

"No, you won't. He gave me a choice, and I did what I had to. He never hurt me or Madeline, and I think in his own way, he came to care for us."

"How can you say that? He forced you."

"No." Her face reddened. "I'm ashamed to admit it, but my body liked what he did. I didn't want to like it, but I couldn't help it. It was the same way with Jerry."

Rye had lain with whores because his body liked it, too. Did he have any right to judge Dulcie for enjoying the same?

"When I finally got back home with Madeline, I swore I would never be dependent on a man again. But"—she glanced away, obviously embarrassed—"but some nights I was so lonely. That's when I'd drink whiskey. It helped me to sleep and forget."

Rye swallowed. "I understand, Dulcie. After Mary died, I did the same thing for the same reason. Only my drinking led to your husband's death."

She smiled sadly. "Everything happens for a reason, Rye. We have to believe that."

As much as Rye hated losing Mary, he realized Dulcie was right. Everything that had happened in their pasts had led them here. To each other. "I'm glad I'm here."

"I'm glad you are, too."

Her face, so close to his, beckoned him. He remembered with crystal clarity how her full lips felt and tasted. Her body heat touched him, stoking the fire she already ignited within him.

"Stay here with me tonight, Rye," Dulcie said.

Her husky voice left no doubt where he'd be sleeping. Although he wanted nothing more than to make love again, Rye didn't want her to think he was like Lamont. "You don't owe me anything."

She lifted her chin. "I know. I want to be with you, Rye, and not only because I love what you do to me, but because I care for you more than I've ever cared for a man."

He knew he should refuse, but gazing into her face, softly molded by the lamplight, it was impossible to walk away. Instead, he cupped her face in his hands. He kissed her gently. "I want to be with you, too, Dulcie."

She took his hand and led him into the bedroom.

$\mathcal{T}$WENTY-THREE

THE following morning, Dulcie dressed herself and Madeline in their best dresses. For the first time in years, Dulcie and her daughter were attending Sunday service. She hoped God understood and didn't judge her too harshly.

The door opened, and Rye entered, sending Dulcie's heart skittering in her chest. Because there were no more secrets or lies between them, their lovemaking had been even more exciting than the first time. Even though her body had reacted to Jerry and Lamont's touches, she hadn't felt anything beyond satisfaction with them. With Rye, there were so many more emotions entangled while they shared their bodies.

For the first time in her life, Dulcie understood what love felt like.

"Wagon's ready to go," he announced.

Madeline ran over to him and held up her arms. Rye grinned and picked her up. "Why look at you, Miss Madeline. Quite the little lady."

She scowled. "I don't know why I gotta wear shoes."

"Because that's what young ladies do when they go to church." Rye glanced at Dulcie, and she flushed at the heat in his eyes. "You look beautiful, too, Dulcie."

She smiled crookedly. "After wearing trousers for so long, wearing a dress will take some getting used to."

He put his free arm around her shoulders. "You're doing just fine."

They walked to the wagon, and Rye lifted Madeline onto the seat then helped Dulcie up. Rye climbed up after them and took the mule's reins.

With Madeline between her and Rye, Dulcie was able to relax and enjoy the morning ride. Not that she wouldn't have minded sitting next to Rye, but with his leg and arm against hers, she would've been far too distracted. This way she could think about what she planned to say.

Last night, after she and Rye had made love for a second time, the idea had come to her. She had outlined her plan to Rye and he had agreed, even though he knew it would be difficult for her. However, knowing she had Rye's support, she didn't care what the God-fearing folks thought of her. Only Rye's opinion mattered now.

The church yard was already filled with wagons and horses since the service had started fifteen minutes earlier. Dulcie intended to arrive late, hoping for a dramatic entrance.

Her heart hammered and her palms were sweaty beneath her gloves. Although she wanted—needed—to do this, it didn't prevent the knot in her belly or the dryness of her throat.

Rye lifted her down from the box and set her on her feet. "You're shaking like a leaf," he said in a low, worried tone.

Dulcie took a deep breath and managed a reassuring smile. "I'll be all right." She squared her shoulders and led the way up the stairs with Rye and Madeline following her. She swept open the door and stepped inside.

The minister fumbled to a stop and stared. It didn't take long for the congregation to turn in their seats to see what had startled him. There were a few moments of shocked silence followed by the gradual rise of whispering voices.

Dulcie ignored them, and the knocking in her knees, and marched to the front of the church. She turned and faced many of the people she'd known since she was a child—Mr. and Mrs. Coulson, the Gearsons, Dr. Wickberg and his wife, and Sheriff Lyle Martin. Then she glanced at the back of the church where Rye stood, his hat in one hand and Madeline's hand held in the other. The feeling of rightness swelled within her, giving her strength.

"I'm sure most of you recognize me. My name is Mrs. Dulcie McDaniel and my father was Frank Pollard." She paused, letting the fragile silence linger and her own convictions buoy her. "He was wrongly accused of Lawrence Carpenter's murder and lynched by many of you sitting here this morning."

Dulcie licked her dry lips and gazed out across the congregation. She expected to feel anger, but there was only pity and disgust. "There's nothing the law can or will do to those of you who were involved in my father's lynching. Instead, each and every day you will all have to live with the fact that you killed an innocent man."

She took a moment to clear the fullness in her throat. "I know my pa drank too much and he was a poor excuse for a father, but he was the only kin I had besides my daughter. And you took him from me." She looked around, but most heads were lowered and faces hidden. "May God have mercy on your souls, because I'm afraid I have none to give."

She caught Rye's admiring gaze, and suddenly she didn't care about anyone else in this town. The only two people who mattered were Rye and Madeline. She noticed Collie get out of a pew and join Rye at the back of the church.

Three people, she amended silently.

Holding her head high, she walked down the aisle. When she reached Rye and the two children, she stopped.

"Your father would be proud," Rye said in a low voice.

She shook her head sadly. "No, I don't think so. But it doesn't matter." She gazed up into Rye's tender blue eyes. "I did this for me, not him."

DULCIE was glad Mrs. Gearson had allowed Collie to return to the farm with them. In fact, the woman had been gracious to the extreme. However, Dulcie knew it was simply Mrs. Gearson's guilty conscience and not affection for Collie that made her so polite.

As Dulcie finished her pie and took a sip of coffee, she

watched Rye tease both Collie and Madeline. Giggles and snorts from the children made Dulcie smile. At this moment, she was the closest she'd ever come to being completely content.

She'd been lonely for years, since long before Jerry died. She just hadn't realized it until Rye came into her life and showed her how decent and loving a man could be.

The only thing that troubled her was the uncertainty of Rye's stay. He offered to go into Locust tomorrow to find a reaper to borrow or rent. Once he did that and the wheat was cut and the corn picked, he'd have fulfilled his promise to stay until the harvest was in. Would he leave then?

Her heart squeezed painfully. She rose to gather the pie plates and carried them to the wash pan. A few moments later Rye joined her, put his arms around her waist and pulled her back against his chest. He kissed the side of her neck, bringing a rush of heat to her belly.

"Are you all right?" he asked.

She kept her gaze on her hands as she washed the dishes. "Why wouldn't I be?"

"You're being too quiet."

She turned her head and found his mouth only inches away. Forcing aside her melancholy, she focused on having him here with her now. "Maybe I just don't have anything to say." She interjected a note of playfulness in her tone.

"I doubt that."

Despite herself, she laughed. "I'm not that bad, am I?"

Rye's reply was lost in the sound of an approaching wagon. Dulcie peeked through the window slats and recognized the doctor's buggy coming down the road. "Dr. Wickberg is here."

Rye released her, and she untied her apron then flung it over a chair. She and Rye, followed by the children, went out to greet the doctor and his wife. Once outside, Dulcie noticed the Wickbergs weren't the only ones who'd come calling. Three reapers following the buggy turned away from the cabin to follow the road leading to the wheat and corn fields. There were also two buckboard wagons filled with people, and more men and children on mule or horseback. Everyone living in and around Locust must have come.

Her mouth agape, Dulcie watched the activity as the men driving the reapers started cutting the wheat. Across the way in the corn, the buckboard wagons stopped. At least two dozen people with large cloth bags slung over their head and shoulders started picking the ears from the cornstalks.

Dr. Wickberg climbed down from the buggy. Both he and his wife wore clothes more fit for working than visiting.

"What's going on?" Dulcie asked the doctor.

"I guess you could say this is our way of saying we're sorry for what happened with your father," Dr. Wickberg replied. Although shame-faced, he held her gaze. "I could've tried to stop the lynching and I didn't. I'm sorry, Dulcie."

Although she'd wanted to have those involved in her father's lynching realize they'd hanged an innocent man, she hadn't expected anything like this.

"Now that the real murderers confessed, you finally believe Dulcie," Rye said, his tone caustic.

"I suppose we deserve that." Dr. Wickberg sighed. "After you left the church, nobody was in the mood to continue the service. Instead, we had a meeting. I know nothing will bring Frank back, but we decided to bring your crops in. With all of us pitching in, we should be able to finish today."

Dulcie knew she should've been happy getting the harvest done so quickly, but now Rye would have no reason to stay. And what reason did she have? She had no loyalty to the townsfolk of Locust, despite this gesture of apology.

"You're right. It won't bring my father back, but I do appreciate the help," she said stiffly.

"If you'll excuse us, we're going to pick some corn." Dr. Wickberg stepped back up into his buggy and started down the road.

Suddenly Dulcie knew what she had to do. She lifted her skirt hems and ran after the buggy. "Dr. Wickberg."

He halted his buggy, and Dulcie stumbled to a stop beside it. She glanced back to see Rye standing back with the children and was glad he wouldn't hear her. "There's something else I'd like you to do, Dr. Wickberg."

"What is it, Dulcie?"

"Ask around and see if anyone would be interested in buying my farm, the sooner the better."

Although Dr. Wickberg appeared troubled, he simply nodded. "I'll do that, Dulcie."

"Thank you."

Dr. Wickberg slapped the reins against the horse's rump and went to join the others. Dulcie walked back to Rye, who gave her a questioning look.

"Does this mean we don't have to work no more?" Collie asked.

Relieved to have her attention stolen by the boy, she grinned. "That's right, Collie."

The boy whooped in excitement.

"Why don't you and Madeline stay outside and play here in the shade while Rye and I finish the dishes?" she suggested.

Collie grinned, and he and Madeline went to plop down on the thick grass to play one of their games with rocks and sticks.

Dulcie took Rye's hand and tugged him toward the cabin. Once inside, she closed the door and wrapped her arms around Rye and kissed him. Rye didn't miss the opportunity to kiss her again.

"Thank you for everything," she said through the lump in her throat.

Rye frowned. "This sounds like someone's leaving."

She couldn't bear to look in his face. "As soon as the corn and wheat are in, there's no reason for you to stay."

Disappointment flashed through Rye's face. "I suppose. Lamont told me of a Creede Forrester down near Robles."

"One of your brothers?"

"Maybe. I have to find out."

"Do you think there might be some land for sale down that way?" Dulcie asked.

Rye frowned. "Why?"

She glanced away and affected a light tone. "I asked Dr. Wickberg to check around to see if anyone would like to buy this place."

"I thought this was your home."

Dulcie thought for a moment. "When I got back to Locust, all I wanted to do was make a home for Madeline by myself. I'd had enough of men, after Jerry and Lamont." She paused and tilted her head, staring into Rye's dark blue eyes. "Then something happened. I met a man named Rye Forrester, and he showed me not all men were alike." She swallowed hard. "He gave me a reason to believe in love again."

Rye's expression softened. "Did he now?"

She nodded, her eyes never leaving his. "In fact, if he asked me to marry him, I'd say yes."

His eyes glimmered with moisture. "I love you, Dulcie McDaniel. Will you marry me?"

Excitement trilled through her, but there was one other thing she wanted almost as much as becoming his wife. "I have one condition."

He frowned. "What is it?"

"I'd like another child."

Rye grinned devilishly and cupped her buttocks. "I don't think that will be a problem."

She laughed but didn't let him distract her. "I mean as soon as we're married. I want to adopt Collie."

Rye stared at her as if she'd just spoken some odd language. Finally, he answered with a husky voice, "I'd like that, too."

Tears blurred her vision, but happiness so powerful it ached filled her. Unable to speak, she answered him the only way she could, with a long, loving kiss.

A month later fields of bare cotton stretched out in front of Rye, just as it had for most of the last week they'd been traveling. Like the other crops, the cotton, too, had been harvested.

After Dulcie's crops had been sold, it had taken only a week for the farm itself to be bought. Although Rye hadn't wanted to use his new wife's money, she insisted it was for all of them to make a new start. He felt a little less guilty, but vowed to pay her back someday.

Madeline's giggle in the back of the wagon caught his attention, and he glanced at Dulcie, who sat next to him on the seat.

"Collie's tickling her," Dulcie said with a smile.

Rye shook his head, grinning at his adopted son's antics.

Two months ago he'd ridden into Locust to pay a debt, and he left the town with a wife and two children who were his in all but blood. Despite the misfortunes that had led to this point, Rye had learned to forgive himself and had no regrets. Gazing into his wife's bright green eyes, he knew she, too, felt the same way.

Holding the mules' reins in one hand, Rye took Dulcie's hand in his other. "Having second thoughts?"

She shook her head, and the sunlight spun her thick red gold hair into golden threads. "Not for a minute. You?"

He grinned crookedly. "Only my stomach. I think a herd of buffalo are stomping around down there."

She squeezed his hand reassuringly. "If he's your brother, he's going to be just as excited to see you."

"I hope so."

Dulcie leaned against his side and kissed his cheek. "He's not going to care about that scar either. He'll love you because you're family."

Rye wished he could be as certain, but was grateful for Dulcie's support. If this Creede Forrester was his brother and he didn't want anything to do with a long-lost sibling, then Rye would find a new place to make a home with his family.

My family.

He didn't realize how much he'd wanted to belong until he found Dulcie.

They rounded a corner, and a well-kept cabin came into view. A man was outside by the corral, and by his side was a child, probably a couple years younger than Madeline. Rye knew he spotted their wagon when he turned to the cabin and called to somebody. A woman came out and stood close to the tall, powerfully built man who lifted his little girl in his arms.

"That must be his wife," Dulcie said.

Unable to speak because of his dry mouth and thundering heart, Rye nodded.

Collie and Madeline stood up behind the seat between Rye and Dulcie.

"Is that your brother?" Collie asked.

"We think so," Dulcie replied for Rye, as if knowing he couldn't speak.

"He's old."

Dulcie smiled. "He's ten years older than Rye. That would make him forty."

Collie wrinkled his nose. "Old."

Rye steered the mules into the yard and halted the animals twenty feet from the family.

"Howdy," the man greeted. "Can we help you?"

Rye glanced at Dulcie, who gave him an encouraging nod. He jumped down from the wagon and took a deep breath. "I hope so. I'm looking for Creede Forrester."

The man's eyes narrowed warily. "You found him. Do I know you?"

"Did you have two brothers named Rye and Slater?"

Forrester's suspicion was replaced by surprise and curiosity. "Yes. They were placed in an orphanage twenty-five years ago." Sadness shadowed his features. "I haven't seen them since."

Rye's gut was coiled so tight he thought he'd be sick. "I'm your brother Rye."

Creede's eyes widened, and he handed his daughter to his wife, whose rounded belly told Rye they were expecting another child. He approached Rye and stared into his eyes. Rye noticed they were the exact same shade of blue as his own. Creede then clasped Rye's shoulders and pulled him close, hugging him. "My God, I can't believe it. Little Rye. All grown up."

Rye's eyes burned with moisture as he wrapped his arms around his big brother. The years disappeared and he was a little boy again, seeing their dead mother as he, Creede, and Slater held tight to one another.

Finally, Creede eased his grip and stepped back, but kept an arm around Rye's shoulders. "I never thought I'd see you again," Creede said, his voice rough with emotion.

Rye cleared his throat. "I looked for you and Slater when I left the orphanage but I didn't have any luck."

"I'm sorry, Rye. I-I did some things I wasn't very proud of, or I would've come back for you and Slater."

"We were there only a month when Slater was adopted."

Creede swallowed, and it seemed he was fighting the same emotional storm Rye fought. If only Slater was here, too. . . .

The tall, handsome woman stepped forward, and though she was wiping tears from her cheeks, she was smiling warmly. "I'm Laurel, Creede's wife, and this is our daughter, Anna."

Rye shook her hand and was surprised by her firm handshake. He quickly moved to the wagon and helped his family down. Dulcie's eyes were as damp as his own. "This is my wife, Dulcie, and Madeline and Collie."

For the next few minutes chaos reigned as everybody greeted one another. As soon as there was a lull, Laurel herded the children into the house. Her husband, obviously as in love with his wife as Rye was with his, followed.

Dulcie joined Rye, who remained standing in the yard.

"I like them," she simply said.

"Me, too," Rye said, a note of wonder in his voice. "Have you ever felt like you've finally come home?"

Dulcie smiled gently. "When you said you loved me."

Rye hugged her, burying his face in her thick, sunlit hair. "I love you, Dulcie Forrester."

TURN THE PAGE FOR A PREVIEW OF THE
NEXT HISTORICAL ROMANCE FROM
MAUREEN MCKADE

A Reason to Sin

COMING SOON FROM BERKLEY SENSATION!

REBECCA Glory Bowen Colfax was out of options. Her worn out shoes muddy and her cheeks nearly numb, she paused at the corner of the street and brushed back a drooping tendril from her face. Nobody needed a clerk or a waitress or even a laundress, which left few alternatives.

Rebecca studied the false-fronted buildings interspersed with large canvas tents that lay across the invisible line separating the respectable from the disreputable. Although it was only two in the afternoon, numerous horses were tied to hitching posts, and men wearing battered hats and noisy spurs milled in and out of the saloons. A piano's off-key notes spilled down the street along with occasional raucous laughter. Rebecca had already experienced too many frontier towns in Kansas, but this one was by far the biggest and wildest.

The sound of gunfire startled her and she lifted her head sharply. Five men raced down the street, and the horses' hooves tossed mud clumps in their wake. She covered her ears as more shots rang out and was shocked to see that few people gave the rowdy men more than a cursory glance. The ruffians halted in front of one of the numerous drinking establishments and went inside, shoving and pushing each other like children.

Her courage wavered and she started back the way she'd come. However, the gravity of her predicament stopped her, reminding her she had no choice. With her heart in her throat, she took a deep breath. Squaring her shoulders, she turned and marched back, crossing the invisible line that would no doubt lead to hell. But she'd made a promise a month ago and even damnation couldn't stop her from fulfilling it.

Rebecca held her head high as she sidestepped a grizzled drunk who staggered out of one of the tent saloons.

"Hey, missy, wanna wet my whistle?" he slurred as he rubbed his crotch.

She swallowed back the bile that rose in her throat and scurried past him. If she stopped to think about what she was about to do, her courage would desert her and she needed every ounce of strength.

She arrived at her destination and stopped to stare at the wooden sign that displayed a rendition of a woman's shapely thigh encircled with a red garter. The Scarlet Garter. A scandalous name but Rebecca had been impressed by the owner, or as impressed as she could be by a man who ran such an establishment.

The double doors taunted her, dared her to cross the threshold. She smoothed her gloved hands down the front of her once-fashionable skirt. Her heart thudded in her breast, and sweat dared to dampen her palms and underarms. Closing her eyes, she pictured him, her reason for living and doing what she never in her worst nightmares dreamed of doing. The image strengthened her resolve and she opened her eyes. She extended her arm and pushed through the door, stepping onto the layer of sawdust covering the wood floor.

Inside it smelled of stale alcohol and caustic tobacco, with more than a hint of body odor. Rebecca fought the urge to press a handkerchief to her nose and breathed through her mouth. Yet she knew the Scarlet Garter had a less offensive odor than most other saloons. Her eyes adjusted to the relative dimness, and she sent her gaze around the room. Although there were a couple of dozen tables, only a few were in use. At one table two burly men drank beer and talked in low voices, and at the second, a thin man balanced a fancy lady on his lap while she whispered in his ear.

Could she do the same if she had to? Rebecca Bowen couldn't, but Rebecca Colfax had no choice.

At another table a dark-haired man sat alone with his back to the wall, shuffling a deck of cards then fanning them across the tabletop. Although he wasn't looking at her, she suspected he'd already catalogued her presence.

She dragged her attention away from the gambler and searched for the owner, but he wasn't in sight. Drawing her shoulders back, she crossed to the bar, her skirt hems brushing aside the sawdust.

"What may I get you, madam?" the bartender asked.

Startled, Rebecca stared at the man whose body was disproportionately small compared to his head.

He wiped a towel across the bartop with a short, stubby hand and smiled. "Haven't you ever espied a dwarf?"

She snapped her mouth shut and shook her head. "No."

"Come closer."

Reluctant but curious, she neared the bar and spotted the plank the dwarf stood upon. He was perhaps three feet tall. "Have you always been this way?"

His eyes twinkled. "When I was eighteen, a barn roof fell upon me." Her eyes widened, and he shook his head sadly. "It was a very tragic day, indeed."

Rebecca suspected he wasn't speaking the truth, but it was rude to accuse him of lying.

Suddenly he laughed. "I am sorry for confounding you, madam. Yes, I have always been short of stature."

Eased by his sense of humor, Rebecca smiled. "No, I'm sorry for being so ill-mannered." She sobered. "I'd like to speak with the owner."

He eyed her, and Rebecca had the impression he could see more than most people. "I shall get him for you." The dwarf stepped down onto a chair then the floor and disappeared through a doorway in the back.

Rebecca's gaze lit on the nearly life-size portrait of a voluptuous nude hanging on the wall, and her cheeks burned.

How could she even consider working in such a wicked place? Yet she couldn't afford to be embarrassed, not with so much riding on her finding Harrison. And to continue her search, she needed money. Badly.

The owner, donning a suitcoat, followed the bartender through the doorway. He was as she remembered him, a man of medium height with thick, steel gray hair. His white ruffled shirt and black pinstriped suit were of high quality, the quality she'd seen in places like Chicago and New York.

"Mr. Andrew Kearny, owner of the Scarlet Garter," the bartender announced.

"Thank you, Dante," Kearny said to the dwarf before turning to Rebecca. The owner's brown eyes surveyed her from head to toe, and there was a hint of a leer in them. "I didn't expect to see you again," he said with a faint Southern drawl.

"I didn't expect to be here again," she retorted, hiding her apprehension behind a façade of brashness.

He came out from behind the bar and leaned against it, loosely clasping his hands across his waist. "I still haven't seen the man you're looking for."

Although she hadn't expected anything else, disappointment rolled through her. Two days ago she'd shown Harrison's picture around in the saloons, but no one had seen him. She buried her frustration. "I'm here to enquire about a position." He continued to stare at her. "I'm in need of a job."

"Perhaps you should try the other side of town."

She fought back impatience. "I did." She glanced down, afraid the moisture stinging her eyes would form tears. "Nobody has anything."

"What can you do?" he asked.

She blinked and brought her head back up to meet his shrewd gaze. No matter what, she couldn't allow him to see her desperate fear. "I can read and write. I can also play the piano."

"I already have a piano player. Can you dance?"

She felt a twinge of indignation. Back in St. Louis, Rebecca had learned everything a young woman of means needed to know. "Of course. I also sing."

He canted an eyebrow. "Well, well. I could use a singer,

but it would only be for an hour or two in the evenings. What I really need are more hurdy-gurdy girls."

Rebecca had never heard of a hurdy-gurdy girl. What if it was another name for a lady of the evening? "What does a hurdy-gurdy girl do?" she asked warily.

"They wear short dresses, smile pretty, and dance with the clientele to get them to buy her drinks," Kearny replied matter-of-factly. "The girls make a nickel for every drink they sell."

Although she had her doubts about the short dress, Rebecca could dance and paste on a smile. However, she'd never touched alcohol other than the occasional glass of wine. "Do I have to drink whiskey?"

Kearny grinned, revealing a gold tooth. "No. The girls drink weak tea, although it comes out of a champagne bottle."

It was cheating plain and simple, but Rebecca wasn't in a position to argue. "Would I be expected to do more than sing and dance?"

The man shrugged. "I don't ask you to, but most of my ladies do make extra money on their backs."

The crude expression sounded odd with his easy drawl, and the image his words invoked brought burning heat to her face. Although she was willing to do what she had to, the thought of lying beneath a panting foul-breathed man while he used her body made her stomach churn with revulsion. "I—" Her voice broke and she cleared her throat. "I'd prefer to simply sing and dance, Mr. Kearny."

A knowing smile touched his lips. "That's fine. Do you have a name?"

Rebecca's tongue stuck to the roof of her mouth. "Glory Bowen."

"When can you start Miss Glory?"

"Tomorrow night?"

He nodded. "That'd be fine. There's one empty room upstairs—fifty cents a night and it'll come out of your pay. Do you want it?"

Relief made Rebecca dizzy. "Yes, I would. When can I move in?"

"Today, if you'd like."

"Thank you." Suddenly uncertain, Rebecca toyed with the strings of her reticule. "What do I need, for work, I mean?"

"Each girl supplies her own black stockings and shoes and, of course, underthings." His eyes glittered with amusement.

Rebecca wondered if she'd ever stop blushing. "What about dresses?"

"There's a room upstairs filled with fancy dresses. I'm sure some will fit you. You'll want them snug." Kearny eyed her modest neckline. "You'll also want cleavage. A man wants to see a woman's breasts when he dances with her. Each girl is required to wear a red garter, too."

Her face burned and she glanced away, only to have her gaze fall on the giggling whore still on the man's lap. Her dress was hiked up high enough that the red garter was plainly visible on her thigh, and her bosom threatened to spill out of the low décolletage.

Rebecca quickly turned away. She couldn't imagine herself acting so brazen yet isn't that what she'd just agreed to do?

"Are you sure you want to do this?"

At his softly worded question, Rebecca looked up at him. For a moment, she was tempted to confess everything, but her pride and apprehension kept her silent. Her stomach queasy, she nodded. "Yes."

He shrugged. "If you're moving in today, you can meet some of the girls this evening. They can answer any questions you have."

"When do I start singing?"

"How about Saturday night? That'll give you and Simon time to go over some songs."

Rebecca's gaze slid to the empty piano seat.

"He'll be here in a couple of hours. You can talk to him before it gets busy."

"All right."

"I'll show you out the back door. You can use that to come and go."

"Thank you."

"Don't thank me yet. Wait until tomorrow night, after your feet have been stomped on a few dozen times." He extended an arm. "I'll walk you out."

Projecting a coolness she didn't feel, Rebecca allowed

him to guide her through the back doorway, past an office and a flight of stairs.

"You can use these stairs when you move your things to your room," Kearny said.

Her mouth paper dry, Rebecca nodded.

Kearny opened the door which led into an alley behind the building. "Last chance. Are you certain you can work in a place like this?"

No!

She ignored the silent scream and met his appraising gaze with her own steady one. "I'm certain, Mr. Kearny."

He held out his hand and, after a moment's hesitation, she gripped it. "Welcome to the Scarlet Garter, Miss Glory."

Not knowing what else to say, Rebecca walked out. The door closed behind her and she stood silently, the damp cold seeping into her. Her breath misted as she fought tears of helplessness, anger, and panic.

What have I done?

You did what you had to for your baby.

In order to get her infant child out of the orphanage, she had to find her husband and tell him about the son he didn't know he had. But would Harrison Colfax, who had gambled away her entire inheritance, even care?

SLATER Forrester shuffled the deck, the motions as familiar to him as shaving. He laid the cards facedown, fanned them across the table, then lifted the end one and brought them back together in his hands. Another shuffle and he dealt four cards face up. All were aces, just as he expected. He smiled to himself.

You haven't lost your touch, Forrester.

He heard the approach of someone and tensed, but immediately relaxed when he recognized the familiar footfalls. Andrew set a cup of steaming coffee down in front of him then pulled out a chair and sat down.

"Thanks," Slater said.

Andrew took a sip from his own coffee then deliberately looked down at the aces. "I thought you didn't deal a crooked game any more."

"I don't, but it doesn't hurt to stay in practice."

Andrew laughed but sobered a few moments later. "Did you see her?"

Slater doubted he'd forget her light blonde hair and almost painfully straight backbone. When he'd first seen her enter the saloon, he thought she was lost. But then she'd pulled back her shoulders, displaying a fine set of breasts, and walked right up to the bar. Yet he hadn't been able to completely shake the protectiveness she'd raised in him. He kept his voice indifferent. "Couldn't miss her. Dresses nicer than most whores."

"According to her she doesn't do that."

"Then why was she here?" Slater picked up his cup and leaned back in his chair, curious despite himself.

"She wanted a job. Says she can sing and dance."

Slater snorted, recalling her shapely figure. "I give her a week before she's on her back upstairs."

Andrew shook his head, his expression concerned. "You never used to be so cynical, Slater."

Slater quirked his lips upward in a caricature of a smile. "Sure I was. You were just too busy fleecing the sheep to notice."

The older man shrugged and glanced down. "I was younger and more foolish. I never thought I'd end up running a straight house."

"We both ended up doing things we never thought we'd be doing." Slater stared into the distance, his thoughts detouring to Andersonville. For a moment, he could hear the endless groans and smell the blood, piss, and misery. His left hand trembled, spilling coffee onto his trouser leg. He set the cup down hastily and shook his head to dislodge the too-real memory.

"You more than me, my friend," Andrew said quietly.

Slater gnashed his teeth, hating the sympathy in Andrew's face and voice. "Yeah, well, like you always told me, a man makes his own bed." He grinned lecherously. "Unless he's got a soft woman to make it for him."

"Women, cards, and danger, and not necessarily in that order," Andrew quoted the description he'd pegged Slater with years ago.

Slater gathered the cards he'd laid on the table and shuffled them, relieved to see his left hand had stopped shaking. It had taken nearly two years to regain his former weight and strength after he'd been released from the brutal prisoner of war camp. However, despite his left hand looking normal, whenever he was distressed it would tremble like an old man's. He hated what he'd become.

"So what's her name?" Although curious about the new gal, Slater was more interested in changing the subject.

"Miss Glory."

Slater barked a laugh. "With a handle like that, she's no blushing virgin."

"I'd bet my last dollar she's not a sporting woman. She talks fancy, like she's been to school."

"Must be down on her luck. That's why women end up in a place like this. And sooner or later, they all end up whores."

Andrew glared at him. "It's not like I force them to prostitute themselves."

Slater lifted his hands, palms out. "I never said you did. But there's a reason the good women steer clear of this side of town."

"Well, if she sings half as good as she looks, she won't have to sell herself." He shook his head and shrugged. "She'll start dancing tomorrow night. After Frannie quit last week, I've been making less money on drinks. It'll be good to have another girl working again."

"I never thought I'd see the day when you were more businessman than gambler."

"And I never figured you'd come back to gambling after you left to join the Pinkertons."

Slater rubbed his jaw, already feeling the rasp of whiskers despite having shaved less than four hours earlier. He remembered how he hadn't been able to shave at Andersonville and how one morning he'd awakened to find a spider had taken up residence in his beard. And then there were the nits . . . He'd shave again before he started dealing, just as he did every evening. "Yeah, well, that makes two of us."

Andrew laid his forearms on the table and leaned forward. "When I took in that skinny sixteen-year-old kid and taught him how to play poker, I knew he'd be better than me someday. You were good, Slater. Damned good. But for you gambling was only a way to make some money, not a way of life. When that Pinkerton agent asked you to join, I could see that was something you really wanted to do." Andrew paused to study Slater. "Why did you leave the agency?"

When Slater had come looking for a job from his mentor three months ago, he'd told Andrew only the facts, that he'd been at Andersonville and he'd quit the Pinkertons. Being a gambler made Andrew more observant than Slater would've liked, and the older man had filled in some of the blanks himself. Of course, Slater had neither denied nor confirmed Andrew's assumptions.

Slater shrugged insolently. "I got tired of having them tell me what to do."

"There's more to it than that."

Andrew wasn't going to settle for anything less than the truth this time, and Slater wasn't about to spill his guts. Not to anyone, not even the man who had saved his life.

The saloon doors burst open and two drunken cowboys stumbled in, cussing and shoving one another and giving Slater an excuse not to answer.

"It's too early for this," Andrew muttered.

"Not when they're moving cattle through and they only have a day or two to blow off steam."

Oaktree was beginning to grow because of the cattlemen and the herds they moved out of Texas. Slater suspected it was only a matter of time before Oaktree and other towns like it would be booming because of the cattle and coming railroad. Andrew Kearny had been shrewd to set up his place here, but with more business came more opportunities for dangerous gunplay among drunken men.

With spurs ringing, the new arrivals strode to the bar.

"What can I obtain for you gentlemen?" Dante asked courteously.

"Two whiskeys, little man," one of the young cowboys ordered.

Slater gritted his teeth, angered by the slur against the dwarf even though Dante had once told him only smaller men than him resorted to insults.

Dante poured two shots from a brown bottle. "That will be fifty cents." He paused. "Two bits each."

Grumbling, the boys slapped down their coins and swallowed the rotgut without flinching. They turned to look around the saloon, and their lecherous eyes lit on Molly, who was trying to drum up some upstairs business. The smirking boys ambled over to her, their path not quite straight, and the shortest one tugged her off the man's lap.

"What's goin—"

"There's two of us and only one of you," the larger of the cowboys interrupted the man who'd been holding Molly.

The man stood, his stance none too steady. "She's mine." He tugged her back against his side.

"Now hold on, boys. Y'all are jest gonna have to take turns," Molly said with a slow drawl and a coquettish smile.

"We don't wanna wait. Been a long time since I done dipped my wick," the smaller and more belligerent cowboy said. He grabbed hold of Molly's wrist and jerked her against him.

"Now just take it easy, fellahs," Molly said, trying to defuse the explosive situation. "You hurt me, and I ain't gonna be able to do anything with any of you." Her voice trembled beneath the bravado.

Slater's cards lay forgotten on the table as his hands clenched in his lap. He couldn't abide a woman, even one like Molly who knew the ropes, being manhandled. Andrew had a bouncer at night to take care of rowdy men, but there had never been a need for one this early in the day.

The short, wiry cowboy kissed her and held her struggling body in a punishing hold while her former "suitor" was held in place by the cowboy's friend.

Before he could stop himself, Slater stood. "I don't think the lady appreciates your attention."

The cowboy lifted his head and wrapped an arm around Molly's neck, shifting her around so her back was against his chest. "Sure she does." He brought his mouth close to her ear. "Don't ya?"

Her face red, Molly nodded but spoke to Slater. "I'm all right."

Although she seemed to be fine, Slater didn't like the way

the cowboy's arm tightened around her neck. Ensuring his sleeve gun was in place, Slater took a step toward them. "Let her go."

The cowboy squeezed Molly's breast, and she gasped in pain. "Not until me and her take care of business."

"You're hurting her."

"Why do you care? She's just a whore."

Slater shook his head, keeping his anger tamped down. "It's not right to hurt a woman, *any* woman."

"You ain't gonna stop me, mister." The cowboy started dragging Molly toward the stairs, moving closer to Slater as he did.

Slater shot out a hand and grabbed the younger man, who released Molly as he struggled to escape. With his other hand, Slater punched the cowboy, dropping him to the floor like a sack of flour.

"I wouldn't," Dante said.

Slater jerked his head up to see the diminutive bartender aiming a sawed-off shotgun at the cowboy whose hand hovered near his revolver.

Andrew stepped forward. "Get yourself and your friend out of here. I don't want to see either one of you in my place again."

Without argument, the larger cowboy pulled his friend to his feet then half dragged him out of the saloon. The few other patrons turned back to their drinks.

"Thanks, Mr. Forrester," Molly said, her face pale except for two splotches of red rouge on her cheeks. She readjusted her breasts within her dress. "I ain't usually afraid of liquored-up cowboys, but that one was a mean one."

"You're welcome, Molly."

She tilted her head to the side and gave him a seductive look. "Let me thank you proper sometime."

Slater merely smiled and returned to his chair as Molly rejoined the man who'd been fondling her earlier. After a few whispered words, she escorted her customer up the stairs.

Slater reached for the cards, but his left hand betrayed him. Instead, he picked up his coffee cup in his right hand while settling his left in his lap.

"It's nice to know some things haven't changed," Andrew commented, taking his previous place at Slater's table.

Slater feigned ignorance. "I don't know what you're talking about."

"Lady Jane."

Slater kept his expression bland although his memory supplied him with a picture of the young prostitute who'd nearly been killed by a knife-wielding customer. Slater had been passing by her room and had taken care of the perverted bastard.

Maybe defending others was Slater's way of trying to make up for not protecting a boy a long time ago. A boy who died because Slater was too frightened to help him.